The critics on Anita Burgh

'A blockbuster . . . an excellent reading experience'
Literary Review

'The mix of suspense, romance, humour and good old heart-tugging pathos is irresistible'
Elizabeth Buchan, *Mail on Sunday*

'A blockbusting story of romance and intrigue'
Family Circle

'The perfect beach book'
Marie Claire

'Its crafted writing keeps you hanging in there until the last page'
City Limits

'Sharp . . . wickedly funny'
Mail on Sunday

'Ambition, greed and manipulation add up to a great blockbuster'
New Woman

'You won't be able to put it down'
Good Housekeeping

'A well-written contemporary story that has all the necessary ingredients to make a great read – and it is!'
Oracle

'Anita has the storyteller's gift'
Daily Express

'Sinister and avaricious forces are at work behind the pious smiles . . . Gripping!'
Daily Telegraph

'A sure-fire bestseller'
Prima

By Anita Burgh

Anita Burgh was born in Gillingham, Kent, but spent her early years at Lanhydrock House in Cornwall. Returning to the Medway Towns, she attended Chatham Grammar School, and became a student nurse at UCH in London. She gave up nursing upon marrying into the aristocracy. Subsequently divorced, she pursued various careers – secretarial work, a laboratory technician in cancer research and an hotelier. She has a flat in Cambridge and a house in France, where she shares her life with her partner, Billy, a bulldog, a Cairn terrier, three mixed-breed dogs and three cats. The visits of a constantly changing mix of her four children, two step-children, six grandchildren, four step-grandchildren, and her noble ex-husband keep her busy, entertained and poor! Anita Burgh is the author of many bestsellers, including *Distinctions of Class*, which was shortlisted for the RNA Romantic Novel of the Year Award.

CLARE'S WAR

Anita Burgh

ORION

An Orion paperback

First published in Great Britain by Orion in 2000
This paperback edition published in 2000 by
Orion Books Ltd,
Orion House, 5 Upper St Martin's Lane, London WC2H 9EA

This edition is for promotional use only.
Not for resale.

Fourth impression 2002

A CIP catalogue record for this book is available
from the British Library.

The characters and events in this book are fictitious.
Any similarity to any real persons, living or dead, is coincidental.

Typeset by Deltatype Ltd, Birkenhead, Merseyside

Printed and bound in Great Britain by
Clays Ltd, St Ives plc

At the end of the 1939–45 war, medals were awarded to the brave fighters of the French Resistance. Of a thousand accorded, six were given to women.

During this war there had been a silent army of ordinary French women who saw it as their duty to their country, their country men, and for the sake of humanity, to help. They carried no guns, they sabotaged no bridges, but went quietly about their work of hiding and feeding the displaced, of moving forged papers, clandestine newspapers, of spying and collecting information. If caught the penalty was deportation to the camps or death.

This book is respectfully dedicated to all those women who felt they had done little, who were awarded no medals, but without whom less would have been achieved.

Puisque ceux qui avaient le devoir de manier l'épée de la France l'ont laissée tomber brisée, moi, j'ai ramassé le tronçon du glaive.
Charles de Gaulle, 13 July 1940

Since they whose duty it was to wield the sword of France have let it fall shattered to the ground, I have taken up the broken blade.

Chapter One

June 1938 – September 1939

1

'You drive, I can't. Better if you do . . .' Felicity was weaving her way down the slippery stone steps, waving the car keys in a vague manner, which reminded me of a carrot and a donkey.

'Don't be silly, I don't know how.' This was not strictly true but I was not about to admit to her that I'd enjoyed the odd spin when I shouldn't have.

'Oh, no? Who says?' She stopped dead and I nearly cannoned into her. Despite the lashing rain I could just hear the strains of Joe Loss wafting after us from the ball we had just left. I hadn't wanted to leave but Felicity was in such a state that when she'd ordered me to follow uncharacteristically I had. 'That's not what David said.'

'He fibs.'

'I don't think so. He says his father went barmy over the state of his Bentley – that you'd been driving and he took the blame.'

'See? I said he fibbed.' I grinned at my sister, who stood swaying gently. In her pale green dress, soaked with rain, she put me in mind of a water sprite. She really was quite lovely, even when she was drunk. 'You're not up to it, that's for sure. All right, then, give me the keys.'

The wind tore at our dresses, the gravel dug through the soft soles of my silk dancing shoes. We leant into the wind and went in search of our father's car, since Felicity could not remember where she had parked it.

Once safely inside I was quite pleased at finding the headlight switch without having to ask. The engine obliged by starting immediately and I did a rather nifty three-point turn, which swung us out of the area our hosts had designated a car-park. I then spoilt the effect somewhat by crashing the gears and going into reverse rather than first, but Felicity said nothing.

'Lovely dance, wasn't it? Did you see what a fright Shirley Chepstow looked?' I had to sit hunched over the wheel for the rain was sheeting down and it was difficult to see as we lurched down the long dark drive.

'Don't even speak of her! Did you see the cow's eyes she was making at Simon?'

'No!' So that's why we were leaving in such a rush.

'I hate him, I never want to speak to him again as long as I live.'

'Fee! You don't mean that. He'd never look at anyone but you.' I heard her sob. 'Oh, Fee, don't cry.'

Just for a second I turned to her to comfort her. A second – that was all it needed. As I looked back at the road ahead I attempted to brake, but the heel of my shoe caught in the rug. I pressed the accelerator instead and we hurtled into the fallen tree that blocked the driveway.

The noise we made was louder even than the storm. The metal of the car screeched and rasped against the felled oak. A branch smashed the window and the glass shattered all over us. With a mighty grating noise the roof peeled back, and the rain poured in. A great flash of lightning was followed by a massive crack of thunder. Then there was an eerie silence.

'Yoicks! What's Dad going to say?' I giggled nervously. I could smell petrol. We should get out, I knew, but my legs wouldn't move. They were trapped beneath the wheel. 'Felicity, we must get out. I can't move – give me a hand.' Even as I spoke she slid sideways slowly and gracefully on to my lap. 'Get up, don't be silly. You weigh a ton!' I couldn't budge her. 'You're going to have a whopping big bruise right in the middle of your forehead,' I told her. The rain on my face was rather pleasant, I decided. I might be trapped but I was in no pain. 'Just look at us, like sardines in a tin.' I laughed, but there was no response from Felicity: she was fast asleep. Honestly! 'Fee, wake up.' She was making a funny snuffling noise, like dogs with short noses make when they're trying to find things. 'Stop it, Fee, you sound like a pug!' I shook her as best I could. 'Fee? Are you all right? Fee?' I could hear my voice rising in panic. 'Wake up, Fee, please wake up!' I cried, but the snuffling noise had stopped.

It had not been my fault. Everyone was constantly assuring me of that. *You mustn't blame yourself.* How many times had I heard that? But no one explained to me how I was supposed to eliminate the guilt. And if it wasn't my fault, why was it that I felt like a pariah in my own home?

My father did not agree with the majority. He blamed me four-square. His ranting was dreadful. I felt shell-shocked by his accusations. Despite this I was sorry for him as he lashed about in his grief, like a poor wounded beast not knowing which way to turn for relief. It was understandable, of course. What was confusing, though, was that as the youngest I had always been his favourite, so I dared to think that he would soon forgive me. But six months after Fee's death he was still not speaking to me.

Felicity had been the middle sister, three years older and three years steadier than me – or so we had all thought. She was the prettiest, most intelligent and the kindest of the three of us. Her row that night with Simon had been completely out of character for her, as if Fate had taken a hand.

Although I grieved for her too, I didn't cry. Perhaps that was the reason no one seemed to understand and take into consideration how I was feeling. I couldn't cry. I wanted to, but the tears wouldn't come and I was left with a great block of sadness locked inside me. When I awoke in the morning, for a split second I would be happy. Then I'd remember, and that solid mass of unhappiness would awaken too. I'd loved her: she was my friend as well as my sister. And none of *them* had been driving; none of them could even remotely be accused of killing her. It amazed me that no one realised how often I relived that awful night and blamed myself for not braking in time. If only I hadn't taken my eye off the road; if only the tree hadn't fallen; if only I had been wearing different shoes . . .

Hope, my eldest sister, at first showed me sympathy and understanding – well, a little. The trouble was that it emerged a bit like a lecture and I wasn't having any of that from her. She was six years older than I was. Too big an age difference for us to be true friends. I saw her as one of the adults, those dreadful people who regarded me as the wild one, and who were constantly trying to spoil my fun. Hope never seemed to have fun, or appeared to want any. At nearly twenty-four she seemed already middle-aged and set in her ways.

There were occasions when I suspected that Lettie, my stepmother, was about to comfort me but then thought better of it. I suppose she was afraid that my father might be angry with her, or that by being nice to me she would appear to be taking sides.

As the months ticked by the atmosphere at home became more and more oppressive. I often wished I could pack my bags and leave. But what could I do? The education I had received had been deliberately planned to groom me for the only choice that had been suggested to me: marriage to someone suitable. I had never worked and never expected to have to. And, in any case, where could I go? I had to hope that it would sort itself out, that Father couldn't carry on like this for ever.

I was wrong. Things became even worse when Cyril Forester, Hope's new fiancé, took a shine to me and we were discovered kissing each other in the summerhouse. All hell broke loose – again!

Hope dissolved into a quivering, blubbing mess, Father snarled, Cyril was contrite. And I wished I was anywhere but there.

'Look, Hope, you can't blame me. It's not my fault if Cyril likes me. I didn't ask him to kiss me, he just did.'

'Nothing's ever your fault, is it? Little Miss Innocent, butter wouldn't melt in your mouth! Don't lie to me!' Hope, the least attractive of we three sisters, looked angrily at me. Her face was puffed up and her eyes were pink, like a ferret's, from all her crying. Then she gave me a shove. 'Get out of my sight. Get out of my life!' she shouted, and flung herself on to her bed. 'You're a two-faced bitch!'

That galvanised me. 'Excuse me! It takes two, you know. Why aren't you screeching at Cyril as well as me?' It was true: he *had* grabbed me. I hadn't meant to let him kiss me, but once he had started I'd quite liked it.

'How else do you expect me to speak to you?' She sat up on the bed. 'I've seen you making sheep's eyes at Cyril when you didn't think I was looking.'

'I never have. He's loathsome. I feel sorry for you ending your days with him,' I spat back.

'You're a foul, selfish, spoilt brat. You've no soul! First poor Felicity and now this. I hate you!'

That hurt. Pretending a nonchalance I was far from feeling, I picked up her powder puff as if inspecting it. 'The fact is, I've done you a favour. If Cyril has a wandering eye, far better to find out now.'

'You cat! I hate you. Hate, hate, hate!' Hope was up and lunging at me.

I was lighter on my feet and danced away from her. 'You know, Hope, you should watch it. You're eating too much. You'll get fat – again.' I left her bedroom quickly.

Her wail of frustration and anger followed me along the passage to the stairs. I had barely started to descend the staircase before I was regretting saying that. I knew that any remark about her weight would upset her. Why was I being so horrible? I really hadn't meant it – I had only wanted to shut her up.

I paused on the stairs, pretending to look at the portrait of my mother when in fact I was listening to Hope, willing her to calm down before anyone else heard her – but I'd hit a raw nerve: her size went up and down as if she were a balloon, one month inflated the next with all the air let out. She was the only one of us who had inherited our mother's interest in cooking, but unlike Mother, she couldn't resist over-sampling.

Mother had been Austrian and it was her genius as a cook that had founded the family fortune. She had baked, and my father, whose expertise was in making money, had capitalised on her talent. Together they had opened a bakery. One was soon two until eventually, today, there was a factory working to Mother's recipes and branches of Trudie's in many English towns. Expansion into Europe was planned.

'What now?' My father, burly, with a bushy moustache and eyebrows that always looked to me like furry caterpillars crawling across his forehead, emerged from his study. The noise from upstairs, if anything, was getting louder.

'Nothing, Father. Hope's a little upset.'

'A little!' The words exploded forth. I admired the way he could make the most innocent sound like swearing. 'What did you expect? Why Cyril? Don't you ever consider anyone but yourself?'

'I didn't do anything, Father. Honestly. Why, I don't even like Cyril – he's so old.' I shuddered for effect. He was twenty-eight, ancient in my seventeen-year-old opinion. 'It's not my fault if Hope thinks he's her last chance.' Oops! That was tactless, but the words had just slipped out before I could stop them. That often happened to me.

'Why are you such a spiteful, wilful child? Have you no shame? No remorse? You're a disgrace to this family and especially to the memory of your dear mother. You are a cross I have to . . .'

I switched off at that point. Since Felicity's death I had heard it all before. He would go on and on now – nothing would halt him. I wished he hadn't mentioned Mother; that was unfair of him. I couldn't remember her: I had been only four when she had died of TB. All I knew of her was what I had gleaned from the others and I had taken their memories to myself, pretended they were my own. I might not have known her long but I felt sure that she would have listened to me, she would have understood, she would have taken my side.

'. . . it's the only possible solution. I trust you agree?' My father loomed over me, peering at me, one untamed eyebrow waggling questioningly.

I hadn't the foggiest idea what he was talking about but I didn't dare admit that I hadn't been listening. 'Yes, Father,' I answered, and hoped I wasn't agreeing to anything too gruesome or arduous.

'Perhaps you'll learn some sense there.' And he returned to his study, leaving me none the wiser.

Paris! There was no need for me to have been so worried. I was to be sent to France for a whole year. I was to improve my knowledge of the language, learn some wifely skills and, presumably, the sense that my father set such store by.

I would have preferred to go to Germany, but I did not argue the point, not at this time, not with Father. Better to settle for what was on offer. I had spoken German before I muttered a word of English, at my mother's knee, and continued after her death with a long line of Fräuleins who never spoke to us in any other language. I was as fluent in it as I was in

English and would not have had to work so hard. Though good at French, it was the tedium of improving it that I did not look forward to.

The miserable summer was replaced by a wretched autumn and then the bleakest winter I'd ever known, as the atmosphere at home became more and more oppressive. I longed to be on my way, but there was Christmas and the New Year to endure – our first without Felicity. And there were clothes to buy, and another school term, which did not start for a month.

I never knew that time could pass so slowly. I was grateful to my stepmother, who helped me shop with studied devotion. Lettie lived to shop, poor dear. I liked her, but I was the only one who did. When my father, at the age of fifty-two, had announced that he was marrying Lettie, thirty years his junior, there was consternation in the family, a near revolt by the servants, and gossip in the community. That had been six years ago and little had changed. I felt sorry for her. She was a pretty little thing, not very bright but always amenable. I suppose that's why Father had chosen her. The one thing she had failed to do was produce the longed-for heir to his bakery empire. She hadn't even managed another daughter. I can't say I was sorry about that.

'I do hope your father is making the right decision in letting you go to France. What if there were a war?' Lettie looked worried.

'Mr Chamberlain has seen to that.'

'But only two months ago those beastly Huns marched into Czechoslovakia.'

'Father says nothing more will happen,' I reassured her. I didn't think it was wise of her to call the Germans Huns: my father's grandparents had been German. But her father had been killed in the trenches in the Great War and I suppose that's why she didn't like them.

'I shall miss you dreadfully, Clare.' We had just returned from another successful shopping expedition, which, this time, had been a triumph for hats. We collapsed wearily into the deep armchairs in her small but tastefully decorated boudoir.

'Me too,' I lied. I was fond of her but knew I was unlikely to pine.

'You're the only one who likes me.'

'That's not true.' It was all very well being told as a child to tell the truth at all times, but how could one do so without hurting people? The times when I had – for instance, when the next-door neighbour had asked me if I liked her hat and I had said no – I had been sent to bed in disgrace. So now I lied when I thought it was necessary. 'Everyone loves you.' What a whopper!

'No, they don't. I think they're jealous.'

'Probably.' There. That was honesty for her. Maybe I shouldn't have agreed with her, for she closed her eyes as if weary of something. It was quiet in her little room, and I sat holding my cup of tea, studying her. There was an air of sadness about Lettie that wasn't related to my leaving. 'You're unhappy, aren't you, Lettie?' I only called her by her name in private: when we were with the others she was Mother. We referred to our true mother as Mama.

'What makes you say that? Of course not. I'm very lucky and very happy.'

'I don't think you are. There's something so sad about you. I wish you would tell me what it is.'

'Dear, sensitive Clare. How sweet you are. I'm fine, really.'

I *was* surprised! No one described me like that normally, and I must admit I didn't see myself in that light either.

'If I look sad, then it's because by tomorrow you'll be gone.'

'But it's only for a year, Lettie, and then I'll be back to annoy Father.'

'What if you get swept off your feet by a handsome Frenchman? You won't be back then.'

'Heaven forbid! Me, with a Frenchman? Never! Nothing will keep me away from England. I bet I shall suffer agonies of homesickness.' I kissed her to emphasise what I was saying. In fact, the idea of a romantic liaison with a Frenchman had already occurred to me.

'If you do find someone, promise me one thing, Clare. Don't marry him if he's much older than you, will you?'

'Lettie!' I meant to sound sorry for her. Instead my voice brimmed with surprise that she should say such a thing – and to me.

Abruptly she stood up. 'I should never have said that. It was grossly disloyal of me. You won't say anything to your father, will you? Promise me.' She clutched at my arm. In a flash of intuition I knew she loved someone else – I was sure of it.

'I won't say a word. Honestly. Did you know him before you married Father?'

'Know who?'

'The person you truly love.'

'Clare, really, you talk such nonsense. I love your father.' She laughed nervously and blushed spectacularly. 'Now, if you don't mind, I must change.'

That blush had said she lied, I would have bet the whole of my savings account on it. She need not have warned me, though: there was no way I would ever marry an old man, I always thought she must have done it for Father's money – not that I held that against her.

In my room I began the last of my packing. As I pottered about, I thought of the Frenchman of my dreams. He was young and virile, slim yet muscular, a fine horseman, I had decided. He would be dark-haired with an accented, rich voice, like black treacle. And if meeting him freed me from this repressive, miserable home, so much the better.

The next morning my father kissed me goodbye, told me to write and I was sure I noticed a tear in his eye. Another surprise! But he didn't tell me he loved me or that he would miss me. It would never be the same between us ever again. It was probably a good thing I was going.

2

On a bright but cold January morning, my taxi pulled up in front of Madame Hortense's. It was, she had said, situated in the very best part of Paris – Passy. It was, but only just! She had sent a print of a watercolour of her house, plus glowing references to her standing and respectability from the cream of French society. The house in front of me did not look like the one in the picture. It was smaller, as if much of it had been torn down, and though it had a garden it was nowhere as large as it had been drawn, and the neighbouring houses – absent from the print – encroached and towered over it. She had been at pains to tell my father that since the death of her husband ten years ago, she had taken to having young guests in her house – not for the money, of course, but for the stimulating company she so sadly missed.

As I stood in front of her establishment and watched her scurrying down the steps, rather like a demented red hen, I knew that I was about to meet another liar.

The immensely tall and ornate gates were wide open for the simple reason that the hinges had rusted and they would not close. The woodwork of the windows and the metal of the verandah and balustrades were covered in curls of peeling paint, like grey lichen. High in the mansard roof were two perfectly circular windows, as if a pair of big eyes were watching the proceedings far below. The garden was untended but I relished its wildness. The driveway in front of the house, along which coaches must once have approached at a spanking rate to halt in a shower of gravel, was now pot-holed and weed-covered. The cream blinds that shielded the elegant long casement windows from the sun looked tattered. The house made me think of a grand courtesan fallen on hard times – and I loved it on sight.

'My dear Miss Springer, welcome, welcome.' Madame, high heels clicking, gold charm bracelets rattling, clattered to a standstill in front of me. Heavily mascaraed eyes scanned me from head to toe, assessing the cost of my clothes, my jewellery, my skin, my age, all in one quick flicker. I took the outstretched hand, freckled with age spots. On several fingers rings reflected the pale January sun. They were such large stones that she was either as rich as Croesus or they were made of glass. Her dress, while smart, looked slightly faded as if it had been washed one time too many. Red was the colour to describe her: red-painted nails, long and probing, red hair the colour of burnished mahogany – dyed, of course, bright red lipstick on Cupid's bow lips, and cheeks with the reddest rouge I had ever seen. As she had lied about the house I was certain, looking at her, that she had lied about her social standing too.

'*Enchantée*, Madame. *Comment allez-vous?*' I asked shyly. I wasn't feeling in the least bit shy, but it had been drummed into me always to appear so when meeting new adults, as a form of respect, I suppose.

'What bliss! You speak French. I am so happy you do – my English is appalling!' She flapped her hands in the air as if drying them, and lapsed into her own language. I had to ask her to slow down; she spoke so quickly that I understood nothing.

'But your accent is perfect. I presumed . . . You are the third to arrive. Come and meet them.' She smiled at me, such a warm and genuine smile that I felt that all would be well here.

Madame did not seem to bother with breathing as we ascended the stairs at a brisk trot. She simply indicated with one of her sweeping gestures which was to be my room, then dragged me on to the next to meet the others, before racing back downstairs to answer a ring on the doorbell.

To my joy, Angelika and Heidi were German. I was only too happy to prattle away to them in their language. The relief on their faces was wonderful as they heard me. They were so German! Their pale blonde hair was braided, and they wore full-skirted pinafore dresses, with starched pristine aprons over the top – fancy dressing like that in Paris! They looked as if they had just come in from herding the cows. If they had yodelled I wouldn't have been in the least bit surprised – or was that the prerogative of the Swiss? They were sweet and welcoming but I was disappointed in them: they did not look the sort of girls to set the city on fire.

'My father will be furious. This place is not at all as it appeared in the prospectus,' said Heidi.

'I think Madame is very poor,' replied Angelika. 'I feel maybe we are being cheated.'

'How? I think it's wonderful. Paris is Paris, whether you're in a garret or in the Ritz. And did you see the pickle she's in downstairs? Blissful chaos.

9

She won't mind us being untidy, will she? I shall feel very much at home. I think she might be fun.'

Both girls looked doubtful, but I meant it. There was something exuberant about Madame Hortense, despite her age – fifty at least, I guessed.

At this point Madame reappeared with the fourth guest, and admonished us for speaking German – it was to be French only. The new girl was introduced, or rather she introduced herself, ignoring instructions, in English.

'Hi, everyone, I'm Mab.' She did not walk into the room but rather insinuated her way in. 'Why are you gawking at me?'

'I'm so sorry. I've never met an American before,' I gushed.

'I just love your English accent,' she cooed predictably.

'I'm rather partial to yours too.' That was better, I was behaving more normally now.

'Ladies!' Madame clapped her hands, which set all her jewellery clanking. 'You are in France now. You are here to learn the language, you really must try. And, Mabel, forgive me, this is Angelika, and this is Heidi, your fellow guests.'

'Where's the cuckoo clock?' Mab asked, as she held out her hand to be shaken, as if bestowing a favour.

'*Bitte*?' the Germans said in unison.

'Forget it.' She waved her hand, not in Madame's agitated and jerky way, but languidly as if already tired of us all. Things were looking up.

My room was perfect, just as I had imagined. French windows, with patterned lace curtains, opened on to a small balcony, which had an elegant wrought-iron balustrade and overlooked the wild garden. The wallpaper, a pretty blue and white with a pastoral scene printed on it, matched the curtains – I had never seen that before. The paintwork inside the house was grey also but with the beading picked out in gold; both colours were as battered and peeling as the exterior. The inside of my door was papered too, making it merge into the walls, so that unless you knew it was there it was hard to see. I made a note to tell Lettie, who was always on the lookout for innovative decorations. My wardrobe was a tall, shelved cupboard – evidently clothes were to be laid flat and not hung as at home. It smelt of mothballs and lavender. My bed was also wooden and looked like a Russian sleigh. It was covered with a beautiful white lace counterpane and a stack of embroidered, frilled cushions. Like Madame herself, the room was slightly shabby. It seemed to me that the whole house was slowly decaying.

'Hi.' Mab appeared in my doorway. 'What do you think?'

'It's lovely.'

'Bit old and faded.'

'That's its charm, don't you think?' But then, coming from the New World, maybe she wouldn't appreciate it.

'Do you think there are bedbugs?'

'Hardly.' I laughed.

'My daddy said he'd been eaten alive by them when he was here.'

'It all looks respectable enough. I'm sure it'll be fine.'

'Have you seen the bathroom? Lordy, but it's bizarre! It's so antiquated. There's no shower and the basin is so low and huge.'

'You're sure that's not the bidet?' I said, trying to sound knowledgeable – my stepmother had told me all about them.

'No, no. I was warned. I think I'll reserve it for my feet.' She gave a glorious head-thrown-back deep chuckle. Everything about Mab was large: she had to be at least five foot eight and towered over my measly five foot two. Her breasts were full and she was undoubtedly proud of them, given the way she thrust them out; mine were small, not that I minded – large ones would make dress fittings difficult. Her eyes were a cornflower blue, mine were grey – though I had written blue on my passport: it sounded prettier. We were both blonde. I wore mine in a roll and I'd had my fringe permed; hers was a bouncing mass of natural curls – pretty if unfashionable. Mine was a silver blonde while hers reminded me of cornfields, though in her case prairies might have been a better description.

'Come and see my room.'

I inspected Mab's room, which was similar to mine, except that hers was decorated in rose, and it overlooked the front of the house. 'Fancy a gargle?' From her wardrobe she took a bottle. 'Bourbon? I've no rocks or branch. Tap do you?'

Unsure what she meant, I agreed with everything. How deliciously decadent, I thought, drinking alcohol at three in the afternoon, in Paris, in a bedroom! My father would have had apoplexy.

'Why are you here? Your French sounds excellent to me,' she asked. From her this was a true compliment for it quickly transpired that she was bilingual, her mother being French.

'My father wanted to get rid of me. I seduced my eldest sister's fiancé and killed my middle sister. He wasn't very pleased with me.' I wondered if this was going to be one of those times where I would regret my exaggeration, but I had discovered that if I joked about it, it was easier to say. Mab's expression of astonishment turned into one of admiration before she choked on her drink. I was rather pleased with myself after all that I had put it like that.

'How absolutely ghastly for you. My poor Clare. I feel, oh, such sympathy for you.'

'Yes, he was pretty grim.'

'Oh, you English!' She laughed at my little joke. 'Actually, I meant the bit about your sister.'

'That was truly grim.' And I explained everything to her and how I had felt and how unfair everyone was, except Lettie, and to my own astonishment I began to cry. Not a gentle, sniffing weep but a full-scale howl. I kept apologising, and saying what must she think of me, and I sniffed and I spluttered but I just couldn't stop.

She took me in her arms and rocked me. 'Do you mind? This is private,' I heard her snarl at someone who had appeared in the doorway.

Still I cried and still she rocked me and began to sing to me a song about cowboys and moons and lone horsemen until I stopped. 'I am *so* sorry!' I apologised, blowing into a hankie and not knowing quite where to put myself.

'Don't be sorry. You obviously needed to cry.'

'I did. You see, I hadn't, not once. And the others all thought I didn't care and I do. But I couldn't cry.'

'I understand. The same thing happened to me when I shot my daddy.'

I never really knew what being poleaxed meant until that moment. Now I did. I was standing and I had to sit down again quickly, unsure if I had heard right. I had.

3

It seemed to me that God had decided he had punished me enough, had looked around and wondered what he could do to help me, then sent Mab. Of course I never said this to her: she might have laughed, she might have misunderstood – she did not strike me as a person who believed in anything, apart from herself. In the light of day this notion seemed silly to me too. But at night when I lay, unable to sleep, fretting about Felicity and going over and over in my mind how things might have been different, then it seemed less so. In fact, it became a perfectly logical explanation. For who else could I have met who understood so well the way my mind was working?

By talking honestly, by crying, I felt the block of sadness in me melt a little. I would never forget Felicity and what had happened. But I was finding my responsibility in her death easier to live with.

I longed to ask her why she had shot her father but I knew that I would have to wait until she wanted to tell me.

We had been joined by two others so that in all we were now six students. The new girls – Joan and Pamela – were English and satisfied with their position in life. They studied my vowels intently, asked a few pertinent questions of us all, made instant friends with the Germans and turned their backs on Mab and me.

'So what's wrong with us?' asked Mab. She was lying on my bed, after a strenuous tour of the Louvre, sipping a glass of delicious champagne.

'My face doesn't fit. And you're American.'

'Bet you a dollar they'll eventually say I'm one of the "sweepings of Europe".' She said this in her languid drawl, which had the effect of making it sound a most desirable thing to be.

'I wouldn't waste my money. They're both so predictable. That sort always are.'

'And what might "that sort" be?'

'Probably distantly related to some nob or other and poor as church mice, but valiantly hiding it from the rest of the world. Daddy probably sold his remaining shares to send them here, or a picture, or the last of the family silver. Sad, really.'

'Grue*some*! And why are you rejected?'

'They were confused at first. I speak the same way as them, if you notice, but where I live is wrong. They wouldn't deign to know anyone from Croydon. But, to compound it, I said my father was a baker. Did you see them shiver with disdain? Trade, you see – it's beyond the pale.'

Mab shook her head in disbelief. 'Are you taught this or do you learn it from experience?'

'That. Last year I met a boy called Tristram. We liked each other a lot. We made plans – you know, silly ones for the future. Unfortunately his mother didn't think me suitable, so he was sent away to a tea plantation in India.'

'How very rude.'

'Exactly.'

'And you didn't go to India to find him?'

'Of course not.' I laughed at the very idea.

'I would have. I'd have searched until I found him. So romantic.'

She would have, I'm sure. How mundane of me that the possibility had never crossed my mind.

'Then why tell them what your father does?'

'Why not? I'm not ashamed of him – I'm proud of what he has achieved.'

'Did you ever tell him how you felt about him?'

'No, you don't go around saying things like that!'

'Why ever not? I told my daddy every day that he was the most wonderful man in the world.'

I looked at her askance. 'In any case I don't want to be like them.' I preferred to continue the conversation on these lines: I felt on firmer ground.

'Good for you. I'm proud of you. What do we want with trash like that? Why are the Germans acceptable and not us?'

'Their fathers are professionals so they just squeeze in. Mind you, I know one family who won't let the doctor use the front entrance. They lump him in with the tradesmen.'

'What a strange race you English are. And money doesn't help?'

'Only if you've masses of it. They'll be in a rare old quandary though when they find out how rich you are. Oh, my, yes.'

'Then I shall just have to be as tight as a bull's ass in fly time, shan't I?'

'Yes, if it means what I think it does.' I laughed.

We weren't allowed alcohol, apart from a glass of wine with our meals, but this did not restrict Mab. On the second day she had found a congenial wine merchant and had hidden in her wardrobe a plentiful supply of wine, spirits and champagne in particular. Since Mab had to have ice with everything – my father would have had a stroke at seeing her drink five-star brandy with it – she had solved the problem by bribing the little maid, Sylvie, to bring us a supply each evening. After dinner, either in her room or mine, we would become gloriously tiddly.

We were not allowed to smoke either, but Mab puffed away oblivious to regulations: rules were for others, not her. I had so wanted to smoke, using a long ivory holder just like Mab's, but, disappointingly, I was sick each time I tried and finally had to admit that smoking was not for me.

Mab was fearless. She did not bother to suck mints or spray herself with perfume to disguise the smell of the smoke – sometimes I wondered if she was challenging Madame Hortense.

'Why should I challenge the dear soul? She knows what I do, she knows I know she knows, but that also I know she won't do anything about it.'

'How can you be so sure?'

'Money, honey. Is she going to want to lose me, especially now the others are beginning to revolt?'

Mab was right. Our fellow students, or rather the English, had started to complain. The Germans, with worried expressions, as if they were not sure they wanted to, faintly echoed the litany. I really couldn't understand them; I loved it at Madame's.

'The standards here are not what we were led to expect. I believe our parents should be informed.' Pamela, overweight, dark-haired and with a faintly malevolent expression, was standing on the rug in the small sitting room. Her feet were planted wide apart as if her horse had just slid out from between her legs.

'Pammie, you sound *so* middle-aged. How truly dreadful for you.' Mab was draped elegantly on a threadbare Louis Quinze occasional chair. She spoke in a concerned tone, as if commenting on some dreadful illness.

'And what does that mean?' Pamela bristled, which had the unfortunate effect of making her look, as well as sound, old.

'I'm worried about you, Pammie. Life is too short and we are too young to be worrying about *standards!* What the hell?'

'How can you say that? There was no hot water this morning. The soup was cold last night. I asked for more soap and was told I had had my ration for the month – the month!' Joan's voice rose in her indignation.

'The boiler's been mended and I had a scalding bath. The soup was supposed to be cold. And if there was no hot water you didn't need the soap, did you?'

'How can we expect a colonial like you to understand the importance of personal hygiene?' Pamela looked at Mab with disdain. I looked at her with interest. Mab's ancestors had gone to America in the *Arebella* – a boat that had sailed in 1632, which, apparently, gave her great social standing – and her mother was of noble French blood. I longed for her to tell them and rub it in. I would have done so, but that wasn't Mab's way.

In one smooth movement she stood up. She loomed over Pamela. 'You know, Pammie, my dear, it's cretins like you who give the English a bad name. And you're such a sad little creature, aren't you? Fancy some bubbly in my room, Clare, honey?'

Pamela was still searching for a smart retort after Mab had left the room. Heidi and Angelika looked perplexed. 'Did you understand any of that?' I asked them in German, for, the conversation had taken place in English.

'Not much.'

I translated for them.

'But these English are so rude,' said Angelika.

'I like Mab, she has a big heart. I hope she's not hurt.'

'No, Heidi, not Mab. She has no time for these two. She thinks them provincial and boring.' I smiled sweetly at Pamela and Joan as I spoke. It was childish of me but fun all the same.

'Are you talking about us?' Pamela demanded.

'What on earth gave you that idea?' I raced out of the room before I spoilt it all by giggling.

*

On her twentieth birthday Mab surpassed herself by taking Madame and me out to lunch at Maxim's, the most expensive restaurant I had ever been to.

What a revelation that was. As we walked in, the head waiter nearly tripped over his feet rushing to welcome her. All his attentiveness was reserved for her as he did a little bow of greeting over her hand. Then, in a complicated forwards and backwards dance, he showed us to our table. He settled us, in a flurry of cracking napkins, and asked solicitously if we needed an *apéritif*.

'That man treated you as if you were an old and respected client,' I commented.

'He can smell the money. Any *maître d'* worth his salt can,' she explained simply, with no hint of censure.

'You are wise beyond your years, my dear Mab.' Madame smiled at her and it was her genuine smile – I had noticed she had quite a repertoire of smiles. As we surveyed the large dining room, she pointed out to us the various celebrities who were packing the restaurant – actors, writers, politicians. 'Ah,' she sighed, with such contentment, 'all of Paris is here.'

The high spot was the arrival of Josephine Baker, a whirl of movement, black hair sleeked to her head like a seal's pelt, carried along by her admiring coterie.

I enjoyed that lunch like no other, and so did Madame who, invited by Mab, was choosing the food and wine for us. I ate *foie gras* for the first time and adored it, while trying not to think of how it had got to my plate, and happily sipped the sticky sweet Sauterne served with it. We had Sole Albert, and I had never tasted fish like it. We drank a white burgundy with that. This was followed by duck with peaches – though where they had come from so early in the year I'd no idea. It oozed blood, which quite turned my stomach until I tasted it and knew I would never eat the overcooked and mangled offering at home ever again. There and then, I declared Romanée-Conti my favourite wine. I ate cheeses I had never heard of and quite disgraced myself over the pudding when I asked for two helpings of the pyramid of profiteroles. Still we were not finished; petit fours arrived with our coffee and Cognac. By this time I knew I was drunk, and Madame Hortense had an even redder tinge to her skin, which did not sit happily with the customary slashes of rouge on her cheeks or the colour of her hair. Mab looked as if she had had one small sherry, not a hair out of place, not a hint of a flush.

'This is the life. I shall have to marry a rich man and come here every day,' I announced.

'Then you will get fat, and if that happens you might just as well be dead,' Madame, slim as a reed, admonished me.

When we returned home, Madame disappeared rapidly to her room, telling all and sundry she was sure she had a chill coming on.

Mab winked at me. 'I suppose you want to lie down too?'

'Whatever for? I hoped you were going to offer me some of your bourbon,' I replied. This was not true, I longed to curl up on my bed and sleep my lunch away, but instinct told me that Mab wanted to talk. We went to her room, or rather she did, and I stumbled along behind her. She poured two generous measures of the whiskey, sat down, put her hands in her lap, took a deep breath, looked at me and sighed deeply.

'It was three years ago today I killed my daddy.' She spoke quietly and apparently calmly. I sobered up in a trice: for her to speak in such a way of this matter did not bode well for her equilibrium.

'I was cleaning his guns. I loved to do them. Of all things, I enjoyed the smell of the gun oil. I liked to polish the stocks until I could see my face in them, and the silver chasing and engraving around the lock. That's what I was doing when he walked into the room, "Happy birthday," he said. "That's my girl." He must have made me jump, I can't remember, and my finger slipped – I didn't even notice I'd pushed the safety catch off while cleaning. Boom! He fell dead.' Mab closed her eyes to shut out the fearful image – I knew that didn't work. I put my arm around her, squeezed her shoulder, trying to inject some comfort and knowing how woefully inadequate it was. I waited, letting her choose when to speak. 'What a cartridge was doing in the breech we'll never know. My daddy was so careful, he never brought a gun into the house unless it was empty. They were always checked. Why didn't I check it too? He'd drummed it into me. "Never fool about with a gun unless you've checked it." It was his favourite shotgun, I never thought . . .' Her voice trailed off. I quite expected her to burst into tears as I had, but she didn't. 'You'll understand, Clare, how I keep on torturing myself. The if only thoughts, I call them. *If only* I had done this and not done that. *If only* I had been someplace else that day.'

'I understand totally,' I said, with feeling. 'Still, it sounds to me that it was a genuine accident. You weren't to know. It was hardly your fault.'

'Don't you bullshit me too! Keep your goddam sympathy clichés to yourself.' She was on her feet and looming over me. 'Of course it was my fault. I didn't do what he told me to. There's no way round it, none at all.'

'I'm sorry. I was only trying to make you feel better.'

'But that's what everyone does, don't you see? My mother, my sister, my grandmother – they talk just like you! "Don't blame yourself, Mab. You mustn't feel bad." How am I *not* to blame myself? That's why I'm here, you stupid fool. I had to get away from the awful sympathy!'

'Could I have some?' My voice squeaked out of me.

'Sorry?' Mab sat down.

'I got nothing but blame. You got the opposite. There has to be a middle way here. You can have some of my accusations and bitterness if I can have some of your mother's understanding.' I didn't know if I was making myself clear, but I couldn't see her face since my eyes were full of the tears I was fighting not to shed. This was her time to talk and grieve, not mine – I'd had that luxury.

I must have said something right, because suddenly she laughed. 'Fair enough, my dear Limey friend. Fair enough.'

She didn't cry, though for her sake I wished she would. I knew how much it would help her, as it had helped me.

4

Madame Hortense's little operation might have been on the shabby side, and everything was done on a shoestring, but we did learn – after a fashion. She plunged into the art galleries with us following somewhat self-consciously behind. She only took us to see the paintings she cared about, speeding past those she did not enjoy with a dismissive wave of the hand, an expressive 'Bah' and a derisive 'Poor brushstroke, no sensitivity, provenance uncertain.' Woe betide anyone who lingered over something of which she did not approve. 'Don't weary your eyes on rubbish!' she would declaim, to the consternation of the tourists. And so we sped past the English romantics, the Dutch interiors, the Renaissance, for it was inevitable that Madame preferred French paintings.

She was sound on china and glass, flower-arranging, how to tie a scarf. Who to introduce to whom and when and how. We learnt to sit and stand, even to walk, which until then was something we thought we had mastered. 'Glide, flow, imagine your feet are wheels!' she would admonish us, fluttering about the room like a scarlet butterfly, annoyed at our giggling, furious that we moved like 'baby elephants'. And she felt and taught passionately on the subject of food and wine.

She had turned the large kitchen in the basement of her house into a demonstration room. A mirror hung over the worktop so that we could see every movement she made. To hear her talk about the mixing and baking of a soufflé was like hearing a mystic talk about God. She would remonstrate with us as we made pastry or kneaded bread. 'Cooking is not for artisans, it is for artists!' she would shriek excitedly, becoming more voluble at every mistake we made. I began to love Madame.

Any plans I had had of meeting a delicious Frenchman came to nothing. There was no time and, in any case, Madame never let us out of her sight. 'Your reputation is your most precious possession,' she announced. 'After your looks, of course,' she added. Mab and I were reduced to ogling the gardener, and both of us developed pashes on the man who delivered the ice, which only showed how desperate we were since he had to be thirty if he was a day.

We did meet men. Three times a week Madame Hortense conducted a *soirée*. Men of letters and the arts were invited, for conversation with them was part of our education – not easy for they spoke in such a courtly, flowery manner that all we wanted to do was giggle. They were old, and scruffy too; food-stained waistcoats were part of their uniform. We were certain that they came because they were starving, and thirsty for the wine Madame served in copious amounts to them – not us. For how could they have enjoyed talking to such young women? What had we to say to philosophers and poets when our heads were full of longing for young men and romance?

Madame, on the other hand, was enraptured by them all. We would sit fascinated watching her coquette with one guest after another. She seemed to shed years as she flirted and fluttered her eyelashes at them. It was, in a way, another learning process.

The days were so full that time raced by. Already three months had passed. To be young in Paris, in spring, with our dreams of the lovers we would surely find, was exhilarating. The trees exploded into blossom, the sun became hotter, as if winding itself up for summer, couples met in parks and kissed, closely observed by Mab and me. It was almost too heady an experience. Sometimes I thought it couldn't last, that something would go wrong.

I had been remiss in writing home. When I had first arrived I had sent a couple of postcards but soon even that seemed too much of a chore. I felt ashamed upon receiving a long letter from Lettie. *They*, she wrote, were worried about me and the rapidly deteriorating political situation. I laughed to myself at her use of the plural. She might be worried but no one else was: if my father really cared he would have written himself. She suggested that in view of the situation in Poland I should return home immediately. I hadn't the least idea what she was going on about. I never read the papers or listened to the radio – I had no interest in any of that boring old stuff.

'Madame, do you know anything about Poland?' I thought I had better check.

'Such divine men! Such thighs – the cavalry, my dear.'

'Ah, I see.' But I persisted. I didn't think that was what Lettie was referring to. 'Is there anything else? Like a political problem.'

'Oh, the Boche huff and puff – they so often do. But there's nothing to worry you. We have our glorious French army with its brave young men who have the courage of lions. And our invincible Maginot Line.' When Madame talked about anything French – food, wine, buildings, history – she virtually stood to attention and declaimed rather than spoke. I often expected her to burst into 'La Marseillaise'.

'So there are concerns?'

'Bah! My dear Clare, never bother yourself about such matters. Leave that to the men. They are so much cleverer than we are.'

At this there was an indignant snort from Mab.

Something was up. That afternoon, Madame cancelled our class and sped from the house with instructions that we entertain ourselves. Mab and I set out for Fouquet's. We bought a *Herald Tribune* and sat with a tisane, watching the people parade up and down the Champs-Elysées, admiring the men and giggling furiously when we noted them admiring us. I would like to have investigated this situation further, but both of us held back, Mab because she said they were all too short, and I because, to be quite honest, the French men with their bold stares and appraising looks frightened me somewhat.

'What does it say?' I asked Mab.

'A lot of verbiage about some Anglo-French-Polish military alliance, which is to be signed next week should Poland need defending.'

'From whom?'

'Germany, I imagine.'

'How thrilling. Does that mean there might be a war?'

'Presumably. A bit unlikely, though, isn't it? After the last one my daddy said there'd never be another.'

'Perhaps it's an April Fool's joke.'

'Remote.'

'I wonder if Heidi and Angelika know.'

'I doubt it.'

She was probably right. None of us knew much about politics, which wasn't on our curriculum. Of course we knew there had been a war in Spain because the brother of a friend of mine had gone to fight in it. But Spain was a long way away and, in any case, it all sounded rather glamorous, not something to worry about.

Mab decided to pop into her dressmaker's to see if her new suit was ready. I opted to stay where I was and write to Lettie. Mainly I told her about Mab and Madame Hortense and the art galleries and the cooking lessons. Then I told her that no one was concerned here about Poland, that if anything did happen I would be on the first boat home. That was a lie: if something like a war happened I had every intention of being here – I wasn't going to miss such excitement. I was about to put my letter in the envelope when I decided to write a postscript: 'Have you done anything about him yet?!? If war is a possibility then you must! Remember, life is too short to turn your back on true love!!' I reread it, pleased with myself and my evident wisdom.

Mab returned. The cream linen suit fitted like a dream, and she announced that such perfect couture should be celebrated, and to make the most of this unexpected afternoon of freedom, where better than the Ritz and champagne? There I gave my letter to the concierge to post for me.

When we returned, the house was in chaos. Cases and boxes littered the hall. Madame Hortense, always a blur of movement, was surpassing herself, whirling about, flapping her hands, screeching, 'Oh, la, la!' at every other second. She would have been mortified to know that she was visibly perspiring.

'What's up?' asked Mab.

'Oh, la, la, don't even ask me!'

'Then we won't,' Mab said, with reason.

On the upper landing we found Angelika in tears and Pamela looking even more sour then usual, something I would have thought impossible. She was officiously ticking off items on a list she held in her hand. So organised!

'What's going on?' Mab and I chorused.

'There's going to be a war,' Pamela announced dramatically.

At this Angelika wailed heart-rendingly.

'Joan and I received telegrams. We're going home on the first boat. Our train leaves in an hour and you're to come with us, Clare.'

'I shall do no such thing.'

'You have to.'

'I don't have to do anything.'

'Your father sent a telegram to Madame.'

Not to me, I thought.

'Clare, they have been so rude to Heidi and me.' Angelika lapsed into German.

'There's nothing unusual in that.' I laughed.

'They called us pigs, aggressors.'

'Don't speak that disgusting language in front of me,' Pamela barked bossily.

'And you stop being so stupid. It's a beautiful language, and it's not Angelika's fault that you're panicking.'

'Could we have some reason here?' Mab asked, from her position at the head of the stairs, lolling against the banisters. 'Has war been declared? Are the Teutonic hordes marching on us as we speak?'

'No, but we're to sign a pact with the French next week that if Poland—'

'We know all that, Pammie. What a fuss. I suggest you all wait and see what happens.'

'Typical of an American, that. Watch and wait, see if it's advantageous to you to join in.'

'Now, you just wait a minute here. We saved your bacon in the last war, remember? Though, quite honestly, having met you two I can't imagine why we bothered.'

'Why we should be grateful to the "sweepings of Europe", I really don't know,' Pamela sneered, and Joan nodded in agreement.

'Yes!' shouted Mab triumphantly. 'What did I tell you, Clare? I knew she'd say that eventually. Poor Pammie, you're so predictable. I can look at you and see your whole future. You will marry and your children will grow up to loathe you. You will be repelled by sex so that your husband will find his comfort elsewhere and who will blame him? Your rear will broaden alarmingly, your bosom will sag, your skin will become rough and mottled. And when you die not even your dogs will be sorry to see you go. As for me, I do hope I shall be around, just so that I can have the pleasure of dancing on your grave.' She turned away from the open-mouthed, furious Pamela. 'Fancy some champers, Clare and my little German friends?' She swept along the corridor. Gleefully, we followed her.

5

Pamela and Joan did not leave without a huge row with Madame Hortense, which we were all privileged to witness. They wanted their fees reimbursed and were noisily adamant about their rights. Madame was equally voluble about hers. 'It's not my fault if your father decided you should return home at the first hint of trouble. You signed up for a year and a year you shall pay for.' Madame and her money were not easily parted.

'You'll be hearing from our lawyers.'

'I await that with pleasure. Your taxi, I think?' She cocked her head like an inquisitive little bird.

That evening we celebrated with a fine white burgundy and salmon in a champagne sauce. I had two helpings.

There was no celebration six weeks later, in May, when Angelika and Heidi were summoned home.

'I shall miss chatting to you two in German,' I said, as we stood in the hall waiting for the taxi to arrive.

'Clare, if the worst comes to the worst, we'll still be friends, won't we?'

'Of course, Heidi. Whatever happens. It's got nothing to do with us, has it?'

'Oh, you two. There won't be a war. What nonsense to talk. The last time was enough for everyone.' Madame fluttered about them, but she looked strained. 'You'll be back in a month, you mark my words.'

That evening we discovered the cause of her worry. Two students who were to have joined us in June had pulled out, and already she had had cancellations for the 1940 intake.

Our numbers sorely depleted, we sat in the kitchen. Madame was in such a state that if we had waited for her to produce dinner, we'd have waited in vain. Mab and I cooked for her and poured her a drink, and made her stay with us and talk to us as we pottered about. We thoroughly enjoyed ourselves and the success we made of it. Perhaps we looked after her a little too well for we had not even finished the main course – aubergine and chicken-liver galettes with a delicate tomato sauce, which looked a bit of a mess but tasted delicious – before Madame began to slur her words. Then her head fell forward. For a moment I thought she had nodded off, but she began to sob and then to wail. We looked at each other, hoping the other would know what best to do. Neither of us did, so we had to sit it out, and very uncomfortable it was – an adult losing control of their emotions is frightening.

Eventually she calmed down, her complexion even redder than usual, black streaks of mascara marbling her face. She was a truly sorry sight. She hiccuped her way back to us, apologising all the time. 'It's the upkeep of the house that is my greatest problem.'

'Can't you sell it?' Mab was always so practical.

'I couldn't do that. I love this house. But, in any case, there are ten of us who own it and the others would never agree. And how could I possibly afford to buy them out?'

'Ten? A business consortium?' Mab asked. I was amazed at the things Mab knew.

'No, of course not. We are all family members. There's my brother and me, and the rest are cousins.' Madame looked affronted, not liking anyone to regard her as a business.

'Doesn't that lead to some confusion?'

'Not really. It is the law here in France. As each person dies so their children inherit in equal shares.'

'How silly. That way if it was a large family then hundreds of people could eventually share a property.'

'Our laws are not silly. They are fair. The family, to a Frenchman, is of the utmost importance.' She sat to attention: it seemed she thought the honour of France was under attack. It sounded a fair system to me and I wished we had it: I had a nasty idea that my father was unlikely to leave me anything but this way he would have to. 'My family are content for me to live here,' she continued. 'Maintaining the property is the price I pay. And that is getting harder and harder.'

'Couldn't you take in some lodgers, if you're sure you can't get students?'

'You wouldn't mind?'

'I don't. What about you, Clare?'

'It wouldn't bother me.'

'How dear of you. And how strange. You see, I had already begun negotiations with a friend and I wasn't sure how to put it to you. I mean, you came here to learn, not to live in a glorified *pension* – even if it is, as you know, situated in the best *arrondissement* of Paris. I was worried what your parents might think.' Mab and I smiled conspiratorially: her customary boast was rather endearing.

'Don't tell them. I shan't,' I assured her, and poured more wine for Mab and me.

Madame did not notice the wine but we noticed the sudden dramatic change in her. She had blown her nose, tidied her hair, reapplied her mascara and announced that her friend was due at any minute. I did think it a bit uncharitable of Mab to whisper to me that we had been led up the garden path.

Tiphaine de Bourbonnais arrived half an hour later. She was small, pretty, and over-made-up. She had large china blue eyes, like a doll, and this similarity had obviously inspired her clothes: there was a touch too much broderie-anglaise for my taste. Her manner was artificially sweet and her voice was girlish. I thought she was dreadful. But I was wrong. After several glasses of wine she was speaking normally and had dropped the little-girl act, but not the giggle – that was natural. She had a fund of funny stories, mainly about men and their private parts. I stopped blushing after the first half-dozen and decided I liked her.

We helped Madame install Tiphaine in her rooms. She had the best bedroom at the front of the house – the only one with a bathroom *en suite*. The room next door, in which Pamela had slept, had been made into a sitting room for her with a connecting door.

'You still think that wasn't a charade we witnessed at dinner? Madame had planned this meticulously. We said everything she had hoped we would – she's as cunning as a prairie dog.'

'I think you're right,' I conceded. Mab was in her bed and I was sitting on it as we had a late-night natter about the unfolding events.

'She's a *hoe*, of course. I'd bet my last dollar she is.'

There followed a conversation of mounting complexity, not helped by the amount of wine we had drunk, as I tried to unravel what Mab meant.

'Oh, you mean a *whore*! It's your accent, I didn't understand,' I spluttered, convinced I would die from laughing, though I was shocked too. 'How do you know?' While aware of the existence of such women and a vague idea of what they *might* do, I had no conception of how they were recognised.

'The tone of the conversation and the look of the woman. And her name! I ask you, whoever heard of a name like that? No, that's as false as her makeup.'

'Is it?' It had sounded all right to me. 'Should we mind?'

'Do we mind? Are you mad? This is the best thing that could possibly have happened to us. In the morning, let me do the talking.'

I was quite happy to agree.

'Madame, we have a proposition,' Mab began, straight after breakfast, having requested a meeting.

'I am all ears.' Madame smiled at us so pleasantly and I wanted to shout a warning to her – I didn't want her hurt in any way.

'We are aware of Tiphaine's profession. That she is a whore.' At least in French there was no confusion about pronunciation.

'That is a very serious accusation, Mab.' Madame looked stern but at the same time very shifty.

'Not nearly as serious as what she and you are doing.'

There was much fluster and bluster, oh-la-la-ing and hands semaphoring. But Mab stood firm and eventually Madame collapsed, exhausted, into a chair. 'And you propose? You will leave?' She looked so sad and small that I really wanted to push Mab for being such a bully.

'Good gracious, no. That's the last thing we want to do. Neither of us minds what you get up to, as long as you don't expect us to join in.' Mab gave one of her full, happy laughs, which lightened the atmosphere in the room. Madame sat up again and looked interested – today she reminded me of an intelligent French poodle, with her black, beady eyes, rather than the bird. 'I suggest that we say nothing to our families. You continue to receive our fees. In return . . .'

'Yes?' She leant forward eagerly.

'We finish as students. We come and go as we wish. You ask no questions of what we get up to and we ask none of you. Agreed?'

'Indubitably.'

And so it was arranged. Mab and I, that very same day, were out shopping and that evening we went to a jazz club, met two men, brought them home with us, gave them brandy and showed them the door when they got too fresh with us.

Everything was set fair, I thought. And then I received a letter from home. I'd wondered why they hadn't replied to mine sooner, but they'd only just received it. Stupidly I had forgotten to put '*Angleterre*' on the envelope and it had been all round France before arriving in England. It was in two parts; the first was from Lettie. Abruptly she told me that she never wanted to see me again – ever. That I had betrayed her. That I had lied. Well, I was most put out. I had not lied, I would have bet my pearls she was in love with another. It was hardly my fault if Father had read her mail; she shouldn't have let him. The second part was from Father, telling me what a spiteful and ungrateful child I was – the usual from him. That he, too, never wanted to see me, that I was to return to England immediately and go to stay with a great-aunt in Devon; he was stopping my allowance forthwith.

It was my turn to wail. Mab came running. She read my letter. 'How unkind,' she said.

'But I'll have to go. I've no money. I can't stay here. I hate the great-aunt – she smells of mothballs. And I hate the idea of Devon. It's full of cows and it rains all the time. And just as we were beginning to have fun!'

'And long may it continue. I can give you money – I've masses and if I run out then I shall just send for more.'

'I couldn't do that. How would I ever repay you?'

'I don't need to be repaid. My daddy always said give money, never lend it, you'll ruin friendships if you do. Just like Polonius, my daddy was. You must stay. What would I do without you?'

And that was that. Mab was an extraordinary friend. Never once was I made to feel indebted to her or obliged to repay her in any way.

We clattered about Paris with a widening circle of friends. We liked exploring Montmartre and the artist colony, where one day we were asked to sit for portraits. I was flattered until I heard Mab bargaining over the price. 'I wasn't aware one *paid* to be painted,' I said, all hurt pride, but Mab laughed and continued her negotiations. The pictures were not exactly what one would hang with pride, but I liked the way we could sit at a pavement café with just one drink and not be harassed to buy more – which happened in the more fashionable haunts.

Best of all, however, we preferred crossing the river to the Left Bank to the clutter of bars and bistros around the student quarter. There were a lot more young people there too, of course, which no doubt influenced us. What I liked about the city, and the people we met, was that *who* you were did not matter a fig. *What* you were was important. Were you amusing? Did you have something interesting to say? We were fully aware that there was another world in Paris, where standing and position and possessions and breeding mattered, but we had decided we didn't want to be part of that.

Most of our friends were American, mainly writers and artists fired up with excitement just from being there. But we had met a fair few French too. We sometimes went to the Café Flore in Saint-Germain-des-Prés, just in the hope that we might see Sartre, Camus, Picasso – not that I knew anything about any of these people but there was always a rustle of excitement when they came in, and I pretended to be excited too.

Our absolute favourite was the Mississippi bar, run by an American called Josh. I liked him even though he was a bit too serious, as if he had huge worries, not that he would ever tell us what they were. It was dark and smoky with a zinc bar that ran the whole length of one wall. Behind it stood many bottles of drink, most of which I did not recognise but which I was determined to sample before I went home. On one side of each white marble table were lovely squishy banquettes covered in leather, so old the stiffness had long worn out, on the other ornate slate-coloured metal chairs, their scrolling ironwork so delicate they looked as if they had been woven by giant spiders. Large white lamps were suspended from a ceiling made dark brown from years of potent tobacco smoke. It was always busy, noisy, no matter the time of day or night.

We spent many hours there having deep, significant conversations about the meaning of everything. Well, they did. I was often bored or lost the drift and I would think about other important matters – like when would I meet someone to love. I never let on, though: I became quite expert at looking interested while I was miles away. I could have wished that our friends washed a little more often, but Mab said they were above such matters. I often wondered why, in order to improve our minds, it was necessary to ruin our stomachs with the seemingly endless carafes of cheap acidic wine. Mab said we had to, that that was what everyone drank and she didn't want to be too flash and order more expensive bottles.

New experiences poured down on me. I went forty-eight hours without sleep. I got drunk. I sniffed cocaine. I was kissed by a Frenchman and he put his tongue in my mouth. I allowed an American to touch my breasts. I

wasn't too sure about the kiss but I liked my breasts being touched –
though no further! I hated being drunk and feeling out of control. And the
drugs, which I admit I enjoyed, frightened me so I decided never to
experiment with them again – I might, I realised, get to like them too
much.

Of course, I often made a fool of myself. A friend of Mab's took us to a
club he had found. It was just like any of the others we'd been to – dark,
noisy and crowded, until my eyes adjusted to the gloom.

'Mab, everyone, just look at those people dancing and smooching. Mab!
They're all men!' I pointed excitedly and was put out when they laughed.

'Honey, they're pansies.'

'What's a pansy?'

This time when they laughed and explained I felt mortified. But, as Mab
kept pointing out, we were experiencing the *real* Paris – even if it was
sometimes bizarre. I thought I would never be so fortunate again.

In a sense it *was* the real Paris for where we went was far from the tourist
route. We moved in a city of narrow, cobbled streets, where houses stood
with shuttered windows – were they keeping the world out or their secrets
in? I loved the noisy markets, the smell of the cheeses, fresh in from the
farms, added to that of the streets, an odd mixture of black tobacco, garlic,
wine and pungent disinfectant. Separately each smell would have been
unpleasant; melded together, they were the unique aroma of a time, this
city, my youth.

If the world was becoming more dangerous around us we were ignorant
of it. It did not concern us. Politics was for fusty old men whose ability to
enjoy themselves was virtually over. We were young, we were having fun,
and we intended to go on that way.

As I got to know her I liked Tiphaine more and more. It was a shock to
find out that Mab did not and, worse, that she disapproved of her. It
didn't bother me what Tiphaine did for a living. She was honest about it,
there was not a hint of hypocrisy in her; she wasn't hurting anyone so
why shouldn't she sell herself if that was what she wanted? What
fascinated me was how she had got to where she was.

'Have you ever lived in a small provincial French town, Clare?'

'No.'

'Then don't, ever. If you haven't done anything bad the old crones will
say you have. So you're damned if you don't so you might just as well
have some fun and do it.' She giggled. 'Only don't get caught. I did and
was virtually run out of town.' This amused her no end so there was
another pause while she laughed. 'I went to the nearest large town and
found myself very popular and I began to think, Why give it away when

there are plenty willing to pay for it? So I came here, where the money is better and the clients classier.'

'Don't you ever want to fall in love?'

'One day when I can afford it and can make my own choice. Until then I've my Henri and he's a darn sight better than walking the streets I can tell you.'

Henri was the only man we ever saw her with; presumably, for a consideration, she kept herself exclusively for him. He was middle-aged, a trader in sugar – but Tiphaine didn't like 'sugar-daddy' jokes. He never spoke to us if we met him on the stairs but Tiphaine was content with him.

I could ask Tiphaine anything. 'I don't understand Hortense. She part-owns this big house and yet she . . . Well, I don't know quite how to put it.'

'Doesn't really fit the house or the neighbourhood?'

'Exactly.'

'It's complicated. She was born in a very poor district of Paris – in Menilmontant, but I doubt if you've ever been there. She hates anyone to know. Her mother, by all accounts, was very beautiful. She was officially a seamstress, only she wasn't – if you understand my meaning. She eventually took up with a rich old man. He was childless and he adopted Hortense and her brother. When he died they found there was no fortune, he'd spent the lot on good living, just this house. She shares ownership with her brother and a gaggle of the old man's nephews and nieces'.

'So why does she pretend to be so grand.'

'For business. You'd never get anyone straighter than Hortense.'

We had several *beaux*, as Mab quaintly called them. But none of them was the man of my dreams – that shadowy dark Frenchman I dreamt about at night. I had been sent out into the world unprepared for men. The only advice I had been given by Lettie just before I left was not to let one 'interfere' with me, whatever that meant. So, just in case I ever met *him*, I thought it wise to have a crash course in the facts of life. I asked Tiphaine to explain everything to me. Which she did with graphic descriptions, a bit too explicit at times, and told me what she got up to. Some things I vowed I could never do. She reassured me that I wouldn't be expected to, not a nice girl like me. She gave me one extra piece of advice. 'Hang on to your cherry as long as you can, Clare. It's a good bargaining counter, that.' Of course, I had to have my cherry explained, and I knew I went the same colour as the fruit as she told me.

Whether it was the arrival of Tiphaine or my growing friendship with her that changed things with Mab, I'm not sure. It was hard to pin down the problem but I began to realise that I needed Mab more then she needed me: that it was always she who took the lead, her opinions that counted. As I became aware of this a distance grew between us. She was as kind and generous as always, which was why I felt guilty even thinking like this.

There was an invisible barrier around her, which I couldn't penetrate. It was as though she were saying, 'So far and no further.' There was the Mab who drank, joked, stayed up all night and was fun, and yet I sensed I hadn't met the real Mab.

If this was the case, why did she bother with me? Sometimes I felt it was because she hated to be alone, which made me sad, I wanted a friendship far deeper than I believed she could give me.

6

By August I was miserable. On 4 July Mab had been invited without me to a reception at the American embassy and there she had met an Englishman, Major 'Tubs' Lyndhurst, and had promptly fallen in love with him to the exclusion of all others – including me.

It wasn't as if Mab had dropped me: she hadn't. I was invited to go to dinner, the theatre, the opera with them. But I felt in the way. And me at the opera? No, thank you! And when they went to the theatre, it was to the Comédie Française, to sit through Racine or Molière – no, thank you, again. They never went to jazz clubs: Tubs, it transpired, didn't like jazz. The likes of Chevalier and Suzy Solidor did not amuse him. And he could not understand the excitement about Piaf. Nor did he like the cinema, so they didn't go any more – and neither did I, after I had once gone alone and half-way through felt a hand on my knee. I turned to give the man a piece of my mind in my best French slang only to find that my molester was a woman. I sped to Tiphaine, who made my hair stand on end with her tales of lesbians and their 'goings-on'. Honestly, the amount I was learning was staggering.

Tubs did not approve of the circle of friends Mab and I had made. That's it, I thought. He's overstepped the mark. Mab will drop him now. To my astonishment, she didn't. She dropped everyone else – except me. 'If I didn't like Tubs' friends he'd do the same for me,' was her answer when I questioned her.

'And you like them?'

'Yes, I do. His friends are charming.'

'How fortunate for you both,' I said, mustering as much sarcasm as I could, but she didn't rise to the bait, merely smiled in that daft way she had, these days.

For a while I tried to keep up with the friends we'd made, but I had never been close to them: Mab had been more their friend than I was. Still, it was hurtful to see the look of disappointment on their faces when they saw only penniless me standing there. For the first time I began to query what the attraction had been: her conversation or the fact that she had picked up the bill. I went out at night infrequently now, but I couldn't spend all my time at Hortense's. I found a job.

The shop I worked in was on the Faubourg St Honoré and sold exquisite, hugely expensive underwear. I was not taken on for my selling ability or my knowledge of knickers but for my language skills: many of the clients were American and German and an interpreter was essential.

They were mostly men, buying these ridiculous clouds of silk, lace and chiffon for their ladies. I was convinced that mostly they were buying for their mistresses: no self-respecting wife would have been seen in some of the garments we sold, although Tiphaine would have given her soul for them.

There were two other salesgirls, both older than I, called Colette and Juliette. I referred to them as the Ettes, which made them laugh and covered up the fact that often I confused them: with their identical dark hair, similar black dresses, and even the same perfume, it was difficult to tell them apart. They wore the underwear we sold because occasionally the customers invited them out and gave them lingerie as presents. I, too, found myself turning down invitations: the men were invariably too old but I took it as a compliment that they bothered to ask me.

Only once did I waver: one day a young man walked in and my heart lurched. It was *him*! The man I dreamt of. No longer a figment of my imagination but there in the flesh. He was French, and Colette, to my annoyance, leapt to serve him.

'And what does Mademoiselle think of this one?' He turned to me, smiling disconcertingly, and held up a sliver of apricot silk. I was so happy he hadn't gone for black or scarlet – they always struck me as vulgar. His voice was deep, just as I had wanted it to be.

'It's lovely.' I knew I sounded mundane. 'I've always particularly admired that set of lingerie,' I added, thinking that that sounded better but wondering for whom he was buying it and wishing it was me.

'Maybe, then, Mademoiselle would award me the honour of allowing me to purchase it for her.' I was aware of Colette glowering at me. I thought I would faint.

'I couldn't possibly,' I said, blushing furiously and, sounding as flustered as I felt, I made a dash for the minute stock room, which doubled as our rest room. I sat arguing with myself, already beginning to regret not pursuing this further. I need not accept the underwear, but I could have flirted, I could have agreed to a drink. 'Monsieur . . .' I was forming the words as I slipped back through the curtain. But he'd gone.

'Just as well,' Tiphaine counselled that evening, as I sat in her room and watched her make up before being taken out to dinner by her 'friend', as she called Henri. 'He might have got the wrong idea. Trouble with men like that is they think that by buying you panties they have a God given right to get inside them!' She giggled. 'But, worse, he might have thought you were on the game.'

'I don't think so.'

'Oh, no? Then what was he doing there in the first place? Those shops are full of amateurs. Why can't they be above board about what they do? Poaching clients from honest girls.' She was applying her rouge in angry little dabs.

'The Ettes? Oh, you're wrong about that. They only go out for dinner and sometimes they're given presents from the shop. They told me.'

Tiphaine swung round on her dressing-table stool, a swansdown powder-puff in her hand. 'And you believed them? Clare! Didn't you listen to a word I said? I warned you about predators like that when you took this job. I told you what those girls were up to.'

'I didn't believe you.'

'Then do. It'll be better for you in the long run.' She laughed – I loved her infectious laugh.

'Tiphaine, is de Bourbonnais your real name?'

'No.'

'Then what is?'

'Never you mind. Now, be off with you. My friend'll be here shortly and he doesn't like being kept waiting.'

Forlornly I went to my room. Without Mab, I was spending more and more time with Tiphaine. I shouldn't. If I replaced Mab with her then, no doubt, she'd let me down or I'd end up missing her too.

Although I resented Tubs for taking Mab from me, I couldn't help liking him. His nickname, Tubs, was a mystery since he was slim and muscular, and I could see why Mab found him attractive. Of course, he was old in my eyes, mid-thirties, but Mab said she didn't mind, that she preferred older men. He was on the staff of the military attaché at the British embassy. He laughed a lot but he could be dreary – his age, no doubt – for he kept on and on at us that we should leave France for England.

'Mab tells me you're half Austrian, Clare, and that you speak fluent German.'

'Almost right, Tubs. I'm bilingual, not fluent. There's a big difference, you know.'

'I stand corrected.' He gave a funny little bow and I had a feeling he was laughing at me.

But I was right to point it out: for me German was not a foreign language, it was as much part of me as English was. 'My mother was Austrian and my father's grandparents were German.'

'You were born in England?' he asked casually.

'No, in Salzburg. My mother was visiting her parents – her father was gravely ill, and I decided to be premature.'

'So you have dual nationality?'

'I suppose I do. I've never thought about it. I mean, I feel English, and my passport is English, so that is what I say I am. I lost my Austrian one months ago.'

'If you mean to stay here – against my advice, given the worsening situation – then perhaps you should apply to renew your Austrian passport. Except, of course, since the Austrians have voted to be part of Germany it will be a German one.'

'Have they? When?'

'Last year.'

'No one told me.'

'You should read the newspapers,' Mab said – quite tartly, I thought. That was cheeky, coming from her. She'd only begun to take any notice of world affairs since Tubs had come on the scene.

'Now you mention it, my father told me. I'd just forgotten.' He hadn't but I wasn't going to let *her* know.

'What do you think?' Tubs persisted.

'I'm not giving up my English one for anybody.'

'Fine, but in the circumstances perhaps a German one too?'

'Don't be such a scaremonger, Tubs darling. You'll frighten us,' Mab simpered. Honestly, sometimes when she was with him I thought she had quite lost her senses.

'It was only a suggestion.' He shrugged, as if it was of no concern to him what I did.

One day in August Tubs and Mab persuaded me to go to the Bois de Boulogne for a walk and a drink. The city was intolerably hot and it made me realise why the French, always sensible in matters of comfort, abandoned the city in that month. This year an atmosphere of tension was added to the heat. All the talk was of war. I just closed my ears to it all.

The Bois was a lovely place to be, yet the outing, for me, was not a success. I felt sad and I didn't know why – it wasn't like me. Perhaps it was the perfection of the day and the place that made being with Mab and Tubs particularly hard. Although I was not alone I might just as well have been for all the notice they took of me.

We had stopped at a café, and as I watched them, so deeply engrossed in each other, I felt more than usually in the way. I made my excuses and told them I was going for a walk. I wandered along one of the bridlepaths, watching the horses, trying to talk myself out of the jealousy I felt towards them. It was stupid to feel like this. Now that I had acknowledged my jealousy I felt better about myself: now that I knew what the battle inside me was about I could rid myself of such a silly emotion. The day brightened, the sadness left me, and I began to take an interest in the riders. How wonderful it would be if one of them turned out to be the handsome man who had come to the shop. What would I do? What would I say? I'd accept an invitation, that was for sure.

Suddenly I heard running footsteps behind me. I turned to see who it was. Before I could register what was happening, a man grabbed at my handbag, which I had slung over my shoulder. 'Stop, thief!' I shouted, as loudly as I could, but there was no one to hear me and impotently I watched him race away with it.

Back at the café it took a few moments for Mab and Tubs to register my agitated state. 'All my papers were in my bag, Tubs. What am I to do? And there was some money – Mab's money.'

'Honey, that's the last thing to worry about.'

'Have a Cognac, Clare, you're shocked.' Tubs called the waiter. 'Have you lost your passport?'

I nodded miserably. Just as the day was improving, this had to happen.

'Don't worry about that. I'll set things in motion for you, but it will take time.' As I sipped my brandy he leant over the table and took my hand. 'Don't look so down, Clare. But take my advice, get that German passport – then you'll have two to lose.' He grinned but spoke quietly, as if he didn't want Mab to hear. 'We should report this to the police. I'll do it for you, if you want.'

That night I thought about what he had suggested. It might be fun to have the two – two passports, two nationalities, why I might even become two different people. The next day, I went to the Austrian embassy, except it was German now, filled in the forms and was met with great charm and efficiency.

Mab was giving a party. Hortense – we no longer called her Madame – was beside herself with excitement. She swept about the house serving food that, these days, she could only dream of, and vintage champagne, which she was certain she would never be able to afford again, and she flirted with all the men. She had suggested sensitively that perhaps it would be a good idea if Tiphaine did not attend. 'Rubbish,' I said. 'Of course she must be there, mustn't she, Mab? She's our friend.'

'If you insist.'

Later I knocked at Mab's door. 'Can we talk?'

'Sure thing.'

'You don't want Tiphaine at your party?'

'I don't object, if you want her there.'

'Exactly, which means you don't.'

'Well . . . I like her, you know I do. But I wonder . . . I'm not sure what Tubs will think.'

'It matters what you think, not Tubs. Oh, come on, Mab – don't pretend. In the past if you'd wanted to invite the devil and someone didn't approve you'd still have invited him. You always did what you wanted till Tubs came along.'

'OK, I'll admit it. At first I found Tiphaine's occupation amusing. Now I'm not sure. People gossip, and you know what they say, "Birds of a feather . . ."'

'I can hardly believe you're saying this. Tiphaine would be so hurt. She's such a sweet, kind soul.'

'The proverbial tart with a heart.'

'You can be insufferably smug at times, Mab.' I jumped up and made for the door. 'You know what, Mab? You're becoming as boring and stuffy as . . .' Frantically I racked my brains. '. . . Pamela.' I dredged up the name triumphantly. 'And it doesn't suit you.' With that I flounced out before she could answer.

Tiphaine resolved it. She declined the invitation, saying how disappointed she was but she had a prior engagement. I didn't believe it and was certain Hortense had said something to her. I wondered if I would ever feel the same about Mab again.

The party was warming up nicely. 'Clare, I've something for you.' Looking mysterious, Tubs beckoned me into a small sitting room. 'Your bag was handed in to the consulate.' He gave it to me: it did not look the worse for wear.

'How super of you. Thank you so much.' I opened it. All my makeup, perfume, money and papers were there – everything except my passport. I don't know why but suddenly I understood everything. 'You arranged for it to be stolen, didn't you?'

'Clare, what an over-imaginative mind you have.' He laughed, but it sounded false to me.

'But why, Tubs?'

'Clare!'

'It's to do with the war isn't it? You think—'

The door opening interrupted us.

'Ah, Clare, let me introduce you to a dear friend of mine, Fabien de Rocheloire.'

I thought I'd never be able to breathe again. It was the man from the shop. Here. Smiling at me!

'*Très heureux*, Mademoiselle.' He inclined his head, and I smiled graciously as I'd been taught. But I felt my knees buckle and my heart pound alarmingly. Despite that, I found myself wondering who he'd bought the knickers for.

'Did your friend like the present?

'Present? I'm sorry, I don't understand.'

'You know, the things you bought in the shop.' Why had I started to ask stupid questions like this?

'My mother adored them.'

I looked at the floor. His mother? I would have liked to believe him.

'But I wish you had accepted them instead.' He smiled, and that was that. I was in love. This was what I had waited for and this feeling would be unique and would never happen to me again.

7

Fabien invited me for lunch. It took me ages to decide what to wear.

'I like this pink crêpe.' I held up the dress for Hortense and Tiphaine, who had presented themselves as my advisers.

'Handkerchief hems went out seasons ago. You'll look like your mother,' Hortense declared.

'This blue?' I was particularly fond of a pale blue dress with just a hint of lace at the collar.

'Pastels are insipid,' she said, so dismissively that I felt quite hurt – being blonde, I tended, to wear them from choice.

'Clare, my dear, what do you want with this Fabien? A flirtation or an affair?'

'I don't know, Tiphaine.' I knew perfectly well what I wanted. Why, only last night, four hours after meeting him again, I'd decided on the names of our children.

'If a flirtation then the pastels are fine. You will appear as an *ingénue*, unattainable. You will be telling him you don't want to go to bed with him and spoil your charm. An affair? That's different. You must wear something bolder, more a statement of your intentions.'

'Perhaps she dreams of marriage?' Hortense looked arch.

I coloured further and wished she'd shut up. 'Don't be silly, Hortense. We've only just met.'

'Aha! Then she does. So, we need . . .' Hortense dived back into my cupboard '. . . style and a hint of sophistication. This charming bias-cut grey is perfect. Absolutely. And wear your pearls to show him you're a woman of substance and background.'

'It's only a date!' Mab, in the doorway, laughed at our antics.

'As the Chinese say, Mab, my dear, all journeys start with a footstep. And all marriages commence with a "date",' Hortense said emphatically.

Fabien took me to La Coupole in Montparnasse. The huge light and airy room was alive with bustle, the clattering of plates, the hum of conversation, waiters skimming hither and thither. I might have preferred somewhere quieter, perhaps more intimate, but on the other hand I liked the excitement and liveliness of the place and the fish I chose was sublime.

I was impatient to be told everything about him. I felt a hunger to know as much as possible as if that would make him mine, part of me. I sat, chin in my hands, hanging on his every word. I knew I was gazing at him adoringly when really I should have been coquettish, teasing. Only I couldn't. I didn't want to play games, for already I knew that this relationship was to be all-important to me.

'And where were you born?' I asked, when he'd finished telling me about his time in the army – in the past, I was glad to hear.

'In the Auvergne. Do you know that part of France?'

'No, I've never been anywhere except Calais and Paris.'

'Then I shall have the pleasure of showing you.' Well! At that I thought my heart would plop out of my mouth, so high had it jumped.

'The Auvergne is the true heart of France, its spirit, its essence. It's a wild country of mountains and valleys, rivers and waterfalls. It teems with wild animals. It is bitter in winter, hot in summer. It's a kind and cruel place. Its people are the proudest and the toughest of all Frenchmen.'

'And the women?'

'Like their men, who have the hearts of lions, they have the hearts of lionesses.'

I loved it when he talked in this way – so passionate, so exaggerated. I couldn't imagine an Englishman talking about the inhabitants of Berkshire like that. It made everything sound so much more fiery and exotic than anything I had ever known. 'Do tell me more.' I leant further over the table towards him, willing him to feel the intensity of my interest, to move his hand and touch mine.

'The Haute-Loire, where my home is, is where the great river Loire begins its journey. My house overlooks it – from every room one can see it. It is the most beautiful area of the Auvergne.'

'And what do you do there?'

'We make and sell cheese. Which is why I'm here.'

That was a bit of a let-down. A cheese salesman? Such an occupation hadn't featured in my dreams: I'd imagined a brilliant lawyer, an actor or a poet – yes, especially a poet. But cheese! Never mind, if that's what he did then I was sure he was the best seller of the best cheese in the world. I settled down with another glass of wine – I must have had at least four – to learn more.

'It's the way he looks at me, as though his eyes are boring into my soul, that he knows what I'm thinking, what I'm dreaming. In that huge, crowded restaurant I felt as if I was the only person for him.' I was sitting on Mab's bed. It was late, for she'd been out for dinner with Tubs and I had spent an impatient evening longing for someone to talk to. Tiphaine was out and there was no way I was going to confide in Hortense – she was too old to understand. I wanted to tell Mab of my lunch and the walk we'd taken afterwards and the small gold and enamel pin of a ladybird he'd insisted on buying for me when I'd spied it in Cartier's window.

'After he'd bought me this – isn't it the most adorable thing you ever saw?' I flashed my pretty pin '– we had tea in the Ritz. Then we went to Fouquet's and we had champagne. And I just know he was loath to leave me. And oh, Mab, I'm so happy. I can't explain how much . . . but you must know and understand.' I added that last bit quickly. I didn't *really* think she could understand. No one in the whole world could be feeling, or have ever felt, this sense of elation. Certainly not her and Tubs.

'Take care, Clare.' She looked up from filing her nails.

'What do you mean?'

'It's too easy to get carried away. You might be imagining things that aren't there.'

'What things?'

'You know.'

'I've no idea what you mean.'

'You don't know him very well.'

'I don't need to.'

'I bet you don't know what everyone calls him.'

'No, I don't.'

'The Lone Ranger.' She looked so smug as she said it, showing me she knew more about him than I did.

'Why?'

'Didn't you know he's got a horse called Silver?'

'Of course I knew.' I didn't but I couldn't let her know that. 'I think that's a silly name.'

'I think it's funny.'

'What things might I be imagining?' I persisted.

'That Fabien might not be, or intending, what you think.' She studied her nails intently. I reckoned she was embarrassed.

'Do you have to speak in riddles?'

'Look, I don't want to upset you, but you should be warned, that's all.'

I felt my heart pounding; did she know something else about him that I didn't? Something serious? That he was a criminal or, worse, already married? I hadn't believed that the lingerie had been for his mother and I wasn't happy about a mistress, but I could forgive him. A wife, though! 'You've got to explain – it's not fair not to.' I was standing up. I don't remember doing so but I was beginning to feel nervous.

'On your head be it. You wanted to know. He's a natural-born seducer. There, I've said it.'

'Don't be silly.'

'He is. He does that eye thing, that boring into your soul, with everyone. It doesn't matter the age or, I'd go as far as to say, the sex. I'm telling you, as your friend, to beware.'

'My friend? No friend would say such horrible things.'

'If you don't like the truth then why demand it?' Mab shrugged and began working on her nails again.

'He might have been once but not any more. Not now he knows me.'

'Oh, yeah? Who says? You with all your great experience of life. Really! Don't be so stupid.' And Mab smiled a particularly infuriating smile.

'You don't even know him.' I was almost shouting. I was furious – at her temerity in saying these things and also because she called me *stupid*!

'No, but Tubs does.'

'Boring old Tubs. I might have guessed. No doubt he's jealous because Fabien is so much younger and has more charm.'

'How petty you sound. Tubs says he's the worst sort of Frenchman. A lounge lizard, he called him, if you must know.'

'Stop it!'

'Tubs says he wouldn't let him near his mother or his sister.'

'You didn't mention his grandmother.' I tried to sound sarcastic while seething with fury.

'Don't get like this with me. It's only a matter of time and he'll be trying to get you into bed. I only want to help you by warning you.'

'Then don't. I don't need your help. You're spoiling everything. I hate you!' And I fled from her room.

Of course I didn't hate her, it was what she was saying I hated. In my own room I blinked as hard as I could, as if by shutting my eyes I could shut from my mind the memory of Fabien saying over tea at the Ritz, 'Wouldn't it be nice to book a room?' I had giggled and told him not to make such naughty suggestions. But he had said it again at Fouquet's, but then he whispered it in my ear just after he'd kissed me so gently on the lips. I wanted to – I almost did. It was an English voice at the next table that pulled me up short, and I was quite sharp with Fabien. 'I'm not that sort of girl,' I said, gathering my dignity around me like a coat. He apologised and it passed, and he delivered me home and kissed my cheek chastely. 'Sweet one,' he said, as he brushed my lips with the tips of his fingers, which sent a bolt of excitement through my body. Something I had never felt before – it was lovely.

I feared he wouldn't want to see me again. That Mab was right. And I found myself regretting I hadn't gone to bed with him and was immediately shocked at myself for even thinking along those lines.

The next day he telephoned.

The following week passed in a whirl of excitement.

As he talked of his cheeses, of his home, I loved to watch his sensuous lips move expressively. What he was saying was actually of little importance: it was his mouth that fascinated me.

Sometimes I wondered why he wasn't more curious about me but, then, I could hardly blame him: there wasn't much about me that was interesting. My life had been so ordinary, so boring apart from . . .

'Fabien, there's something I have to tell you.'

'And what's that, my sweet? he asked, pausing, as he did so, in stroking my hands. He spent ages doing that: outlining my fingers, my palms with the most delicate of touches, kissing them, licking them softly with the deftest of touches. I was glad I had nice, well-cared-for hands.

'I'm frightened to tell you in case you no longer like me. But if I don't then someone else will.' I meant Mab, but of course I didn't say so. If Tiphaine had taught me anything useful it was that men did not like a woman who was catty about others.

'What on earth could you have possibly done? Are you about to tell me you have robbed a bank or you're a murderess.' He laughed. I didn't.

'The latter.'

'The what?' The caressing hand stopped.

'I killed my sister,' I said, far too baldly, but I was in such a hurry to get the words out.

'But not intentionally?' He said it so kindly and with such a warm expression in his beautiful eyes that it was the easiest thing to unburden myself to him. 'Try to forget it ever happened,' he said, when I had eventually finished my confession. 'Don't let such unhappiness from your past mar our present happiness.' He kissed the tip of my nose.

'It's hard.'

'It must be. But you have me to protect you from both your past and your brutal father.'

That did it, of course. That set me off and I howled away but if I'm honest it was from sheer relief at the way he had taken it and not from guilt – that had faded, or seemed to have. But I thanked God for sending me this kind, sensitive man.

It amazed me that he chose to be with me. He was so clever and I was far from that. He was sophisticated and, though I tried to be, I never quite achieved it. He was handsome, the sort of man any woman would have been proud to be with, and while I was not bad-looking I was no great beauty. Why me? I asked myself constantly. Why should this wonderful man have chosen me?

Mab, I had thought, was to be my salvation, but I'd been wrong: it was Fabien. When I was with him I felt such a sense of comfort, of security. He could not be with me without needing to touch me, kiss me. I felt cocooned by his sensuous interest in me.

But, as I was to learn, whenever I was deliriously happy, something always happened to change it all.

'You won't believe this, Clare,' Mab rushed into my room, 'I just heard. Tubs called me. Britain has declared war on Germany. Wow, isn't that thrilling?'

'Oh, no! The beasts! How could they? They might have timed it better!'

Chapter Two

September 1939 – January 1942

1

The next few weeks were a time of indecision. Many Parisians packed and
fled to the country, parking themselves on astonished relations whom,
until then, they had always pitied for having to live out in the sticks.
When nothing happened – the bombs didn't fall and the Germans had
not arrived – many scuttled back. The citizens who had stayed felt
remarkably superior to those who had run, and gloated at how sheepish
they looked.

This fear and panic passed me by. In a way I felt like an interested
observer of someone else's catastrophe, which had nothing to do with me.
It was a war that belonged to them, not me.

And yet I was involved. Immediately war had been declared Fabien had
rejoined his regiment. I didn't want him to go – after all, we had had
barely a week together before he reported for duty. But my disappointment was tempered by my pride in his bravery and how wonderful he
looked in his uniform. But that didn't ease my misery, or my longing for
him when he was sent away. I worried about him, not Europe, not France,
not England but my Fabien.

From England came a blizzard of postcards, letters and telegrams.
Everyone, it seemed, had been mobilised to write. My sister nagged, my
stepmother was concerned, though I detected a coolness in her words, my
godmother, the dreaded great-aunt in Devon, wrote to tell me where my
duty lay. Since I hardly saw her and, apart from a bracelet at my
christening, she'd given me nothing, I ignored her. When the cook
dropped me a line suggesting that I return I realised that the agitation had
reached its height. Good. Then my father wrote, demanding my presence.
Not a wise move. A second letter went further: he almost begged me to
return. But he said nothing of love or forgiveness, so I tore it up.

All this attention came as a surprise. I had resigned myself to my family not caring for me or loving me, and that probably I'd never see them again. Then this bombardment of mail. The problem for them was that I'd adjusted to not being part of them any more; I'd learnt not to mind. I didn't need them. I had Fabien. Now, with my job, I didn't even need my father's money. I confess, though, that I gleaned a bushel of satisfaction that my father had *begged* me to return.

'But I'm fine, Father. There's nothing to worry about.' He had telephoned me, an even greater indication of his concern: it was expensive, it took time to arrange, and when he was finally connected we spoke through a background of static that sounded like rusty nails being shaken in a bucket.

'Clare, you can be so stupid! The whole of mankind is teetering on the abyss . . .' I rolled my eyes. I sometimes thought he would have made an excellent fire-and-brimstone preacher. And I didn't like being told I was stupid: it made me see red. His saying it showed me that nothing had changed at all.

'Paris is calm. I've food and a roof over my head. I've even got a job.' I paused, expecting him to respond with pleasure, but he didn't. 'The French army are being enormously brave. They won't let the Germans in. They pummelled them with their guns at Saarbrücken last week.'

'Have you no consideration for others? I'm worried for you.'

'If I'm not worried for me then there's no point in you worrying, is there?' I surprised myself at the way I was talking to him. I could never have done that face to face.

'You're thinking only of yourself again.'

'That's not fair.' If only he knew of the hours I spent worrying about Fabien – not that I could tell my father about him: he'd be on the first possible ferry to haul me back.

'Clare, sometimes your selfish stupidity . . .'

There it was again. That hateful word. I scratched the receiver with my fingernail to increase the noise of interference. I dropped my voice to a whisper as if the connection was fading and then I cut him off.

'Your daddy's right. You should go home,' Mab said, as we tested a Manhattan in the Ritz bar.

'You're here,' I retorted, over the rim of the glass.

'My country isn't at war, is it?'

'Bah. It'll be over by Christmas now that the British army's arrived.'

'You hope. That's what everyone said last time, and that war lasted four years.'

I placed my glass on the table between us. 'Tubs has changed you. He's making you middle-aged like him, and frightened.'

'Tubs is not middle-aged, and I'm being sensible.'

'Well, it doesn't suit you.'

'Tubs says he reckons it's only a matter of days before the Germans are on French soil.'

'Fabien says the British wouldn't allow the Duke of Windsor to be here if there was any risk to him *and* he's to visit the front line.'

'I should think the Limeys could think of nothing better than something happening to him of all people.' Mab giggled.

'That's a disgusting thing to say.'

'You never like the truth, do you? You live in your own little dream world. Tubs—'

'I know. "*Tubs says.*" Don't you have any opinions of your own?'

'And I could say the same of you. You're all "*Fabien says.*"'

We sat in brooding silence. I didn't want this. I didn't want a row. It was all Tubs' fault, we'd been such good friends until he appeared.

'Tubs has asked me to marry him.'

The 'Oh, no!' was out before I could stop it. 'I didn't mean that,' I added hurriedly.

'Yes, you did.' But to my relief I saw she was laughing at me.

'I don't want you to go further away from me.'

'Then come to England with me.'

I looked at her with horror, for I'd meant emotionally, not physically. 'You're leaving?'

'Yes. Tubs is genuinely worried and he's in a position to know a lot more than we do at how bad things could become. I'm to stay with his mother in the country.'

'You'll hate it.'

'Maybe, but I can always move to London if I get too cranky. He understands about your problems with your own family and his mother says you can come too. Oh, do, honey, we'll see this through together.'

'So how many people have you told my business to? I'd rather you didn't. I can't go – I can't leave Fabien.'

'Look, Clare, the last time I tried to talk to you was a disaster and you were very angry with me. I don't want a repeat and I didn't want to tell you this . . . but . . . in the circumstances I must. There's someone else in Fabien's life.' She leant forward as she said this, taking my hand in hers to comfort me, I suppose.

I withdrew it sharply. 'That's a malicious thing to say just to get me to return to England.'

'It's the truth, and this time you should listen. He's engaged to marry this other girl. Her name is—'

'I don't want to hear it.'

'You must. She's called Céline de Fonteille de Villeneuve. She's beautiful, good family and rich. Tubs knows her.'

'I don't believe you.'

'If you stay you'll be hurt. To him you're just a bit of spare. A shop girl he picked up.'

'He might have thought that at first but not any more. He knows who I am. He loves me. And how dare you lie about him?' I stood up, knocking over the remains of my Manhattan – which was a shame, I'd liked it. 'I'll speak to you again when you apologise.'

The October night was drawing in as I walked out of the Ritz – I walked everywhere these days to save money. The blackout imposed for the raids that didn't come echoed my mood. I had said he loved me. He hadn't told me so, but I just knew he did, that it was only a matter of time before I heard him say the words.

It took me a good half-hour to reach Hortense's house. I raced up the stairs fearful of meeting anyone. Mab, who'd taken a taxi, was waiting for me on the landing.

'Look, Clare, I'm sorry. But you had to know—'

'I don't need your lies. Take yourself and your money-bags and your vulgarity to England. You won't last five minutes with his mother – I know the sort.'

'Clare—'

'Oh, shut up, Mab. I thought you were my friend.'

I flounced into my room, slammed the door shut and promptly burst into tears. Why had I said such horrible things? But I'd said them and she deserved them, lying about my Fabien so viciously. I flung myself on to my bed and, for the first time, knew real loneliness.

'Mab tells me you're engaged,' I said this lightly, as if I couldn't have cared less – and was astonished at how convincing I sounded.

'She what?' Fabien, who was removing his greatcoat, his back to me, swung round looking astonished. He was back from the front, and very tired, but we had a whole precious weekend together.

'She said you were engaged to a Céline – I can't remember her surname, it was one of those long ones you French go in for.' There it was again, light amusement in my voice. I was good – maybe I should go on the stage.

'Céline!' He laughed. 'Oh, the gossiping women.'

'Tubs told her.'

'So? What is the difference between gossiping women and the busybody Major Tubs?'

'It frightened me.'

'Of course it did, my poor darling.' I was sitting on my bed. I'd asked him to my room so we could talk in private. It was difficult downstairs, with all the comings and goings. Fabien sat beside me and took me into his arms. I breathed deeply: he smelt of earth and fatigue, tobacco and sweat – it was a heady combination. 'Let me explain. My mother would love me to marry Céline. She is a sweet girl. Pretty too, of good family. But we have known each other since our cradles so there's no spark, no surprises. She is like a sister to me.'

'Not like me?'

'Not at all like you,' he said, in his wonderful voice, and in English. I loved it when he spoke my language with his adorable accent. His hand, which had been round my shoulder, had slipped to my breast. As he touched me there he kissed me. I seemed to melt. My blood felt as if it had turned to honey and my brain as if it had shut down. When he lifted my jumper and his mouth searched for my nipple beneath my camisole, I let him. I wanted him to touch me everywhere. There was one moment when sense returned, just as he began to enter me: the pain alerted me to where I was and what I was doing. And then I thought, So there's a war and everyone says I should be worried. If there's danger, if there's fear, what's the point in saving my virginity? So I bit my lip to stop myself crying out and endured the pain. But then the bliss of him on top of me, moving back and forth inside me, the amazing hardness of him and the smoothness. Then in a flash it was over and I felt bereft as he withdrew from me and I longed for something more, though I had no idea what it was.

'Are you all right, Clare?'

'Thank you, it was lovely.' I grinned to myself in the dark: I sounded as if I was thanking him for my tea! 'There's just one thing . . . No, it doesn't matter.' I changed my mind, too embarrassed to say what I wanted.

'We should be completely honest with each other. What is it? You can ask me anything.' He stroked my hair.

'It's . . . Well . . . I was wondering . . . We shouldn't be making babies yet, should we?' Not that I had any idea how not to, knowing only that what we had just done could.

He laughed loudly. I blushed. What silly thing had I said?

'Sweet one, don't worry about such matters. There's no need. You see, I can't have children – a riding accident when I was a boy.'

'How awful for you.' I felt sad, thinking of all the babies whose names I'd chosen and who would never be born.

'I didn't realise you were a virgin. I'm sorry. I shouldn't have—'

'I'm glad I was. That I waited for you. I never wanted another man to do

46

that to me,' I whispered. As I snuggled into his arms it crossed my mind that he had been surprised I was a virgin.

2

Although we were at war, life continued in much the same way apart from my not seeing Fabien as often as I wanted to. I could even say that, after the initial shock and excitement, I felt somewhat let down.

In November Mab had left for England. I missed her dreadfully. Although I had vowed I wouldn't speak to her again, of course I did. She had hugged me tight and assured me she had only spoken out of concern for me. I listened and accepted, and in turn reassured her that she'd nothing to worry about: Fabien had explained everything to me. 'So that's all right,' I'd said, in an emphatic tone, which I hoped would put an end to her speculation like a full stop.

'Of course. And I *hope* you find happiness with him. And if things go wrong you will come, won't you?'

I'd said I would. It was only later, when reconsidering our conversation, I realised she'd emphasised that word 'hope' as if she was certain I wouldn't. I had presumed she was referring to the worsening of the war situation with her 'if things go wrong' but I began to think that 'things' meant not an army but my lover. I was glad I hadn't told her we were lovers, it might have set her off again. One resolve I made, though, was that when this was over I would be more wary of her in the future.

Each day I went to work at the shop. At least I could understand most of what the other girls gossiped about now that I was a real woman too. Sleeping with Fabien had changed me; I had known it would. I felt more confident, assured of his love for me since he had wanted to sleep with me as much as I had with him. I wasn't just me any more, we were one, we were us. I had told no one what had happened even though I thought Hortense had suspicions. It was my secret, a very precious secret, which I hugged to me and which helped me through our separations.

Christmas and New Year were dismal. Right until the last moment I'd hoped Fabien would come to share one or other with me, but he hadn't. Tiphaine was out at a party – she went to so many, these days – so it was Hortense and me alone who saw in 1940.

Early in the new year Fabien was promoted to staff officer and, wonderful for me, I was able to see a little more of him since he had frequently to return to Paris to 'liaise' – not that I was sure what that implied. I didn't care, though, not if it meant we were together. Sometimes it was only for an hour; a night was bliss; a snatched weekend was Paradise.

We didn't talk about the war. I didn't want to know about such ugly things and I sensed he didn't want to go over it either. My job, as I saw it, was to help him relax and enjoy his time away from his duties. It made me feel very grown-up.

Phones still worked, and the post still got through after a fashion so I was in contact with my family. They continued to nag me to return, while I endlessly reassured them that I was fine, but to see a letter with an English stamp on it always lifted my spirits.

Hortense, whose initial flapping and panicking I had expected to subside, seemed to be getting worse as time passed. Admittedly she had grounds: the Germans were only a hundred miles away. But while I was convinced that our troops would rout them, she was equally certain that the Germans were coming after her personally. For some time I avoided her: agitation, I had quickly learnt, was contagious. I had to laugh when I found her in the garden one day in early April, dressed in heavy boots and an old coat, carrying a spade and looking remarkably furtive.

'Hortense, why on earth are you dressed like that?' I'd never seen her anything but impeccably turned out.

'None of your business,' she snapped, in a most uncharacteristic way. 'I'm sorry.'

She put her hand on my arm. 'As I am. I was rude. I should tell someone. And I trust you. The English are many things but I think you are trustworthy people.' I waited patiently for her to get to the point. 'Come.' She led me through her wild garden behind the house until we reached a part even wilder than the rest, beside a particularly lovely chestnut tree. She pointed dramatically to the ground. 'There. If anything should happen to me, it's there, and I rely on you to get it to my brother, and if he is dead then his family . . .'

'Yes. Of course.' But she said no more. 'But what, Hortense?'

'My silver, you silly girl. The Hun has invaded Denmark and Norway. It'll be Belgium next then us. They're not getting their hands on my possessions, that's for sure.'

'Ah, I see.' It was worrying, though I thought she was overreacting.

Hortense didn't stop with the silver. Paintings were taken down and stored in the cellar. Rooms were stripped of furniture. Heavy curtains were pulled over windows in the daytime and, most dramatically, the chandelier was lowered to the hall floor where it lay like a great crystal octopus.

In the cellar Hortense had furnished a little shelter for us, well stocked with tinned food and, of course, wine. The sirens sounded often, which sent everyone scurrying to their bolt-holes, but no bombs fell so we soon learnt to ignore them.

Fabien's intermittent visits came without warning. He might appear at any time, which put me in a quandary. I wanted to stay in in case he turned up but I didn't want to miss any of the fun if he didn't. I made a rule not to go out unless there was a telephone number where I could be contacted – a bit like a doctor, Hortense said.

Since the arrival of the British Expeditionary Force the previous autumn, my social life had picked up. There were some gorgeous officers strutting about. Like most women I was excited by the sight of a man in a well-cut uniform. Not, of course, that I showed any interest in them – not with Fabien in my life! But there was no harm in looking, was there?

Tubs, missing Mab, had been seconded from the embassy to the British Military Mission. He was based five miles outside Paris near the Château de Vincennes, which housed the French General Headquarters with whom they liaised.

Tubs was not my favourite person because of what he'd said about Fabien, but when he invited me to a party there, curiosity got the better of me. The Duke of Windsor was part of the group and I was all agog to see him, and especially Wallis, to judge for myself what all the fuss had been about.

'Oh, they won't be coming.' Tubs chuckled at my evident disappointment. 'We hardly see him ourselves. He pops in for an hour late morning then potters back to his missus. Not that there's much to do. If this is war I must admit I rather like it. We call it the Great Bore War.'

After that I went whenever I was invited. Tubs always saw me home but my main reason for going was the food.

'You eat well, I must say.'

'The chef comes from the Hôtel Crillon, that's why. Fabien said trust the Brits to snaffle one of the best chefs.'

'Fabien's been here?'

'Why, yes, several times. He was here last night.'

'I didn't know.' My heart sank.

'Well, of course, he's busy. I mean back and forth to the front. He was probably in a rush. He probably didn't have time. He—'

'Please don't say probably again, Tubs,' I said, in a very controlled manner, I thought.

'Sorry. Of course.' His face was crumpled with worry, as if it had been screwed up like a piece of paper.

'Was he alone?' I asked, hoping I'd made it sound like an innocent question.

'Alone? Why, golly. Yes, of course.' I didn't believe him.

The minute I returned from my dinner I sat and wrote to Fabien. I asked him why he hadn't told me he'd been to the Mission and why he hadn't contacted me. I waited with even more impatience than usual for his reply, in which he explained that he'd been pressed for time and in any case everything was very hush-hush. I tried to believe him.

'I think Tubs was covering up for you.' I hadn't meant to quiz Fabien, but when he eventually came to see me, a demon inside me drove me on.

'What could Tubs possibly be concealing from you? I wasn't aware that I had to report every movement I make.'

'I think you were with a woman. Were you?'

'Oh, really, Clare. What a funny little cabbage you are. This Pouilly Fumé is really excellent.' He topped up my wine-glass. We were eating at the Crillon. The restaurant was crowded and busy; only the sight of so many men in uniform indicated that a war was on.

'You didn't answer my question.'

'I wasn't aware you had asked one.'

'Well, I did.'

'So . . .' He shrugged in the way I normally adored, but which tonight annoyed me.

'You need not go all French with me.'

'I would find it extraordinarily difficult not to.' He laughed. I didn't. He leant across the table and gazed deep into my eyes, the look that always sent shivers through me since it was how he looked at me just before we made love and always when he was inside me. I moved my bottom, imperceptibly, I hoped, on my seat. That look always made me incapable of sitting still. 'My little one, these are not normal times. I wish they were, that our lives were calm and settled. Not war. Not this awful war.' His expression changed and he looked bleak. He shrugged again, his trademark shrug. 'But these are the times in which we live and we must learn to adjust to them. You understand?'

'Yes,' I said, though I didn't, but I thought it was what he expected me to say. I did wonder about the bleakness and what he might have seen of the fighting. For fighting there was: it was just that I didn't know about it or even think about it because I didn't want to.

'Are you having dessert? Or shall we go and find our bed and make love?'

I felt the colour rise in my cheeks. But I knew my eyes sparkled at such an invitation.

Fabien had a small two-room flat at the very top of a building in the sixteenth *arrondissement* – the best place to be. It was sparsely furnished for, as he told me, it was only somewhere to sleep – not that we did much of that. There was never any food there – but who needed food? There was always wine and champagne, however. Fabien told me it was how all his bachelor friends lived. It needed a woman's touch.

It had become one of my pleasures to buy things to decorate it and make it seem more a home, lived-in – more permanent, I suppose. I scoured the flea-markets for inexpensive little presents to surprise him with when he came back to Paris. It was our secret place. Whenever I entered it I felt I had come home.

'Why don't I move in here?' I asked, as I was placing a lamp with a pretty coloured-glass shade that I had found, trying to find the ideal spot for it. 'I wouldn't feel so lonely when you're away. I'd feel close to you. What do you think?'

'I'm never here without you and I couldn't bear to be at the front and to know you were here without me,' he'd explained, so I decided not to make an issue of it, but I was disappointed.

His longing for me was such that the minute the door closed he would sometimes tear off my clothes and take me there and then, often in the small hallway; he couldn't wait to get me to the bed, he told me. It made me feel so proud. That's not to say that there were not times when I longed for him to seduce me slowly by candlelight, soft music playing on the wireless. But that wasn't Fabien's way.

'There's so little time. We could all be dead tomorrow. I want you now, this instant!'

I would like him to have told me he loved me. Whenever I told him he always kissed me and told me how sweet I was.

'Do you love me?' One day, from somewhere, I found the courage to ask him.

'So many questions you ask me. Have we not just made love?'

At night we lay in each other's arms after we were satiated with love. We always talked then and caressed each other gently as if we were calming ourselves. We learnt about each other, our pasts, our dreams. For if I sat down and worked out how many hours I'd spent with him they were not many so it was imperative that I used the time we had to learn as much about him as I could.

'There's just one thing, my darling. Before you go.' I looked at Fabien as he dressed in his uniform at the end of the bed. 'Please tell me you weren't with another woman when you saw Tubs.'

Fabien threw back his head and laughed long and loud. 'Oh, my sweet one. Already you sound like my wife!'

He couldn't have made me happier. I pulled that sentence to me, I

51

stored it in my mind, I remembered it again and again. It gave me such happiness and such comfort.

It was much needed a few days later when the news came that Fabien had been reported missing.

3

When Tubs telephoned with the news that Fabien was missing, my legs buckled, my stomach churned and I felt physically sick. Yet, at that point, I was unaware of the awful fear and loneliness that lay in wait for me.

Finding out what might have happened to Fabien was a nightmare. I went to his regiment's headquarters but because I was not related to him they would tell me nothing. I felt myself brushed aside by the officer I spoke to as a person of no importance. For the first time in a long while I felt a foreigner, that I didn't belong.

But while much had changed some things never did. Paris for one. I sat in the park, the early spring sun warming me, looking about me at the chestnuts, the lilacs, all beginning to blossom. The beauty of the city, to me at her most lovely this year with danger looming, almost broke my heart. I watched the children playing . . . such a short time ago and I had been one of them – look at me now!

For nearly eighteen months I had been in France. So much had happened to me. I'd learnt to eat and drink with discrimination. My French was fluent. I'd met Mab and Tiphaine. I had become more sophisticated. I had a job. War had been declared. I'd lost my virginity and I had fallen in love. I was no longer a child but a woman. Now I had lost my love and I felt as bereft as any widow.

'Clare, I know you think I nag like an old woman but, really, you'd better go home. Be realistic. Belgium has fallen. Maybe in a week or two the Germans will be here in Paris. When I leave who will be here to protect you?'

'Tubs, how can I leave, not knowing what has happened to Fabien? And don't scare me, you'll stay, you can't go. The British will stop them, you know they will.'

'I'm afraid it's going to be more difficult than you realise. And it could be a long time before Fabien . . . if–' Abruptly he stopped speaking.

'If he's ever freed. That's what you were going to say, weren't you?'

'No. I mean, if he had been taken prisoner we'd know.'

'Then you think he's dead?' My voice rose at that. The idea had occurred to me, of course, but I had squashed it at once. I couldn't think that, I wouldn't. I hated Tubs for making me.

'No. We'd probably know that too. My fear is that he's wounded and hiding somewhere. Or he may have gone for a run.'

'Deserted, you mean? Fabien would never do that. He's a man of honour. He would never leave his men. I know him, you don't.'

'Clare, calm down. I'm just trying to list all the possibilities for you. I'm trying to help you.'

'Well, you're not doing much of a job, are you?'

'No. I'm not. I'm sorry. Forgive? It's just I don't know what to say. I like Fabien. I know you think I don't, but I've actually got a soft spot for him. And I do understand your feelings. If Mab had gone missing I'd be worried sick.' He looked so genuinely upset I felt ashamed at my reaction.

'It won't help if we fall out, will it?'

'No, Clare, it won't.' He squeezed my hand to comfort me. I squeezed back. It didn't work, but I knew he was trying. 'Things are getting serious, Clare. The French had this blind faith that their famous Maginot Line was going to keep out the great German hordes. They wouldn't listen to us. The Germans are on French soil now, you've heard surely?'

'Don't say that!' At which, childishly, I clapped my hands over my ears to shut out his words, as if that would stop it all happening. 'Fabien didn't say much to me about what was going on – I didn't want to know,' I said miserably, wishing I'd asked now.

'Like us he believed the German tanks would come through the Ardennes forest – while his superiors had an ostrich-like idea that the forest would hold them back. The last thing I want to do is to frighten you, Clare, but I really do think that, if you stay you could be in danger. While there's time let me arrange for you to go home.'

'I'm staying,' I replied, lifting my chin to show how determined I was while quaking with terror inside.

Money was becoming a problem. My job had come to an end. The owner of the shop, a woman from Provence, returned there in early May leaving us all in the lurch. Hortense had been a brick and told me not to worry about money, something would turn up. I had kept going by doing the odd piece of translation, though not nearly enough – I'd helped out in the Mississippi bar, and in the house as much as I could but domesticity, I'd be the first to admit, was not my forte.

I watched Tiphaine with envy, I'll admit. She seemed to have more money than before: she was obviously widening her circle of 'friends'. Men of different nationalities began to appear, some in uniform. 'My war work!' she'd say with a grin.

*

Hortense devoured news. Whenever I saw her she was either glued to the wireless or telephoning her friends to see what they thought. Often, though, I decided, it was to see what they feared – as if she needed constantly to feed her own terrors.

'All is well!' she said, dramatically flinging her arms wide as she met me in the hall one evening in May, on my return from delivering some translations. 'Our dear Marshal Pétain has returned and is now our deputy prime minister. France need no longer worry.'

'Who's Marshal Pétain?' I asked, as we crossed the hall, skirting the chandelier, making a bee-line for the kitchen as I did each evening. I was always hungry these days – food was becoming harder to find.

'You don't know about the Hero of Verdun?' Hortense had stopped in her tracks. Her face was a collection of surprised circles – mouth, eyes. 'I cannot believe you are not aware of the greatest living Frenchman . . .'

Oh dear, I thought, I wished I'd known about him, then she wouldn't have got so worked up. Now she'd go on and on, no doubt, about the glory of France! 'Any bread?' I asked, finding that the long pine bread-box on the wall was empty.

'There was none . . . He would do nothing that would hurt France. He—'

'No bread?'

'The army comes first. The Marshal . . .'

And that's how the war affected me. Endless worry for Fabien and no bread.

4

Hortense was right. Something did turn up. The Germans.

All through May we had watched their advance with mounting horror: the unthinkable was happening. This was no longer Tubs' Bore War for the fighting was fierce. The Germans were winning, and our troops were being pushed back relentlessly.

By mid-May the British troops had been ordered to begin to retreat to the coast taking many French troops with them. We couldn't believe they were leaving us – deserting us! By the twenty-first the Germans were only sixty miles north of Paris.

Tubs made a last effort to get me to leave but still I refused to listen.

'Here, you'd better have this.' He handed me my British passport. 'Someone might make you see sense and it wouldn't be funny to land in

England without one and find yourself under suspicion by the British themselves, would it?'

'You had it all along, didn't you? It wasn't stolen by a thief, was it? Why?'

'We thought it might be better if you had both.'

'Who's we?'

'Well, me, really, it was my initiative. I thought that if a situation like this occurred – you refusing to leave France – it would be expedient if you had a German one too, should the country be invaded.'

'Then why keep my British one?'

'You were more likely to get a German one if I did.'

'Are you sure you didn't think of turning me into a spy? Dual nationality, bilingual, I must have appeared ideal.'

He laughed – a little too loudly. 'What on earth gave you that idea? Spies have to be trained. You don't just set up shop and start spying.'

'No doubt you would have. What made you change your mind?'

He studied his boots, planning what to say, no doubt. 'I've grown fond of you, Clare. I want you to go home.' I felt touched: it wasn't the reply I had expected. 'Take care. If you stay perhaps you'll be recruited.'

It was my turn to laugh. 'You tell your masters I wouldn't dream of doing such a thing. I'm not putting myself at risk for anyone. I want to find Fabien, that's all. So thank you, Tubs, for my British passport but I'm not going, not until we're together again.'

'Your family will be desperate.'

'My family don't care about me. They might pretend they do, but I'm sure that's only for appearances' sake. They hate me.'

'I'm sure they don't. They'll have forgiven you by now.'

'Forgiven me what?' I asked, hearing the sharpness in my voice.

'Clare, I know about your sister. You must stop blaming yourself.'

'I don't, they do. That's my problem. But who told you?' I had a sinking feeling that I knew the answer.

'Why, Mab, of course.'

'She had no right to do that. I told her in confidence.' I was hurt that she should tell. It had been disloyal. So why shouldn't I do the same to her? 'I've never told anyone about her father,' I said slyly.

'What about her father?'

'That she shot him.' And then I spoilt it. Shocked at the enormity of telling him I added, lamely, 'By accident, of course.'

Tubs guffawed. 'She told you that? The minx. Her father would be interested to know. He was fit and well when I spoke to him last month.'

I had to sit down, I was so shocked. But more than that I was hurt – deeply. How could she have played such a game with me?

*

Paris was chaotic. For days every train that arrived at the Gare du Nord and the Gare de l'Est brought refugees – Belgians, Dutch, Danes, from Luxembourg they poured in. They were a sorry bunch, frightened and confused, clutching their children, dogs, cats, birds in cages, and their bundles of possessions. Paris had welcomed them with open arms, until the Belgians surrendered. Then the anger was dreadful to see.

'Bastards!' shrieked Hortense, as a family of Belgians were evicted from a neighbouring house, their baggage unceremoniously hurled after them. I wasn't sure whom she was yelling at, the neighbours or the Belgians, but she looked so angry I decided to make myself scarce.

The exodus from the city, which had been a trickle, became a flood. It was a jumble of people, rich and poor, young and old, healthy and disabled. The roads were clogged with this tide of humanity and the rich man's limousine was as impeded as the poor man's cart. Slowly and laboriously they moved south like a great army of ants.

'They say five million are on the road,' Tiphaine remarked, over the inevitable glass of wine. We were drinking a lot now: as our worries mounted so did our intake.

'I heard nine,' I said.

'Bah! There aren't that number of citizens in Paris.'

'I think they mean in total – from other parts of France, from other cities.' Honestly, if I listened to Hortense I'd soon think there was only one nation on the planet, France, and only one city, Paris, and only one group of people, the Parisians, who mattered.

'Where will they all go? Times are hard everywhere. How can the poor relations in the country cope with an influx like this?' For once Tiphaine looked serious.

'No doubt the peasants will charge them and make a hefty profit!'

'Hortense, you're such a cynic,' I laughed.

'I know people and how they behave, young woman. I read in the paper that there are many lost children. You'd think parents would be more responsible, wouldn't you? Truth be told, I expect some people are losing their children on purpose – let someone else feed them.'

'Hortense!' both Tiphaine and I exclaimed, shocked to the core.

'Well, I'm not going anywhere,' Hortense concluded, stood up and collected another carafe of wine she'd carefully decanted earlier. 'I've no intention of allowing the Boche to drink my dear husband's best claret. Now this is a particularly fine Medoc – *deuxième cru*, no less. You remember what I taught you, Clare?'

'But of course.' I didn't, but I was not about to let Hortense know and risk another lecture on wine vintages rather than drinking it.

'To peace.' Hortense raised her glass.

'Amen to that.' Tiphaine lifted her glass.

'Will you go, Tiphaine?' I asked.

'No. My parents wouldn't welcome me,' she said, with a melancholy expression.

'Then you're lucky, Tiphaine. Why, you'd pine away in the country. I hate it. All that green!' Hortense shuddered. 'Such a vulgar colour.'

'I like green – think of emeralds.' Tiphaine grinned, her sadness gone.

'No. Sapphires for me. I've always preferred them.'

How strange, I thought, the Germans on our doorstep, the sound of heavy guns audible and we talk of precious stones. But then why not? There's nothing we can do to alter anything. 'Do you prefer gold or platinum?'

Devoid of so many people, the city felt strange. With little traffic it was a pleasant place to walk, some said, but I missed the crowds with their noise and bustle, even the traffic.

Air-raid sirens continued to wail and we were used to hurtling to Hortense's shelter. But when nothing happened we began to ignore them. Until, in early June, we were bombed and over fifty people were killed. We took the sirens seriously after that.

As if that wasn't bad enough, the news the next day that the British had left France, rescued from the beaches of Dunkirk in an armada of little boats, made me deeply depressed. I think I hadn't believed it would happen. That Tubs had been scaring me. That somehow they would turn back and stand and fight and beat the Germans. It was a sobering jerk into reality. This was no game.

'How brave of the government to scuttle off to the Loire with the Germans so close,' I said, feeling quite bitter about everyone who was leaving me in the lurch.

'You've no right to talk. What about your army fleeing?'

'They had no choice. And they took most of your French army with them. So there.' I regretted that immediately: in the circumstances it sounded so childish.

'Hortense! Clare! Falling out amongst ourselves isn't going to help, is it?'

Of course Tiphaine was right.

'I'm sorry, Hortense.'

'I accept your apology, Clare.'

'How about a glass of wine?' Tiphaine said quickly.

'Fine.' I'd have liked to have said more but I was in no position to do so, I depended on Hortense and her hospitality.

'You should have gone home, Clare. When Tubs came and begged you to go,' Hortense said suddenly.

'And what if Fabien turns up?'

'And what if he doesn't?'

'Hortense, please, don't say that.'

'Sometimes, my dear, I wonder if you are less in love with Fabien but rather in love with love.'

'Hortense, that's a horrible thing to say!'

'One often prefers not to hear what is true.'

'At least you speak German, Clare.' Tiphaine changed the subject. I was grateful. At that moment I would have liked to slap Hortense. 'Knowing their language will be useful. I bought myself a phrase book last week.'

'You'll probably need it.' We all laughed. In Tiphaine's trade I suppose a man's nationality or which side he was on in a war was of no importance.

'Thank heavens Tubs made you get a German passport, Clare. That will be most valuable for you.'

'Oh, I don't like this talk.' Hortense looked annoyed. 'It's defeatist, Tiphaine. I'm sure Marshal Pétain will come to some accommodation with the Germans, you mark my words.'

'Pétain! Stupid old fart!' Tiphaine spat the words venomously: she'd obviously decided to ignore her own advice about confrontation. Hortense bridled. I was sure she was in love with the Marshal. In pride of place on the kitchen wall she had hung a large framed portrait of the blue-eyed old charmer.

'I forbid you to speak of our heroic Marshal in such a way in my house!' She was standing now, holding the back of her chair like a shield.

'Heroic! Who's sidled off to Bordeaux now, even further away? Who told Churchill that a union with Britain would be like a marriage to a corpse? Some hero!'

'He never did! How rude,' I added, not that they seemed to notice.

'You don't remember the last war. I do – my brother was killed, four cousins too. Our Marshal will do anything to stop a repeat of that slaughter.'

'Capitulate, you mean?'

'No. Peace with honour. He will arrange it, I know. I have faith in him.'

'Misplaced. He will sell us to the Germans. He will—'

'Anyone fancy cheese on toast?' I asked lightly, trying to defuse the situation.

It was a strange time for those of us left in the city. There was fear, of course, but over and above this was an almost placid resignation as people waited for the inevitable, as if this was what they had expected all along. It was like that strange, heavy calm in the air that one feels before the onset of a storm.

To add to the sombreness, a constant pall of black smoke hung in the air. Government departments were burning papers by the truckload and to add to that the petrol depots had been set alight. 'By the Germans,' Hortense declared, which seemed somewhat illogical. More likely it had been done by the retreating British and French armies, Tiphaine and I agreed, but we thought it politic not to tell her.

On 14 June the Germans marched into Paris. I stood in the crowd that watched them goose-step down the Champs-Elysées. It was an eerie experience for no one cheered this triumphant army. There was only the thud of their boots, the rumble of tanks as they passed by. I saw women clutch their children close with terror. I saw hatred in some faces, yes, and fear in others. I watched men cry and I cried too – but what and whom did I cry for? France? Fabien? Myself? The world? Or just because so many others were crying?

5

With all these German soldiers in the city I had great hopes that my American friend, Josh, would give me a permanent job. His bar – close to one of the ministries that had been requisitioned by the military – was busier than ever. A translator would be an asset, I pointed out to him, as we sat perched on beer crates in the tiny store room that doubled as his office.

'Clare, I'm so sorry, but I'm closing.'

'Closing? But why? You've never been busier.'

'Right, but with the wrong clientele as far as I'm concerned. I'm going home.'

'This isn't America's war. You don't have to go.'

'I do. No, we're not involved and long may it stay that way. But I'm Jewish, you see.'

'Are you? I never knew. You don't—' I stopped abruptly, about to say he didn't *look* Jewish, which was fairly silly of me since I had no clear idea of what a Jewish person looked like; I was not aware I knew any. 'But what's being Jewish got to do with it?'

'I can't take their money, it's like taking blood money.'

'Really?'

'Oh, Clare,' Josh laughed, 'don't you know anything? Don't you ever read the papers?'

'Of course I do,' I lied. I didn't, well, hardly ever. Once I hadn't read them because I wasn't interested, now I didn't because I didn't want to be scared. I knew I was ignorant, but admitting that to oneself was not the same as confessing it to someone else.

'The Germans regard us as vermin. There's been a steady stream of refugees for several years, but now it's become a flood. Jews deserting their homeland, their possessions, their families to get away from those thugs.' He nodded his head towards the bar, which was noisy with the laughter and jokes of the young soldiers crowded into the small room.

'It does seem a shame when you've worked so hard to make this place a success.'

'Some things are more important than money, Clare.'

'Yes, I suppose they are,' I said doubtfully. My painful lack of it, at the moment, made this concept hard for me to grasp. 'But isn't someone buying it off you?'

'I'll leave it on the market, yes. If someone buys it, fine. If not I'll come back when this madness is over. Unless you'd like to buy it?'

'I wish I could. I liked working here.' I watched Josh and realised that what I'd thought was mere shuffling of paper was in fact Josh straightening his affairs. 'I could manage it for you,' I suggested, with more confidence than I really felt. But then, I reckoned, it probably wouldn't be that difficult – buy the beer and wine from the wholesaler and sell it for more than you paid for it. I reckoned I could do that.

'What would that solve? I'd still be taking tainted money, wouldn't I? Is there no way you can escape too? You could come to Spain with me. The idea of you, of all people, being left alone here is enough to give me goosebumps.'

'And what does that mean?' I bridled.

'You're so young, and, well – innocent.'

Just as I hated being called stupid, so I hated being patronised about my youth. I stood up. 'I'm sorry you're leaving, Josh, I'm sure you're making the right decision.' I tried to sound dignified as I said this and hoped he realised I meant entirely the opposite.

It was harder for me than the French to feel any animosity towards this army of occupation. Of course, like everyone else, I resented the new restrictions – the blackout, the curfew, the difficulties in getting food, the lack of transport. To the French these Germans were the usurpers of their homeland, but not to me, for I was a foreigner here too. With their memories of the Great War still fresh, the French looked on the occupying army as arrogant monsters. But, unlike most of them, I could listen to these 'monsters' talk. On the buses, walking in the parks, sitting in a café I would eavesdrop on them. They gabbled about the sights they'd seen, the photos they wanted taken to send home. They thought Paris wonderful, beautiful. They raved about the food, the wine, the pretty, elegant women. They were just like any other group of visitors who had fallen under the spell of this city. It was a shame that the French did not know what they said, how they felt. But they also spoke of how they hated their senior officers, the boredom of their duties, their hurt at the unfriendliness of the French. They spoke of the jobs they'd left, the farms they longed for. Of the girls they were desperate to return to, the country they pined for. Monsters? Not to my ears. They were just young men a long way from home and, quite honestly, I felt sorry for them, not that I ever let on to anyone, especially Hortense and Tiphaine.

Tiphaine had heard talk of a broadcast from England. '"The flame of the French resistance must not go out . . ." That, apparently, was what he said. Isn't that inspiring?'

'Who said?' Hortense looked up from her sewing.

'Someone called de Gaulle, he's in England.'

'Then it's all right for him to talk.'

'But he's correct. Every time I see one of those awful red flags of theirs flying over *our* buildings, I want to tear it down. We must do something.'

'My friend Josh says that in his bar it's quite a game for people to bump into the tables of the Germans and knock their drinks flying. He says they must think the French the clumsiest nation on earth.'

'Did he find you a job?'

'Sorry, Hortense, no. He's leaving – tomorrow, in fact. He says it's not safe to remain here.'

'But he's American,' said Tiphaine.

'He's Jewish too.'

'Then he's far from safe, poor man.'

'It's the Jews who have caused all these problems.'

'Hortense!' Tiphaine and I protested in unison.

'That's a dreadful thing to say – I can't believe you said it.'

'You mark my words, Tiphaine. You're only pro them because of your precious *friend*. They're in cahoots – Freemasons, Communists, gypsies, they're all tarred with the same brush.'

'For someone who is normally quite intelligent you can sometimes be incredibly stupid!' I had never seen Tiphaine so angry before.

'I heard that someone misdirected a whole platoon of Germans when they asked the way. Imagine that!' Though as shocked as Tiphaine, I hoped to defuse the argument that was boiling up between them.

'Oh, I've heard that one too – several times. It's a rumour, I expect.'

Tiphaine was probably right. Rumours abounded. There were tales of murder, rape, of babies slaughtered, of poisoned sweets being given to children. I'd never met anyone who had witnessed such an event but I was constantly being assured that a friend of a friend of a friend had seen such atrocities.

They often argued now, Tiphaine and Hortense, as if we didn't have enough to contend with. The worst argument had been in June when Marshal Pétain had surrendered to the Germans and agreement was reached that there should be an unoccupied zone in the south. People wept openly that day and took sides, and bitterness began to fester between them. Hortense, though weeping, had defended the actions of her Marshal with a noisy passion while Tiphaine labelled him an appeaser, a traitor, and declared herself for de Gaulle.

I left them to it. I had no opinion either way. All I wanted was to have my Fabien back safe with me. I couldn't have cared less who was in charge so long as that happened.

To be English was not the most popular thing to be when the French fleet was bombed and a thousand poor sailors were killed.

'It must have been done for a very good reason, Hortense.'

'What good reason? You English have always hated we French. You wait until now to gain ascendancy – you've lusted after us for centuries.'

'That's just not true, Hortense. I'm sure that it was done with a heavy heart.'

'*Bah!* You are no better than the Boche – and your language is equally disgusting.'

There seemed little point in arguing with her when she was like this so I kept out of her way.

Soon all foreigners were being treated with suspicion in case they were spies. My situation worsened when, after the bombing of the fleet, France severed diplomatic links with England. Even I, optimist that I am, saw that my position was difficult. I couldn't be English since neither country liked us now. And I couldn't be German for that would alienate my French friends. In a country where papers were needed for everything in order to survive, I had none I could show without getting into trouble. I virtually didn't exist.

Hortense, who had forgiven me the destruction of the fleet – I'd no idea why – assured me that my French was excellent. 'You have a mere trace of an accent and it would take an ear as finely attuned to the nuance of our language as mine is to hear it. If it is ever queried it would be best to say you're from the south where an accent is to be expected.' She said this with such a haughty mien that I had to hide my smile.

There were problems for me, certainly, but all that concerned me was trying to get news of Fabien. I besieged the special office in the National

Archives set up by the Germans to find out if he was a prisoner-of-war. He was on no list. I tried the Red Cross; he wasn't on their lists either. The lack of information was destroying me – better to know even if it was bad news than to be left in this limbo. Letter-writing was banned but I could use the special cards printed with lists of words one could tick to make up a message. All I could tell him was that I was well; there were no words for describing my longing and love for him. These I posted to the Red Cross and prayed that somehow they would reach him.

The rest of my time I was fully occupied keeping body and soul together. I was able to pick up translation work: so many documents had to be filled in, permits for everything – more even than the French had demanded. Tiphaine said she was amazed we didn't need a special pass to pee. People needed to write letters to the German authorities to put their case, to explain why they were lacking this piece of paper or that, and were glad of someone like me who could write for them. It was very boring but it meant I was earning. I made enough to pay Hortense for my room and to get some extras on the black market that had sprung up alongside the shortages and the stringent rationing, and which, for me with no ration cards, was a lifeline.

At first all the restaurants, theatres and clubs had closed, but they soon reopened. Hortense said it was to show their contempt, but I thought it more likely that the French could no longer bear being cooped up in their apartments with no social life.

Tiphaine was treating me to a drink in a café. I felt nervous when three German soldiers clattered up to the table beside ours. Nervous because the café was empty. What were their intentions? And nervous for Tiphaine who, despite the ban on the French national colours being displayed, was wearing a blue dress with a white collar and a red belt and shoes.

'Which one do you prefer? The sassy one in blue, red and white or the little one with the nice eyes?' My heart leapt into my mouth at the soldiers' words. They weren't blind or stupid.

'The older one looks like a bit of a tart to me – she might be diseased. I like the look of the girl – she could be one of us with that hair. Nice legs.' I just knew I was going to blush.

'I reckon they're both whores. We could have them both and offer them treble – no tart will turn that down.' The third one laughed loudly.

'Tiphaine, we're leaving.' I quickly placed some money on the table.

'Why, I was enjoying myself, apart from the louts at the next table.'

'Tiphaine!' I said, through my teeth. She stood up, puzzled.

'Leaving, ladies? How very sad,' one said, in passable French.

'Yes, Oberleutnant. You really should be more careful what you say. We are not tarts, but even if we were, I doubt if you could afford either of us, let alone together,' I said, in my perfect German. 'Come, Tiphaine.' We left the soldiers wide-eyed with astonishment and, I was gratified to see, a hint of embarrassment.

Slowly we adjusted to each other and the new circumstances. Slowly people's fears lessened – the rapes and atrocities remained only rumours. The Germans weren't nearly as bad as everyone had feared. And the French, in their pragmatic way, began to make the most of this new, constrained life. And many of those who had fled south began to trickle back.

6

During the first winter of occupation there was a marked shift in our feelings towards the occupiers. The pragmatism of the summer months was harder to maintain. Even the weather, it seemed, was in league with the Germans for no one could remember a winter as bitterly cold as this one. How to keep warm and where to find food became our main concerns. The dark mornings did not help: French time had been changed to German. London was being blitzed, battles fought, but Hortense and I were more interested in the latest rumour of a supply of flour at one bakery, some rabbits at the butcher's, a load of wood from the forest, all of which might be acquired at a price and if we got there before everyone else.

The Germans were warm – very warm – burning our fuel, eating our food; the Germans had first priority for everything the country produced. While at the beginning I'd felt sorry for these lads so far from home, now I regarded them as overfed robbers of my comfort.

With few buses and taxis I walked or cycled everywhere – on the Métro the Germans tended to check papers more often and since I had none I avoided it. In a shed in Hortense's garden I'd found a bicycle, rusted and filthy, but once I had cleaned it up, I had my own transport. I found two large baskets, one for the front and one for the back: one never knew when one might find something useful to buy or pick up.

To us it appeared that the occupiers' main business was devising new regulations to make our lives more difficult. What none of us had been prepared for was the attitude of some of the French. When the Germans invited people to inform on their neighbours they were deluged by an avalanche of accusations.

'It's appalling. My friend Fifi has been denounced as a black-marketeer by her lover's wife. What is the world coming to when a Frenchman can't have a mistress?' Tiphaine was indignant.

'And is she a black-marketeer?' asked Hortense.

'Only in the smallest way.'

'Then she should have been reported,' Hortense said firmly.

'But—'

'Yes, Clare?'

'Nothing.' I got up from the table. I couldn't survive without the black-market and Hortense wasn't above using it either. But some things were best left unsaid.

'Were you about to comment on my purchases last week? If so, you should understand, Clare, that there is a difference between buying and selling.'

'I don't see it. If no one bought they wouldn't have any customers to sell to and then they'd be guilty of nothing.'

'Sometimes, Clare, you are such a child.'

I left the room. Hortense made me angry when she spoke to me like that.

'You'll never guess what's happened.' Tiphaine burst into the kitchen, cold from the December wind but grinning. 'There was a big ceremony at Les Invalides today. The Germans have returned the ashes of Napoleon's son. What crap! And we're supposed to be grateful?'

'I'd have preferred it if they had sent some coal rather than ashes,' Hortense hooted.

The cold was pernicious. It gnaws at you, creeps into your bones, makes your head ache. I felt for the very young and old, for fuel was in dangerously short supply. But Hortense was nothing if not inventive.

'What on earth are you doing?' I asked, finding her kneading torn-up newspapers in a bucket of filthy water.

'Coal-dust briquettes.'

'Oh, yes? And how are you going to dry them to burn in this weather?' She sat back on her haunches. 'Ha, I hadn't thought of that.' I quite expected her to cry. Instead she laughed. 'I suppose they'll dry eventually.'

The execution of the first Frenchman, just before Christmas, was a dreadful shock to us all. He had been found guilty of pushing a German on the pavement. For so many that had been the game to play.

'They've put up posters announcing his death. As if advertising a spectacle at the theatre,' Tiphaine told us, with disgust. 'But as soon as they put them up they are defaced and the people are laying flowers in front of them, like a shrine.'

The fear that, for a time, had lessened returned, renewed in strength.

There seemed little to celebrate that New Year of 1941. Cold, hungry, afraid, and with no news of Fabien, it was a bleak time for me. I didn't even bother, in February, to tell anyone it was my twentieth birthday.

Queuing became part of our lives. At the merest hint that something in short supply might just be available a queue formed.

'You could earn money, Clare, queuing for people. I've heard of some doing it.'

'Not me, Hortense. I'd never get up in time.' We needed money. I knew that Hortense had begun to sell things to buy food and I was aware that my contribution was not enough. 'Did you notice the house opposite has Germans billeted? Why not us?' I diverted the conversation.

'Oh, they came. I said I was full with family and they believed me. I'll say that for as long as I can get away with it.' Hortense sighed. 'Well, perhaps you should try to get work with the Germans. You should see the queues at their offices – they haven't enough translators.'

'And how would I explain myself?' I said shortly. I didn't want to work for them. 'If I did that it would be disloyal to my French friends.' The real reason was that I wouldn't have time: I needed that for my constant search for Fabien. 'I've my principles.' I swathed myself in self-righteous dignity.

'They don't keep you warm,' Hortense replied.

We both worried about Tiphaine. Her sugar-daddy had long fled, down through France to Portugal and then America.

'Henri asked me to go with him, but his wife wouldn't agree,' she'd told us, and looked hurt when we'd burst into laughter.

To replace him she'd had to start going out into the hotels and bars – on the prowl she called it. 'I hate doing it, you never know where they've been!' I could never sleep until I knew she was safely home.

As things became worse I began to regret my foolhardiness at staying. If only ... I would find myself thinking. Sometimes I would dream of drinking coffee – real coffee, great steaming cups of it, sometimes black, sometimes white, always delicious. They were cruel dreams to wake from for Hortense's efforts with chestnuts, acorns, chick peas and even lupin seeds had not been a success. Her tea made from apple skins was no better. At least I didn't smoke: only men were allowed tobacco and when that ran out they smoked dried oak leaves, lettuces, even Jerusalem artichokes. It didn't matter what was used, they all stank to high heaven.

I caught a cold, which I just couldn't seem to shake off, and when spring came I was still coughing. Hortense said it was my own fault for going out with wet hair. And I had chilblains which I'd hoped the warmer weather would relieve but they itched so much I thought I would go mad. And I hated the silence of the city when curfew came. At curfew time windows had to be closed, which was easy in winter but awful in summer. Yet the closed windows didn't stop me listening even harder, and innocent noises easily become ominous ones when you are afraid. The sound of footsteps meant soldiers, for no one else walked in the dark. The swishing of car wheels was upsetting since only the Germans drove at night. I would lie wondering if they were going to stop at our house, if someone had told them about me. Careful as I was, there were people in the neighbourhood who knew my nationality. I feared that it was only a matter of time before I was found out.

Tiphaine talked a lot about resisting the enemy. I thought this rich coming from her, for, although she hadn't said so, Hortense and I were pretty sure that she was sleeping with Germans. She always had cigarettes and money and no Frenchman had either of those in abundance. In any case I didn't see how one fitted in 'resisting': staying warm, searching for supplies, trying to stay healthy, this took up all my time.

With spiralling prices I was the first to admit that, without her, it would have been doubly hard: when she had money she shared it with us.

'It hardly seems fair, Tiphaine. You do the work and we get your money.' Hortense was counting out a wadge of notes that Tiphaine had given her at the rumour of a delivery of black-market coal to a friend of a friend and, no doubt, several other friends along the line.

'You'd share with me if it was the other way around.'

'You know, Tiphaine, I've wondered about that. I'm not so sure I would – it's easy to say, much harder to do. I'm not a good person like you.'

'Good? Me? Are you teasing me?' Tiphaine put her hands to her face to cover her laughter, or was it tears? 'No one ever said anything so nice to me before.' At that she blew hard into her hankie.

'Hortense is right,' I said, wishing I'd had the sensitivity to say something to her but I could hardly admit that it hadn't crossed my mind. 'I'll never forget what you do for us. Perhaps I should do more. I should help.'

'No, you don't,' Tiphaine almost shouted. 'If you even thought about it I would . . . I'd – I'd slap you, Clare. I really would.'

'Dear Tiphaine. I didn't mean men, I meant maybe I *should* go and try and get a job with the Germans.'

'Perhaps if you chose the right department – food supplies or fuel – you might be able to pick up the odd misplaced item.' Hortense looked eager.

'I need some boots . . .'

'No, Clare. You can't. If you help them, even translating one little form, you're collaborating with them.' Tiphaine was standing, thrusting her pretty face forward at me.

'Bah! Tiphaine, what rubbish. She wouldn't be.'

'I could mistranslate.' If translating was collaboration, what on earth did she think sleeping with the enemy was? I wondered.

'But you wouldn't because you'd be afraid they'd find out. No, Clare, I beg you, don't. Look what their people are doing to us – I heard of a whole family starved the other day, all found dead in their flat.'

'Wild rumours always abound in wartime,' said Hortense.

'Henri was no rumour. He's disappeared.'

'Sugar-daddy Henri? But you said he had fled to America.'

'I said that because I didn't want to frighten either of you and also because I needed time to come to terms with what had happened. I learnt from his neighbour that they came in the night and took him and no one has heard a word since – it's over two months now. And his poor wife is terrified . . .'

'And I suppose you gave her money?'

Tiphaine looked sheepish. 'Well, yes, but, then, over the years he's given me enough.' She grinned at the ridiculousness of the situation.

'Tiphaine, I adore you.' I raced round the table and gave her an enormous hug.

Henri was not the only person we knew to disappear. A whole family further down the road had gone in the night, and we hadn't heard a thing. The following morning we learnt that they had been hiding German Jews for months, and we had never suspected a thing. But someone had reported them to the authorities.

'They must have been denounced by a foreigner. No French person would stoop so low,' Hortense declared confidently.

'Wouldn't they?' Tiphaine asked cynically. Of the two, I tended to believe Tiphaine; she went out more than us and she saw and heard more than we did.

Hortense's old men still came, even though the wine did not flow as it had once. They sat for hours discussing what they could and should do to resist, to object. Too old to do much they took up their pens and, like so many intellectuals, began to write subversively. A network for distributing these writings grew up. Their age was no protection: one was arrested, then a second.

'You can't come here any more if you are going to keep up this nonsense,' I overheard Hortense lecturing them one day. 'It's not fair on me. I risk being arrested for being one of you – and I'm not. This is a silliness that has to stop. What good do you think you are doing?' But one and all they left and never returned: their writing to them was more important than their friendship with her. Hortense missed them more than she was prepared to admit. I wondered sometimes if she regretted banning them.

Fabien had been missing for twenty months and my efforts to find him had come to nothing. There were no parcels to send to the Red Cross now, for there was little to put in them. I still wrote – but less often. I was giving up hope, I knew.

Sometimes my longing for Fabien was a horrible ache. Then I couldn't settle to anything and I found myself being irritable and short with people when I didn't want to be and could not understand why I was behaving so.

'You're frustrated, my sweet. You need to help yourself or it will make you bad-tempered and we don't want that, do we?' Tiphaine smiled at me.

'Help myself do what?'

As Tiphaine explained exactly what she meant I listened with fascinated horror. There was no way I could do that to myself, touch myself there! Never! But I did, and she was right and it helped take away the ache.

7

Nineteen forty-one ended on a higher note when the news filtered through that America was now in the war. Hortense was in a quandary. She had verbalised her loathing of that nation too often to show any gratitude. 'Well, maybe that will mean Mab will return and that would be very nice,' was about as far as she would go.

There was a postal service of sorts. Cards, with a restricted number of lines, were permitted but, never receiving any, I was surprised one day, to find a note for me on the hall table. It had no stamp. It's from Fabien was my first thought, but while it had been written in a French hand, it wasn't his.

'Have you seen this, Hortense? Was it delivered by hand?'

'It was on the mat, the envelope was open as you see it now. I've no idea how it came to be there.'

'Have you read it?'

'My dear Clare! My breeding would never permit me to do such a thing!' She managed to look indignant while lying through her teeth, I was sure. 'Come and have a glass of wine to fortify you before you open it.'

In the kitchen, where we spent most of our time, and which was the only room with a vestige of heat, I sat down, too scared to open my letter fearing bad news. 'You read it, I can't.' My hand was shaking as I held it out to her. I held my breath as she scanned it.

'It's signed M. I think it's a woman from the writing.' Hortense waved the card at me.

'M? Surely not . . .' I grabbed it from her.

How are you? I think so often of the radiance of your smile, and dream of it often. I am flying about all over the place. I'm just not made to be amused by the countryside. So I do what I must do. The Lone Ranger is well with his cheese. How's the houe? Love, M.

'It's Mab,' I shrieked with excitement. I turned the card all ways as if it could tell me how it had come. 'She's telling me that Fabien is alive.' I clutched the card to me as if it had come from him. 'But why write in French? She must be in France.'

'She could hardly write to you in English, could she? It might be intercepted and then the Germans would arrest you for being a spy.'

'Heavens above, Hortense. Don't even joke about it!'

'I'm not making a joke. Popping a note like that through a letter box is bad enough – but in English! What if we had Germans living here? We might all be shot!' Poor Hortense, she could see the black side to a rainbow if you let her. 'How you can surmise from this that Fabien is alive I do not understand. And all this nonsense about your smile.'

'I think she was trying to sound very French – you know, the flowery terms you always write in.'

'The French write with an elegance that is fast disappearing.'

'It certainly manages not to sound like Mab, doesn't it? And Mab calls Fabien the Lone Ranger. He's a character in American films.'

'Ah, American films!' Hortense managed to imbue the words with a distinct distaste, as if she had never enjoyed one.

'I wonder if she's here? Or if she got someone else to deliver it for her.'

'People are hardly coming on day trips, are they? But what is all this nonsense about garden instruments?'

'Oh, that. Well, that really proves it's Mab. It was a joke we had.' I'd no intention of explaining that the translation of *houe* was 'hoe'. And what that meant to me.

'Strange humour you have – you and the Americans. So what will you do?'

'Why, go and find him, of course.'

'But you don't know where he is.'

'I do, Hortense. He's at home with his cheese.'

I wanted everything to happen immediately but, of course, in time of war that was impossible. I had weeks of worrying and waiting for an appointment with the right German officer to give me the necessary papers to travel.

At last my German passport came into its own. To travel anywhere outside one's immediate area was difficult and not encouraged. The pass to allow me to travel from the occupied into the unoccupied zone was particularly difficult to obtain. But I had high hopes that by putting on my German mantle, for the first time, I would have less trouble.

I was frightened as, finally, I sat waiting outside the relevant office. I'd been scared enough venturing here but Hortense's conviction that I would be immediately arrested as a spy, and the memory of the passionate embrace she had given me, as if saying farewell for ever, had done nothing to help me be calm.

'Fräulein Springer, if you could explain your reason for this journey?'

I looked modestly at the carpet beneath my feet. 'Do I have to tell you?' I raised my eyes, opened them wider and looked pleadingly at the upright, handsome German colonel on the other side of the desk. 'You promise not to tell? I mean, if my parents found out . . .' I smiled nervously. 'I have a lover they don't approve of. I'm forbidden to have contact with him. But I've heard from him. He's been sent to the coastal region in the south-west of the unoccupied zone.' I had spent hours concocting this story and now as I trotted it out I congratulated myself at how plausible it sounded even if it felt strange to be speaking in German again.

'But that area is severely restricted. I can give no permits to anyone to go there.'

'No, no. I understand . . .' Obviously I should have spent more time on my tale. 'I didn't mean *there*!' I laughed nonchalantly at the very idea while my mind raced; I needed the name of a place. 'He's suggested we meet at . . . Lyon.' Geography had never been my strong point and I sent up a silent prayer that Lyon was a possibility.

'A long journey to make, right across France. Couldn't you have thought of somewhere nearer our coastal defences?'

'He's a historian . . .' I said, after the merest of pauses. 'He wants to do some research about . . . the silk trade in Lyon,' I gabbled hurriedly, aware the palms of my hands were wet with sweat. I must have gleaned that snippet of information from Hortense without realising.

The officer laughed and I relaxed. 'If you were my girl, I don't think I'd want to be bothered wasting my leave on dull history.' He pulled a form towards him – I forced myself to breathe normally.

'What I don't understand, Fräulein, is what a nice German girl like you is doing in Paris in the middle of a war. You should be home in . . .' he glanced at my papers '. . . Salzburg. A lovely city.'

'Blame Jürgen. He's fluent in French, you see. He did a degree in French – before his history one.' I felt sick at the easy mistake I had made. 'We gambled on him being posted to France. And it's paid off.' I allowed myself a grin at this point, that last bit I had rehearsed in front of the mirror – grin and all.

'And your parents. How have you explained your absence to them?'

'Why, sir, I told them I'm working for you.'

'A devious young woman. But, then, love should be allowed to conquer all, shouldn't it? Perhaps when you return it might be a good idea if you made that a reality. I would be happy to find employment for you here.'

'Thank you, sir. I'll do that. The minute I return.' I stood up aware that the backs of my knees were damp with sweat. I took the document he offered me and thanking him again, I turned to go.

'Not so fast, Fräulein, I've a question or two.'

Sometimes I thought my heart was on an elastic band the way it plunged around in my body. 'Yes?'

'Where did you meet your young man, Jürgen . . .?'

'Schiller.' I grabbed a name from the air. 'Here, in Paris.'

'When?'

'In nineteen thirty-nine.'

'The year you had your passport renewed?'

'Yes.'

'But you have been home since then?'

'No.' Should I have said yes? I felt bile rising in my throat.

'So that would explain why you haven't an entry stamp?'

'Of course.' My relief was so strong I thought I would faint. But it was short-lived; he still had not finished.

'So how can your parents object to someone they have never met?'

'But they have. They came to collect me. They drove. I ran away . . .' I gabbled.

'Quite an adventurous young woman, aren't you?' He smiled and I grimaced – I just couldn't get my smiling muscles to work. 'It is strange that in the circumstances your parents have not asked us to find you.'

I saw a black hole of despair open up. 'I phoned them after they got back. I said I was fine. They said they never wanted to see me again as long as I lived.' At least that was only a half-lie. 'And, as I just said, they think I'm safe working for you.'

'I see. So apart from this passport we have no record of you. Have you been living with this Madame Hortense all that time?'

'No, no. She's no idea I'm still here. She'd have tried to send me home. She wouldn't have wanted to anger my parents.' God, I thought, lying is so complicated, tell one and you spawn ten more. 'So where have you been living?'

'At the bar Mississippi.'

'When you return from your rendezvous, Fräulein Springer, I suggest you register with us immediately.'

'I will, I will!'

At the door I barged into a soldier, so anxious was I to be away before the Colonel could think of anything else to ask me.

'I wish you weren't going. I'll worry.'

'I'll be fine, Hortense. See? All my papers are in order. I'm a nice respectable German girl off to find her brave soldier lover – which is true, it's just that he's a different nationality.' I laughed gaily, feeling quite drunk with excitement.

'But there might be such dangers. You are used to the civilisation of Paris. The wild countryside you are going to – God knows what brigands await you. The Auvergne is the wildest area of all France!'

'Oh, really, Hortense. You do exaggerate.'

'The countryside's a dangerous place,' she said gloomily, though I was strongly of the opinion she'd never set foot in it. 'At least can't you write to him, tell him you're coming?'

'I don't know his exact address and you know what the post is like. In any case, I want to surprise him.'

'Tush! Not knowing where he is, it's all wrong.'

'Men hate surprises,' Tiphaine offered.

'Not if they're nice ones,' I countered.

'Take this.' Tiphaine pushed a purse across the table to me.

'I can't,' I said, but knew full well that Tiphaine would insist, which she did.

'What if you can't find him? You'll need money then.'

'But I will. I know the town he lives in – Rocheloire. I'll find him with no trouble.'

'What if he doesn't welcome you?'

'Oh, Hortense, why wouldn't he?'

'He hasn't written to you himself.'

'No, but he might have. Dear Hortense, you do worry unnecessarily.'

'You're too trusting and, well—'

'Naïve? Was that what you were going to say? I'm not. I decided ages ago not to divulge my name to strangers, and I haven't.'

'Extremely wise. But I do wish you'd take things more seriously, Clare. This war isn't a game, you know.'

I muttered a response. Really, older people could be so patronising at times.

'When will you be back?' Tiphaine asked.

'Never, I hope.' I grinned at them. 'Oh, forgive me, I didn't mean it like that.' I put out my hands and grabbed theirs, ashamed of myself upon seeing their crestfallen expressions. 'I mean I'll be back to visit you. I just hope—'

'I understand, my dear Clare. But remember always. Whatever happens we are always here for you, aren't we, Tiphaine?'

'To be sure.'

Chapter Three

January – April 1942

1

The journey to Lyon, which should have taken part of a day, took three. The train was constantly starting and stopping – and no one ever knew why. At each stop yet another official would board the train to check our documents. It was crowded so this was never a rapid process.

Although my papers were in order and I was blessed with my German passport – I'd never be able to thank Tubs enough for insisting I get it – I could never quite control the idiotic nervousness whenever a German soldier demanded them. I soon realised I was not alone in feeling this way. The others in my compartment visibly tensed and looked as anxious as I. It was odd, for the only man in the carriage who looked unconcerned was the one who was arrested at the stop before we passed into the unoccupied zone.

His noisy departure – I'd seen stark terror for the first time in my life – frightened us all. We rode in a strained silence for some time after that.

The atmosphere in the carriage was not helped when, ordered to show my passport and papers, to the other passengers I appeared to be German. I talked to the soldiers. They, content to find a young 'German' woman, joked and flirted with me. But my companions were less impressed with this. They glanced at me in a most unfriendly way. When they shared food and drink they offered me none. I longed to let them in on my secret: I found it uncomfortable to be so disliked.

Once in free France we were sure everything would speed up. It didn't. There were as many stops and as many checks as before.

At Lyon I found there was no train for Le-Puy-en-Velay in the department of the Haute-Loire, the nearest big city to where Fabien lived, until the following day and even then, I was told by a sympathetic ticket man, there was no guarantee. So I changed my suede court shoes for the

75

brogues I had brought from England, and never worn, and decided to walk.

On the map, which Hortense had insisted I bring, it looked to be only seventy or eighty miles. I intended to hitch-hike, and, presuming I would quickly get a lift, set off in high spirits carrying my case, a large canvas bag and my purse. It wasn't long before I was wishing I'd packed fewer clothes.

In the occupied part of France we had often thought of the fortunate ones in the unoccupied zone as we queued for food and walked for lack of petrol. How wrong we were! There was little traffic: I soon discovered that petrol was in short supply here too.

As I toiled up and down the steep hills I decided that, beautiful as the scenery was, it was best viewed from a train or car. Over the following days I did get some lifts, in a variety of vehicles, a couple on lurching tractors that were on their last wheeze – I thought my spine would never feel the same again. I experienced an exciting hour in a van full of road-menders. Strapped on the side was a metal contraption, which had constantly to be fed with wood to power the engine; I decided it would be a close-run thing whether we were gassed by the fumes or incinerated when it blew up. I had rides on several horse-drawn carts and once in a smart little trap. What all these vehicles had in common was that they were worn out – even the horses looked as if they were about to drop dead – and they were so crowded that not even a mouse could have squeezed on. One lift of relative comfort, compared with the others, was in the car of an official of the Vichy government, but I could not enjoy it for he asked too many questions, so I pretended to be very vacuous. But the other people were friendly once I had dissipated their initial suspicion by telling them I was French. They didn't even complain about my luggage as I clambered on board amongst the rabbits in hutches, the sacks of potatoes and, on one memorable occasion, a large pink pig.

The first night I found a room in an inn but I was too much an object of curiosity. The second night I was offered a bed by the man who had given me a lift on his cart. But to reach his farm we had to go far from the main road, and his wife was the nosiest person I had ever met. After that I contrived to sleep in barns. Sleeping on straw was easier than I thought, and surprisingly warm, even if the scurrying noises took time to adjust to.

In the occupied zone we were aware that the information we received was only what the Germans wanted us to hear, so the newspapers and the radio were full of their victories and the failures of the Allies. I was not alone in wondering what was really going on in the world outside this country. I had hoped that by being in the unoccupied zone I would finally find out how the war was progressing. But here it was the Vichy government who censored what the populace was told and I found that no one believed them much either.

It was January and bitterly cold, but dry, and there was much talk of snow. I prayed it would hold off until I reached a town called Vorey, which Fabien had often talked about.

I had never really liked the countryside – not that I'd ever let on to Fabien – but he had not exaggerated the beauty of his homeland. I found myself in awe of my surroundings. At times the inhospitable wildness frightened me. There were thick forests, which I could have used as short-cuts, but I did not dare enter for fear of the animals that might lurk in them. Cascades of crystal clear water hurtled down the hillsides to tumble into the Loire river, which snaked placidly along like a great stream of mercury between the gorges in the valley it had carved itself.

This river was a comfort to me. The road was built alongside it so I rarely lost sight of it. I knew from what Fabien had told me that his house overlooked it. It was a moving ribbon that, if I kept close to it, would lead me to him.

It was hard, but the moment I considered giving up I had only to think of Fabien and my longing to be with him and I found new energy from somewhere. As I trudged I'd imagine our first meeting, the expression on his face at first sight of me, the tender words of love we would exchange. The advantage of being alone was I could talk to him out loud, practising the fine phrases I would shortly be using to him.

By the sixth day I was tired and had reached the point where I wondered if I would ever arrive when, breasting yet another steep hill alongside my faithful Loire, I looked down and there, clasped in a wider valley, was the little town of Vorey. Just seeing it lying huddled between the hills, the pungent smell of woodsmoke rising from the many chimneys, I was rejuvenated and could have walked it all again – well, so I told myself.

My pace quickened as I almost ran down the hill past the graveyard. I longed to shout, 'I'm here, I'm here.' I didn't but, oh, how my spirits lifted.

The town seemed deserted. I padded down the rough, rutted main street looking for a hotel, a shop – signs of human life. Further down, a door opened and I saw a shaft of light. It was a bar, judging by the hubbub coming from within.

As I stepped over the threshold I entered total silence. It was dimly lit by a single candle on the bar and a couple of noisome smoking oil lamps. The lack of light was not helped by the pall of acrid cigarette smoke. The room was half full of short, square-shaped men in the distinctive blue overalls of the French farmer, and they all had equally square faces.

'Good evening,' I said politely. One had the grace to respond. The others just stood and stared.

At what? Nervously I brushed my hand through my hair. I must look a sight. Certainly I was filthy and in need of a bath. I walked through the silence to the bar.

'Do you have a room for the night?'

'I might have.' The patron looked at me suspiciously – I must look worse than I thought.

'I can pay in advance.'

'I'd expect you to.'

'Ah.' I wasn't sure what else to say to that. There seemed little point in indignation. 'Do you serve food?'

'Yes.'

'I'll have whatever you're serving.'

I sat down at a table and tried not to notice the staring. No one said anything. I studied my hands. When I looked up they were still gawping at me. I began to feel angry at such rudeness. Who did they take me for?

'I'm trying to find a Monsieur Fabien de Rocheloire,' I said quite loudly. Once they knew who I had come to see they might stop peering.

'And who might be asking?' a voice demanded. At least, that was what I thought he said, but the accent was so thick that I couldn't be sure.

'A friend from Paris,' I replied. I was put out at the snorts of derision this generated. Was it my being a friend of Fabien or the mention of the city?

They began to speak amongst themselves, not that I could understand since they now spoke in a patois, but I sensed, uncomfortably, that they spoke of me. I was tired, hungry, and had never felt so alone in my whole life.

'My father says you're wanting a room?' A young woman of my own age had appeared at my table.

'Yes, please.' I stood up. Her smile, in that room, was like the sun breaking through.

'Perhaps you'd be more comfortable eating there too? This lot are too curious for their own good.' She laughed. 'I'll lead the way.' She picked up my case. I was grateful – I don't think I could have carried it another foot. 'You see, we don't get many strangers here and not many women venture into the bar. Especially pretty ones like you. With your blonde hair they probably thought you were German.'

'Good gracious! Me?' I laughed uncomfortably. She was probing, I was sure. 'I'm from Paris,' I said, and I hoped my accent stood up.

She pushed open the door of a small room dominated by a large cupboard and a wooden bed – just like the one at Hortense's, shaped like a sleigh. 'It's not very grand.'

'It looks like Paradise to me,' I said, sinking gratefully on to the bed.

'Paris, you say. Do you like it there?'

'I love it. Well, I loved it more before the Germans came. But it's still the best place in the world to be. It's so beautiful.'

'You're looking for His Nibs, Fabien, they say.'

'Fabien de Rocheloire. Yes.'

'He lives at Rocheloire. There's no bus and it's a good six miles. I'll lend you my bike in the morning, if you like – I warn you, it's a tough uphill ride, but fun going down the other side. Still, you'll be wanting some food. Sausage and lentils be all right? I'm Simone, by the way.'

'Clare,' I said. She looked surprised, but I didn't want to say my surname – it sounded too foreign for comfort.

The food, when it finally arrived, looked the most unpleasant dish I'd ever seen. 'These are our famous green lentils,' Simone informed me. They looked more grey to me. 'The sausage is safe.'

I was glad she'd said that for Hortense had sent me off with strict instructions to avoid sausages at all costs since one never knew what was in them. Alone again I gingerly sniffed a forkful. I was too hungry not to eat, so I shoved it in, closed my eyes, and found it was delicious. I even enjoyed the wine, which was young and rough. Hortense would have declared it vinegar.

I was so tired that by seven thirty I was in bed.

Sleep, however, was a long time coming. My room was directly over the bar and the floor of my room was its ceiling. So for the next few hours I could hear every word from below. It was probably as well that I couldn't understand anything that was said.

2

Of course I did eventually sleep, a wonderful deep sleep, and when I awoke, although it was still dark, I felt refreshed. I unpacked the clothes I intended to wear – I'd been too tired the night before. Everything was crumpled. In the kitchen I found Simone who was already up and cooking. She lent me an iron to press my suit and jumper – a blue and heather fine tweed and pale blue cashmere. Fabien loved me in blue, he always told me. Simone thought it funny that I didn't know how to heat the iron on the large kitchen range. 'Here let me. You'll scorch it.'

I sat at the table and watched her deftly manhandle the heavy iron. She used two – one heated while she worked with the other. 'Have you known himself long?' she asked, not looking up from her work.

'Over two and a half years,' I said proudly. Which, of course, was true, even though in that time we'd spent only thirty-six days and eight and a half hours together. I'd worked it out ages ago, but I wasn't going to admit that to anyone.

'He's handsome.'

'Yes, he is. Well, I think so.'

'A real ladies' man.'

'He likes women, yes.' I didn't like that comment, or the sly little smile that accompanied it. 'But what Frenchman doesn't?' I wish I hadn't said that, afraid it made me sound not French.

'Some more than others.'

'I don't know what you're trying to imply but you're not succeeding.' I knew I sounded haughty.

'Why, nothing, Miss.' She looked down at her task.

'Good.' I felt a bit foolish. 'May I still borrow your bicycle?'

'You can hire it.' She slapped the flat-iron down on the hotplate with a rattle and a tight-lipped expression.

'How much?'

The short journey took ages – hills again, but also it was a dreadful old bone-shaker for which I'd had to pay an exorbitant fee, not that I minded: I had no intention of being friends with anyone who made snide remarks about my Fabien – she was probably jealous. Eventually, on the brow of the last hill, I was standing looking across at Fabien's village. On this overcast day in winter it looked lovely; in sunshine it would be beautiful.

Rocheloire was situated in a loop of the river. On a lush flat meadow, where the road snaked into the village, there were a few houses and a couple of farms. The village proper was on a very steep hill. The Roman tiles of the houses were red, baked a warm, faded colour by the sun. The roofs were layered one above the other as if the houses had tumbled down the hill and landed teetering over their neighbours. They were built of a mixture of white, fawn, brown and, in some cases, coal black stones, some as big as boulders. The thick mortar that outlined each block made the walls look as if they were made of giant slabs of nougat.

In the centre of the village I could see the tower of a church around which the houses were clustered more densely, as if for comfort. Towering above them all and near the summit was a small château, which looked as if it protected the church and the dwellings gathered at its foot.

Further north, where this great river finally flowed, the châteaux were white, elegant, airy and fairy-tale-like. But this one was of a different style:

it stood four square, made of the same dark stone. The windows were small, deep-set in the evidently thick walls; the turrets were squat. It had been built for defence, not as an aristocrat's conceit.

I paused to get my breath back, wondering which was Fabien's house. I found myself wondering if . . . No, it couldn't be. Although his name was the same as the village. But, then, a cheese salesman would hardly live in a château.

Getting back on the bicycle I freewheeled down the hill. The wind in my hair, the excitement of the speed made toiling up the hills seem worthwhile – well, almost.

A shepherd approached with a flock of sheep that were being herded noisily by two spiteful-looking dogs of indeterminate breed. I stopped to let them pass. The shepherd did not stare but smiled pleasantly and touched his cap with his stick – a good deal friendlier than anyone had been last night. I pedalled on, aiming for the centre, and the square and the bar I knew I would find there.

The houses were pressed so tightly together that obviously there were more inhabitants than I had first thought. A network of tiny streets led off the main route, though none of the surfaces were made up. Some weren't roads but steep flights of steps, great grooves worn in them from the centuries of boots that had trodden on them. The main square was small and cobbled. On one side stood the church, dark-stoned and old, with a bell clanging discordantly. A bar, its windows steamed up so it was impossible to see in, was on the other side. Obviously a man could go to church and come straight out to the bar. A cluster of shops looked empty of wares but were still open. The only noise came from the fourth side of the square where stood the austere façade of the school, with *Garçons* carved in the stonework on one side and *Filles* on the other. To my mind French schools always looked more like barracks than schools.

I pushed open the door of the bar and entered, expecting the silence of the night before. There was a silence, but only a momentary one as the small group inside registered my arrival. Then there was a chorus of 'Good morning,' which was cheering.

I asked the woman at the bar for a cup of coffee. It was a silly request, but it was my automatic reaction to being in a French bar. Who had coffee these days? I was just about to apologise.

'With milk?' the woman asked, to my astonishment.

'Thank you.'

'Come from Vorey, have you? They told us you were coming.' She was a friendly-looking woman, plump and smartly dressed in a bright red dress. She'd have been quite pretty but for an unfortunate cast in her eye, which made it difficult to know if she was talking to me or one of the men behind me.

'Originally from Paris.' Did they appear friendly because they had been warned of my pending arrival – reassured by the citizens of Vorey that I was not a German spy?

'Well, there's a surprise. We don't get many from that far these days. That would explain your accent.'

'Probably.' There was a definite silence now as the men listened avidly to my responses.

'I'd have bet you came from Lyon. Good job I didn't.'

'Yes. Still, I came via Lyon.'

'And how did you get here? There've been no trains for days.'

'I walked and I had a few lifts.'

'Young thing like you. You shouldn't have done that all on your own. What must your mother be thinking?' She leant on the zinc bar.

'I was fine. My mother is dead.' Now why did I tell her that? She was so nosy, she'd be asking my age next.

'And how old are you?'

'Twenty-one next month.' Why hadn't I told her it was no business of hers? But I grinned at how right I'd been.

'You look younger.'

I was at an age when that was not a compliment, so I took my coffee and sat at a table close to the fire. It was wood-burning and looked like a large black bucket situated in the middle, its flue looping dangerously low across half the room before venting on the outside. Now that the conversation was over the men began to chat again, in patois, and from the odd surreptitious glance in my direction, it was obvious they talked about me. Even though they were friendlier they still looked like the men in the bar last night – just as short, just as square, the same faces, virtually as if they'd all come out of the same jar. Perhaps they had: perhaps they were all related or even interrelated. But Fabien didn't look a scrap like any of them.

The woman approached with an ashtray. 'I'm Fleur Collange.'

'Clare,' I replied.

'That's a pretty name. You don't hear it often these days, gone out of fashion, I suppose. And your surname?'

'My mother was a romantic,' I joked, sidestepping the need to say my German-English-sounding name.

'Come to visit Fabien?' Her question almost made me choke on my delicious coffee.

'Why do you ask?' I said warily.

'A pretty young woman, smartly dressed, nice pearls, well spoken, slight accent. You don't have to be Maigret to work out who you've come to see.' She looked at me with an arch expression.

'I was a bit puffed after my cycle ride from Vorey. I needed to catch my breath.' I had to say something: it was beginning to alarm me how people spoke of Fabien, as if he had a bad reputation.

'I expect you didn't want to arrive looking dishevelled, did you?' She smiled in a conspiratorial way. I smiled back as if agreeing when it hadn't even crossed my mind. 'The toilet's at the back. There's a mirror there if you want to tidy yourself. Meanwhile I'll get one of the men to put your bicycle in the store room. It's too steep a climb for you to ride up to the château and it'll get stolen if you leave it outside.'

'Stolen? Here? Surely not.' I laughed, but was pleased she'd told me where Fabien lived without my having the embarrassment of asking.

'Bicycles are at a premium everywhere.'

In the somewhat smelly lavatory at the back of the bar I studied my face in the mirror: her insistence had worried me. But I didn't look too much of a mess, after all. I tidied my hair, dashed a spot of powder on my nose, practised a smile and snapped my handbag shut.

So, Fabien did live in the château. I was most excited about that.

3

A long shallow flight of steps led to a massive wooden door. Half-way up I wondered if, perhaps, this was the right way in. If it was often used, the steps surely wouldn't have been so slippery from the moss that covered them. I also had a horrible idea that I was being watched, but the windows were so deeply set it was impossible to know for sure.

I lifted a huge knocker – in the form of a lion that looked as boss-eyed as Fleur in the village bar. It banged down and I could hear it echoing through the interior. That made me giggle – it sounded like something from a Boris Karloff film! I bet myself that I would hear rusty bolts drawn and the door would creak when opened. I was right. The old woman who peered up at me looked taken aback to find me laughing, somewhat hysterically, on the threshold.

'I'm so sorry. So rude of me . . .' I flapped my hands, desperately trying to stop laughing. 'I wonder . . . I've come to visit Fabien de Rocheloire . . .'

The woman held the door open wider. Luckily it made no more noise. She ushered me in and pointed silently to a chair for me to sit. Was she dumb, I wondered. Slowly she moved across the room, her back so hunched that she was bent to an angle of forty-five degrees as if permanently searching the ground for something. If dumb at one end, she wasn't the other. I had to put my hand over my mouth as at each step wind rat-a-tat-tatted from her rear. She finally disappeared through a door and I allowed myself to laugh, then made a conscious effort to control myself.

The hall was dark with little light coming from the two windows. I was aware of dark beams above me and a black floor beneath. And it was cold. I pulled my coat close around me.

The door reopened. A middle-aged woman appeared. Razor slim, immaculately groomed, two rows of expensive pearls hanging on her neat navy blue jumper, heels clicking smartly on the flagstone floor. A scarf was draped elegantly over her slim shoulders. She didn't look a scrap like the tweedy English countrywomen I'd met. 'May I be of help?' she asked, without smiling.

'I'm looking for Fabien de Ro—' And then a dreadful thing happened. I couldn't remember his name. 'I do hope I've come to the right place,' I said, too quickly, hoping she wouldn't notice.

'But of course.' She said no more but stood waiting politely as if for an explanation.

'I'm a friend of his. From Paris. I've been so worried. I've been so afraid,' I gabbled. Then, to my absolute horror, I burst into tears. I felt so foolish standing in this strange hall, blubbing in front of a woman I didn't even know. She looked shocked and actually took two steps back, as if faintly repelled. 'I'm so sorry. I don't know what's the matter with me.' I fumbled in my pocket for a handkerchief, and blew mightily into it. 'I'm tired,' I added feebly, and still she said nothing. I felt she was assessing me as if deciding whether to let me move further into her domain. 'I'm Clare Springer.' This wasn't the sort of person I could not use my surname to.

'You're not French?'

'No.' Unsure who she was, I wasn't prepared to say more.

'I'm Fabien's mother.'

I smiled with relief, she still did not respond. 'How do you do?' I offered my hand, which she took reluctantly. She had a weak and flabby handshake, and from her expression she did not appreciate my strong one. 'Then it's safe to tell you I'm English. If you wouldn't mind keeping that to yourself. These days in France . . .' I shrugged, thinking an explanation unnecessary.

'Have you travelled far?' She held up her arm indicating I should follow her in the direction she pointed. How odd that she didn't comment: it was unlikely that many English people turned up on her doorstep now.

'From Vorey this morning.'

'A pretty little town with the Loire and the Arzon meeting. Inevitably it is prone to flooding. But the hills are delightful and . . .' She chatted away about the scenic beauty as I trotted along behind. It struck me as even odder, in the circumstances, that she chose to sound like a tourist guide.

We passed through several rooms, all small, dark, heavily beamed and with tiny windows. Eventually she opened a door leading into a drawing room, in which several oil lamps were burning so it was not as gloomy as the others. A small log glowed in the large stone fireplace. Honestly, it was so big you could have cooked an ox in it. The furniture was heavy, uncomfortable-looking and worn, as were the rugs and the curtains. She invited me to sit on an upright wooden chair with red velvet upholstery on the seat but no give at all. Still, it was good for my posture, I reassured myself.

We had to wait while the windy one brought in an extra glass, although there were four others on the silver tray. I studied the ceiling carefully to keep myself under control since there was no reaction from Madame to her servant's digestive problem. Fortunately it was painted with stars, moon, crescents and small flowers, and, although in need of retouching, was quite enchanting and distracted me sufficiently to dampen any giggles. 'I see you are admiring our ceiling. Quite ravishing, isn't it? Sixteenth century.'

'Really?' I didn't want to know about the ceiling, nor the portraits on the wall, which she was now explaining – rattling off names and titles, those long French ones I always got lost in the middle of. She told me who had been guillotined and who hadn't. And I had to get up to study a small Fragonard since, obviously, it was her prize possession. I wanted to be told about Fabien. I wanted her to be impressed by the long trek I had made to find him. But she was too imperious for me to interrupt and ask the questions I desperately needed answered.

'Are you cold,' she asked suddenly.

'No. I'm fine. It's warm in here.' It wasn't, but it seemed polite to say it was. 'I had a marvellous cup of coffee in the bar in the village,' I continued, without thinking.

'You went to the bar? How extraordinary. You came from Vorey, you have accommodation there?'

'Yes. I found a room.' I sensibly avoided saying where.

At this information she allowed herself a glimmer of a smile, as if the news that I had a room was the first thing to please her. She then began a subtle interrogation. A throwaway remark about Paris to elicit which area I'd lived in – acceptable. A name or two mentioned, as if in passing, to ascertain whom I knew. But I could name no aristocrats, no society people, so this was not as acceptable. A reference here and there to restaurants and shops I might patronise – most acceptable, thanks to Mab. She was doing what Hortense did, and the mothers of my English friends, probing, dissecting, placing me socially in the scheme of things, judging my background, my suitability.

The reason for the two extra glasses became evident as the door opened and two other people entered, one a woman, slightly younger than Fabien's mother, I guessed, and the other a dusty-looking cleric. I immediately stood up.

'Might I introduce my sister-in-law, Violet Chambrey, and this is Father Gilbert. Miss Springer is a friend of Fabien . . . she says.' I was already smiling at them but I felt the smile freeze at the subtle pause and subsequent implication of her words.

'Then welcome, my dear.' Fabien's aunt shook my hand in a friendly manner. She was a complete contrast to her sister-in-law, quite plump for a start. She had faded blonde hair and large, innocent-looking blue eyes. Her nose was small and upturned. She was remarkably like the pug dog that had followed her into the room – except the dog's eyes and nose were brown, and the woman was prettier.

The priest's hand was dry and scaly. He bowed over mine. He had the obsequious air of an over-zealous waiter. Black was an unfortunate colour for him to have to wear since his cassock was scattered liberally with dandruff. It was as if he was so desiccated that he was gradually flaking away.

'Have you come far, Miss Springer?' the priest asked me, and I trotted out the bit about Vorey but this time I also explained about my walk from Lyon.

'But, my poor child, you must be exhausted.' The priest looked so concerned that I thought he was going to cross himself at any moment.

'Then you must be a very good friend of Fabien.' The aunt smiled. I liked her smile: it was genuine. At least these two seemed pleased to see me.

'Where did you meet my son?'

'I was introduced to him at a party given by an American friend of mine, but I'd already met him before.'

'As if you were destined to meet?' The aunt clasped her hands together.

'Exactly. That's what we thought. The first time he came into the shop where I worked, and then at Mab's party. Fabien said it was meant to be.' I felt all melty telling them this and a bit embarrassed so I stared at my hands in my lap. When I looked up I wished I hadn't told them. His mother looked appalled. His aunt smiled sadly at me and the priest coughed.

At this point, with no one seeming to know what to say next, the door opened again.

'Are the drinks poured? I'm freezing.' And Fabien, my tall, strong, beautiful Fabien, came into the room.

He was still beautiful, but he was thinner and he looked desperately tired. It was him and yet it wasn't him. The strong, handsome face was gaunt and his expression was wary. He had changed, in the months since I had last seen him. He looked as if he had aged ten years. As he walked I realised he was limping. At first he didn't see me.

'Fabien!' I cried with joy, a lift in my voice. I jumped to my feet.

He stopped in his tracks. 'Clare? What the hell are you doing here?'

'Fabien,' I said, on a descending note this time, burst into tears again and sat down abruptly.

4

'My poor, sweet darling. Will you ever forgive me? What an oafish welcome.' Fabien was covering my face with little urgent kisses, his tongue licking my tears which now, once started, I couldn't stop.

'I'm sorry . . .' I blurted out.

'What have you to be sorry for?' He gave me his handkerchief. I covered my face with it inhaling the smell of him. He was right. Why was I apologising? It wasn't my fault I was crying. 'Why are you crying so?' he asked, as if he'd read my thoughts.

I began to say, 'Sorry,' again, but stopped myself in time. 'I'd imagined our meeting so many times, Fabien. I knew what it was going to be like and then it wasn't,' I said, while blowing my nose and dabbing my eyes and fretting at what a mess I must look. It was at this point that I registered we were alone in the room. Thank heavens, I thought. What must his family have thought of me, making a scene like that? They must have left from embarrassment.

'It was such a shock seeing you standing in our drawing room. The last person I expected to see here.' He stroked my face as if to make sure I was really there.

'But surely I should have been the one you knew would come and find you.'

'Sweet darling. How could I presume any such thing? I'd thought you'd be long gone.'

'Where?'

'Why, to England, of course. I never for one moment thought you would have stayed. I mean, the danger you're in . . .' He shook his head. I liked his concern.

'I couldn't possibly have gone until I knew you were safe.' This statement led to a very satisfactory kiss. 'How long have you been here?' I asked when, sadly, it was over.

'Six months.'

I sat up straight with shock. 'Six months!' I repeated, like an idiot, but I was so shocked. 'Then why didn't you contact me? I've been so miserable with longing and worry for you. Why?' I felt more tears dangerously near.

'What would have been the point? I didn't have your address in England. I'd no idea you'd be so silly as to stay in Paris.'

'I had to stay. You might have come. You might have escaped and come to me.' I said this forcefully to cover up my annoyance at that word. *Silly!* Why had he said it, spoiling such a precious moment?

'I don't deserve such devotion.'

'You could have written to Hortense?'

'And compromise her? That wouldn't be fair. Harbouring the enemy—' he kissed the tip of my nose, as if pointing out how silly was the idea that I could be regarded as *enemy* '– or not reporting the whereabouts of an escaped prisoner-of-war, that could have got her into serious trouble.'

'I'm thinking only of myself, as usual. Of course you couldn't write.'

'But how did you know I was free and to come here?'

'This.' From my handbag I took the card.

'But it says nothing of me.'

'It does. You're the Lone Ranger.' And I had to explain yet again about the film and the man and the horse called Silver.

'I don't find that very complimentary. Me! An American cowboy!'

I wanted to say for goodness' sake not to be so stuffy. I thought all things American were bliss but I realised not everyone, especially the French, agreed with me. 'I think it's from Mab. There you see, it's signed M and it was only *she* who called you that.' Snide of me I knew but, then, in the circumstances?

'Yes, that would make sense with her excellent French.'

'What do you mean?'

'They're using her. She must have been sent over.'

'Mab? What? As a spy, you mean? Are they doing such things? Golly, how exciting!'

'And dangerous. It will require much courage.'

'Of course, that too,' I said hurriedly. 'But I could do that as well, couldn't I? I should go home and volunteer.'

'You? As a special agent? Oh, my darling, don't be silly.' And to add to the insult he laughed.

'Was it bad?' I needed to change the subject to cover up the hurt that he had called me *silly* again. And what better than to get the conversation back to the subject of himself?

'Being a prisoner? The most frustrating year of my life.'

'I was going crazy with worry. I couldn't even find out where you had been captured.'

'We were sent into Belgium to help shore up the defences there. I was captured near Liège. I was interrogated by my hosts then thrown into a temporary prison.' He made light of it all but I shuddered at what might have happened to him.

'Do you want to talk about it?'

'No, not yet.' I could have wept, he sounded so brave. 'I was later moved to a camp just inside Germany.'

'Did you get any of my cards? And I sent you a couple of parcels.'

'Not a thing. Where did you post them to?'

'The Red Cross. I didn't know what else to do and I hoped they might find you. I felt I was doing something. They gave me a kind of hope.' Don't cry, I told myself firmly, he'll get fed up with you if you do.

'I hope some other poor sod got them, then. If only I'd known what you were doing for me. How happy that would have made me. I thought of you often and longed for you . . .' His voice had taken on that wonderful husky tone I loved so much and sent shivers down my spine. 'I escaped for you,' he said dramatically, and I thrilled at his words.

'How?'

'We were being moved from one PoW camp to another further into Germany. The guard was distracted and four of us ran. That's when I was shot.'

'Shot? Oh, my poor darling. Where?'

'Here.' He pointed to his thigh. 'It shattered the bone. I nearly died.'

He'd been wounded and I hadn't known. I should have known, I should have sensed his pain. I felt so bleak that I hadn't; it was as if I had failed him in some way.

'But how . . .?'

'Did I survive? My friends, my incredible friends, carried me to safety. Fortunately we were still close to the border with France and in the night we slipped over, undetected. A farmer gave me shelter – he had no cause to love the Germans, he'd fought in the last war. I stayed there, tended by the local doctor, nursed by the wife until I was strong enough to move under my own steam. Then I just walked . . . sheltered by courageous people on the way, until I got home.'

'From northern France?' I was astounded, I wouldn't boast about my walk from Lyon ever again. 'And now your leg is better?'

'Much. I had a bad infection, otherwise it wouldn't have taken so long to heal. I walk miles each day to strengthen it. I hope in a few weeks to be fit enough to serve again.'

'Oh, no, Fabien. You've done enough.'

'One can never do enough for one's country.'

I wasn't surprised to hear him say that, not that I really understood his reasoning. I didn't see I owed any country anything. But, then, he was French and I'd learnt quickly that they felt differently about such matters. 'Still, there's not a lot you can do, is there? Not with the Germans in half of France and the controls here in Vichy France.' I brightened up at this.

'The moment the doctor says I'm fit I shall go to England and join de Gaulle. We shall fight on. We shall never be defeated . . .' I sat listening to him as he talked of this other general, of the Free French army he was collecting about him. I listened because I loved the sound of his voice and because I thought I should. But, oh, how I longed for him to talk of love and longing and us – really important things.

'Has your little friend stopped crying, Fabien? Ah, yes, I see she has, I am so glad.'

'Mother,' Fabien said, frowning crossly at his mother as we joined them for an *apéritif* before lunch. War or no, some things never changed in this country.

'I was concerned about her. That is all.' She poured us each a glass of port. I noticed that mine held half the quantity of Fabien's.

'I must apologise for my behaviour, but I was so tired and so overwhelmed at seeing Fabien safe. I'd dreamed of our reunion so many times.'

'Ah,' sighed Madame Chambrey. The priest coughed drily.

'Quite,' said his mother.

'I was wondering, Mother, if Clare could come and stay here?'

My heart leapt with joy at Fabien's words.

'Here?' his mother asked, as if *here* was the oddest place in the world for anyone to stay.

'For a few days.' Plop . . . I felt my heart tumble. Still, a few days were better than none and she might change her mind. 'I'll ask Georges to collect her luggage.' Flip . . . There, my heart was soaring again, for he spoke as if the matter was settled. 'Where were you staying, Clare?'

Oh dear, I thought, confession time! 'The hotel in the centre of Vorey,' I said vaguely.

'Hotel? There is no suitable hotel in the centre.' Madame looked at me closely. I felt myself redden.

'Well, actually, it's a bar more than a hotel.'

'Really, Miss Springer. Well-brought-up young women simply do not enter bars, especially those full of coarse working men. You took a great risk. But, then, perhaps you are used to such company?'

'It was night time and I didn't know where else to go . . . Madame.' Two could play at the pausing game. Really, what a crabby old snob she sounded. They might have stared but I hadn't felt threatened by them in any way.

'I'll speak to Georges.' Fabien was on his feet. I wished he'd speak to him later. I didn't want him to leave me alone with his mother. Even though the aunt and the priest were there I doubted they'd defend me. What an odd way to be thinking, I realised. Or was it? I'd have had to be totally insensitive not to know that she wasn't delirious about my presence. The reason for this evaded me for the time being. I'd seen enough of her to establish that she was the one in control. Fabien deferred to her – though that, of course, was probably out of respect. I thought Madame Chambrey looked scared of her. And the priest? He'd hardly said anything yet the clergy I'd known in the past had been a fairly talkative bunch and I'd no reason to think that Catholic priests would be any different. No, I sensed he said nothing for fear of putting his foot in it.

'You said you worked in a shop?' she asked, soon after Fabien had left the room. Aha, I thought, straight in on the attack. I drained my glass. 'I don't think I have ever met anyone socially who worked in a shop. Have you, Violet?' Bless the aunt, for she coughed and could not answer.

'Yes, but only temporarily. My father was cross with me and had stopped my allowance. I needed some money.' I wished she'd offer another drink, but at the rate everyone else was sipping theirs it seemed unlikely.

'And why should your father be cross?'

'Because of Fabien,' I fibbed.

She looked surprised at this. 'Fabien?'

'Yes, he didn't approve of our relationship, you see.'

'And might I ask why he did not approve of *my* son?'

'Oh, he thought he was a gold-digger,' I answered blithely, silently laughing at my judicious lie. To my satisfaction I heard a snort from behind me where Madame Chambrey was sitting but it might have been the pug.

'I've never heard of anything so preposterous in my life.'

'Silly, isn't it? You know and I know he isn't, but try telling that to my father.' I made myself laugh to imply that this was a common occurrence. 'Of course, he's right. All Father is doing is looking after my interests, isn't he? Being so rich he's learnt to be careful . . .' I left this nugget of information hanging in the air. She said nothing, merely looked haughtier, as if to show me she was not stooping to take the bait. I wish I hadn't said it now, it was pretty vulgar of me and not something I would normally do, and untrue – I was resigned never to see a penny of my father's money. But since I couldn't slap this woman physically I suppose I was trying to do it another way. I hoped then, as I looked at the threadbare carpets and curtains, that she might have registered it for future reference, that it might still stand me in good stead.

'What does he do?' Madame Chambrey asked.

'He owns a chain of baker's shops, and a factory too, of course.' At this I am certain Fabien's mother shuddered. Trade! 'Still, once he gets to know Fabien they'll have a lot in common, won't they? Since Fabien sells cheese.' I smiled sweetly, and this time I was sure it wasn't the dog snorting.

'How very interesting,' Madame de Rocheloire said, coldly, and she appeared to sit even straighter in her chair, if that were possible.

'What were you doing in Paris?' Madame Chambrey asked.

'I was at finishing school,' I replied, though the idea of Hortense's being an ideal establishment made me want to giggle. I hoped this would be approved of and perhaps counteract my father's occupation. After my last thrust at Fabien's mother I should have been feeling confident, but I wasn't. It had seriously misfired. I sat tense, certain that more sniping would follow.

For a time I was relieved of being the centre of attention since the old woman with wind appeared and said something incomprehensible. Since everybody else stood up I did the same. And, in a solemn line, the priest bringing up the rear, we trooped into the dining room where Fabien was waiting. By now I was starving and looked at the well-set table with anticipation.

As the priest intoned a long and seemingly never-ending grace my stomach rumbled, which made Madame Chambrey titter and me grin, only to be rewarded by a scowl from Madame de Rocheloire and a serious frown from Fabien.

The meal was the best I had had in months. A rough but delicious terrine was followed by small fillets of *sandre*, a fish I didn't like since it tasted of mud. Luckily the next course was a casserole of meat I could not identify but wolfed down with enthusiasm. Then we had cheese, which Fabien told me with pride was their own. Dessert was a small portion of tart – I think it was pumpkin. 'That was wonderful, Madame.'

'This is not a restaurant. There is no need to comment on the food. You'll be remarking on the furniture next.' She looked irritated.

'I didn't wish to appear rude—' That wasn't true: I was rather glad I had annoyed her. 'What I meant was that it was the first five-course meal I've had since we were invaded. Thank you.'

'Invaded, you said? I was not aware that England had been invaded.'

'No, I meant here . . . France.'

'I see. I was confused by your use of *we*. I thought there must have been a mistake. After all, as we saw at Dunkirk, you British are really only good at running away, aren't you?' She smiled graciously. The silence around the table was uncomfortable. I wanted to hit her, instead I sat mute.

'British?' the priest said eventually, with curiosity.

'English?' Madame Chambrey chorused, but looking worried.

'Mother. That's not fair.'

'What's not fair? What have I said?'

'Your remark about Dunkirk was tactless.'

'You don't agree? I am surprised!'

'Of course I don't. The British fought brilliantly. If we'd listened to them . . . That apart—'

'Well, that's a matter of opinion, to be sure.'

'That apart,' he glared at her, 'I don't think you should broadcast to the world Clare's nationality. It's not fair on her. It puts her at risk.' Probably what she intends, I thought, but through it all I carried on smiling sweetly.

'Don't be so over-dramatic, Fabien. Violet and Father Bernard are hardly anyone. I didn't realise it was a secret.'

You bitch, I thought. You knew darn well. I asked you not to tell anyone. I decided there and then not to mention my German passport. This woman was not to be trusted.

5

The room I had been allocated earlier in the day was in one of the turrets. Disappointingly it was stolid and square, not a romantic round one as I'd hoped. To see out of the window I had to climb on a chest of drawers to peer out, so high was it set in the wall. A sheer drop to the river below made me shiver, but it was a stunning view, though not much use when I had to go mountaineering on the furniture to see it.

They live like troglodytes, I thought later, when, a light supper and a very sticky evening over, I returned to my room. I made several attempts to light the oil lamp on the bedside table before I could blow out the candle I'd been given to see me to bed. Didn't these people know about electricity – even with the cuts?

Apart from the lighting the room was lovely even if the furnishings were tatty. The tapestries on the walls were faded. There was a huge and very comfortable bed – I'd bounced up and down on it to test it. I unpacked my clothes into an intricately carved cupboard. No maidservant to do it, so they weren't as grand as Madame would like me to believe. Best of all, by the empty grate was the first comfortable chair I'd encountered so far. The bathroom, unfortunately, was one floor and a long corridor away but, I'd noted on my travels, the stairs were stone and if Fabien . . . Well, there'd be no danger of creaking boards!

Washed, dressed in my nightie, I sat in the bed and wondered what to do now. It was only nine fifteen – but I could not have borne another moment of the company downstairs. In bed at nine! In the old days Mab and I would have been just setting out. Mab. That's who I needed now. She'd have put Madame in her place for me.

How could the woman be so blatantly against me? Where were the courtly manners on which the upper-class French prided themselves? But maybe she wasn't as upper class as she would like me to think . . . Oh, shut up, Clare, don't think about her.

Though not a great reader, I now wished I had a book to while away the time. There were some books in the room but they were all worthy tomes by Balzac or Victor Hugo, people like that, nothing worthwhile or interesting.

It was fiercely cold. I shivered. I needed more clothes on but I didn't want Fabien to find me bundled up in layers of jumpers and cardigans looking like a shapeless blob.

The evening, I had to admit, had not been a great success. Seeing the priest putting on his bicycle clips to leave had reminded me that I'd forgotten about returning the bicycle I'd borrowed in Vorey. That was bad enough, but then I had to confess that Fleur, the owner of the bar in Rocheloire, was looking after it for me.

'You went to the bar in the village? Consorted with our tame black-marketeer!' Fabien found this highly amusing. 'Clare, you're impossible!'

'I didn't know she was. And I didn't know not to.'

'This isn't Paris, you know.'

'I fear your friend has much to learn of our ways, Fabien.'

'Which she will,' he said, so staunchly that I could have hugged him.

'She will hardly be here long enough, will she?'

Her remarks were like cold water sloshed in my face. Each time Fabien lifted my spirits she crushed them.

'I think she should stay here and not return to Paris. In the circumstances it is much too dangerous for her.' There. What a whoosh of joy at his words! I was on top of the world again.

'Then she should have thought of that before she decided to stay when this wretched war broke out.'

'For me, Mother. She only stayed because of me.'

'Be that as it may,' she evidently thought I had lied, 'her actions make everything difficult for everyone. It's most irregular. And now this wretched bicycle.' Aha, I thought, she's got no answer. She's twisting the conversation back to the bike because she knows she is losing the argument.

'It's no problem, Madame. I'll cycle over to Vorey with it in the morning,' I said, all sweetness and light, as if unaware that I was such a problem to her.

'And what good would that do? Someone will still have to go to bring you back . . .' And I was reminded of the lack of petrol, the price of feeding the horse, the inconvenience caused, on and on. She could have been related to my father from the way she nagged.

'I'll walk back,' I interrupted her.

'Don't be *so* stupid!'

Well, if that wasn't rude I didn't know what was. Fancy calling someone you'd just met, *and* a guest, *stupid*. For all she knew I was a blue stocking with a degree in mathematics from Cambridge – maybe I'd pretend I was. The ludicrousness of this idea at least made me smile.

'And what is funny? Pray share with us what amuses you.'

'It's nothing,' I replied, which only made matters worse.

Everything about me appeared to annoy her. I inadvertently sat in her favourite chair. I didn't play bridge. I was not knowledgeable about literature, the arts in general. 'You show no interest in anything, Miss Springer.'

'That's because I'm not really interested,' I replied. She was cross at that. She sniped about England all evening. To my utter astonishment, since I thought I didn't care a jot, I had been seriously insulted and hurt – only I hadn't let her see that: it would have meant she'd won.

Fabien, I thought, might have come to my rescue again but he just sat grinning – looking quite doo-lally, I thought.

The best part of the evening was when she and Fabien had a furious row about Vichy France. I hadn't been listening to the conversation that led up to it: I was just gazing at Fabien, wondering how long I'd have to wait before he kissed me and if he had the same delicious feeling of anticipation in his stomach as I did, when his mother shouted 'Rubbish!' Most unladylike, I thought gleefully, and pricked up my ears.

'Sometimes, Fabien, I'm glad your father isn't alive to hear such subversive rubbish.'

'My father would be in agreement with me.'

'If he did then he'd be as stupid as you.'

'Do we have to talk about my poor brother in this way?' Madame Chambrey looked upset. At least I wasn't the only one Madame deemed stupid.

'We should be on our knees daily thanking the dear Lord for our Marshal Pétain.'

I thought Fabien muttered, 'bollocks', but I couldn't be sure.

I smiled at him with admiration.

'At least the *curé* has gone or no doubt you *would* be on your knees,' he added.

'Fabien!'

Better and better I thought.

'All the Marshal is doing is upholding that which is right, and which the Jews, the Communists, the Freemasons and progressives like you wish to see crushed.' Why, she sounded just like Hortense, only nastier.

'Planning to deport Jews, you mean, Mother? Taking away their livelihoods? Stealing their possessions? Oh, quite right, I'm sure.'

'That is wild rumour. I don't believe it for one minute. I know of no Jews who have been affected in any way whatever.'

'Because you don't know any – you've made sure of that. Do you not realise Jean Martin has lost his job because he's a Jew?'

'Nonsense. It was because he was an inadequate teacher. In any case, I refer to the Marshal's principled stand for the values of the home, the glorification of motherhood. Don't you ever listen to his talks on the radio?'

'Not if I can help it.'

'Then you have no grounds on which to argue.'

'What like *Kinder*, *Küche* and *Kirche*?' I offered helpfully.

'You speak German?' His mother glared at me. I could swear her eyes were blazing with loathing.

'Only a little,' I thought it politic to say.

'What has happened to *Liberty*, *Equality*, *Fraternity*? The *old* values, Mother! Replaced now with *work, family, country*! I defend the old, Mother, it is you who are upholding the new. Capitulating. A government we hadn't even elected had the audacity to hand over France to the Germans, agreeing to restitution that we cannot afford for the privilege of having half our country occupied. All negotiated by your hero!'

'He has not capitulated. He has saved us. We are safe here.'

'Mother, don't you understand anything? Those Vichy morons are doing the Germans' work for them. They police us, control us, ration us, restrict us so that Hitler can control the whole of this great country with fewer soldiers than we have police! Oh, yes, such a patriot!'

'I will not have the Marshal spoken of in these terms in my house.'

'No, Mother. *My* house.'

Oh dear, I thought. I had enjoyed their rowing at the beginning but not now: it was becoming distinctly nasty. Watch it, Fabien! I longed to shout. Don't say things you'll regret. Madame Chambrey, I saw, was sitting quietly, a hand to her mouth, but she didn't look as anguished as I thought she might.

'Get out!' I heard Madame scream.

'With pleasure.' Fabien jumped to his feet.

I made quick excuses and followed him.

'Not now, Clare,' he said and shook my hand off his arm – as if I were a dog, I thought. He stomped off – well, limped – into another part of the house. That's when I had taken myself to bed. It seemed safer there.

Now I waited and still he did not come but, then, he had been very upset. He needed time on his own to think. Poor Fabien. I turned off the oil lamp – I can't say I liked the smell it made – and settled down under the blankets . . . He'd be along soon . . .

Only he didn't come. I woke the next morning alone. Immediately I felt sad. Last night had been horrible. I must try to make things better today.

As I dressed I lectured myself on the subject of Fabien's mother. I must try to like her: even though they rowed, he must love her and I must learn to love her too. After all, it was only a matter of time and we'd be related. At that thought I hugged myself and had to grin at the uphill task I'd set myself. No doubt, I decided, it was the worry of the war and Fabien's leg that was making her so bad-tempered.

'Good morning, Madame,' I said, as I met her in the dark hallway as I searched, hopefully, for breakfast.

'We eat at eight. It is now nine.'

'I'm sorry . . .' But she had already swept away and I was left standing, feeling foolish as well as hungry. I wonder how many times I'd said, 'Sorry,' to her since I'd arrived.

'Psst . . .' I swung round. Madame Chambrey was beckoning me from a doorway. 'I saved you some bread when you didn't appear.'

'Nobody woke me. I didn't realise it was so late.' Gratefully I followed her into the room. 'You've bread! Yum, yum,' I said, seeing a large piece, some jam and, unbelievably, butter neatly arranged on a plate. 'I haven't seen butter for months!' I began to eat with relish.

'Don't let Constance upset you, my dear,' Madame Chambrey suddenly said.

'But she isn't,' I began, but at the look of disbelief on her face I said, 'Well, she is, but I'm busy fighting it.'

'She has a lot of worry. This house. Fabien. The situation . . . The Marshal.'

The bloody Marshal again, I thought.

'And Fabien talks of going to England so she is afraid.'

'Of course.'

'She has others dependent upon her.'

'I realise.' I hadn't, but I thought it made me sound sympathetic if I pretended I had. 'And then I come blundering along – another mouth to feed.'

'Exactly. But more than that – you're young and beautiful and you've come for Fabien.'

'Well.' I looked dutifully bashful.

'She will fight you. She has chosen whom she wishes him to marry.'

'Céline?'

'You know her?'

'Of her.' I pulled a face. 'But Fabien says I'm not to worry about her.'

'French mothers have a knack of getting their own way, you know.'

'Not this time,' I said, trying to exude confidence, knowing it was ebbing away fast.

'And, of course, to compound everything, it is that time in her life.'

'Sorry?'

'She is having a particularly bad time. She should have all our sympathy. It's a difficult time for women. But, then, Constance is her own worst enemy.' She laughed, I joined in, though I hadn't the foggiest idea what she was talking about. 'But be careful, my dear. Your being English has not endeared you to her.'

'I know.'

'She could make things difficult for you. She, well . . . I'd best not say.'

'Do, please.'

Madame Chambrey looked about her as if to check whether we were being spied on. 'She has friends – important friends. They and she support Vichy passionately. They could be dangerous for you.'

'But Fabien doesn't.'

'No, there are so many families like this one, horribly divided in their allegiances, fathers against their sons, brother against brother, and I fear it only becomes worse. Some have shocked me – it's as if it has taken this war and occupation to see people as they really are.'

'You are kind to warn me. It must be a difficult position to find yourself in. But, please, don't worry, I won't be here long enough for her to harm me. I shall be in England.'

'Then I am happy. I hope your plans are successful, Clare. But while you are here trust no one. Do I make myself clear?'

'As crystal.'

Fabien walked every day, adding another kilometre to his total. 'At this rate you'll end up spending all day walking,' I teased, as I panted along beside him.

'Once I can do twenty of your miles I shall be content.'

'In one day! How ghastly.'

'It's nothing of the sort. It's a pleasure for me. There is always something new to see – the wildlife, the plants.'

'Of course,' I said, hurriedly – I'd almost boobed there. I'd presumed that, like me, he preferred the city. Now when I saw him in this environment, I realised how wrong I was and remembered how much he had talked about this place in Paris. 'You love the country more than anything, don't you?'

'I find cities restrictive.'

'Just like me,' I lied through my teeth. Behind the château, there was a huge park on the plateau of the hill. We had marched – you couldn't call the pace Fabien had set walking – across the grounds and we were now entering a wood that swept down the other side of the hill.

'My mother doesn't understand me. She pines to be back in Paris. She says she only feels alive there.'

'Doesn't she normally live here?'

'No, in the past she visited as rarely as possible. But when the Germans were advancing I insisted she come here.'

'Is that what makes her so bad-tempered?' Oops, I thought as I clapped my hand over my mouth – much good that would do, the words were out. 'I'm sorry.'

'You only say what's the truth. She is bad-tempered. But I don't remember a time when she wasn't. Being here doesn't help – and neither, of course, does her age . . .'

'What's her age got to do with it?'

'Clare, you're innocent of so many things, aren't you?' He kissed my cheek. What did he mean? 'I shudder when I think of you, alone, plodding along the road from Lyon. You shouldn't ever be on your own.'

'I didn't plod, I walked with my usual elegant step. I don't mind being on my own, but I'd rather be with you any day.' I blushed at my forwardness. But it worked.

'Sweet Clare.' He took me into his arms. 'I longed to be with you last night. Longed to come to you.'

'Why didn't you?'

'In my mother's house?'

'But you said it was yours.'

'I'm afraid I was in a temper. I just . . . It's too difficult to explain. But come . . . Along this path there's an uninhabited old cottage. I used to play there as a child. Let's go!'

Let's go! I wanted to run to it like the wind, lock the door and throw away the key.

To reach it we went down a precipitous slope – I pretended it was hard for me so he helped me, just as I had planned. At the bottom was a tiny lush valley with a stream cascading over rocks. It was surrounded by trees so that if you didn't know it was there it would have been impossible to find. The cottage was more a small barn than a house. The living quarters were a room with a partition behind which animals had once lived. 'To give warmth,' Fabien explained. It must have been a mite smelly, I decided, but said nothing. A ladder led to another room in the loft. The floor was dirty, the range was black, the tiny window covered in cobwebs, but to me it was a palace as I felt his body against mine, his mouth on my throat, his hands searching for my breasts. At last. This was what I'd come for, this was what I'd dreamt of. 'Oh, Fabien. I love you so.'

'Clare,' he said, on a sigh.

6

'You can't stay, you do realise?'

It was a fortnight later. Two weeks in which everything had become progressively difficult with his mother making her dislike of me ever more obvious. We had reached the point where she barely spoke to me and often when I entered a room she would leave it. I was wretched that it should be like this, but I wasn't going to give up until someone told me I had to.

And it had not been easy with Fabien either – I seemed to annoy him. I didn't mean to, and I tried not to, but the harder I tried the more I seemed doomed to irritate him. There was nothing big, we had no rows. It was inconsequential things, my not knowing about Francis I of France – why should I? That I didn't appreciate wine as he thought I should – I tended to drink it because I liked the feeling it gave me, not for the taste. Several times the fact that my legs were shorter than his and it was hard for me to keep up – especially if I was tired – made him angry. He always said sorry after he had snapped at me, and I endeavoured to forget what he had said but it was difficult: each little spat or snarl seemed to me to chip away at our precious love as if a chisel was attacking a lovely block of marble.

All these days I had been expecting Fabien to say I had to go. Now the words hung between us in the silence that ensued.

'I know.' I hung my head. I didn't want to look at him and let him see how sad I felt. It wasn't fair: this was hard for him too. We were sitting on the blankets that Fabien had carried to our little cottage in the woods. Now we'd a Primus, a saucepan, some china. Once we had lit the fire in the range, even if it was a bit smoky. With each item we'd brought here – or, rather, smuggled – I'd allowed myself to hope that it was a sign that somehow this little house was to become a permanent base for us. Such a silly dream. I pulled my coat closer to me – I was naked beneath it and it was snowing outside.

'I warned you that once the snow comes it can last right through to April. A few serious falls and we won't be able to get through to here even. And with the atmosphere at home . . .' He gave one of his expressive Gallic shrugs.

'Yes, you said.'

'I don't want you to go back to Paris. It's far too dangerous.'

At that I looked up sharply. 'Neither do I. I couldn't be so far away from you.' I could feel the all-too-familiar prick of tears, which I fought: crying wouldn't help.

'But your papers? You can't exist without papers.'

'That's no problem. I've permission from the Germans to be here for a month. I've checked them and I can easily alter the dates.'

'Clare, my darling . . . it's . . .' He took my hands and held them tight, as if he was transferring what it was he wanted to say. 'I'll worry.' I felt, I don't know why, that this wasn't what he really wanted to say. 'If anyone finds out about these German papers of yours – then I fear for you, here.'

'No need. I won't tell anyone. Only you know. And I'll get a job,' I said, though I couldn't imagine what I would do.

'You're so brave.'

'No, I'm not, I love you.'

'But, sweetheart, you know I'm going to England.'

'When you do I'll go with you. It's my home, after all.' I had finally had the courage to tell him what I planned – I hadn't dared until now. I glanced at him. He didn't seem too put out.

'It will be a difficult trip over the Pyrenees.'

'You'll need me when you get there – your English is so bad. I'll be your personal translator.' I chose to ignore the reference to the Pyrenees.

He began to dress, much to my disappointment. I didn't want to go back to the château. 'In the meantime I'll see what I can do for you, locally. I don't want you to go either.' He put on his trousers. 'I'm glad you understand. Ready?' He kissed the tip of my nose. 'You're so cold. My poor love . . .' He bundled me into a hug, sweeping his greatcoat around me, holding me tight, kissing me, feeling me – just as I wanted. Quickly we began to take off the clothes we'd only just put on.

'Thank you so much for having me, Madame.' A few days later I stood, quite meekly, I thought, in the dark, gloomy hall, my case at my feet.

'It's been a pleasure, Clare. It's nice for Fabien to have his friends to stay. I've been so worried about him. But your visit has cheered him immeasurably.' She shook my hand. I don't think my mouth dropped open but it was a miracle it didn't at the hypocrisy of her little speech. 'You will take care, won't you? These are dangerous times. Now, off you go. You'll miss your train.'

That was more like it, I thought, as she literally pushed me towards the door.

Fabien and I slithered and slipped our way down the steep hill into the village. I wished he'd hold my hand but, then, coming from such a formal family I wasn't surprised that he didn't.

'Won't your mother be cross when she finds out I haven't left and that I'm at the doctor's house?'

'If she knows, so what? It's none of her business.' Although I liked what he said I had the feeling that she would make it her business.

'Only your aunt said—' I stopped. Maybe it was not a good idea to tell him and cause more trouble in the family than I had already.

'What did my aunt say?'

'Nothing.'

'Honestly, Clare, I find it most annoying when you do that. She must have said something.'

'Only that I mustn't trust people, and—' I stopped again.

'Quite right too. And? You were about to say something else.'

'Nothing.'

'Clare! Will you stop being so nonsensical?' His lips were set in an angry line.

'I don't want you to be cross with me.'

'Then you're not going about it in the right way. What did she say?' I could hear the studied control in his voice.

'Only that your mother supported Vichy.'

'Everyone knows that – a lot of people do.'

'She said she could be dangerous for me.'

'She said what? The ungrateful old bitch. How dare she?'

'She was only trying to help me.'

'And be disloyal at the same time.'

'What would you prefer? That she didn't warn me and I got into trouble?'

'Yes.'

'Fabien, you don't mean that.'

'I do. Loyalty to me is a sacred trust.'

'But it doesn't extend to me?'

He stood towering over me, frowning. 'Of course it does. It's just, well, you see how difficult these times are, how divided we become.' With relief I felt him searching for my hand. He gave it an encouraging squeeze. 'There's no need for you to be afraid. I have spoken to my mother and have made her promise never to divulge your nationality to anyone.'

'And she won't?' I admired his confidence in his mother. I didn't share it.

'Once my mother has promised she never goes back on her word.'

We carried on walking. 'I nearly died laughing when she so obviously thought I was catching the train. Did you tell her I was?'

'No, she just presumed.'

'The priest!' I skidded to a halt – bang opposite the church too. 'What if he tells on me?'

'He won't. Politically he does not agree with my mother.'

'He never said so when you were arguing.'

'He's polite. Stop worrying. If she does find out you're here she's not going to eat you.' To my joy he kissed me right there in the street. If only she'd seen him do that!

Dr Robert Forêt was in his late thirties, a short, comfortably padded, genial-faced man. His deep voice, which seemed to rumble up from his diaphragm, a bit like a volcano erupting, welcomed me.

I had expected him to be an old man, like my doctor at home, and was glad to see he wasn't so *very* old. But his house was. It was crammed with knick-knacks, and heavy curtains hung at the windows. The furniture was overstuffed and covered at strategic points with crocheted antimacassars. The wallpaper was dark, heavily patterned and varnished, which made it even more sombre. It was as if an ancient couple had just moved out, for it smelt of the elderly, and this young family had arrived but only temporarily. All was explained when I learnt that the doctor had only recently taken over the practice when his own father had died.

'So you're an Auvergnat too?'

'Yes. We all come home eventually, to our roots, you see. I worked in Paris, but you know . . .' He shrugged, as if further explanation was not necessary. 'And what should we call you, Mademoiselle?'

'Clare will do fine.'

'Then Clare it is. Now, these are my two adorable monsters – Yvette and Dominique.' The two children, beautiful in that black-haired, dark-eyed, sharp-featured style of the French, bobbed me a little curtsy.

That made me laugh. 'Please don't.' I waved my hand in confusion. The two girls watched me with solemn, sad eyes. Yvette, I knew, was eleven, her sister nine, and while physically they looked their ages their faces seemed older.

'Children, perhaps you would like to show your new governess to her room and then, Clare, when you've unpacked I should like you to meet my wife.'

Politely the children carried my case and I followed them up the stairs to my room. Governess, he'd called me. Crikey, that was something to live up to! It was a charming room, large, furnished with windows that opened inwards and well-oiled shutters – light at last! The wallpaper was a bit fusty-looking but the white lace bedspread made up for that. Best of all, I could look up and see Fabien's château. At night I'd be able to sit here and watch his oil lamp go on and off – if I could identify from all the windows which room was his.

'Have you been a governess long, Mademoiselle?'

'To be honest, Yvette, I'm not really a governess. I've never taught anyone anything in my life. And I don't know very much – but I'll do my best.'

The girls stood wide-eyed with shock. This was evidently not what they'd expected to hear.

'But it might be fun, mightn't it?' Tentatively they smiled and then they giggled, rather as if they weren't used to laughter. 'Come on, cheer up!' I leapt on them and began to tickle them, wrestled them to the floor and continued until they were shrieking with joy.

'What on earth is this racket? Stop this minute! Have you no consideration?' The door had been flung open and a large old woman stood glaring fiercely down at the tangled heap we had become. 'Yvette, Dominique,' she barked. They stumbled to their feet.

'*Pardon*, Grandmother,' they said, dropping the same little curtsy they'd given me.

'And you, Mademoiselle, is this the behaviour you intend to teach my granddaughters?'

'I'm sorry, Madame, but they looked so miserable.'

'Well, really . . .' And the woman flounced out as much as her bulk would allow.

Wrong again! I was doomed, it seemed, to be the sort of person who, if she could put her foot in it, would do it with both feet. The girls' mother was seriously ill – no wonder they looked so sad. But, as usual, no one had told me. Well, Fabien had said the doctor needed help with his daughters since his wife was poorly. Poorly! She was mortally ill, poor soul. She'd been this way for months, and her pain was becoming her family's too.

'My husband tells me you want to be known as Clare . . . nice. I've never been one for . . . formality myself.' She was propped up against a mountain of pillows on which her emaciated body barely made an impression. She had the black hair and eyes of her daughters, but hers lacked the sheen and healthy glow of theirs. Her face, which must have been beautiful, was now ravaged by her illness and her expression was pinched with pain. 'They've been so excited at you coming.'

'You know, I'm not really a governess. I think I should make that plain.'

'They don't need one at this time in their lives . . . They need someone to take their minds . . . off me . . . Someone to make them enjoy life again . . . I apologise for my mother, Madam Chadrac. She . . . wants to protect me . . . but I was so happy to hear your . . . laughter.' She spoke in short bursts as if gaining strength in the pauses to get the next sentence out. 'And if you're to be Clare, then I insist I am Pauline, to you.'

'Thank you. I'm honoured.' I was more than that: I was overwhelmed – an older person asking me to use their Christian name had only ever happened to me once, and the circumstances with Hortense had been somewhat different.

'Sit . . .' She patted the bed. 'Tell me all about yourself.'

'There's not much to tell, really,' I began. And then the most extraordinary thing happened. I found myself telling her everything – absolutely everything. From day one of my life. Now why was that? I didn't know her or anything about her. But I just knew I could trust her. *Trust.* I shivered inwardly. Madame Chambrey's words were still fresh in my mind. Maybe it was because Pauline was dying and that soon my secrets would have the utter security of her grave.

'Clare, I'm honoured you speak to me in this way . . . but promise me you'll never do this again . . .' I felt quite silly sitting there as she warned me of all the things I already knew – that I might be risking a lot. She said death, but I thought that was an exaggeration.

7

Quickly my routine was settled. I had to be up by seven, which initially was a nightmare for me. Since her daughter was incapable, Madame Chadrac was in charge of the household management. She was so strict she could have run an army without undue effort. It was she who insisted on the early breakfast – even the doctor had been heard to mutter that it was too early. In consequence it was, thankfully, a silent meal.

By eight the girls and I were at our lessons. That was a rather grand way to describe our time together. Having learnt so little there wasn't an awful lot I could teach them, so we read books and talked. Languages I could help them with since they were both interested: their progress in English and German was rapid.

Fabien had been right: once the snow began it was relentless – I was convinced it would never stop. But one morning I awoke to find it had: the village was beautifully dressed in white and the hills appeared to have changed shape under the snow blanket.

I learnt to ski. Yvette and Dominique were expert and patient teachers. The hard bit was having to climb the steep hill, our heavy wooden skis on our shoulders, but it was worth it for the sheer exhilaration of whooshing down whooping with joy. I had acquired a fine collection of bumps and bruises but, my goodness, how fit I was becoming. The girls also had toboggans, which I adored hurtling about on, and in the garden of a large shuttered house was a frozen pond on which they taught me to skate – cause of yet more bruises.

Whatever we were doing we had to present ourselves at noon with hair brushed, hands and nails clean, ready for lunch. I rather resented the implication that I was not capable of washing my hands without a reminder. I did not like Madame Chadrac treating me like a child.

Before the war the doctor's household had consisted of a cook, a maid, an odd-job man and a gardener. Now there was just Madame and an aged woman from the village, who came for a couple of hours three times a week.

For such a large house – it had ten bedrooms – this number of staff was woefully inadequate, and I could just imagine Lettie complaining, but maybe the same thing was happening in England. Here, with so many men prisoners-of-war or fighting with the British, it was left to the women to tend the land and the animals. Both the cook and the maid had had to leave when their brothers had been captured and their old parents left to cope with their farms alone. Goodness only knew when they would be back.

This part of the Auvergne was a maze of small farms, often with a cow, a pig, a few chickens and an acre or two of land to cultivate. There were no great estates of hundreds of acres with fields rolling to the horizon. Here the landscape was on a grand scale while the farming was '. . . rather like your Scottish Highlands with its crofters,' the doctor had told me. I had nodded in agreement, but to be honest I hadn't a clue how the Scots farmed. Why should I? I'd never been north of Oxford.

There were, of course, shortages of certain foods, sugar, coffee, olive oil, but since we were in the country meat and vegetables were plentiful. After the shortages in Paris it was as if I couldn't get enough to eat.

'In its wisdom our government agreed to supply the Germans with sufficient petrol to collapse our transport system,' the doctor said one day, with a wry smile. 'By the terms of the agreement we are to send produce to the occupied zone. This is difficult when the transport is almost at a standstill. I was told the other day that only fifty per cent is getting through. Good!'

'Good!' we all echoed round the table.

The food was delicious. I had been used to Hortense's cooking and what Madame Chadrac called, disparagingly, 'Parisian food'. This, she taught me, was the real food of France, plain, honest, cooked with love and care. She looked almost human when she talked about cooking, not nearly as fierce. There were hearty casseroles with meat so tender it melted in the mouth, soups so thick and nourishing they were meals in themselves, even a cheese soup, tarts and flans with pastry light as a whisper, and rough pâtés and terrines that just begged you to eat more of them. Certainly I'd never tasted rabbit as she prepared it, and wild boar – no wonder she was so fat. And I risked being so too since, after the hunger we had endured in Paris, I looked forward to our meals and often had two helpings.

Given the size of the house and Madame Chadrac's age I reluctantly decided after only one week that I had to help her. I had never done any housework in my life. Madame was surprisingly patient with my attempts, but I was mortified when it became evident that I didn't even know how to sweep a room. But I learnt.

'You're a good girl, Clare. I don't know how I managed before you came here.' I glowed in Madame's praise – no one, as far as I could remember, had praised me like that before.

'I don't expect you to do housework too,' the doctor said one evening.

'I don't mind. I enjoy it,' I replied honestly.

A couple of times a week I saw Fabien – those were precious moments. We had nowhere to be alone so we stayed in the doctor's parlour and touched each other's hands at the least opportunity. We would sit on the overstuffed chairs, with their lace antimacassars, talking politely, while I was longing for him to rip off my clothes and make love to me there and then on the doctor's prized Turkey carpet. In a strange way that I didn't really understand, I liked the agony of wanting him but not being able to do anything about it. For me his visits always culminated in the narrow front porch when Fabien would squeeze past me, his body making contact with mine and his eyes full of the lust I, too, felt.

He visited on my birthday – my twenty-first. Now I was free of my father and could marry whom and when I wished. I thought Fabien had remembered, and had come on purpose, but he said nothing. I sat in an agony of suspense, working out how best to introduce the news.

'It's my birthday,' I blurted out instead.

'You should have told me. Many happy returns.'

'I hoped you would remember.'

'I'm useless on dates.'

'It's the big one – twenty-one. You know, key of the door and all that.' I prayed he would understand what I meant by *all that*.

'Still, you've had the key a long time, haven't you?' He was supposed to talk of marriage, our future. 'They say more snow is coming.'

How I wished it had been a leap year and I could have asked him. But perhaps they didn't have that in France. I hated that visit.

I took to sitting with Pauline during the afternoons. It gave her mother a break from the relentless nursing, but also I enjoyed being with her and talking to her. It was she who explained why Fabien's mother was as cross as she was. 'And that happens to every woman when they get to their forties?' I asked.

'Or their fifties. Yes.'

'But why do they become so bad-tempered?'

'I've always thought it's because of the sadness they feel. In a way they are grieving for the children they cannot have.'

'But you can't have more children and you're not bad-tempered. Oh, my God, I'm so sorry, what an awful thing to say!'

Pauline, bless her, laughed. 'I'm a realist. But I feel for them, for they also are saying goodbye to their youth. They fear that they will become unattractive and unloved. Some women find it hard to deal with.'

'When I marry Fabien we won't be able to have children. I'm determined it's not going to make me crabby.'

'And why will you have no babies?'

'Fabien can't have them. A riding accident when he was young.'

'He told you that?'

'Yes. Poor Fabien.'

'Clare, my dear, take care.' She took hold of my hand. 'Some men will say anything to get what they want.'

'I expect so.' I wasn't sure what she was talking about, and I was surprised she didn't sound more sympathetic. 'Still, if my husband no longer loved me because I had grown old then I think I would hit him!' This made Pauline laugh, which was a mistake as it made her gasp for breath. It never failed to amaze me that I could be having conversations with her like this until I worked out that she was only a few years older than Hope – not that I could imagine talking about periods and 'the change' with *her*. For me it was such a relief to have someone I could tell everything to. I often talked to her about Felicity and my father, and all the things that normally I had to keep bottled up inside me.

'Your poor father. This way he has now lost two daughters. He must grieve for you dreadfully.'

'I doubt it.'

'I'm sure he does. It is easy to stick by one's principles when you know you will shortly see the person you love. With this enforced separation I'm certain he has buried all his anger.' It was sweet of her to try to reassure me in this way and I thanked her, but I didn't really believe her. 'Do you miss England?'

'Sometimes,' I found myself saying, to my surprise. I'd thought I didn't. 'It's silly things, like toast – French bread is lovely, but the toast it makes isn't the same. And bacon and the rain. And the birds sound different. And church bells . . .' And I couldn't go on, I was crying.

Pauline comforted me. 'It must be hard for you, so far from your family.'

'I didn't feel like this before. I can't imagine what has got into me. I love France.'

'Of course you do. But maybe it's because before this wretched war you could go home whenever you wanted. Now you can't. So now you realise what you've lost – rather how your father must be feeling.'

When she explained things to me I sometimes thought she was the wisest person I knew. I loved talking to her, and dreaded her leaving us.

The thaw came slowly, so slowly. I was able to get away occasionally to see Fabien in our little cottage in the woods. I don't know why, but everything seemed different to me. We made love, just as before, but sometimes I thought that he was thinking of other things. Our journey, no doubt.

I consoled myself that soon we would be free to be together for we would begin our trek to Spain and then to England. Fabien's leg was healed. He was waiting for his arrangements to be finalised: contacts had to be made, friendly houses found to stay in and guides to get us over the mountains.

'I'm so excited, you and me, refugees, trekking through the mountains together. It will be so romantic.' I looked up from the maps we had been studying for the umpteenth time.

'Sometimes, Clare, you are such a child. This will not be a game, this will be dangerous and hard.'

'I'm strong and fit. And I realise the seriousness.' How unkind he could sometimes be.

'You might slow me down.'

'What rubbish! I'm fitter than you.' I saw him frown. 'I mean your poor leg,' I added feebly.

'I've been thinking. With your German passport you should go to Switzerland. Take refuge there.'

'Don't you want me to come?' With shock I began to fear he meant it.

'Of course I do, but I worry about you.'

'Don't be silly. I can't wait until we can go – together.'

One afternoon the doctor joined Pauline and me. I liked it when he did so because I knew how much she longed for him to have the time to sit and talk with her. Their love for each other was wonderful to see, for it shone in their eyes and in the touching courtesy with which they spoke to each other. Usually I got up and left them to be alone.

'Clare, don't go. I want to talk to you.' The doctor stopped me leaving. 'I know you spoke to my wife in confidence, but I'm sure you'll forgive her for telling me your true nationality.'

'I don't mind you knowing.'

'You should, really. Your secret is safe with us, but you never know . . . Don't tell anyone else.'

'I won't. In fact I don't normally.'

'We've been talking and we think you should have French papers.'

'But I can't get any. You see—' I began.

'No, *you* can't. But *I* can.'

'I don't understand.'

'I have friends – that's all you need to know – who are willing to make you a set of papers, give you a new identity.'

What a splendid offer! French papers might help smooth my journey with Fabien.

Two weeks later I was Clare Saulle. I had been born in Moulin, I'd married a Lyonnais who was now a prisoner-of-war. I'd moved into the area after finding work at the doctor's. I had no family here.

'But everyone round here knows my real name is Clare.'

'Which is why we incorporated it. It will be less confusing for you.'

'But the stamp mark says it's been issued here. Isn't that risky?'

'Not particularly. The mayor is my brother. He's the pharmacist in the square.'

'But what about the policeman?'

'My cousin.'

'Ah, I see. Then I'm safe. And French. I like that. Now that is an honour.'

At that the doctor did the oddest thing. He put his arms about me and hugged me so tight I could hardly breathe. When I looked up I could see he was crying.

These weeks of waiting were marred by two things. It rained – my, how it rained. And one afternoon, on an errand for Madame Chadrac, I met Fabien with a young woman. She was my age. She was dark. She was pretty. But, worst of all, her arm was linked through his.

'Let me introduce my cousin, Céline. This is Mademoiselle Clare Saulle.'

Him calling me by my false name would normally have made us giggle. It didn't today as I shook hands with Céline, eyeing each other up and down. We made small-talk and parted.

'You should have warned me she was coming,' I ranted at him in the cottage the following afternoon.

'I didn't know she was. My bloody mother sent for her to come and say goodbye to me before I left for England.'

'But she shouldn't have done that. It's wrong for Céline to know your plans, no one should. That could have put you in danger of being arrested.'

'I sometimes think my mother would rather I was in a French prison than with the "enemy", as she puts it.'

'I don't understand some of the French at the moment. We should be united.'

'Exactly. And neither do I.'

'But Céline, she won't tell?'

'No, she loves me too much.' He grinned at me.

I hit him. 'Beast.'

'But she can't have me, can she?' And he was grabbing for me, tearing at my clothes.

'I'd kill her if she tried.'

Fabien had several setbacks, which delayed our departure so that spring arrived and we were still there. On one walk he had twisted his ankle, not too badly, but then he contracted a fever, the cause of which the doctor did not know. He was understandably irritable during these delays. Once again I annoyed him, and I didn't know why or what to do about it. It was the fault of the hold-ups, I reassured myself. But I found I was no longer looking forward so much to this trip with him, not if he was going to be like this. What if we arrived in England and I found that he was just as grumpy with me? What would I do then? No doubt, once we were there, everything would be fine. I told myself to stop worrying.

Then, in the same way that the war had intervened before when I was happy, catastrophe loomed just as I was hoping to be happy again. Pauline had a relapse.

Poor Robert was at his wit's end. She was in such pain and he had little to treat her with. As a doctor he had a small petrol ration and had used precious fuel to drive to Lyon to try to get drugs for her. The few he obtained were soon consumed by her agony. She was so brave. I watched her clutching at her bedclothes, smothering her cries of pain in her pillow so that her daughters would not hear.

'Fabien, I can't go with you.' It was late April and he had arrived with the news that we were to leave the following day, that the network of people willing to help across this vast country were all ready, and papers, money, everything was in place. 'I can't leave them. Not now.'

'I have to go.'

'Couldn't we delay a week? Robert says – he doubts she can survive.'

'No. It's too complicated. Everything is arranged. We leave tomorrow or not at all.'

I felt such turmoil, as if war was being waged inside me. I wanted to be in England but I didn't want to leave France. I wanted to be with him yet I knew I couldn't leave this family. Not now. It wasn't just Pauline, it was the girls: their faces were becoming more strained and afraid. I knew what they were going through – I knew what it was like to be motherless. 'I'm sorry, Fabien, you'll have to go without me. I'll follow as soon as I can.'

'Clare, don't be ridiculous. How could you possibly do that journey alone?'

'Of course I could.'

'I thought you loved me.'

'Oh, Fabien, how can you even say that? You know I do. It's just, the family—'

'You prefer them to me? You think more of them than you do of me?'

'Fabien! They need me. I can't desert them.'

'I need you too.'

'But in a different way. Please don't make this more difficult than it already is for me. Why, a month ago you were trying to persuade me not to go with you.'

'That was then. This plan has cost a considerable sum, you know.'

'If it's a question of money I'll give you a note. You can take it to my father. I'm sure he'll pay you whatever I'm in debt to you for.'

He had the grace to look shamefaced at that. 'I'm sorry, Clare. I didn't mean it like that. I want you with me. I shall miss you.'

This, of course, was music to my ears but, lovely as it was, I couldn't allow myself to listen to it. And the oddest thing was that, although I said I was heartbroken to be left behind, I wasn't. The truth was that as I spoke I felt a great sense of relief that I was not going – but I had no idea why.

'My mind's made up, Fabien.'

'Well, selflessness wasn't something I ever expected to see in you.' He picked up his coat and thrust his arms roughly into the sleeves.

'Fabien!'

'Goodbye, Clare. Good luck.'

'Fabien, I love you—'

But he'd gone. He hadn't even waited for our little game in the porch of pressing our bodies close. He'd gone in anger. He'd left me in pain. And, worst of all, he still hadn't said he loved me.

That night when I looked out of my window up at the château above the village I found myself wondering why I had ever thought it stood benignly protecting the village below. Now it loomed ominously above the houses as if threatening them.

Chapter Four

May – November 1942

1

That strange feeling of relief at not going with Fabien soon disappeared and I began to miss him. I wondered if I'd imagined his irritation with me. Perhaps I had been over-sensitive – it had been a difficult time for both of us with all the delays. Now, two months later, I found I could barely remember any unpleasant incidents in detail, just the good times.

It was a worry that we had parted on an argument, a foolish thing to have done. I wrote to him, sending my letters c/o General de Gaulle, London, and sealed them with a kiss. It was a foolish thing to do, for even as I dropped them in the post-box I knew they would never reach him, but writing them made me feel that little bit closer to him. Each post I looked out for a letter from him, hoping that somehow one would find its way to me. But nothing came and I felt a ridiculous and quite illogically hurt that it hadn't.

In Paris, during our first separation, I'd been buoyed by the certainty that this war would soon be over and I would find him again. Now, here we were, over two and a half years into a war to which we could see no end.

A choice of problems kept me awake at night. Pauline's condition was one, and fear for Fabien and his safety another. But added to these was a real and growing fear for myself, which had taken me by surprise. What had all seemed fun – the false papers, my false name, congratulating myself on hoodwinking the German and French authorities – was rapidly becoming serious. Hortense's conviction that here in the unoccupied zone the life of France continued as before was a fantasy.

As the Vichy government tightened its grip and an unending flow of rules, regulations and moral codes rained down upon us, people became afraid and resentful.

'Whenever I see you, these days, you have your head in a newspaper or your ear to the wireless,' the doctor said one evening, when he returned from his rounds.

'I need to know because of Fabien.'

'What is there to know? It's all bad news and what is truth and what are lies? How people are managing I can't imagine. I saw a patient today whose husband is a prisoner-of-war. She worked in the *mairie* to support herself, her two children and her mother. Now that women are no longer allowed to work in the civil service, what is she to do? How is she to feed them all?'

'It's wicked, isn't it?' I began to busy myself laying the table. 'Doctor, these newspapers, I think that they're not telling the whole story. They only print what the government wants them to.'

'I should say that's the case, Clare.'

'Well, I couldn't help but notice that sometimes I've seen you reading another paper and I wonder if you would let me read it too.'

'And I thought I was being so careful and that nobody knew!' He smiled. 'If I let you, there's just one thing. I'd prefer you didn't mention it to anyone – especially my wife. I don't want her worried.'

I promised. I had been right: it was a clandestine paper I had seen him with. It wasn't a proper newspaper, merely a sheet with masses of errors in it and, from its print, it looked as if they had been running out of ink. I didn't ask who had written it or where it had come from. As I began to read I almost wished I hadn't. It told of camps where people were being sent by the government – not by the Germans but by Frenchmen – here in unoccupied France. Jews, Communists and people who did not conform were incarcerated. The conditions were dreadful and getting worse as more people were crowded in. It was June and the heat of the sun didn't help, but the situation would deteriorate even further as the summer progressed. I began to wonder whether, if I was found out and my false papers exposed, I would be sent there too.

Pauline clung to her sad and painful life with extraordinary tenacity. She would relapse and we would all prepare ourselves for the worst then she would recover only to relapse again. Fabien had been gone for nearly three months, and still she survived. As I watched this close, loving family I realised she would not let go because she could not bear to leave them.

There were days when her pain was so severe, their concern so intense, and their frustration at their inability to help her so evident, that I wished she would stop fighting and die. Then her agony and everyone else's would be over. I always felt guilty thinking along these lines especially if suddenly she had a good day, when the pain lessened, her family gathered about her and they could talk and laugh together. I always felt in the way then, but how I envied the closeness this family had.

Then I'd start to think of my own family, which always made me low: we had never had even a pale shadow of the love these people felt for each other. Had my mother lived, would everything have been different? It was a pointless question – who could tell?

The poor doctor's suffering was the worst. He knew better than we what was happening to her poor body. He would often climb into bed with her and kiss her. I was shocked the first time he did this, thought that he should not bother her. I was wrong. When he held her, her pain seemed to lessen and she even slept.

Despite the strength of her spirit it could not go on. The day finally came when her flesh won the fight. I was in my room, supposedly taking a nap for we had all had a bad night with her. Most unusually for me, I was praying. I was asking God to do something, to make her better or to take her. And he took her.

I hope that I helped them. In truth I didn't know what best to do. Madame Chadrac took to her bed in grief. The good doctor was like a crumpled bear: he couldn't sleep or eat but paced the house, round and round endlessly. The children were so brave but they cried at night, when they would creep into my bed and I held them tight.

The morning of the funeral was a perfect July day. The air was heavy with the scent of flowers. It was so hot even the bees buzzed lethargically. It was a day for picnics, for dozing in the summer sun, for enjoyment – not for burying someone you loved.

The girls, I had presumed, would not be attending. In my family, and every family I knew, only men went to funerals. But, no, here it was different. Never having been to a funeral, I was a mixture of nervousness and curiosity.

It seemed as if the whole village had turned out. Many of the doctor's friends had come from far afield despite the problems of transport. We formed a ragged cortège behind the elaborate black and silver hearse, which was pulled by two horses, which should have been coal black, but instead were two stocky mountain ponies, whose heavy faces looked somewhat comical under black plumes attached to their harness.

The doctor walked, head bowed, not looking to right or left, clutching the hands of his daughters. In the square, people had lined up on the pavement. They crossed themselves as we passed by, the men doffing their caps. There was total silence apart from the tramp of our feet and the clatter of the horses' hoofs on the cobbled stones.

The silence made the shout 'One bloody Jewess less!' even more shocking. The doctor stopped and, walking behind him, I nearly cannoned into him. There was a general murmur of disapproval from the crowd. All of us except the doctor, who stared unwaveringly ahead, turned towards the group of men gathered outside Fleur's bar. They shuffled their heavy boots and looked intently at the gutter, as though it were full of objects needing their immediate close attention.

The service was long and in Latin, so went completely over my head. I had sat at the back, fortunately, for near the front I saw Fabien's mother.

When the service was finally over the cortège re-formed and we trudged along a dusty unmade road to the cemetery on the outskirts of the village. It had a breathtaking view, which to me seemed wasted. Not all the congregation came to this part of the service, just family and close friends; I was proud to have been included.

In the church I had felt curious and strangely detached. The chanting, the sombre bell, the choking incense, the ritual, none of it seemed to have anything to do with Pauline. Looking down into her grave was a different matter altogether. I felt such an overwhelming sense of loss and knew I could not hold back my tears. Neither could the little girls, though the doctor behaved with impeccable dignity. I was useless. Poor Madame Chadrac's legs gave way and she had to be supported. It was a relief when everything was over and we were leaving the cemetery.

'Clare, girls, go home,' the doctor ordered, when we reached the square. I started down the hill but something made me turn and, telling the girls to carry on, I ran after the doctor.

He didn't just enter the bar, he stormed in. It was packed and he had to push his way across the room, apologising to no one. As the others registered his presence they fell back making a passageway for him rather like Moses and the Red Sea. Finally he was looming over one particular table. He'd chosen correctly for a man sat white-faced and perspiring. Fleur ran round the side of the bar, dressed in black rather than her customary red.

'Doctor . . . It was . . . A drink? Pastis?' She fluttered about him like a funereal moth.

'Ernest Blanc. You are scum!' the doctor bellowed. The man was cowering now, but I didn't like the aggressive way he was clutching his glass as if he intended to grind it into the doctor's face. 'I would beat you to a pulp only it would not dignify the memory of my beloved wife.'

This statement appeared to enable the man to summon up some courage. 'I say what I think, Doctor. No one can silence me!' He looked defiant.

'Think? You haven't a brain to think with!' There was an audible snigger at this. 'But I'll tell you one thing. You may say what you think, but I treat whom I wish. The next time you or your decrepit mother, or your alcoholic father, or your licentious sister is ill, find someone else to treat you. Don't call me. You understand?' With enormous presence, and with Fleur still flapping about him, he strode from the bar to a ripple of applause.

When we returned, the house was full of people who had come to pay their last respects. Since I had been warned that this would happen, I made straight for the kitchen where I had prepared some food. I collected a tray of canapés and went back into the hall.

'And what are you doing here?' Fabien's mother stood in the hallway. My heart did the nose-dive it invariably did in her presence.

'I'm helping the family.'

'How commendable.' This woman had an enviable talent for turning a compliment into a sneer.

I chose to ignore it. 'Do you know if Fabien got to England safely?' Maybe there was still a chance we might be friends.

'My son's whereabouts is no concern of yours.'

'You're mistaken, Madame.' Hell! Where had I found the courage to say that? 'I have every right to know.'

'You? You arrived at my house uninvited. Then when we would much prefer you to have gone you insisted on remaining. I can assure you, such behaviour doesn't give you any rights whatsoever – quite the contrary.'

'You knew I was here?'

'Of course I did. You don't imagine that you could hide in my village? In any case, you made little attempt to be discreet, did you? Of course I'd have known, even if Fabien hadn't told me he was having a problem with you.'

I forced myself to smile sweetly, as if what she had said was of no concern to me, when I could quite happily have stuck a knife into her and twisted it too.

'I'm only surprised you didn't force yourself on him and tag along.'

'He wanted me to go but I had responsibilities here.'

'I'm sure the dear doctor is very grateful to you for your – how best to put it? – ministrations, shall we say?' Haughtily she looked at the tray of canapés I was holding in my hands, but her meaning was evident. I felt myself blushing – from anger, but I knew she would interpret it as guilt.

'Really, Madame, you can be so rude.'

'When necessary.' She picked at an invisible fleck on her sleeve.

'Why is it so hard for you to accept that Fabien and I love each other and intend to spend our lives together?'

She laughed, such a hateful, superior sound. Suddenly she stepped forward and grabbed my arm, making the tray wobble precariously. 'It isn't me, you stupid girl. My son has been playing with you. He does not love you. You are merely a sexual plaything for him. He will never marry you. Do you understand?'

Stupid! There it was, that damn word. 'I'm not stupid. How dare you speak to me in this way? And you insult your son by speaking of him like that. We love each other.' I needed to say those words, even if she was about to deny them, as if they were a talisman that would protect me from her. I shook my arm but she would not let go. Instead, her grip tightened but I was not going to let her see that she was hurting me.

'You will not marry him because you are not a suitable person. You are uneducated, the wrong class, the wrong religion. It would be a disaster for him and you would ruin his life.'

'That is rubbish! How could I ruin his life?'

'I suggest you listen most carefully to what I am about to say. I can make things very difficult for you. The authorities, I'm sure, would be interested to know you were here.'

'Don't try to blackmail me.'

'But I'm not, I'm *telling* you. I do not want you in my son's life. I will not say it again. Get out of all our lives . . . or else.' Taller than I, she leant threateningly above me, her face distorted with anger. 'Ah, my dear Doctor . . . I was devastated to hear of your sad loss . . .' And she wafted into the parlour, oozing sympathy alongside her hypocrisy.

I didn't follow with my tray of canapés. I left them on the hall table and rushed for the kitchen where I stood shaking with fear and anger and feeling very, very sick.

'Clare, are you all right?' The doctor, his guests finally gone, entered the kitchen. 'I was not thinking, I should have warned you she would come, doing her gracious Lady Bountiful act! I'm so sorry. Please don't upset yourself.'

'I'm fine, Doctor. Really. It's just that she said such awful things. She threatened me. I'm so frightened.' I just could not stop shaking, I had to hold one hand with the other to keep it still. He put his hands on mine, which helped a little. 'Robert, I'm afraid she's going to tell the authorities about me.' I was so agitated that I barely noticed I'd used his Christian name.

'I'll have a word with her.'

'But that might make matters worse. Anyway, would she listen to you?'

'Don't worry, she'll listen. For a long time I've had a little snippet of information about her that I thought might be useful one day. I'll simply threaten her that if she gives you away then . . .' He gave one of his shrugs, which were often, I thought, more expressive than words.

'Good gracious me, what's she done? Had an affair with the *curé*?' I laughed at the very idea.

'Much worse than that. Taxes!' he said, and smiled at my disappointment. 'You've been such a loyal friend to us, Clare. I know you would have preferred to leave with Fabien and that you selflessly opted to stay with us . . .' I had to look at the floor, I was so embarrassed. I was so used to being called selfish that this was almost too much. 'I hate to say this, Clare, especially now, but in these circumstances I really think you should leave. Do you know Anliac? It's a small city south of here, about thirty miles south of Le Puy. I've friends there, I'm sure they will help you. In a city you can hide more easily.'

'But, Doctor, the last thing I want to do is hide. I want to go home to England. I want to find Fabien.'

'And how do you propose to do that? It might prove far more difficult than you think.'

'I don't know for sure, but I'll find a way. I'm quite resourceful, you know,' I said, quite sharply, fed up that he, too, was speaking to me as if I was foolish. 'When Fabien left we rowed, you see. I didn't have time to ask him how he had made his arrangements and who to approach, but I don't think it should be too difficult.'

'I wish I shared your optimism. I mean, where do you begin? Where will you go?'

I gave a shrug, though mine was not nearly as expressive as his. 'I don't know. I'll catch a train, get rides and walk when necessary – just as I did when I came here. It shouldn't be too difficult to get down to the south and when I'm there I'll find a guide to help me over the Pyrenees into Spain. I've been saving.' I patted my purse.

'Do you really think you're being wise? There is a big clamp-down on movement out of one's area. I hear it's getting harder to cross the borders. Let me arrange for my friends to help you. You could stay with them until this war is over.'

'I can't hide all my life, can I? And end up feeling guilty all the time. It's been marvellous helping you but it isn't enough. When I get home I can join up and be useful.' I waved my hand vaguely, not in the least sure what I could do or what use I could be.

'It could be so dangerous for you. I'm not sure . . .'

'Doctor, if I tell you something to set your mind at rest, you promise not to tell a living soul?'

'I promise.' He laughed a little, no doubt at the urgent way I spoke and the seriousness of my expression.

'Well, it's like this. You thought I told you and your wife everything. I didn't. You see, I've got this German passport . . .' and I told him all.

2

The odd thing was, and I had noticed this before, that when I shared my secrets with someone I always felt far more relaxed, at ease and less scared. So I was quite content, having told the doctor, to leave my arrangements to him.

A fortnight went by before he had news for me. His mother in-law had left that day for her home in Lyon. With the children in bed and dinner over, he called me to his study and sat me down with a map. 'I've been in touch with my friends in Anliac. See? It is here. They are happy to put you up until the next stage of your journey.'

'I can't just go to the south?' Anliac didn't look that far away, so what was the point in delaying there?

'No, Clare, you can't. I told you, it's no longer easy to flee the country. There are things to be arranged. How much money do you have?'

I thought he was being a bit nosy but I told him all the same.

'Take this.' He pushed a small purse towards me. 'You will need it. Guides will have to be paid, and perhaps people bribed.'

'I couldn't possibly accept.'

'This is no time for such niceties, Clare. I'm indebted to you, not you to me. Now, where were we?' Together we studied the map, he pointing out possible routes for me. 'You must be extra careful near the Spanish border, there will be many police there looking out for people just like you.'

'That's when I can become a German. I'll travel through France, until I reach the very south, with the papers you gave me, and the rest of the way on my German passport – the police won't bother me then.'

'If you do that you risk being taken for a spy.'

'So what am I supposed to do?'

'You must take the advice of my friends. France is a very dangerous place for you. In these country areas strangers stick out. The population is being encouraged to inform on each other. Some of it is being done out of malice – scores to be settled, that sort of thing. But a lot of people think they are doing it for the safety of France. We live in confused times and there are many who believe that Marshal Pétain is only doing what is best for us all.'

'And you don't?'

He paused, as if selecting his words carefully. 'I think he is an old man who is out of his depth. He behaved, he thinks, with honour but rapidly it becomes dishonour.'

'Then why doesn't he resign?'

'Because he, too, now believes he acts for the best for all. And then, of course, there is the matter of his pride.'

'Of course, the oh-so-famous pride! I know all about that and Frenchmen.' I laughed.

'I love to see you laugh but, Clare, you must begin to take everything more seriously. This isn't a game, you know.'

'But I *am* being serious.'

He shook his head as if he didn't believe me. 'The people who will put you up will have a cover story for why you're there to quell the curious. They are going to say you are a niece from Lyon. You understand that to protect them you must stick with this story?'

'Yes.'

He sat silent for a while, shuffling the map around. Then he coughed, I assumed he had finished with me and stood up.

'There's just one more thing, Clare.' I sat down again. 'This is difficult for me . . . I want to ask you an enormous favour. If you don't wish to do it please say so, and I will understand. I will not think less of you.'

'Whatever you want,' I replied, wondering what it could be.

'Would you please take Yvette and Dominique with you? To Spain. My sister lives in Seville.'

'Certainly,' I answered, with no hesitation whatsoever.

'You should think about it a bit more. It's a great responsibility. And they might put you at risk. It would be much easier for you on your own.'

'No, they will be company for me,' I said blithely. He looked up sharply, as if about to say something, but stayed silent. 'Why do you want them to go? Why are you so anxious?' Of course I could guess the answer, but I felt I had a right to be told.

He took a deep breath then slowly lit a cigarette. 'At the funeral, you heard that evil creature who shouted out about Jewesses.' I nodded. 'I don't know how he found out that Pauline was Jewish, or from whom. But it is true.'

'I thought it must be. But I don't understand, the service was in a Catholic Church.'

'Pauline was Jewish by birth, by her mother, but her father was Catholic. It was something that I don't think any of them thought about – we are not and never have been a religious family. No, this is about race, you see. And that made her Jewish and thus, by definition, her daughters. And with things as they are . . .'

'You mustn't worry so much, Doctor. When I was in Paris I read that the definition of a Jew was one who had two Jewish grandparents.'

'I know . . . grandparents who *practised* the religion. I'm aware of that.

That was the German ruling. Vichy's, while also based on two grandparents, is based on race, not religion.'

'Yes, but you said . . . that the girls only have their grandmother. So?'

'And how long before these regulations are changed and all you need is one Jewish grandparent to be regarded as a Jew? How long before they make it one great-grandparent? I can't take the risk. I don't trust the bastards – I'm sorry, please excuse my language.'

'You know in English we have an expression when you swear, you say, "Pardon my French."' I laughed.

'Clare. This is my family.' As he looked at me I could swear he was close to tears.

'I was trying to lighten your mood, that's all,' I said defensively. 'But your mother-in-law, what about her? Should she come with us?'

'I begged her to go last year when our government ordered that census of Jews. You might not remember but the following month their property was confiscated. I asked her, "Why are they doing that, what for?" There had to be a reason, a plan. She ignored it and didn't fill in the forms. She said there was no way she was going to leave Pauline when she needed her. She now says she's too old to go careering around the world. She'll take her chances in Lyon, she trusts her friends. I only hope she's right.' He looked gaunt with worry. 'You see, none of this is a joke.'

'Doctor, I *do* realise the gravity of the situation. It's my Englishness – we always joke when things are bad. If you must know, I'm scared silly most of the time. If I joke, it's because I don't want you to know just how scared I really am.'

'Thank God you said that. I'm sure in these times that fear can be a valuable shield.'

Yvette and Dominique were excited about the trip. We were to travel light with one bag each. Our story was that we were going on a short holiday to stay with an aunt since their mother had just died, and too much baggage might look suspicious.

'When this war is over I'll return to collect the rest of my things, Doctor.'

'How will I know you've arrived safely?'

'I'll join the army and I'll finish the war single-handed. Then you'll know.'

'Clare!' He kissed me on both cheeks. I turned away as he said farewell to his daughters for he was crying and I didn't want to embarrass him by letting him know that I had seen his tears.

The trip to Anliac was quite a let-down. I'd imagined us trekking across treacherous countryside, being whisked through the night by car, lorry, tractor, horse or even by donkey. Instead we took the train to Le-Puy-en-Velay. We had to wait for a connection and there was time to explore the lovely city.

The carriages of the next train were packed and we were lucky to get seats – even then we had to give them up several times to aged crones who didn't have the courtesy to thank us. It smelt too, for in France when people moved anywhere they took food with them. On this train geese and chickens were among our fellow passengers. However, the guard drew the line at a goat coming on board; that led to a fine rumpus and a big increase in my vocabulary of bad French words. We passed through some breathtaking scenery – but the train was so slow, stopping frequently for no apparent reason, that I thought we would all die of boredom.

Our papers were checked. Twice the policeman flirted and twice I flirted back. There was no need to worry about the girls letting slip anything. I don't think either had ever asked my surname and since the doctor had sensibly used my real Christian name on my false papers I hadn't had to school them in to calling me by a strange name. They had been told they were going on holiday; we had simply not told them that the aunt lived in Spain. When we got to the south, the plan was for me to leave them and to take a boat for England. It would be blissfully simple. I couldn't think why Fabien had made such a fuss.

We stood somewhat forlornly on the station platform at Anliac. The bustle of departing passengers was over. There was no one to meet us as arranged. The latter part of the journey had been uncomfortable: my rear ached from sitting on the wooden benches. I had never in my life travelled on such an uncomfortable train. It was blisteringly hot, we were two hours late, and no one was here. Some friends!

'Clare, Yvette, Dominique!' A young woman – I guessed a little older than me – dark-haired, slim, dressed in grey, hurled herself at us. 'At last you're here,' she said loudly. I felt like saying the same to her but instead I allowed this perfect stranger to kiss me. The two girls looked wide-eyed with surprise. 'Oh, the pretty little cabbages, you've forgotten me. I'm your aunt Arlette.'

'Oh! Hello!' they yelled equally loudly, and she made as much noise answering them back. I began to wonder if she was deaf – she seemed incapable of speaking in a normal tone.

'Come on.' She picked up my bag as we began to walk along the platform. 'Oh, shit!' she said, under her breath, as we approached the barrier at which stood a group of police.

'Papers.' One held out his hand. He began to check our documents. It was not the cursory glance we were used to but a long and close study of them. As they checked I became aware that Arlette was not just tense but terrified.

'And you are Madame Saulle? What is the reason for your visit?'

'She's not married. She's not a madame.' Dominique giggled as she spoke.

'I'm the girls' governess.'

'You said you weren't a governess.' Dominique again: at this rate I'd end up strangling her.

'If you're not that, then, what are you?' the policeman asked.

'I am. Don't listen to her. She's just being silly.'

'Is she your governess?' he asked Yvette.

'She doesn't like to be called one but, yes, she teaches us and very well.' I could have hugged her.

'And tell me, why don't you like to be called governess?' He emphasised the wretched word, making it sound sinister.

'I hardly like to tell you, Officer, it's so silly. But it's just that I think it sounds so middle-aged.' I batted my eyelashes and somehow managed to smile. It was a miracle I could for my stomach was churning and I was certain I was about to be sick. The nausea didn't subside when the policeman smiled too.

'No one would dream of thinking you middle-aged, Madame.' He handed me back my papers.

'She's not a—'

'I'm so sorry, Dominique. Are you hurt?' Arlette was picking her up from the platform where she had judiciously pushed her.

Fumbling nervously I stuffed our papers back in my handbag. I picked up my case. Instinct was making me want to run.

'Walk slowly,' Arlette whispered, out of the side of her mouth. I forced myself to do as she ordered. It was not easy for I was convinced they were watching us as we walked across the concourse, certain I could feel eyes boring into my back. I don't think I could have said a word: nausea still surged in me.

Anliac was beautiful if not quite as lovely as Le Puy. I wished I had arrived in a less tense frame of mind the better to appreciate it. We were walking along a wide boulevard lined with plane trees, which gave us welcome shade. Across the road was the customary square in front of the fine town hall. In the centre stood a large fountain, in which Poseidon and several nymphs and dolphins looked forlorn, their mouths gaping but no water tumbling forth. We took a side road and moved from one century into another. Here the streets were narrow, the houses tightly packed and so tall it was like walking down a canyon. We were in shade for the height of the buildings protected us from the hot sun. The road was cobbled and the wooden shoes that Arlette wore made a loud clattering sound, which echoed off the ancient buildings.

'This is wonderful!' I exclaimed, as the road ended in a small square. The houses that bordered it were all different shapes and sizes. They were painted in varying pastel colours, the only unifying feature the deep red of the Roman tiles on the roofs. In the centre was another fountain with another dolphin parched for water. None of the window-boxes had flowers in them but were planted with vegetables instead. 'Why?' I asked.

'One can see you've been living in the country. In the city getting fresh vegetables is difficult because of the transport problems. I'm fortunate, I have a grandmother who lives quite near. When I can go to her she gives me vegetables and good things like ham and eggs. But unfortunately we can't go there every week, it's too complicated a journey.'

Arlette stopped in front of one of the buildings, painted a lovely faded rust colour. There was a shop on the ground floor, a milliner's, I saw. She pushed open a dark green door in great need of paint. We entered a dusty stone hallway cluttered with bicycles, a pram and, incongruously, an old sewing-machine. The stairs were of stone also and poorly lit since there were no windows and the bulb must have been of the lowest wattage possible – it barely glimmered. Worse, burdened with our bags, we couldn't move quickly enough before the timer switch cut out and plunged us into darkness. Since Arlette lived on the fifth floor it rapidly ceased being a joke.

With our limbs miraculously intact we finally reached the door to her flat, which was perched on the top of the building. The sitting room was huge and had large floor-length windows with muslin curtains gently billowing in the breeze. It was a light, clean and wonderfully airy room. Stepping over the low window-sill we were on a large terrace, shaded by an awning.

'You've a farm here!' Yvette clapped her hands with excitement at the sight of a goat and two chickens.

'We've rabbits over there that need feeding.' Arlette handed them a bag of grass and the girls rushed across to the hutches. 'Don't let them escape.' Now I could see livestock on other balconies and terraces too. 'We used to have a pig but it was a little too smelly at such close range. I've an aunt, though, who keeps one on her balcony. It makes me laugh – she was always so fastidious. What changes war can make! But I'm prattling away and you probably want a drink. I'm afraid I only have acorn coffee to offer you.'

'Which reminds me.' We were back inside. I dug into my case and produced a bag of coffee beans. 'I don't know where the doctor got these but they're for you.'

'From Fleur in the bar, I expect.'

'And this?' I handed over the bag of sugar, a pot of jam and another of *foie gras*, some dried sausages and ceps. 'I'm afraid I couldn't carry any more.' Her joy as she swooped on them made me ashamed at the fuss I had made about carrying them, and I thought of the ham, the cake and the bags of salt and pepper I'd refused to bring.

'It gets worse in the cities. The shortages are serious. The government does nothing except cut our rations further. I don't know how people survive if they don't have relations in the country.' As she spoke she was stowing away the produce into cupboards, which I saw were bare.

'I've a confession to make. There was other stuff. I left it. I felt I couldn't carry it.'

'And why should you? You've brought a feast as it is. And your case was horribly heavy. Now, coffee – real coffee with sugar. I shall think I have died and gone to heaven.' She pottered about grinding the coffee, measuring it. I would have liked to ask her how old she was. It was difficult to tell. At the station I'd thought her older than I but now, at home in her kitchen, she looked much younger. Her face was more relaxed here – she really has been worried at the station. 'Fleur is amazing, isn't she? She can always get hold of something. It's best not to ask her how she does it. I hope she's careful. They're coming down hard on anyone involved in the black-market.'

'You know her, then?'

'Of course. She's my cousin.'

I smiled at that, for if there was one thing I'd learnt whilst living in the country it was that it was unwise to say anything critical about anyone. Sure as eggs were eggs, you'd find out they were that person's nearest and dearest. To me it seemed as if the whole of the Auvergne was one giant family.

At the sound of a key in the latch I turned round. An older woman appeared, shepherding two children, both of whom looked as if they had been crying.

'Oh, my God! No luck?'

'They didn't come.'

'Ah.' Arlette frowned. 'This is Clare, Mother, she's come with Robert's children. And lots of lovely things to eat.'

'You're most welcome, my dear, and thank you. I'll just settle these two. Sam, stop crying, do!' She sounded exasperated.

'I'll make them some tea, shall I? Put them in my room, if you want.'

Arlette returned to making the coffee. I watched as the children reluctantly followed the older woman.

'Can't they play with the girls?'

'I don't think it would be a good idea, Clare. You see, they're not supposed to be here. I'm sorry about this. Some people are so unreliable. I feared this might happen.'

'Yes?' I was curious, but she didn't enlighten me.

'I've some lemonade for the girls. I managed to get a lemon last week.'

I wished she'd hurry with the coffee, but she seemed agitated and older again, less inclined to talk. I wandered back to the terrace, sat in the shade and watched the girls playing with the animals.

3

It was late in the evening. All four children were settled in bed. Something was wrong. I'd have had to be as stupid as people thought I was not to notice. Arlette and her mother had spoken only of inconsequential things as we ate dinner.

'Now we can talk, Clare.' Madame Bonnard had put the last of the dishes away. 'I'm always afraid to say too much in front of the children in case they let slip something at the wrong time. I realised you had grasped what we were doing when you didn't ask any questions.'

'Of course,' I said. What a hoot! *Of course*. In fact I hadn't understood anything: I was just being polite and English.

'Did you have any problems at the station this afternoon, Arlette?'

'Problems! We must find somewhere else to meet. I nearly had a heart-attack when I saw the same policeman standing at the barrier who was on duty when I picked up Sam and Sarah. That friend of yours in the police station was wrong about him being off duty. They must have changed the rota.'

'Did he recognise you?'

'No, I don't think so. But I was so nervous – he might have picked up on that. Honestly, I think they're trained to smell fear.'

'But I thought we had decided you should be late and the police would have gone once the train was clear.'

'That's what I thought too. Fortunately I used the entrance from the market and saw poor Clare standing on an almost deserted platform. They stood out like a beacon. I had to barge in.'

'Weren't you told to go through the ticket barrier, Clare?' asked Madame Bonnard.

'No. All I was told was that someone would be at the station to meet me.'

'We were lucky this time.'

'I'm sorry.'

'My dear child, it's not your fault.'

'The doctor said I would be safer here in the city.' I managed an ironic laugh.

'In many ways you are – with the crowds, it's normally easier to come and go – but the police are stricter with their checking of papers. No cousins in the force here, I'm afraid, isn't that so, Arlette?'

'Unfortunately. You see, Clare, I'd picked up the other two children only a couple of days ago. That particular policeman asked who they were and I said my cousins so, of course, I was terrified today that he might remember and think I'd far too many relations coming to stay.'

'I understand. And I nearly died when Dominique said I wasn't a madame, nor their governess. Still, we're safe now.'

'There will be other checks *en route*. She might say the same thing again.'

'I'll tell her I married Fabien in secret. That should shut her up.'

'Fabien, did you say?'

'Yes, you know him too?' I noticed that they glanced quickly at each other. It bothered me.

'Of course. We helped him on his way.'

'You did! Oh, you wonderful, marvellous people.' I had to jump up to kiss and hug them, in thanks for helping him and also to relieve my agitation at the look that had passed between them. What could it mean? At mention of Fabien I wanted to be on the move again, as quickly as possible. 'Do we leave tomorrow?' There it was, that glance again. 'Do we?' I said, more emphatically.

'That was the plan.' Madame Bonnard was avoiding looking at me, I was sure.

'*Was?*'

'The other children not being met by the contact today has made things more complicated,' Arlette explained.

'But how does that affect me?'

'Because the man who had promised to take them did not arrive, it is necessary to alter the arrangements.'

'I wasn't aware anyone was escorting me.'

'They aren't. But . . .' Madame Bonnard paused. I hated that sort of pause: it usually meant that something I didn't want to hear was about to be trotted out. 'We wondered if you would take Sam and Sarah with you?'

'To Spain!'

'No, just to Lourdes. They are to be met there. But, you see, if there are five of you to be put up instead of three, we have to rearrange the journey.' Arlette's mother was speaking rapidly, as if not wanting to give me time to respond. But this was the last thing I needed. No, I thought, I don't want to do this. Why should I? These children were nothing to me, not like the girls. And, in any case, I didn't even like them: all they had done this evening was snivel and cry and look miserable. No, I'd say no.

'I feel sad for the little scraps. They have had the most appalling time. Their parents were taken in the middle of the night from their home. Fortunately they were sleeping at their grandparents'. I think their parents, poor souls, were celebrating their anniversary – sheer chance the children were not at home. A kind neighbour got to them and warned them despite the curfew. It was a courageous thing to do. In one cruel night the children's lives were shattered.' The words tumbled out of her in a breathless stream as if she was aware of my thoughts. 'God knows when they will see their parents again – if ever. Have you noticed that Sarah hasn't spoken and Sam cannot stop crying? It's the trauma, you see. The awful trauma.' The torrent stopped and she sat looking at her hands as if they might reveal the solution to the problem.

'Yes.' I heard myself say. 'I mean . . .' I didn't want to say yes, I hadn't intended to, so what was happening? Why should I put myself at risk for two brats I didn't even know? 'Yes, I'll take them.'

'I knew you would.' Arlette exhaled as if she'd been holding her breath. 'Bless you, child.'

'Why were the parents taken? What had they done wrong?'

'They were born. They were Jews.'

It took over a week to rearrange my journey. In that time I came to know Arlette and her mother, and my admiration for them grew. For over a year they had been helping people escape to Spain.

'It started with a friend of my brother,' Arlette told me. 'He'd been a prisoner-of-war and escaped and wanted to join the Free French. My brother was in the same camp. He was wounded so he couldn't escape with him, but he gave him our address. One became two, then three. Then, of course, this awful business of the Jews.'

'Aren't you scared?'

'All the time. But we couldn't just stand back and do nothing, could we?'

'What about the neighbours?' I asked, thinking that I'd be perfectly happy to do nothing. I was still reeling from amazement at my momentary madness in agreeing to fall in with their plans.

'I hope they can be trusted, that's all. I share my eggs and rabbits with them – a little bribery goes a long way. Mother prays a lot too. I'm sure that helps.' Arlette laughed. 'The adults normally come at night, but we can't do that with the children – it would look suspicious. So, when asked, we risk saying they're relatives and hope people don't count how many have been here.'

'I think you're so brave.'

'Me? Rubbish. It's the least I can do. What about you? You're brave, travelling across country with them, through all the checks.'

Brave! Me? It was a nice thought, and I hadn't seen it like that. 'I'm just helping the doctor out. I'll soon be in England and safe. But you won't, will you?'

There were other things I learnt, too, during that long week. These two women were more involved in clandestine activities than I had at first realised. Arlette distributed an underground newspaper – perhaps that was where the doctor had got his – taking a few copies at a time hidden in the basket of her bicycle – it had wooden wheels and must have been agony to ride over the cobbles. I'd never have dared, I decided, I would have been too scared.

Nor was she a milliner. It was a front. She had been at the university but had been forced to leave when her father, a teacher, had been arrested for anti-Vichy activities. 'What did he do?'

'He refused to submit a list of children with foreign names. Nor did he like the state interfering with the curriculum and he told them so. They arrested him on some trumped-up charge. We lost our home, of course – we lived in a government house. Fortunately my mother had this building.'

'How awful for you. In Paris, we all envied you in the free zone.'

'It's not free. Just a different form of occupation.'

'Aren't you bitter about your studies?'

'No, I shall return to them when this war is over. Unless we do something, it will take even longer.'

'I suppose so,' I agreed, but I knew there was no way I would put myself at risk as she was doing.

Listening to the BBC was banned but that didn't stop them. It was why they were so much better informed than I. It was odd to sit huddled over the Bakelite wireless, the windows closed so that no one would hear, and to realise that the faint, often barely audible voices, had been beamed from London, from my home, where Fabien was, I reminded myself.

It wasn't all fear and hiding, though. Several times in that week Arlette and I went out leaving the children with her mother. We went to one bar in particular, the Golden Bear, owned by a friend of hers David Pointe. Sometimes I saw a look pass between them and I wondered if they were more than just friends. But she didn't say and I wouldn't ask. There were always people she knew there. We even managed to enjoy the cheap, bitter wine – we had to for there was nothing else to drink. But we sat in the sun, under the gay umbrellas and flirted and chatted. It was almost as if there was no war, and I was not sitting here in this strange city with forged papers in my handbag, such a long way from home.

It was time to go. Yvette and Dominique were bursting with excitement to be on the move again, though sad to say goodbye to the animals. To say 'sad' was an understatement, they sobbed their hearts out. It was just as well we were leaving before they discovered that all the creatures were destined for the pot.

Although I knew that eventually I was going to Spain, no route was given to me or the names and addresses of anyone along the chain. 'For security reasons, I suppose?'

'It's not that we don't trust you, it's in case you're picked up and questioned by the police. If you don't know you can't tell them, can you?'

'But I wouldn't.'

'Maybe you would have no choice.'

I had a shrewd idea what Arlette meant. But I didn't want to know for certain.

4

Some adventure! It was blisteringly hot, I was bored, and a lot of the time we were hungry. Keeping four children amused was not easy for me: I soon realised I lacked the patience to deal with them. And people wanted to be parents! Indeed, I had once thought I wanted to be a mother. Now, the knowledge that Fabien could not father children was a source of relief. And, if I thought about it, that news had never bothered me as much as perhaps it should have. It was puzzling, unless it signified that I was not meant to be a mother.

Had it not been for Yvette there would have been a lot more tears but she was wonderful with the others, reading to them, playing with them. I longed for this journey to be over so that I could hand them on to someone else.

We had set off by car. A policeman friend of Arlette, with a petrol allowance, drove us on the first day. So there were good policemen as well as the bad, bullying sort. Then we were handed from one family to another down the country getting closer and closer to the coast with each day. I had slept in cleaner beds and I had eaten better food, but I had never met kinder, more concerned people than these. I thought them so brave and they thought they did nothing.

Boring? That was until we arrived at a small station in the back of beyond and were all ordered off the train. No explanation was given but, judging by the resignation of the other passengers, this was a common occurrence. I bundled the children into the waiting room to get out of the sun.

'Clare, how long will we have to wait?'

'I don't know, Dominique.'

'Clare, see what I've got.' From his pocket, with a conspiratorial look, Sam produced a matchbox and opened it to show me.

'Isn't he lovely!' I said, at sight of the large black beetle inside, sitting on a bright green leaf. 'Does he have a name?'

'Beetle,' Sam said, with a childish logic that made me laugh.

'Jewish, is he?'

'I beg your pardon?' I looked at a squat, red-faced man, who was pointing his walking-stick at Sam, an unpleasant expression on his face.

'He looks like a Yid to me.'

'What on earth do you mean?' I felt a huge surge of anger that I knew I must control. Sam rescued me by sneezing loudly, dropping the match-box, out of which the beetle scurried to freedom.

'Beetles are the Jews of the insect world.' Deliberately the man brought his boot down on the hurrying insect; there was a sickening crunch.

'Beetle!' screamed poor Sam, bursting into tears.

'You bloody fool.' A woman, evidently his wife, swiped the man across the head with her handbag.

'That's what I'd do to all of them,' he said belligerently, glaring with undisguised hatred at Sam.

All the children began to cry. 'Shut up, say nothing,' I said sternly, as I stood up. I couldn't put up with any more of this, even if it did put us at risk. 'You—' I began.

'You, sir, are a disgrace to this nation.' A tall, angular woman towered over the man and said it for me.

'Mind your own damned business – nosy old cow.'

'How dare you speak to my wife like that?'

'And you a Frenchman . . .'

'Jew lover . . .'

'Collaborator . . .'

'Communist . . .'

'Pétainist . . .'

'Gaullist . . .'

The other people in the waiting room took sides as all that divided this nation was noisily debated, and insults were hurled and countered. What I feared would happen did: the police appeared, hurriedly summoned by a railway official.

'Stop this!' the gendarme bellowed. As the recriminations and defences to the policeman began I collected the sobbing children and left the room, unsure what I would say if questioned or for how long I could keep my temper. The train was ready and I ushered them on.

'We'll find another beetle, Sam, I promise.' I sat on the train hardly able to believe I had just been part of that scene. If some ordinary people thought in this way, and about children, what hope was there? I pulled Sarah on to my lap and hugged Sam tight. No one was going to hurt these children, not if I could help it. I felt an unfamiliar but strong need to protect these little ones, no matter what.

'Why did that man kill Beetle, Clare?'

'Because he's sick in the head, Dominique. I suppose we should feel sorry for him,' I said, though I knew I never could.

Finally we arrived in Lourdes. I had been looking forward to seeing this unique city, as I had Mendes, Rodez, Albi and all the other places we had stopped at or near to on our journey. Instead, here as there, I was too tired and hot to bother. I sat in the park where I'd been told to go and, where the children, as subdued and exhausted as I was, could not even summon the energy to play.

There were few people about, so spotting my contact should not be difficult. I'd been told to look for an elderly woman called Désirée – no surname had been given. She would be walking a white poodle with a red collar. I was to say my dog had a collar just like that, and she would reply that it was of poor quality. I wondered if I would be able to keep a straight face. She would take Sam and Sarah and hand us over to a guide to take us over the Pyrenees. We would have to walk most of that stage, not something I was looking forward to.

Suddenly Sarah was on her feet and racing across the gravel. 'Uncle Ben!' she was crying. I yelled at her to come back but she raced on towards a young man. I ran after her, cursing her for drawing attention to us.

'Sarah!' I was overtaken by Sam, shooting off in the same direction. The man bent down and scooped Sarah into his arms, covering her face with kisses.

'Excuse me.' I eventually caught up with them. 'I presume you're the uncle?'

'I'm so sorry. Clare?' Tears were cascading down his face and he could barely get the words out. 'I have my papers to prove . . .' He delved into a pocket.

'Not here, it'll look odd. Kiss me too, make out you know me.' I must say he did that most effectively and, for good measure, put one arm round my shoulder as we walked back to the bench where the girls awaited us. 'Yvette, will you take the others to play? I saw a swing back there. This gentleman and I have to talk. Please, Sam, just for a minute. Sarah?' But there was no budging these two: they clung to the man like limpets.

'My papers—'

'Honestly, I don't think there's any need. Just look at Sarah – that's the first time I've seen her smile.' And she was sitting on his lap and stroking his face as if she could not really believe he was there. 'There's no doubt in my mind that she knows you.'

'I was so afraid she would have forgotten me. I haven't seen them for nearly a year. Mademoiselle, I have to thank you, you—'

'Please, it was nothing.' I felt quite ashamed at the number of times I'd been bad-tempered with them now. 'I'm to meet a woman here. I hope she won't be cross that you've turned up, that it won't wreck her plans.'

'Désirée? I'm sorry, I'm afraid she has been arrested.'

'Oh, my God, no!'

'I came earlier than arranged. I'm glad I did now, otherwise you would have had no one here to meet you.' He spoke French but with a marked Italian accent. 'I was with her when she was taken. They were unnecessarily rough with her and she is an old woman. I tried to stop them. I fear for her.' At this he began to cry. Oh, really, I thought, this isn't helping. Doesn't this family do anything but blub?

'Why weren't you arrested?' I asked, when eventually he stopped. I thought that was quite smart of me in the circumstances. Arlette had warned me to be suspicious of any change to our plans. I thought he was OK, but best to check.

'I'm an Italian citizen. They let me go.'

'How did you explain why you were here?' I was confused. Italy was on the side of the Germans so why hadn't the French arrested him too?

'I said I had come to meet my niece and nephew.'

'You what!' I exploded at that. 'How could you be so – *stupid?*'

'I was in a panic. I couldn't think. They accepted it.'

'I hope you're right. When was this?'

'Last week.'

'When? Oh, really!' I was so exasperated I could have hit him. If Arlette and her friends could contact each other to set up our escape, why on earth couldn't they have been contacted about this catastrophe, which was putting us all at risk? 'And what have you been doing meanwhile?' Not mooning about Lourdes, crying, I hoped.

'I only returned yesterday. I went—' He stopped as if close to tears again, but instead he took a deep breath. 'Fortunately Désirée had told me she was to meet you here in this park, and the time.'

'You went all the way back to Italy?'

He looked uncomfortable. Was he lying? 'I . . . It's difficult to speak . . . I had heard that there was a camp close to the border where Jews are being sent. I went there . . .' He put his hand over his mouth as if to suppress words. 'The conditions . . . They are hard to describe . . . The heat! Mademoiselle, you cannot imagine the stench. And my sister, she is such a fastidious person.'

'Is she there?'

'I couldn't find out. But if she is she will die. She's a diabetic. You cannot imagine what I have seen – and here, in France. What is to happen to them? What about the children?' I was about to say he shouldn't be talking like this in front of the children when I saw that both of them were fast asleep curled up close against him. I must say, this time I didn't blame him for crying.

'Did Désirée have time to tell you how to contact our guide?'

'No.'

'So now what do I do?' Then an awful thought struck me. 'Your arrival hadn't put Désirée at risk? Was she arrested because of you?'

'Please don't even think that. No. She told me herself that this was the last time for her, that she thought the police were suspicious of her, that she was being watched.'

Despite the July sun, I suddenly felt bitterly cold. Had I come last week, as arranged, or had the police chosen this week to arrest her, I would have been with her. I would have been arrested too.

'If she talks she could compromise the chain.'

'Désirée? I doubt it. She's an indomitable woman.'

'And the dog?' I can't imagine what had made me ask that.

'They shot it.'

Ever since I had come to France there had been moments, like the changing of the gears in a car, when my view of my life and what I was doing shifted, turning-points, and this was one of them. This was all so dangerous. And Arlette? I shook myself in an attempt to dispel my mounting fears, for her, her mother and others like them.

'Well, somehow we have to find someone who can take us over the mountains,' I said briskly.

'No need, I have a boat.'

'You've hired one?' I was cheering up by the minute.

'No, I bought it. It's near Perpignan, at a small fishing village. I drove here in a friend's car. I have to go to Genoa, but I don't mind taking you to Spain first. How could I, after all you have done?'

'But that's miles and miles away.'

'The roads are practically empty.'

'What about petrol?'

'I've plenty.'

'Won't there be patrols at sea?'

'I shall keep close to the shore – an innocent fisherman.'

It was all going to be all right, after all. I sank back on the bench and felt relaxed for the first time in ages. Spain, England, home . . .

Then I leant forward. 'Could I ask you a favour? Would you take just Yvette and Dominique. You can phone their aunt, she will come and collect them,' I heard myself saying.

'And you, Mademoiselle?'

'Things have changed. It was the dog, you see. I have to go back. There are so many children – I've no choice, have I?'

5

The door to the apartment opened slowly. At the sight of me the anxious expression on Arlette's face changed in a trice.

'Clare! I don't believe it, it's you!' At which the door was flung wide open and I was being enthusiastically hugged. 'Mother, look who's here!' she called excitedly, as she ushered me into the sitting room.

'But we thought you'd be in England by now. Has something gone wrong?'

'I changed my mind, Madame,' I said, grinning broadly. I was gratified at their pleasure in seeing me. But Madame Bonnard looked quizzically at me as if about to ask for an explanation. 'Who wants to go to boring old rainy England? Just look at the weather here,' I joked to forestall her.

'This calls for a celebration. Maman, may I open that last bottle of Tokay?'

I was even more pleased with myself. It meant that I was the something special they'd been saving that bottle for. While Arlette saw to the wine and her mother gathered together the olives she had also been saving, I asked if I might tidy myself up and was shown into my old room.

Inevitably they were going to ask me why I had returned. And yet, more than a week after seeing off the children, I was still unsure of the exact reason I was here. I had acted on the spur of the moment. I knew I was not of the stuff of which heroes were made. I wanted to get to England, to be with Fabien, not stay here in the vastness of France where, as everyone said, the situation was getting worse each day. Didn't I? I was a fool, I had said that to myself so many times. And yet . . . There was something else but I was not prepared to think about it, not yet at any rate. 'Clare, the wine is ready,' Arlette called.

We chatted about the weather, the friends at the Golden Bear, about the animals, as if we were all putting off talking about the serious things.

'Why have you returned, Clare?'

'Would you believe it, Madame? I don't know.'

'I'm sure you have an inkling.'

This was the subject I didn't want to discuss but when Arlette's mother looked at one with her penetrating but kind eyes it was difficult not to. 'I'm very confused. I had no intention of doing this but then suddenly I knew I had to return, even when part of me didn't want to.'

'Just like me. I want to help but half the time I wish I didn't and I could go back to my safe old life.' Arlette's admission, while surprising me, relieved me also.

'That is it exactly. You see, I don't think I believed everything that I had read and heard. It couldn't be true that the France I loved could be changing so much. In Paris I could blame everything that was happening on the Germans, but I can't do that here since there are none. And then, on the trip, I witnessed a scene with Sam that shook me. I had never seen a look of such hatred as was directed at that poor child. It had all seemed a game, but suddenly it wasn't. And I'm sure this sounds silly, but the police shot Désirée's dog and in a flash I knew that it was true, that there are cruel and bad French out there too, who are hurting people and, for all I know, enjoying their new power. Poor little dog.'

'Clare, so English!' Arlette chuckled.

'And so, because of the little dog—'

'I knew I had to stay. You were putting yourself at risk with the children and I couldn't turn my back on you too. It's the bleakness in their eyes. Children shouldn't look like that.'

'Dear girl.' Madame smiled at me with such warmth that for a moment I thought I *had* done the right thing. 'And there's another reason?' There was that look again, as if she could see right into my soul.

'No, Madame Bonnard.' How could I explain to these people who, dear as they were, did not know me nor what had happened to me in my life? How to explain that which I did not want to face? That I was afraid to see the man I loved in case he no longer loved me, in case my love for him was not the wondrous thing I thought it was, in case the anticipation was greater than the reality.

We debated long into the night about what to do with me now I was here. With the arrest of Désirée everyone was nervous. These women risked being sent to the camps, those awful places Sam's uncle had described. If Désirée had confessed everything, they might be implicated too.

'What will you do?'.

'We are lying low for the moment. It won't help anyone for us to play heroes at a time like this. No more escapees, no more children. If we are not doing anything we can't be accused of anything, can we?' That was an echo of the words Arlette had used to me, except then I had thought she was being melodramatic. Now I knew she wasn't.

'And the paper?'

'Arlette has stopped her connection with that. A little more tisane to help you sleep?' I thanked her. I had seen the look on Arlette's face. Her mother might think she had stopped but I'd wager money she hadn't.

'I haven't helped much, then, have I? Blundering back with my notion of being a sort of Pied Piper of Hamelin – I'm sorry.'

'Don't be. We're delighted you're here. But we've been thinking. Désirée, hoping you had got to England, might have given your name to the police to keep them happy. I think you should have a new set of papers, a new identity. I can arrange it.' So much for not being involved any more, I thought.

'Also, Clare, I don't want you to be hurt by this but we both think you should take a room elsewhere, just in case.'

'That's common sense. I don't want to put you two at risk. What's the news?' I asked, since I wanted to cover up my dismay. I had so little money left and how I was to afford to rent a room I had no idea.

'Nothing good. They arranged for the first prisoners-of-war to be returned to France. Really, I don't know what this government is thinking of. Three French workers are going to be sent to Germany for each prisoner returned. One doesn't have to be a mathematician to work out that to get them all home virtually the whole population of able men will be forced to work in Germany. It's ludicrous. And our beloved deputy prime minister struts around as if he were a genius.' At this she said something in argot that I didn't understand but which made Arlette laugh. 'I've also heard that Jews from the camps are being loaded into trains and sent to Germany. God knows what awaits them. And our dear neighbours the Swiss have closed their borders to Jews. Not a happy litany.'

'I could wish I hadn't asked, Madame.' I smiled wanly. I *should* have gone home!

'And in the occupied zone matters become much worse. Reprisal shootings. Little food. My heart bleeds for them.'

'It's not all doom, Clare. All this is having an effect. People are becoming disillusioned. They're starting to think, We *must* do something.'

'My great fear is that the Germans will move south. I've always thought this unoccupied zone was a strategy to enable them to entrench in the north while Marshal Pétain did their dirty work in the south.'

'That's what Dr Robert thought.'

'Good gracious. Arlette, we're becoming weak in the head. We forgot to tell you. His daughters arrived safely – which was why we were so convinced you were safe too. He had some trouble with Fabien's mother – it was a problem over a letter for you. But he calmed her down apparently.'

'For me? Who from? Where from?' My first thought was that it had to be Fabien, for who else would be writing to me?

'He didn't say. It wasn't necessary. Like us he thought you were safely away.'

'Can I contact him, get it from him?'

'He's not there.'

'Where's he gone?' I was annoyed. The least he could have done was give my letter to someone else if he was going to swan off.

'He's been arrested.'

'The doctor!' Now I felt awful, how could I have been thinking that way!

'Apparently he is accused of buying drugs on the black-market and profiteering.'

'What rubbish! If he did, it was to help people and I doubt he made a penny from it. Why, I often heard his mother-in-law nagging him about not chasing unpaid bills from the poor.'

'Some people don't care, provided they can bring some trumped-up charge. Don't worry, I'm sure he will be freed.'

I had a horrible struggle with myself. Half of me was appalled at what had happened and worried about him. And the other half, my demon half, was frustrated that he had been so stupid as to get arrested and be unable to give me my letter. My thoughts made me feel very uncomfortable.

'Are you all right for money, Clare?' Arlette asked.

'I'm fine.' How stupid of me to lie and to be proud at a time like this.

'I asked only because I think David might have a job for you at the Golden Bear. But since . . .'

'No, I lied. I was being stupid,' I said. 'I would love a job.'

Working in a bar again – how I longed for my father to see me.

The beauty of my new job was that it came with a room. I had imagined living alone in a garret talking to myself in a mirror for company. But at the Golden Bear there was always company if I wanted it. Nor was I employed in the bar: David needed me to supervise his cleaning staff and to do paperwork for him. Me as a housekeeper? Now that would have made even my stepmother laugh.

The bar was in a medieval building of thick walls, winding stone staircase, stone arches and frescoed walls. The beams were black with age and the fireplace in the dining room was so huge you could have walked into it. The pathetic attic of my imagination was, in fact, a fine room. The sloping floors made dropping anything hazardous for it rolled away to disappear under furniture or my large bed. The window overlooked a cobbled square, off the main boulevard, and in the older part of the town. There was yet another fountain – dry, naturally – and there was a large cross made of wrought iron, slightly askew so that it looked as if it was about to tumble at any moment. However, I was assured it had been like that for five hundred years. On three sides there were other buildings like this one, different periods, different sizes – it reminded me of a cardboard village I had had as a child. On the fourth side loomed the dark stone cathedral. And there lay the only disadvantage: it had a chiming clock that bonged the hours through the night.

'You'll get used to it, everyone does,' David assured me.

'I hope so. At the moment it's driving me potty. I think there's something wrong with it – it chimes thirteen when it's twelve.'

'It's meant to. That thirteenth chime is to remind us of the dead souls.'

'How lovely,' I said, while thinking, How weird.

'Arlette explained I have to go away quite a bit on business? I'm on the council.'

'Yes, she did.' He looked far too young to be anything so boring as a councillor, I thought, as I eyed him surreptitiously, liking what I saw. He was my type of Frenchman – dark-haired and -eyed, with that bold look that sent shivers down my spine, like Fabien.

'You came here with Arlette, didn't you? But not recently.'

'I've been visiting family down south.'

'Arlette says you've lost your papers.'

'I'd prefer to say I've mislaid rather than lost them,' I told him. What else had she said? What did he know? Could he be trusted? So many questions I had to ask now. Pray God they'd be ready soon.

'I'll need them quickly. I have to register that you're working for me. And I'll need your ration cards.'

'As soon as I find them, you'll have them,' I assured him.

Why had I worried? Within a week Arlette had my new papers. I was now Clare Dupont. I came from Givors near Lyon. My parents had recently died – father had been a minor executive in the silk industry in Lyon. I was grieving, and had decided to sever my links with my home town. I had worked as a receptionist in an hotel. I was taught the names of my old schoolfriends, my teachers, even the name of my nanny.

'Arlette, I don't want to appear to be telling you what to do but a couple of things bother me. Isn't it dangerous that I'm still called Clare? People forget surnames more easily than Christian names.'

'True, and we debated long and hard but we decided you were too scatterbrained to be given a different one.'

'Me?' I felt quite offended at that. Once yes, but no more.

'You said there were a couple of things.'

'When I was Clare Saulle my details were sketchy. It would have been difficult to check up on me. This is so precise.' I tapped the papers laid out on my bed.

'And safer. Clare Saulle could so easily have been found out to be false. Those papers were arranged for you by people not as expert as we are. There really is a Clare Dupont.'

'Has anybody asked her if she minds me becoming her?'

'But she *gave* us her documents. She wanted them to be used. She's gone to England to join her fiancé. Why, she even looks like you.'

6

In his position as a councillor, David was allowed a small petrol ration. In early September he offered to drive Arlette and me to her grandmother's home out in the country. He was to attend to business while we collected some food.

Their relationship continued to puzzle me. If they were in love they never showed it, and sometimes I thought that Arlette was indiscreet in front of him about her underground-newspaper activities. He was a councillor, which must mean he supported the Vichy government. But if he didn't and was involved with Arlette's friends, why didn't they tell me? It would have been kinder for I was always on edge with people, afraid that they would find out about my forged papers. I had kept my word to the doctor and no one knew of my English and German origins.

It was a long ride to Arlette's grandmother, who lived in a typical Auvergnat farmhouse. The main room served as kitchen, sitting room and, with a cupboard bed in the corner, as a winter bedroom too. It was dominated by an enormous fireplace. A long old pine table, well scrubbed, stretched down the middle of the huge room, which was heavily beamed. It was dark: in common with many buildings here, the windows were small to protect from the heat as well as the cold. Although it was only eleven, the table was laid for four.

'You can't come here without Gran feeding you. She's convinced I'm starving.'

'As you are, my girl! Just look at you, not a pick of flesh on you.' She turned to me. 'I hope you like rabbit, young woman?'

Once, having been raised on Beatrix Potter, I'd have refused it, but the war had changed that. I ate anything now. 'My favourite.'

At the sound of a car, she bustled out. 'That'll be that David of yours. He does too much – he'll be getting into trouble.'

'*Your* David? Trouble?'

'She hopes we'll get married,' she said, ignoring my last question.

Madame Pierre returned with a young couple. Arlette greeted them, kissing them, but in a restrained way as if she didn't really want to. She introduced them as her cousins – Paul and Marie Brives. We shook hands and they smiled in a friendly enough way but the atmosphere had changed.

'And to what do I owe this honour? Managed to find your way here at last? Bought a map, have you?' The old woman's attempt at sarcasm was embarrassing.

'You know how it is, I'm always so busy.'

'Informing on whom?'

'Aunt! That was a filthy rumour.' Marie leapt to defend her husband.

'We just happened to be in the area.'

'In the area? With the petrol rationing? Don't give me that. What do you want? Food?

'Anything you can let us have, Aunt. Times are hard.' He had cheered up at this.

'I've a ham, some pâté, potatoes, *marc* . . .' As she listed the food, just like a shopkeeper, I could swear that the man's eyes shrank and became piggier. 'You'd best come with me.'

While we waited I made idle conversation with Marie. Arlette ignored her. It was an uncomfortable five minutes until Marie clapped her hands at the sight of her husband and Madame Pierre, returning from the cellar laden with food. 'You're a saint, Aunt, you really are,' she squealed.

'So I've been told.' She took a pad of paper and a stub of pencil and began to write, making an exaggerated show of counting on her fingers. 'That's what I make it.'

Paul's smile rapidly transformed into a scowl as he scanned the list. 'This is a bill!'

'That's right.'

'You are playing a joke?'

'No, I'm not.'

'But we're family.'

'Some family!' She snorted.

'This is usury.'

'This is supply and demand. I'm no fool, Paul. If it wasn't for this wretched war the next time you would have come this way would be for my funeral – just on the off-chance there might be pickings. All these items are the results of my labour. I'm not overcharging you. I think you will find that is the going rate. That's what I want or you go empty-handed.'

I was glad I had not taken to Paul when he arrived or I might have felt sorry for him, as he fingered his wallet with such a sorrowful expression – but he paid.

'Cheeky bugger!' Madame Pierre made a washing movement of her hands as we watched their van bump down the potholed lane. 'He's one of those who say we peasants are exploiting them! Rubbish. I'm not a charity.'

'You should be wary of him, Gran. He could make trouble, report you for trading in rationed food. You know how thick he is with the Vichy toadies.'

'Who's going to arrest me? Young Georges in the village? I'm no fool, Arlette – I know who to *give* things to.'

Back in the house Arlette unpacked the bag she had brought with her – some soap, the remains of the bag of coffee beans I had given her, candles and a silk scarf. The old lady fell upon them with pleasure. 'See, Clare? This is how things should be done. I give what I can and they give to me what they can – nice and simple. I've already packed up the things for you to return with.'

We ate when David returned, looking pleased with himself, but not saying where he had been.

'Arlette tells me you came from Paris? Nasty dangerous place. It always was, let alone now,' the grandmother suddenly said when the meal was over.

I looked sharply across at Arlette. No one was supposed to know. I came from Lyon, that's what she'd said I was to say – to everyone.

'Long time ago,' I said evasively.

'I thought you said last year, Arlette.'

'Did I?' At least she had the grace to look a bit apologetic.

'David, talk to my grandmother do! Tell her to be more careful about Paul Brives. She won't listen to me.' And she recounted her cousins' visit.

'Madame, you were right to treat him in that way. But Arlette is right too. He could be a dangerous man to cross. He is involved with that vicious bunch the Ordre Légionnaire, which Pétain has formed. I know for certain that your nephew has informed on two families. He's evil.'

As they argued I fumed with exasperation. David must be involved! And yet he'd asked me questions as if he knew nothing – maybe they were testing me, maybe they didn't trust me. But hadn't I proved myself with the children?

'It's this young woman you should be worrying about. She looks the restless type to me. What if she goes haring back to Paris?' Madame Pierre's voice broke into my thoughts.

'But I shan't. I'm content here.'

'We wouldn't let her go, Gran. Would we, David?'

'She'd break my heart if she went.' David grinned at Arlette, who pushed him playfully.

Although I had said I was content, it was not strictly true. Madame Pierre had been right: I was becoming restless. I wanted to be doing something – rescuing people, being useful. I had made the big sacrifice of coming back but, often now, I asked myself why.

My work was not onerous, but the office jobs I did for David were tedious: ordering the stores, keeping an inventory – how surprised my father would have been! Rules and regulations seemed to proliferate in the night while we slept. As soon as you were sure that you'd got the hang of one set, another lot would appear. I needed my wits about me, that was certain.

The Vichy government had long ago decreed that a woman's place was in the home, and only allowed those with no man to support them to do cleaning jobs. 'How do women alone cope on this sort of money?' I asked, as I peered at the pittance in my wage packet.

'God knows, ask *them*.'

I had noticed that whenever there was something untoward, or something they did not approve of, the French always blamed *them* those faceless people in Vichy, rather as the Parisians had referred to the Germans.

'They deny it, but a friend of mine is certain that the teachers have been told to concentrate on the boy pupils and fail the girls,' Arlette contributed from across the room, where she was helping me count the money.

Such information enraged me. I had always been content with my lot – I had never wanted to be a boy, and I looked forward to marriage – but not as a second-class citizen. Frenchwomen didn't even have the vote – not something I had given much thought to, but I would have been furious if I had been denied it. I had never worn much makeup but now that it was frowned on by the authorities, Arlette and I, on principle, paid a small fortune for some powder and lipstick and plastered it on. We had worn trousers too, and shortened our skirts – because *they* had said we shouldn't. We enjoyed not only the satisfaction of doing what we wanted but a lot more attention from the men of Anliac. Not that I should have been quite so pleased. Fabien, I reminded myself. But our satisfaction was short-lived when we realised that *they* had actually told the women of France it was their duty to be attractive so that their men would make them pregnant. Well, really!

To stave off boredom I sometimes helped in the bar at night. We were seriously short-staffed, and though there was a shortage of alcohol we always had some, and even on the days when we ran out, people still crowded in. For companionship, I suppose.

Men flirted with me and I enjoyed flirting back. It bothered me that I did. I hadn't once. Just the thought of Fabien had been enough for me not to want to. But now? The truth was that though I thought about him I often had to remind myself to do so. And, worse, I couldn't remember clearly what he looked like.

As the nights drew in there seemed to be a collective lurch of the population towards despondency, as if the whole nation was suffering from a great depression. It wasn't just the advancing cold, it was the realisation that the war had now been our lot for three years, and nothing was getting better – in fact, everything was getting worse. I wanted and needed to be doing something.

'David, I couldn't sleep last night. There were noises in the roof.'

'Rats, probably.'

'Don't be disgusting.'

For three nights my sleep was broken. If these were rats then they were wearing hobnailed boots. Finally, infuriated and exhausted, I took my candle and climbed the stairs to the attic. I pushed hard at the door but it wouldn't open.

'Clare, what the . . .?' David had appeared on the steep staircase.

'I told you, I can't sleep. There's someone in there and I've come to give whoever it is a piece of my mind. And don't patronise me by telling me it's rats. Rats don't cough.'

'Some things are best not explained.'

'You've people hiding there.'

David stared long and hard at me, then without a word unlocked the door. 'My friend, you have to try to be quieter. You woke Clare.' To my astonishment David was speaking heavily accented but passable English.

'I say, I'm awfully sorry, Miss.' A young man peered at us.

'You're English,' I said, rather pointlessly.

'Yes, I am. Suppose it's obvious.' He grinned. 'Caught a bit of ack-ack and had to jump. But you're English too – well, I'll be damned.' He grinned even more broadly. It was odd to be hearing my language again, after such a long time.

'Are you hurt?'

'Not me. Landed like the proverbial butterfly. Jolly nice people took me in. I had a bit of a job with the old lingo – but we eventually sorted ourselves out. I'm hoping to get to Gib. Peter Toptree.' He held out his hand.

'Clare Dupont,' I had the wit to say, when Springer was on the tip of my tongue.

'I'm glad you know, Clare,' said David. 'He's not the easiest person to understand – he seems to talk in gibberish half the time. At least I can let him out now.'

We sat in the kitchen, with a bottle of wine and some cheese. The curtains and shutters were safely drawn. I was hungry for news. He told me of the bombing but assured me Croydon was all right – I wasn't sure that I believed him. He talked of the spirit at home and how determined everyone was not to be beaten. 'It's a bit hit-and-miss, but we'll win in the end.' This was wonderful to hear, especially in our present mood.

'Are you one of those clever people they're beginning to parachute in? You know, speak the old Frog talk like a native. Are you a spy?'

'No, don't be silly. I sort of got trapped here.'

'She has taken Jewish children to the safety of Spain.'

'Gosh, that's jolly brave.'

'Not really. Nothing much happened. It was a bit of a let-down, to tell the truth.' But for all that I found myself blushing. And, speaking English without warning after so many months, I had a sudden whoosh of homesickness, like being kicked in the stomach. Suddenly, with a great ache of longing, I wanted to be there. 'I couldn't come with you, could I?'

'As far as I'm concerned, the more the merrier.'

'No, Clare, that's not possible,' David interrupted.

'Who says?'

'I do.'

'I took the kids.'

'That was different. This is far more dangerous. For a start, he doesn't speak a word of French.'

'Then I'd be best placed to help him.'

'And you would have the added danger of being more likely to lapse into English with him. And be found out.'

'David, please. I'm doing nothing here – I want to so badly.'

'It'll come, and we'll need you then. Sorry, Clare, it's all been arranged and I don't want to change things.'

I felt so disappointed that my throat ached from fighting back the tears. 'Next time, then?'

'We'll see.'

'Chin up, Clare. I'll give your love to England.' Peter's words only made me feel worse.

'Could you take a letter for me?'

'Only too happy.'

'I've no address. He's with the Free French.'

'No problem, I shall just tootle along to Carlton Gardens – that's their headquarters.'

'When do you go?'

Peter looked at David, who looked at his watch. 'In four hours.'

Straight away I began my letter to Fabien. I told him how I missed him, how I loved him, how I longed for him – yet when I reread it, the words seemed false. It was as if they were referring to someone else not me. What was happening to me? How confused I was becoming. I added a postscript that I was coming home any day now. I returned to the kitchen where the two men were finishing the wine.

'You didn't put an address?'

'Oh, really, David, what do you take me for?'

Later that day I confronted David in his office. 'Why didn't you tell me he was there? Don't you trust me?'

'It's not that, Clare. It was just that the fewer who knew the better for everyone.'

'Did Arlette know?'

'Yes.'

I felt ridiculously hurt that they had chosen not to tell me. 'Did you know I was English before last night?

'Yes.'

'Might I ask how you knew?'

'Arlette told me.'

'How interesting. And who told her? I didn't. I have told no one here. You see David, this trust, it's a two-way thing.'

'I'm sorry if you're offended. I think Dr Forêt told her ages ago.'

'He promised me he wouldn't. And did he impart anything else interesting about me?'

'Yes.'

'What?'

'You know.'

'I'd like to know for sure.'

'That you were also German.'

That was unforgivable, I thought. How could he have betrayed me? And then, in one of those flashes that I sometimes had, I saw it all quite clearly. 'You've known all along, all of you. You won't let me help because you're saving me in reserve, aren't you? Just in case I might be *very* useful to you, like if the Germans overrun the southern zone – just as you were saying the other day. Well, I'll tell you one thing, David, you lot can whistle in the wind. I'm not helping. If you couldn't trust me over Peter why should I trust you? This isn't my country, this isn't my concern. So there!'

'Clare, Dr Forêt was in town last night. He couldn't see you – he has immense problems.' Arlette had just entered the Golden Bear.

That was typical of this bunch of French, I decided. I take his kids to safety and he doesn't even have the courtesy to see me. 'What problems?'

'He'd been arrested, as you know, but managed to escape and friends of ours are helping him hide. But he gave me this for you.'

In the envelope Arlette handed me there was a fulsome letter of thanks from the doctor, which made me feel ashamed at my initial reaction. And also the letter that had come for me way back in the summer. My spirits plummeted when I saw it was from Hortense – deep down I had hoped it would be from Fabien.

It was written in the formal style Hortense admired. She told me that, in the circumstances, they were well. That Tiphaine was busy, that the drawing-room ceiling had fallen, and asked when I was returning. All rather boring and then . . . I screamed. 'No!' I shouted, flapping the letter in my excitement. 'She's seen Fabien!'

'She says that?'

'No, she wouldn't want to put him at risk. It's in code, listen— "I finally saw the Lone Ranger—"'

'And?'

'She means Fabien. I've got to go. I've simply got to go.' Already I was rushing around my room like a demented creature, flinging things on my bed to pack.

'Hang on, Clare, it's not that simple. Getting a pass to cross into the occupied zone is getting harder and harder. It's dreadful in Paris. Stay here, where you're safe.'

'I'll be fine, and aren't you forgetting one thing, Arlette? I *am* surprised when you seem to think it's all right to tell everyone my business. I've got this.' And I waved my German passport in her face.

7

Both David and Arlette tried everything to persuade me not to go to Paris. They felt I hadn't thought out the consequences of returning to the occupied zone. This annoyed me. It was bad enough when older people treated me like a wayward child but it was worse when they were close to me in age. When insulting me didn't work they tried scaring me with tales of people starving to death, of Parisians collapsing in the streets.

'I'll take food with me.'

They described graphically the swish of tyres made by the black cars the Gestapo used as they slid ominously into the streets at night. Of people being taken by them and never seen again.

'I've done nothing so why should they come for me?' I closed my ears to the reminders of false papers and Jewish children. Surely that would not be enough for me to disappear?

What, they asked, if I was denounced as an English spy? I'd be shot, they said.

'And who will denounce me? Hortense? Tiphaine? They would never do such a thing.'

They told me of Germans killing babies. 'That was said in the last war to scare everyone senseless. The Germans would do no such thing. And you, two more than most, should be wary of scandal-mongering.'

They left the best until last. What if the Germans caught me and tortured me and I told them about their activities in Anliac?

'For a start, what do I know? You are always so secretive with me. It's highly unlikely I'd be arrested. And if I was I wouldn't tell. And this is the unoccupied zone. The Germans can't get at you here and, in any case, I doubt they'd be interested.' I said this with conviction but the truth was that I wasn't sure what I would do in such circumstances. I had this nasty idea that if someone threatened to hurt me, I'd tell them anything they wanted to hear – I'd even make things up. Not that I was about to confess this to them. And I was talking off the top of my head: I had no idea where the tendrils of the Germans reached. It was one of those things I preferred not to think about.

They finally shut up. I knew they thought me irresponsible, selfish even, but I couldn't help that. I was going, but I accepted the address of a friend of David's – just in case, he had said. After all, I no longer had any idea who or how many of my friends remained in Paris. I might need a friend.

On the train north I had plenty of time to think for the intervening year had not improved the delays in the journey. They were worse. I wondered if, back in 1939, I had known how restricted and uncomfortable my life would become whether I would have stayed on so blithely.

Whichever angle I looked at it I reached the same conclusion. Yes. There were many times when I had wished that if only I'd had a crystal ball, if only I had been certain that Fabien would go to England, I would have gone. But, then, luckily I hadn't, for if he was here now. I would only have been left in England pining for him. David had pointed out that I didn't even know if he was still there. I'd be devastated if he wasn't, or so I told myself. For niggling doubts had begun to form. I still couldn't remember what he looked like and, worse, I wasn't even sure that I cared. But I had to find out. What a muddle I was in!

What was annoying was that Hortense had written in June, the letter had reached me in October and it had taken until now, November, to get my pass. Still, what consoled me was the thought that it must be difficult for Fabien to have got into the country so he was hardly likely to be leaving in a hurry.

The carriage was uncomfortably full. There were more people than there were seats and the corridor was jam-packed too – at least I wasn't the only person who didn't mind going back. The luggage rack was bulging dangerously with the weight of the things stuffed into it. On top of one bag in the rack a small child was wedged uncomfortably between what looked suspiciously like a ham, and, from the smell, a sack of onions. It was unheard of for anyone leaving southern France not to take food with them.

The crowded conditions had one advantage: it was difficult for the French police, who boarded at regular intervals, to check our papers. To do so they had to push and shove and no one was very obliging. The inspections were cursory to say the least. I was travelling on my French papers; if asked the reason for my journey I planned to say that I was returning to Paris to see my dying sister – the real Clare Dupont had a sister who lived on the outskirts. I would just have to pray that no one checked with her. I remembered the looks I had got with my German papers when I had travelled south. Now the attitude had hardened and it would have been unwise of me to travel on them. Who knows? I might even have been thrown off the train.

There was another advantage to the squash. It was bitterly cold and there was no heating, but we kept each other warm.

Once we crossed the demarcation line the inspection of papers was not nearly as slap-happy. The train was stopped and we were all made to clamber down and line up on the platform while our papers were scrutinised. There was no attempt by the Germans to be friendly. They did not smile; they were rude and rough. They shoved an old lady who did not move quickly enough and their dogs snapped at her heels. There was a time when I would have shouted at them to stop but, like everybody else, I just stood and watched, saying nothing, but feeling wretched and ashamed at my cowardice.

'Nice legs,' said one young soldier to me. It took all my control not to slap his face at such impertinence. Instead I smiled.

'So, you understand? You speak German?' he asked, grinning back.

'Only a little,' I put on a heavy French accent.

'Maybe we could meet in Paris?'

'I'm sorry . . . My German . . . Very poor.' God, why had I even let on I understood? I'd regret this. I felt an almost uncontrollable urge to pee. I was rescued by a commotion further along the line. Someone had run for it and was being chased. As all hell broke loose he handed me back my papers. But I had learnt a good lesson: he was much more interested in my smile than in my papers. The odd thing was that when I managed to get to a lav I couldn't pee after all.

Three times this procedure was repeated. Three times we all had a good moan. And three times more people were led away from the train. We all wondered who they were and what they could possibly have done. But our conversations were discreet. David had warned me that innocent-looking people were sometimes put on the trains as plants to spy on us – that was a horrible thought.

Paris looked sad, not helped by the bleakness of the day. The few people walking on the pavements were huddled up against the chill. Their complexions were grey from lack of food and the cold. Their clothes added to this greyness, for everyone was dressed in dull colours – black, brown, and that ubiquitous grey. I knew why: such colours showed the dirt less and, with soap virtually unobtainable, they were necessary. But there was one bright colour impossible to ignore that had not been there when I left for the Auvergne. I was jarred with shock when I saw the first gaudy yellow Star of David on one old man's coat as he shuffled along. Then I saw another and another. Others seemed not to notice, as if they were now too commonplace; I hoped I never saw them as such. German staff cars whizzed by and soldiers strutted on the street. Where before there had been curiosity, resentment, belligerence and some fear in the passers-by, now all I saw was fear.

There was a long queue for transport – mainly pedal cabs. The wait was longer now for each time a German soldier appeared he immediately took precedence. They had to have the thickest skins not to be aware of the acrimony caused. Probably they simply did not care.

Once in my own pedal cab, my case strapped on the back, I enjoyed the ride – it was something new. It was like being in a high-speed pram, I decided, as we swept along at a spanking rate. Comfortingly a statue of the Madonna was strapped on the handle-bars along with a small vase of artificial flowers. My driver was young, but a couple we overtook were old men, wearily pushing the pedals round. It shouldn't be allowed, poor things.

'You look brown,' my driver – I couldn't think what else to call him – shouted over his shoulder.

'I've come from Anliac. We had a late summer.'

'You've come here voluntarily? You must be mad.' I caught his laughter as it zipped past me.

There were so few people about. I remembered these streets heaving with people and life but now, with no private cars, the city was almost silent. Then on the pavement I saw a woman dressed in blue, a wonderful hat with a bright red feather pulled rakishly to one side over her blonde hair, scarlet high-heeled shoes clicked on the pavement – a true, chic Parisian at last.

'Whore!' my driver screeched at her, and spat in her direction. 'Collaborationist bitch!' he added, for good measure. I wondered how he could be so certain. I also noticed that he'd looked about him before shouting, no doubt checking if any Germans were in earshot.

There were more German flags flying than there had been before I left. Presumably more buildings had been requisitioned. At every turn I saw the now familiar scarlet flag and black swastika. When I had left they had been just flags; now they were more ominous. The news that had filtered down to us in the south had disturbed me, despite my bravado with David and Arlette.

We pulled up in front of Hortense's house. The garden was wilder, the paintwork thinner, but it was the nearest I had to a home now. Twice I knocked – the bell-pull was not working. I was about to knock again when the door opened a crack and Hortense looked out – her face less suspicious than frightened.

'Hortense, it's me.' Still the door didn't open. 'Please let me in. I'm not going to eat you.'

'What on earth are you doing here?'

'Well, there's a welcome! Can I come in? I'm freezing.' Almost grudgingly, it seemed, she opened the door. The hall was exactly the same as when I had left, the same clutter on the console table of bills and letters, the chandelier still stranded on the floor. If anything, it was colder in than out, I decided. But the welcome was not what I had expected. Where were the hug, the squeals of delight I had imagined on the journey? I dropped my bags on the floor, put my arms up and hugged Hortense, but she stood rigid as if made of wood.

'Hortense, what is it? Aren't you pleased to see me?'

'You should never have come.'

'But I had to when I eventually got your letter.'

'My letter? Why?'

'The letter about Fabien. You must have known when you wrote it that I would have to come.'

'Fabien? What are you going on about?' She moved towards the kitchen.

'That you had seen him. That he was here.'

'I never did.'

'You told me.' Oh dear, poor old Hortense, was she going doo-lally? 'You said you'd seen the Lone Ranger – remember? My code name for Fabien.' I spoke patiently.

Hortense's eyes widened, she clapped her hand over her mouth. 'My dear child. Sit down. I saw the film – I meant the film. I thought it would amuse you.' I didn't sit down, she did. I felt my smile freeze on my face.

'You're lying. Why are you lying to me?'

'Clare, I'm sorry, I'm not.'

'I don't believe you!' My voice was rising, shrill and ugly.

'Even if I had seen him I wouldn't have told you.'

'What does that mean?' Why was she talking in riddles to me, now and at a time like this? She looked so distressed that I knew it was true: she wasn't lying to me, why should she? I was about to cry, there was no way I could stop myself. Then I noticed Hortense herself was crying.

'Oh, Clare, why have you come, and at a time like this? It's Tiphaine, she's been arrested!'

8

We were in the kitchen. It would be difficult to say who had cried the most. Certainly we both looked dreadful, with puffy eyes and streaming noses. I felt foolish now that I had come running in the way I had. I kept getting echoes of David and Arlette telling me not to go. I could be safe in the Auvergne – that, I realised, was why I cried.

Hortense, with a last mighty blow into her handkerchief, began to busy herself making coffee. Though it was awful, I drank it; I didn't want to upset her further. The anxiety that emanated from her filled the room like an invisible fog. I began to feel more edgy myself. It was such a shame. This kitchen should be a place of refuge – we had spent so many happy hours here. Surely some of that joy had seeped into the brickwork, and if so, why wasn't it fighting back? Sitting here it was easy to conjure up Mab. Yet again I wondered where she was and if she was safe. I wished that she could come back and we could begin again with no disagreements, caused by men, between us. Mab wouldn't have allowed herself to be contaminated by Hortense's nerves.

Twice I had asked why Tiphaine had been arrested. But this had been like pouring petrol on a raging fire. My questions left Hortense almost prostrate with emotion so I thought it best to wait until she brought up the subject.

'Hortense, please stop fiddling and come and sit and talk to me,' I begged.

'You should never have come.'

'So you keep saying. I'm sorry if I've put you out, I thought you would be pleased to see me.'

'Pleased? Why should I be pleased? As if I haven't problems enough. And how am I to feed you? Have you thought of that?'

'I'll get a ration card. My papers are in order.'

'Ration card? What good will that do?' Hortense proceeded to wash up the cups. She had already done so once. I wished she would stop repeating herself – she spoke to me as if I were an idiot. But finally she sat down on the chair opposite me. 'Have you heard what we are permitted – when it's available? When it's edible? You were safe in the south and you come here on a wild-goose chase. You're mad! You're stupid!' Each sentence her voice went higher, as though another gear was being engaged. I could have done without being accused once again of stupidity, but in the circumstances, and given her rising hysteria, I'd forgive her – this time. At her tirade I didn't know where to look, certainly not at her: she resembled a wild thing and it was too upsetting. 'You only ever thought of yourself. You've always been selfish. Nothing about you has changed, has it? Has it?' That last phrase was a virtual shriek.

Of course, at this point I wanted to stand up, cool, calm and dignified, and tell her, fine, I'd go where I would be welcome. But where? The little money I had would not last me long. And I had no idea if any of the friends Mab and I had made were still here. 'I'll go back, then,' I said.

'Good.' She stood up, crossed to the old porcelain sink and began to bang saucepans about noisily. This was hopeless. I got up and followed her. The kitchen was dimly lit, the bulb the dimmest I'd ever encountered, dim even by French standards.

'Hortense, please. What have I done to make you so angry?' I put my arms around her stiff shoulders, I felt her trembling and I heard a strange rustling noise. 'It isn't just that I've turned up, is it? It's something else. Tell me, maybe I can help.'

With a mighty wail, she swung round and was in my arms and was sobbing and shaking and talking incoherently. I stood feeling awkward, holding this weeping woman. I led her to the chair and eased her into it as if she were an invalid. Looking down I saw, with a shock, that at her parting were very grey hairs. She was one of those people I had thought would never be old, but she was. That, more than anything else, made me feel such a wave of protectiveness for her.

Burrowing in my case I found the bottle of *marc* I had brought her, wrapped in my undies. It was a particularly potent liqueur brewed from plums in the Auvergne, this one by Arlette's grandmother. I poured one large measure and a small one for myself – I hated the taste. 'Look, Hortense, I've a treat for you.' Hortense, seeing the drink, stopped crying. She picked it up, downed it in one, coughed, thanked me then eyed the bottle greedily. I poured her another. 'My bag is terribly heavy. I brought you so much food. You see, I didn't come empty-handed.' I smiled encouragingly at her. 'I've a pâté, rillettes, a terrine, a small jar of peaches in brandy – a host of things.' As I listed the food her expression changed, the tears dried, she was interested. Now I was glad I had paid the small fortune the food had cost me and lugged it with me, cursing the weight. 'Tell me everything, Hortense.'

'Where to begin?' She flapped her hands in that well-remembered way of hers. I noticed her beautifully manicured nails were no more – they had been bitten to the quick. 'When did you go? Were you here last autumn?'

'No, Hortense. Don't you remember? I left in January. I've been gone nearly a year.' Oh dear, I thought, her mind really was going.

'Then it was so different. Then there was a sort of mutual respect between us and the Germans, though laced with a healthy suspicion. There was even an odd sort of larkiness – do you remember Tiphaine knocking over Germans' drinks and misdirecting them, silly harmless things like that? We were all congratulating ourselves that they were not nearly as bad as we thought they would be. But everything began to change. I think they lost their respect for us. They asked for informants, you know, and they were snowed under with letters. Neighbours reporting each other. Wives denouncing their husbands' mistresses, their husbands, even. People accusing people of being Jews when they weren't. It was madness – they looked at us differently after that.'

I nodded sorrowfully. I knew this, I didn't need her to tell me but she seemed to want to let it all out.

'Then there's the food. Clare, you have no idea what a problem it is. I spend my life queuing for rations and then when I get them, often they are bad, rancid, but still we have to eat them, maggots or no.' She shuddered and I joined in. 'And now the cold. I've never known a winter like this, and we've so little fuel. Listen to me.' She stood and wriggled and I heard that distinctive crackly noise again. 'Newspaper! I'm lined with newspaper. Me! I always took such pride in my appearance.'

'Like a drawer?' I laughed, I couldn't stop myself. Hortense frowned and I thought I had gone too far; but then she smiled.

'Yes, just like that, only not scented.' And she began to laugh and once started she seemed unable to stop. 'Forgive me, but how I need to laugh.' She wiped away tears of mirth, took another appreciative sip of the *marc* and began again. 'The transportation is so bad, you see. How is food to be got into the city when there is no petrol for the transport? The rations have been cut so far that soon we shall be living on air. Why, they even sent out a warning that it might be damaging to our health to eat casseroled cat. In Paris! With our traditions!'

Dear old Hortense. I could have hugged her. Depressed, hungry, cold, she was still trumpeting the superiority of the French.

'Now is bad enough but what is to happen in the future? Our health is poor – and the children, what about them? What problems will they have in the future? It hardly bears thinking about.' I poured more *marc* – really, she had the most amazingly strong head. 'But now life is becoming intolerable. Hotheads have been killing German soldiers. It started last August.'

'Actually, Hortense it was a year last August it began.' I tried to correct her but she wasn't listening.

'Well, they won't put up with it. And who can blame them? But it is excessive to my mind to shoot fifty Frenchmen for one German.'

'Perhaps. Apart from reprisal it's to show they despise you.'

'I don't understand.'

'That Frenchmen are worthless compared with Germans.'

'Fortunately they have only shot Communists so far.'

Oops! I laughed again, I couldn't stop it bubbling up. She peered at me through the gloom. 'It's not funny.'

'Sorry.' I remembered her saying, when the Germans had first invaded, 'Better Hitler than Stalin.' I wondered if she still thought that.

'We've all had enough. We're exhausted. I thought when the Americans joined in last year that it would soon be over. But where are they? Where are the British? What are they doing? Safe and smug on their little island. They never liked us. It's all Napoleon's fault.' One thing hadn't changed: Hortense could still go off at a tangent.

'I expect they're trying.' How strange that I should refer to them as *they*, as if I was no longer English.

'So why don't they invade and liberate us?'

'They are being bombed rather badly and they do have other fronts to fight on.'

'Bah!'

'And Tiphaine?' I ventured to ask, and held my breath in case I set off the hysterics again.

'The silly girl. She's got in with the wrong people – it's their fault. They've been influencing her.'

'I can't imagine anyone being able to influence Tiphaine.'

'Then you don't know her very well,' she retorted.

'How did they?'

'It started with silly childish things. She always carried a piece of chalk and wrote Vs on paving stones and walls. On the Métro if she was near a German she would fold her ticket into a V shape. I warned her. I said she'd get into trouble. But that was her business and she's an adult so I didn't mind so much if she didn't listen to me. Then she began to make it my business. Hiding them here right under their noses. Well, that is plain dangerous and stupid and not fair on me. Perhaps a tiny sip more?' This time she didn't wait for me to pour her a drink but helped herself. 'I have two Germans billeted here, you see. Oh, they're nice enough and polite, they don't bother me and I don't bother them. It seems the best way to be. And then she does this. I've begged her. Don't you think I'm right?'

'I'm not sure what she's doing. Who is she hiding?'

'I don't know and I don't want to know – then I can't tell anyone anything, can I?'

I didn't believe her. 'But you must have known what she was doing?'

'I did not!' She raised her voice angrily. 'I go to bed at the curfew. There's nothing else to do, especially if there's a power-cut. Bed is the best place to be – it's warmer there. She waits until the Germans and I are asleep then brings these wretched people here – into my attic. Mine! She's made a hidden room up there as if it were her house. It's got beds, and chairs, she even put some pictures on the walls to brighten it up for them.' There were a lot of loose ends here; for someone who pleaded innocence she seemed to know an awful lot. But I knew Hortense: one could usually learn more from her by just letting her talk. 'I loathe these new friends of hers – I'm sure they are all left-wingers. They're very shady sorts. She talks of fighting back, of resisting the Germans. I told her she's mad. What can we do against their might? If we don't harm them they'll leave us alone. We can get on with our lives.'

'What lives? You've just been saying—'

'If you'd been here you'd have known exactly what I'm talking about. I don't have time for anything but survival. Let the politicians argue, the armies fight, I'm only interested in where I can get potatoes, bread, a scrap of meat. That's life too!'

'Sorry, I'm in no position to speak out.'

'Exactly.'

'Do you know where they've taken her?'

'No.' She spoke too quickly. She was lying again.

'When did this happen?'

'Last week.'

'And you did nothing?'

'What could I do, at my age?'

'I'll go to the police and find out.'

'You won't.'

'Then the Germans.'

'No. You're not going anywhere. It's none of your business. Leave well alone. If you go blundering in they will arrest you too and then come here and get me. Don't you see? They haven't been here, so she must be spinning them a tale. You'll spoil everything.'

'OK. Let's have some pâté, shall we?' She was working herself into a state again – far better to divert her.

'A veritable feast!' Hortense was up and busily collecting plates, easily distracted.

We had gone to bed too late the previous night. My head was clear but I had had to help Hortense. On the stairs we met one of the German officers. He was drunk and looked lecherous, but fortunately, just as he slurred a greeting, the lights went out and he was left to fumble and grumble his way to bed alone.

The bedclothes in the morning were a tumbled mess, for I had tossed and turned my way through what was left of the night. There was so much to assimilate and worry about – Tiphaine, the conditions here, what I

could do. And in the darkness, without Hortense and her chatter, I had
had to face it: my trip had been for nothing, Fabien wasn't here. But what
had made it worse had been Hortense: at the end of the evening, very
drunk, she had pointed out things to me that didn't want to hear.

'Clare, my dear, I fear Mab was right. This young man has played with
your sensibilities. You say he never mentioned marriage?'

'Now isn't the time with a war on.'

'This is exactly the time. Nothing could be more romantic, a brave
young soldier, not sure if he would live or die . . .' She was away now,
rhapsodising about love, lovers of her own, but also how I was wasting my
time. I poured her a huge drink to shut her up.

In the night, however, I thought about myself and Fabien. When I had
found he wasn't here, I hadn't really cared, if I was honest. So, why had
been pretending to myself all those months that I loved him and him
alone? I remembered Hortense, ages ago, accusing me of being in love
with love, and I'd been so angry with her. Had she been right? And if
didn't love Fabien, I was alone in the world and that made me cry.

After breakfast – if you could call it that: one dry biscuit and a cup of he
execrable coffee – without telling Hortense, I set out to find David's friend
They had the same surname, I wondered for the first time if they were
related, though David hadn't said.

Didier Pointe lived in a tall building in the Place des Hirondelles
Swallows Square. What a pretty name, I decided, as I turned into one of
those little squares that are such a delight to find in Paris, hidden behind
the great sweeping boulevards as if the planners had forgotten all about
them. It was a sad little square now; without their leaves even the plan
trees seemed defeated, and their mottled bark, which I normally admired
looked today more like disease than beauty. One shop was open and
outside stood a dispirited queue of women, clutching their baskets.

'Papers.' A German soldier stopped in front of me. As I dug into my
handbag I noted the gun he was fingering, almost lovingly, as if he wanted
to get it out of its holster and shoot someone. My heart did a nose-dive
and I had to force myself to breathe normally as he ponderously studied
my papers. He handed them back to me without a word and moved on.
watched him stride off. He stopped no one else, so what had made him
pick on me? Was it because I was the only woman in the square without
basket? I must get one fast.

Number twenty-two had no lift, but if there had been one it wouldn't
have worked. Hortense had told me that a working lift was a rarity these
days – unless it was in a building used by the enemy. I climbed the narrow
staircase, passing scuffed, anonymous doors. Long ago I had learnt never

to be influenced by these scruffy hallways for such a door might lead as easily to an apartment of exquisite taste as to a student garret.

Puffing, I knocked on the door on the sixth floor – the maids' rooms they called them. I heard soft footsteps, which paused. There was a spy-hole and I tried to look as natural as possible while being observed. It wasn't easy. Numerous locks clicked, squeaked and rasped and the heavy steel door finally swung open.

'Didier Pointe? David sent me,' I said, normally enough, for I was sure my knees had buckled. He was gorgeous.

Chapter Five

November 1942 – March 1943

1

Didier Pointe was not tall, nor was he dark – rather, his hair was a nondescript brown. So why, I wondered, as I watched him pouring us both a drink, did I find him so attractive? He was not at all like the men I usually admired and yet . . .

'Thanks for this.' He raised his glass of the *marc* I had brought with me. 'I can't remember when I last had a drink.' He had a pleasant voice. Odd, I found myself thinking, how voices were so important to me. 'David told me to expect you.'

'You've seen him?'

'We get about.' He smiled. It might have been the smile that appealed to me, it crept lazily up his face and lit his eyes. Yes, the eyes, very dark and large – eyes that I could imagine crying as well as laughing.

'I brought some biscuits with me from the Auvergne, too.' He pounced on them eagerly – like everyone here, he was hungry. He was thin, as most Parisians were nowadays, but not gawky: he did not look emaciated, but lean and lithe. 'You should have seen the train. I think there were more kilos of food than people on it.' I prattled away, but something was wrong – very wrong. My imagination was going haywire. I found myself wondering what he looked like with no clothes on, and how I would so much like to see. Help! 'Paris has changed a lot since I was last here.' I forced myself to talk of other things. I had never, in my whole life, reacted in this way to anyone. I had to control these mad thoughts, or goodness knew where they would lead. We talked of this and that. At least, we tried to, but it was a very disjointed conversation as if his thoughts, too, were elsewhere.

'So you know the Auvergne?' He had the most lovely mouth with a full lower lip. Mab had once told me that was a sure sign of a good lover. I brushed at my hair, feeling agitated.

'I was born there, in Le Puy.'

'You're not as short as some of them.' My hand shot to my mouth. That wasn't very polite. He didn't seem put out. He had lovely hands with tapering fingers and I could just imagine . . . 'Is David related to you?'

'He's my cousin.'

'Naturally.' I laughed. 'Isn't everyone related in the Auvergne?'

'You have a wonderful laugh.'

'Do I?'

'Oh, yes.'

I had to look away because he was staring at me with such intensity. While I liked it, I also found it disturbing. I straightened my skirt as if to straighten my thoughts. 'How long have you lived in Paris?' It was a banal question but interesting topics of conversation were not uppermost in my mind.

'Would you like to go for a walk?' he asked abruptly.

'Why, yes, that would be nice.' I'd be safer from myself outside.

It was not the ideal day for a stroll in the park: it was cold and misty and rain threatened. Neither of us was aware of it. The park, which in peacetime must have been lovely, was different now: the trees and roses would get no pruning this year and the flower-beds had been dug up and planted, no doubt, with vegetables.

'I expect they have to put guards on the vegetables in the spring.'

'Sorry?' he said, as if miles away. 'Oh, yes, probably.'

'I love Le Puy. I long to have time to explore it. I've only managed to spend a few hours there.'

'Did you like the red statue of the Madonna? It's made from the bronze cannons captured at Sebastopol, you know . . .' We were on safe ground as he told me of his home town, how he missed it, how he longed to return to it. 'One day, when this is all over.'

We sat on a bench and we talked and talked. When had there ever been so much to hear and say to a person? I wanted to know about his family, he was an orphan; his work, he was an architect. At that a naughty thought popped in – better than cheese! – but I squashed it flat. I didn't want to think about Fabien now. But I had to. He asked me where I was from, and I told him – no lies, no fabrication, I just knew I was safe confiding in him. Inevitably he asked what I was doing here so I had to explain about Fabien, though how I wished I didn't have to. But it was all right for he'd had a big love affair too, which, I was happy to hear, hadn't worked out, but he and the girl had remained friends.

'That's nice,' I said.

The November days were short. Neither of us noticed that the light was fading, the curfew approaching; we had too much to learn about each other.

'Oh, my God, look at the time!' I jumped up from the bench.

'Where are you staying?'

'In Passy.'

'You'll never make it.'

'I know.' I wish I could have controlled the stupid smile that insisted on appearing.

'You'd better stay with me.' I saw he was grinning broadly too.

'How kind of you.'

Back in his apartment, tucked beneath the roof, he lit a candle, explaining he could only afford the one. He apologised for having no food. Who needs food? I thought, but I didn't say it. If anything, I decided, he looked even more attractive in the candlelight. I rather hoped the power-cut would last all night.

Hortense was going to be cross, that was sure. But there was no way I could contact her. And thinking of Hortense made me realise I had forgotten why I had come here.

'Do you know a Tiphaine de Bourbonnais?'

'Who? What a name!' He laughed, but I'd noticed a slight pause before he answered me. Was he lying?

'It's not her real name.'

'And why does she have a false one?'

'She's . . . Well, it's a bit delicate, but she's a prostitute.'

He really laughed at that. 'And you know her?'

'There's nothing wrong with knowing Tiphaine. She's a lovely person. She does what she does because there is nothing else for her.' Don't spoil everything, my inner voice said.

'I didn't mean it nastily. I'm sorry if I offended you.'

I was so glad he'd said that. 'She's been arrested and I have to find her to help her.'

'Better you don't. They might arrest you.'

'Why? I haven't done anything.'

'Clare, you don't need to have done anything to be arrested these days.'

He had no suggestions as to where I should look or what I should do. Just as well I liked him so much or this would have been a wasted journey.

I'm not sure how it happened. We had started the evening sitting opposite each other but then, after a while, we were sitting nearer until finally we were side by side. I enjoyed it when his hand accidentally brushed mine. I loved it when he leant across me to get a book he wanted to show me.

'Clare, forgive me. I've got to say it. I want to make love to you.'

'I beg your pardon?' I meant it to sound indignant, it emerged like a simple question.

'I'm sorry. This is unconscionably rude and unforgivable of me. But when I saw you standing—'

'I know. I felt the same.'

'You're not cross?'

'How could I be?' And it was true. I didn't understand what was happening to me, only that it was real and genuine. I felt no fear with this man. And Tiphaine's arrest had affected me more than I realised. In this city with its ever-present sense of danger, none of us knew where we would be next week, let alone next month, or year. Why risk living with a mountain of regrets? I thought, as I slid into his arms.

He took me with such gentleness, finesse, and so slowly that my body felt as though it had never been touched before. Never been loved before. Never been awoken like this. I surrendered myself and my senses to him. As we climaxed together he withdrew from me with an agonised cry, and I scrabbled at him begging him to enter me again. But where he had been, now he put his mouth and caught my tumbling climax, miraculously reigniting it and caressing me to a point of such insanity that I had no idea existed. I became my body alone, and in my body just that one place as if the rest of me didn't exist.

We lay exhausted in each other's arms, and guilt and shame began to worm their way uninvited into my mind. I kissed him to try to blank them out but it did not work.

He sat up in the bed and, leaning on one elbow, looked down at me. 'I shouldn't have done that. I'm sorry. I don't want you to think I make a habit of this.' He smiled as he apologised and I felt confused: he was saying the words that should have been mine.

'I was about to say the same. I don't know what got into me. Only that it was right at the time – it's only now . . . But I can't say I regret it.' I blushed, then stretched. As I moved, my hand found that my stomach was sticky.

'A moment.' He leapt from the bed, to return with a flannel and gently wiped me clean. I flinched. 'I'm sorry, is it too cold? I've no hot water.'

'Why did you take yourself away from me?'

'I didn't want to take any risks with you. I didn't want us making babies – not yet.' His smile was almost shy. 'And this bloody war – there are no rubber sheaths for us.'

'Oh.'

'What did you do before? You know, to prevent getting pregnant.'

'That was no problem, he was sterile.'

'Was he?' He smiled a funny little smile that I didn't quite understand. I was embarrassed; it felt wrong to be talking of one man in another man's bed.

I felt suddenly chilled and shivered, and it wasn't just the cold. I didn't understand that either. Didier was out of bed again and from a cupboard he produced a large black overcoat. We huddled down under that.

'Is that better?'

'Much.' I snuggled closer to him.

'Thank you, my darling Clare, for giving me such happiness in the midst of all this unhappiness.'

If for one moment I had been ashamed of my actions his words made such thoughts flee. It had been the right thing to do.

Half a day later we emerged from his bedroom. We were both elated. He loved me! He hadn't told me once but countless times.

'If only we could stay here like this for ever.' I sighed.

'Forget the Krauts, the war, everything, just you and me.'

'But we can't, can we? For a start I have to find Tiphaine.'

'Look, Clare, I meant it last night. These are dangerous times, and you risk a lot if you go searching for her. They'll immediately think you're in cahoots with her, and before you know where you are, you'll be arrested too.'

'You know her, don't you?'

'I'd rather not say.'

'Then you do. Where is she, Didier? I have to know.'

I could see he was fighting with himself whether to tell me or not. So I added, 'Please,' to help him make up his mind.

'We think she's in prison, perhaps Fresnes, and that's one place you're not going. I'll make sure of that. And, yes, I do know Tiphaine, as you call her. She's a wonderful woman.'

'How?'

'Clare, you've been with David and Arlette – you know that the fewer people who know things the better it is for everyone.'

'This is different. I love her, I need to know.' That was strange. Once I had said it I knew it was true – I did feel like that about her.

'Do you know she's been helping Jews escape, hiding them in her attic?' I nodded that I did. 'Did you know she's Jewish herself?'

'No, I didn't.'

'That's put her in greater danger. I'm afraid they'll deport her to the camps – there's little to choose between that and shooting her.'

I screamed that I couldn't bear it. We had been so happy here and now it was all disappearing too fast. He held me tight. 'I shouldn't have told you that. I didn't want to frighten you. Oh, shit, what have I done?'

Stupidly I was crying. I didn't mean to, I didn't want to, it wasn't going to help anyone, least of all Tiphaine. I was shaking and I couldn't seem to stop. 'How did they find out? What about our friend Hortense?'

'She's probably safe. Tiphaine . . .' He smiled. 'I find it difficult to call her that. To me she's Becca, you see – Rébecca Weil. She told me she chose Tiphaine because it sounded more exotic and she never wanted her family to find out what she did. Anyhow, Tiphaine, like so many of the Resistance, had a second apartment where she was known only as Weil. They are bolt-holes to go to if one is found out, stocked with food and clothes and usually different papers.' Was he in the Resistance? God, I hoped not. Having found him, the thought of losing him appalled me.

'I knew that her main home, and where she hid the people, was with Hortense – not that I ever met her. It's best, these days, to keep parts of one's life separate. Normally she never hid anyone in the flat, but with the deportations stepping up . . .'

'Deportations?'

'They're sending the Jews east to Germany to camps there, even the children. That's how Becca got so involved. For the past year she's been helping the odd person escape south. But last July fifteen thousand of them were rounded up and held at the Vélodrome d'Hiver. Men women and children, the kids torn from their mothers' arms. Becca had gone there to look for someone and she saw it happening, saw the French police helping them separate the children from their parents. She heard them screaming, witnessed their agony, saw the brutality. She was devastated.' He was crying now, as he relived what Tiphaine had seen. 'She stepped up her efforts. That must have been why she had begun to use her flat as well. It was so tragically bizarre. Her neighbour is a very proper devout old woman and she reported her to the police. There were so many men coming and going the old woman thought she was running a brothel! She was raided and instead they found the refugees she was hiding.'

'That's awful!'

'Becca laughed. She actually told the old woman not to be sad, that it was closer to the truth than she had realised.'

'And the old woman?'

'She felt dreadful, understandably. But, you know, it's odd how things work out. She's very rich, she has an estate in the country and she's handed that over to us to use to hide people.'

'Us? Didier, no!'

'My darling, until this business with Becca blows over I'm keeping low. There's nothing to connect her with me. I, too, have an alias. Please don't ask me what it is.'

'I don't want to know. Didier, I'm so scared. To have found each other and now this.'

'But we *have* found each other and that's the important thing. Imagine all this misery surrounding us if we were without each other.'

For someone who was keeping low Didier had a lot of visitors – the shady people Hortense had talked about. I heard much talk of fighting, of guns. I didn't want to know. They planned how to transport people to the new house in the country. I didn't want to go. They whispered about air drops, of the Resistance. I wanted to be safe. To my shame I did nothing about Tiphaine – I was too scared.

'Hortense, I've met someone. I'm moving in with him.'

'Well, I hope he's an improvement on that Fabien.'

I let it pass. I was in no state to think about Fabien. 'He's a friend of Tiphaine.'

'Oh, one of them!' Hortense sniffed dismissively. 'You watch your step, Clare. They didn't do Tiphaine any good, did they?'

'He's not involved in you-know-what,' I lied. 'Anyhow, I've come to collect my bag. I wondered if I might leave a package here.'

'What?' She asked suspiciously.

'Just some letters. I'll hide them up the chimney in my room.'

'Love letters?'

'Yes,' I lied again.

'How romantic.'

I felt guilty as I secreted my German and British passports. I didn't want to put Didier at risk by having them in his flat. But I had to face the fact that I was placing Hortense in danger. I shrugged away the thought and consoled myself that, with her soldiers billeted there, it was unlikely she would be searched.

On Armistice Day, with their perfect timing, the Germans swept south. It was the end of the unoccupied zone. It didn't matter where one was now, everywhere was dangerous.

2

Everything in my life was turned upside down. From being alone to having this great avalanche of love, which I now received day in and day out, was a happy adjustment to make. There was one thing that marred it, though.

'I wish I'd never met Fabien,' I said one day, soon after we had met, as we lazed in bed where we spent most of our time.

'That's silly. You loved him once.'

'But not like this. It was different. I thought it was the most I could feel but I was wrong. If only I'd known it could be like this I'd have waited for you.'

'I know. I understand. All the sweet nothings we say, if only we were saying them for the first time. If only we had saved all those kisses, hugs, love.'

'Exactly, and if only I had saved myself for you.'

'But that past has made us as we are now. What if we'd met two years ago? We'd have been different. Maybe we wouldn't have felt the same way, maybe we wouldn't even have liked each other.'

Of course he was right. I could hardly expect him to love the empty-headed creature I'd been then. And I worried frequently that there was not much improvement now, that one day he might find out how awful I really was. 'How could you even say such a thing!' I remonstrated instead, and hit him with the bolster. He pretended to be knocked out and then we tumbled, and then, as was so often the case, we ended our play with passion.

'If my father could see me now!'

'In bed with me?'

'And living with you, my reputation sullied for ever more.' I could grin at this for, unlike Fabien, this man had talked often of marriage to me – when this was over.

'And what would he do?' Didier asked, as I snuggled down in the bed beside him.

'He couldn't disown me, he's done that already.' I laughed, for it *was* funny: the one thing Didier and I didn't need was a lot of money. We needed nothing but our love and a bite to eat and wine when we could get it.

'I think it's sad that you have no contact with your family. When this is all over . . .'

'But I don't need them, I've got you.'

'Maybe the day will dawn when you will need them.' He looked sad as he spoke and I knew why: he still missed his parents.

'Not unless you leave me for another woman!' To make him smile, I sat up naked and made a pretend frown at such a preposterous idea.

'As if I would.' He pulled me down beside him just as I had intended him to do.

We often talked of our future and what we would do. 'Not that my services as an architect are much in demand at the moment,' he joked.

I loved the way he made light of everything.

'Still, think of all the rebuilding there will be when we win.' We always talked like that. None of us contemplated defeat.

For now he made money using his knowledge of art: charging a small commission he advised people what price to ask when selling their paintings – it was how many people survived nowadays. He even helped the Germans find paintings they wanted to purchase – always at an inflated price, he told me, with a hefty commission for himself. It was his way of getting his own back: it could in no way be regarded as collaboration.

'Will you build us a house when this is over?'

'No. I want to find us an ancient but crumbling manor built of butterscotch-coloured stone, its windows overlooking a wild garden, with a white-panelled hall, a well, south-facing and covered in wisteria. We shall save it and restore it.'

'So exact.'

'Nothing else will do.'

'Will you build houses at enormous cost for other people?'

'No. I don't think I ever want to do that again. If I'm honest, I only studied it to please my father. I want to deal in art, I've enjoyed doing that far more. I'll have a gallery in Paris, or maybe Le Puy, where I shall make our fortune. And you will be in our lovely house caring for our babies, and each evening, when I return from my work, you'll be dressed in white and smelling of lilies.'

'Oh, my darling, let it be over soon!'

It was an odd thing but we never refered to 'the war' always 'it' or 'this', as if we did not want to acknowledge what was going on out there, or allow it to impinge on our happiness. Inevitably it did, no matter how much we longed for it not to.

His friends, the shady ones, had not been much in evidence for several weeks. There had been a retrenching after the wave of arrests in which Tiphaine had been scooped up. For Christmas and New Year there were just the two of us and, without doubt, I think it was the best Christmas of my life – 'So far,' he said. Didier had acquired a pigeon and an onion – the latter I sniffed for ages for the sheer pleasure of its smell – and we casseroled it, since we were unsure of the age of both bird and vegetable and I honestly declared it the best meal I had ever eaten. I had knitted him some socks as a present – purple: it was the only colour wool I could find. He gave me a tiny St Christopher which had belonged to his mother, and because of this it meant even more to me. 'Until this is over, who knows how many miles we shall have to travel?' he said, as he clipped it round my neck.

For my twenty-second birthday we had a small party; somehow Didier had found a bottle of wine. Louise, a dear friend of his, made me a carrot cake, and his other friends gave me little presents, a scarf, a book. They were used and old, but no less precious for that.

It was not a time free of guilt, however. There was the problem of Tiphaine. I hadn't even tried to look for her. I had no right to be so happy and she in prison somewhere. I would be punished if I didn't do something. Once more I broached the subject.

'My darling, Tiphaine would be the first to agree with me. If you attempted to find her, they would arrest you too. And now, if you did that, they would arrest me as well.' Didier was adamant. So I did nothing, saying to myself that because of him I couldn't, but deep inside me, in that uncomfortable place where fibs don't work, I knew I didn't because I was too afraid.

While we were enjoying this glorious time I knew it could not last. By mid-January 1943, his friends were joined by others full of determination and vigour. This was a momentous time for them: at last all the small Resistance groups, throughout France, were to be united as one. There was much work to be done to accomplish this. Before, Didier explained, no one had trusted anyone, and had fought and made trouble alone. They were to be united and organised, and as a result, they would be receiving far more help from the British: they would have guns, dynamite, radios and agents trained in sabotage. While he was excited and elated at this news, I was full of fear.

These meetings weren't always in Didier's apartment – that would have been far too risky. They met in different places, cafés, parks, others houses, on different days and at different times. Like the group I had known in Anliac, no one used their real name and certainly no one asked them. When Didier went out I was filled with terror until he returned. When they met at Didier's I would make them coffee, or what still passed for it, and would sit quietly pretending not to listen. I didn't like any of this, I didn't want my Didier involved.

'I don't think your girlfriend should be here,' one burly man we called Luc X complained one day. He was Louise's lover. 'These meetings should be confidential.'

'And where's she to go? It's bitter outside. We have only this one room.'

'Couldn't she go to a friend's?'

'I have no friends,' I piped up, indignation beginning to boil up at the implication. 'You are my friends now,' I added, in the hope that I would make him feel guilty.

'Women talk.'

'And men don't?' Honestly, I could have hit him.

'If something should happen . . .'

'It's not going to, Luc. You can trust her, I promise you. She worked for a group in the south, you've nothing to fear.'

'I heard she spoke German.' At this the other two men in the group looked up, concerned. So did I. Where and from whom had he heard that?

'As I do. I learnt it at school where she learnt hers. Don't be so suspicious, Luc.'

I stood up and advanced towards the table. 'May I say something? Luc, I love Didier, I would die to protect him. Could you say the same for your girlfriend?' Louise had confided to me that she thought he was having an affair with someone other than her. He flushed at this. I knew I'd won.

'I'm sorry if I insulted you, but we can't be too careful. And you're not one of us.'

'That's quite simple. I'll become one of you.' This was the last thing I wanted, but what else could I have said? I prayed, as they went into a huddle to discuss this idea, that they would reject me out of hand. I had been a fool to challenge them for unfortunately they didn't. I was recruited as a courier – a reluctant one but I had only myself to blame.

Due to the differing venues, and the differing times – so that no routine was established – couriers were needed to inform others where to be and when. There were often documents to be transported across town and, of course, the underground press. I was given a bicycle with a basket on the front and a pannier on the back. At least this one had tyres, unlike Arlette's incredibly uncomfortable wooden-wheeled one – but they were solid not pneumatic, so it was still a bumpy ride when so much of Paris was cobbled.

Each trip I took, I became more nervous instead of more relaxed, convinced my luck could not hold out. As I cycled along trying to appear nonchalant I felt sick to the pit of my stomach. German soldiers filled me with terror, as did the police, and even innocent passers-by I eyed with suspicion in case they were spies for the authorities. Every time I returned I vowed never again, but it would have taken more courage than I possessed to refuse to turn out for them. Often my situation astonished me: instead of being safe at home in England I pedalled about this city, my mind shrieking with terror.

The groups liked to have women couriers since there was nothing unusual in the sight of a woman on a bicycle equipped with a big basket for shopping. And they liked young and attractive ones so that if they were stopped by the Germans their looks were more likely to distract them. I had a nasty idea, too, that some of the men thought it easy work, suitable only for women. But if discovered we were likely to be shot just the same so I felt this was more than unfair.

One day in mid-February I was pedalling along with a message for Luc. It had been received from the BBC the night before by our radio operator. There were four clandestine newspapers and a set of forged papers for someone called Claude – always the most frightening thing to carry. It was also an unusual amount for me to transport and I presumed something big was on, though I didn't ask. It was far better that I knew as little as possible. The papers were covered by a small bag of potatoes, some knitting, some baby clothes and a light romance I was reading.

A German staff car overtook me, at speed and on a corner. I knew I was going to fall off before the bike even wobbled.

With a crash I fell to the road, the contents of my basket falling out all around me. Quickly I looked up, hoping to God that the car had swept on. What did it matter to them if they knocked me over? However, it was my misfortune to have been knocked down by a gentleman, for racing along the road back to me was an *obersturmbannführer* and his scared-looking driver.

'Mademoiselle, are you hurt? I do apologise. It was entirely this stupid driver's fault.' He was worried as he helped me to my feet and put a protective arm round me. 'Pick up the young woman's possessions, you fool!' he snapped in German to his driver. I moved, desperate to pick them up myself. The newspapers were in a parcel but I could see that the forged papers had burst free of their envelope. 'No, Mademoiselle, you must not bend down, let him pick them up for you. See, you've hurt your knee badly.' I looked down. Blood was pouring from a gash in my leg – I hadn't even noticed the pain. Fear had blanked it out.

For what seemed hours I had to stand and watch as my incriminating cargo was stuffed back in envelopes and then into my basket. 'How sad. Those lovely baby clothes are made dirty. Are they for your baby?' he asked, with too much interest.

'Yes,' I lied, hoping to put him off and amazed that I could say anything since my mouth was dry with terror.

'Let me at least buy you new ones.'

'That won't be necessary. They'll wash.'

'You are most understanding, Madame.'

'It was an accident.' I was out of his grasp now and taking my bicycle back from his driver. I went to get on and unfortunately winced from the pain of bending my knee.

'Let me give you a lift?'

'No. Please. I'm fine, really.'

'But I insist. Hans, tie the bicycle on to the back of the car. Where are you going? Your wish is my command.' He clicked his heels and bowed in a way that in other circumstances would have been charming.

Why is it that in such situations one's mind goes a complete blank? In fact I was meeting Claude in a church where a funeral was taking place – funerals were good cover. Stupidly I couldn't think of anywhere else to say, all road names disappeared.

'You're not concussed?'

'No, a little shaken. The *tabac* on rue Victor Hugo. That's where I was going.' I grabbed a name from the air.

Somehow I sat in the car, making polite conversation, and cursing myself for not having chosen a café round the corner. But finally we entered the street. 'Perhaps we could meet again?'

'I'm honoured, Herr Obersturmbannführer, but I don't think my husband would agree,' I said demurely.

'You know, you spoke my rank like a native.'

'Really? I can't think how!' I scrambled out of the car, and grabbed my bike the minute the driver had hauled it down for me. I clambered on, forcing myself to ignore the pain. The wave of relief I felt, as the car sped off and the young officer waved cheerfully from the window, was immeasurable. A group of people on the pavement outside the bar spat at me and screeched that I was a whore.

3

'I want you to stop this courier business. It's too dangerous.' Didier was pacing the sitting-room floor, he'd been doing that since I had finally returned from my trip, bloodied, looking a fright but with everything safely delivered.

'It was a scare and I thought my heart would burst from pounding, but I hoodwinked them.'

'You did no such thing. You were lucky, more like. If the driver hadn't been so stupid he would have twigged what those papers were. If the officer hadn't been lusting after you he most certainly would have.'

'And what does that mean?'

'I've seen you flirting, and don't try to deny it. But with a German! It makes my blood run cold.'

'What would you have preferred? That he arrest me and shoot me just so that you need not feel jealous?'

'I'm not jealous. I was concerned for you.'

'You have an odd way of showing it. I resent your accusations. I've never looked at a man since I met you. But if that's what you think of me then I might just as well. Maybe someone else would appreciate me and what I do more.' I flounced across the room to where a curtain was pulled across the alcove where our bed stood. I wrenched it back. 'And trust me!' I yelled, before I flopped on to the bed. I bit my lip to stop myself crying. There was no way I was going to give him the satisfaction of seeing me in tears. Ideally I wished we lived in a huge mansion, so that I could have stalked off with more style – a one-room apartment did not give one much scope.

I lay on my back and looked up at the ceiling, overwhelmed with misery, then turned on my side and studied the wall. How insufferable of him, and I had thought him different, I had thought him perfect. I'd pack and go, that's what I'd do. I'd show him I didn't need him, that I needed no one, least of all him . . .

'Clare, I'm so sorry. I'm behaving like a fool. Forgive me.'

'Didier, how could we? Forgive me, please. I love—' There was no time to finish my sentence for his mouth was on mine and we began to make love in such a hungry way, as if we had just been reunited after too long an absence from each other. In the two months we had been together, I had lost count of the times we had made love. I had been certain that we had reached the apogee of pleasing each other, but that evening, through into the night, we made love with an even greater intensity and need for each other than ever before. Had I died at that moment it would not have mattered to me one iota.

The following morning I was out early on an errand for the group – delivering some papers, I knew not what. I left him sleeping. I didn't want him to think that by setting out on this little assignment, so soon after our disagreement, I was crowing. It took less than an hour and I pedalled back, happy that I had found some bread. I would creep in and wake him for breakfast in bed . . . I had a scrape of jam . . . We would make love . . . We . . .

As I rounded the corner of the street I saw the ominous black car parked at an angle as if it had stopped in a hurry. I stood transfixed, my legs astride the worn saddle of my bicycle. I leant on the handle-bars and fought for breath. 'No!' I said in a whisper. 'They could be in any of the houses,' I told myself firmly.

They weren't. They were in ours. I watched with mounting horror as I heard the clatter of boots on stairs, the guttural shouting of orders and I saw my darling, my Didier, the sleep still in his eyes, his hair tousled. He was dressed only in a shirt – he would still have the smell of me on him

175

. . . Involuntarily my hands shot out as if I could stop them, as if my arms were stronger than their fearful-looking guns, as if I had some power they lacked. I wanted to shout. I opened my mouth, I formed the words: 'Stop! Didier! No!' But no sound emerged. My face must have said it all for me. In this street where people stopped and stared impotently, no one noticed a lone woman on a bicycle, with a stricken expression and her precious piece of bread in her basket. He was bundled, roughly, so roughly, into the back of the car. The engine roared, the soldiers – so many for one man – piled into the troop carrier behind. The small convoy began to move, it neared me. As I stood there ineffectual, powerless, he looked out of the window and he saw me, and not by a flicker did he betray me.

Only when they were safely out of the way did the little crowd that had gathered mutter and curse. I stood still with my bicycle. I was sure I had been paralysed, that I would never move again. Why had I gone out so early? If only I had been there and they had taken us together. I didn't want to live a minute of this life without him by my side.

Sense kicked in and my brain woke up. Messages were tumbling around in my head, and chaos shrieked at me. I wanted to pedal after them hell for leather, catch up with them, try somehow to rescue him. My other instinct was to go to the flat, throw myself on our sheets, inhale the scent of him, roll and cover myself with the odour of our love. But what if someone was there, waiting for me? I turned the bicycle round. I had to warn those of the group I knew, who in turn would warn others. I was aware of the code – they hoped he would hold out for forty-eight hours, and after that, if he talked, they would have scattered to the winds, papers would be destroyed, printing presses dismantled, radios hidden. I was not paralysed as I feared but cycled away from the scene as if all the demons in hell were after me.

'Having hysterics isn't going to help anyone, Clare.'

I could hear the words, the concern in Luc's voice, despite the irritation that overlaid it. I knew I should listen, I knew I should stop this noisy wailing – but I couldn't. The slap across my cheek was a shock sufficient to silence me momentarily. The hysteria changed to a sobbing despair.

'I'm sorry, Clare. I had to do that.'

I nodded that I understood and I waved my hands impotently in the air as if in some way they would help indicate to him the confusion and terror I was feeling. 'I love him,' was all I could say, over and over again. It was odd the way I was behaving. When Luc had opened the door to me and I had barged in I remembered that I had reported to him reasonably calmly all that had happened but once the words were out, once the warnings were given, I collapsed into a weeping, useless heap.

'Here, drink this.' Louise handed me a glass. 'It's Cognac. I've been saving it for the liberation. I'll have to find another somehow. You need it.'

'Thanks.' I gulped at the drink, hoping it would calm me. I didn't like to be out of control in this way: how could I be of use to Didier like this? 'I wish I had been with him. I don't know what to do.'

'Did he have an alternative place?' Louise asked. I blinked, unable to grasp what she was saying. 'You know, a bolt-hole, another identity? Only we must get to it and clear it before *they* get there.'

'He told me he had another name but I don't know it. I don't think he had any other address, he never said.'

'He was planning to go to the south, to Lyon. He was to join a group there. There wasn't much point in having an alternative,' Luc explained. I hadn't known that. Was he going without me? I felt the skin of my face tighten with this shock. 'He planned to ask you to go with him, we discussed it only yesterday.' I could have leapt up and kissed Luc at that point. 'You were to leave tomorrow.'

'Oh, no!' I wailed.

'How cruel!' Louise said. She was sitting at a table neatly and methodically folding children's clothes. It was such a normal thing to be doing at such a nightmare time. I found it calming, far more so than the brandy.

'Thank you for not losing your head, Clare. I've already got messages going out. You'll have saved the members of our cell with your prompt action.'

'When?' I felt confused.

'You were in a state for a good hour. Luc was able to get out to his contacts.'

'Was I?' How extraordinary. I glanced at my watch. She was right. An hour had passed and I thought I had only just this minute arrived, given my message and cried for a minute or two. I needed to pull myself together. I sat up straight to help me clear my mind. 'Can we rescue him?'

The look that passed between Louise and Luc was my answer.

'We would have to find out where they have taken him. If it is to a prison, then there's a slim chance. If to the Gestapo headquarters in avenue Foch or rue des Saussaies, then . . . Look, Clare, it's best not to hope too much. We'll do our best, but . . .'

'I know. I understand.' There was an awkward silence. Why had I said that? Why weren't they doing more, now, this instant? No one seemed to know what else to say. 'Still, I must get going. You'll be wanting to hide yourselves.' I stood up.

'Have you any money?' Luc asked.

'Back at the apartment.' I was putting on the coat that I did not remember removing.

'It wouldn't be wise for you to go there, Clare. Tell me, have you any incriminating papers there? Anything that would point to you?'

'No, nothing. Didier made sure of that. My clothes, my things, that's all.'

Luc crossed the room to a bureau, opened a drawer and took out a pile of money, which he stuffed into an envelope. 'Take this. We owe you more but it's all I have. There's a small hotel on the rue Savarons. They're discreet. Go there and lie low. Just in case.' I took the money. I needed it – I hadn't a centime on me. Louise kissed me, we all wished each other luck. Luc showed me to the door.

'Luc, how could they have known?' I said, before he opened the door.

'I don't know. There must be someone in the group who's collaborating. It's all I can think.'

'But who do we know who could do such a thing? Who could be such a traitor?'

'The bastard Germans, they find out things about people. They blackmail them, threaten to deport their families unless they help. I've seen it happen before. And who can blame them if their kids are at risk?'

'Then they shouldn't be involved.'

'I'd agree there. It's why I think single men only should be in the Resistance, no married men, no wives or girlfriends involved. That's why I won't let Louise take part. But, Clare, if it was because of one of our own that Didier was arrested then I think you should be very careful for the foreseeable future. What if they come after you?'

4

The receptionist at the somewhat seedy hotel close to the Gare de Lyon had not been welcoming. He did not like my lack of luggage and asked too many questions for comfort.

'Look, do you want my money or not? There are other hotels,' I said finally in exasperation.

'Feel free to patronise one of them.' He began to close his visitors' book.

I had a moment of panic. 'I'm sorry, I didn't meant to sound so abrupt.'

'I can assure you, you would meet the same reluctance elsewhere, Mademoiselle.'

'I realise,' I said, in a subdued tone when I wanted to scream at him. I rocked from one foot to the other. It was late morning and already I was exhausted. I needed to be alone.

'I have to be careful these days.'

'Yes.'

He reopened his visitors' book. 'You have your papers?'

'Of course.' I clipped open my bag, registering the look of surprise on his face.

'Well, that's something.' I handed over my identity card and he laboriously filled in my details.

'I'll pay you for a week if you want.'

'That won't be necessary, Mademoiselle. I am sure you have no idea when you will need to move on.'

My room was dreadful. The paper on the walls was damp, pock-marked and peeling, the window was filthy, it stank of stale tobacco and the bedding could not have been changed in weeks.

In normal times all this would have bothered me and made me storm out to give my opinions loudly to the *patron*. But today it would not have mattered if I had ended up in a sewer. Where I was and how was irrelevant to me as I sat on the dirty bed and gave vent to my misery.

I wept. I hoped my tears would act as a balm but they did not. I stormed at God and his injustice to me and Didier. To give us just two months of happiness then to snatch it away. I ranted at Didier, blaming him, cursing him for being involved with these madmen, for risking his life for his country when he had me. I hated him for ruining our happiness. And then the weeping ceased and I longed for rest. If I could sleep I could forget, but sleep was denied me. I sat on the bed and stared into space. I saw nothing but desolation and despair, and I wished I was dead.

When, eventually, I became aware again of my surroundings it was night time. I cursed myself for wasting precious hours. There was one saving grace to this hotel: it was situated overlooking the railway shunting yard; when the curfew came, the sound blanketed those fearful night-time noises that Parisians had learnt to dread. The roar of powerful car engines, the tread of soldiers' boots, the random shots, the knock on the door . . . If they came for me I would not hear them coming and I found I didn't care if they came or not.

Sleep did come, though I don't know when. I awoke and in those precious moments between sleep and waking I was happy, content until I recalled what had happened and where I was.

It was still dark as I fumbled along the dark corridor to where the man had shown me the showers stood. I felt sick at the sight of the green slippery slime on the tiles, the stench from the adjacent lavatory.

Hurriedly I washed myself and felt a little better for being clean. If only one could wash one's soul as easily.

'You're late!' Luc welcomed me in the café where we had agreed to meet.

'I'm sorry but I had to go there.'

'To the apartment?' He looked alarmed.

'No, to Gestapo headquarters.'

'You fool!'

'I'm sure that's where he is.' That was all I said. Luc was not the sort of person to whom I could explain how I felt drawn there so strongly. That nothing could have stopped me from lurking and watching. How I was sure that if I could get close enough and think long and hard of my love Didier would know somehow that I was near, that he was not alone.

'And what if you were seen?'

'So? What if? There were quite a few sad people there, no doubt for the same reason as me. I needed to, all right?' I snapped. 'Have you found out anything?' I spoke more politely. I couldn't fall out with Luc. I needed him.

'He's at rue des Saussaies.'

'How do you know?'

'We have the place watched for comings and goings. He was recognised.'

'By whom?'

'I can't tell you that.'

'Are you any closer to knowing who betrayed him?'

'No, no one has any idea.' He looked about the room as if checking who was there. There was something in that glance, as if he was avoiding my eyes. Did he know something? But, then, what if it was him? What if he was the traitor? I felt my heart begin to race. 'You settled into the hotel?'

'Yes. It's filthy.'

'Not the Ritz, I know. Still, the *patron* won't betray you. We keep him well supplied with goods.' So that was how it was done.

'I don't know what to do, Luc.'

'I'm afraid there's little you can do but wait.'

'What are you doing?'

'What I advise you, waiting.'

'Oh, really!' I stood up. 'I can't just do nothing. I thought you were his friend.'

'For the moment there's no information. Look, I don't want you repeating this to another soul, but we do have a contact on the inside. I see him later this week. Meanwhile, like I say, be patient.'

Back at the hotel the *patron* was waiting for me in the front hall and he was in a highly agitated state.

'Mademoiselle, you must leave immediately. They were here.' There was no point in asking who *they* were: one only had to see the fear in his eyes to know that the police and the Gestapo had visited. 'We might still be being watched. I should never have taken you in. My wife said there would be trouble. As it is, I don't think they believed me when I said you had left early this morning. Here,' he delved down behind his desk and gave me a battered card, 'go to this hotel. It's just five hundred metres from here – it's run by my sister-in-law. She'll have you if you say I sent you. But take my advice and get yourself a bag of some sort – you look too suspicious wandering around like that with no luggage.'

'But how did they know I was here?'

'Contacts. Trust no one, Mademoiselle, not a living soul, if you want to survive. If those bastards have a hint that you're involved . . .' He held up his hand at this point. 'And don't tell me what you've done, I don't want to know. But, mark my words, they won't rest until they find you. If I were you I'd get out of Paris as quickly as I could.' He began to usher me to the back of the hotel. 'It's safer if you go this way.' He opened the door on to a cluttered yard, then a gate, glanced up and down the back road, and pushed me out. I didn't even have time to thank him.

Once I allowed the fear that I was being followed to enter my mind, the vague feeling of suspicion quickly became a certainty. As I stumbled on, my panic mounting, I remembered how Didier and the others had sometimes talked of how they checked to see if they were being followed. I remembered the trick of bending down to tie my shoelace, even though I had none. Of stopping to look in shop windows so that I could glance sideways. There was never anyone there but I could not stop myself thinking there was. I had never been so afraid in my life.

The *patron*'s relative's hotel, was, if anything, worse than his. Madame also served food so as well as the appalling state of the place there was an overlying stench of boiled cabbage. On the way I had managed to buy a canvas bag and a couple of newspapers. Somewhere, I can't remember where, I had read or been told that if one lay on newspapers the bedbugs were less likely to bite.

The tears had stopped. This time when I sat on the one chair in the room and surveyed my dismal surroundings I was able to think a little more clearly. There must be something I could do.

Luc was wrong. The key was to know what was happening at the Gestapo headquarters. When I had stood there this morning I had noticed vehicles coming and going. One had been a black van. I had wondered what it was for. It had made two trips in the short time I was there. I would wait there again, and follow it on my bicycle.

My bicycle! Dear God, how stupid of me to forget something as important as that. In my rush to flee I had left it at the first hotel, in the hallway for safety. Even though I was more afraid than ever, I had to get it back.

'I'm sorry to bother you, but my bike, I forgot it.' The *patron* looked heartbroken – no doubt he had intended to sell it for bicycles in Paris sold at a premium. 'Sorry.' I felt I had to apologise for his disappointment.

'Just go!' He waved his hand urgently at me. He was so agitated that I quite expected to hear the Germans squeal to a halt outside, but no one did and I pedalled calmly away.

It took three days to discover where the black van went and what it carried. I could only follow it so far before losing it, so I waited at the last point along its route and followed it a little further each time. To my horror I found out that it went to the morgue by the Gare de Lyon. I began to ride away but then stopped. At least if he was there, or had been there, I would know that he was dead, that his suffering was over. For the hardest bit, I now knew, was the uncertainty. Of not knowing what had happened to him. And, in circumstances such as this, one's imagination could be cruel and terrifying.

The man in charge didn't want to know. Despite my pleading, despite appealing to his honour, despite anger, he refused to give me the name of anyone who had been brought there. 'Do you want me to join them?' He pushed me towards the door.

'What if I stole in when you weren't looking and had a peep?'

'There are sights in there no woman should see.'

'I need to know. I'm looking for my husband.'

'Look, Madame, I can't.'

'Please. You don't know the torment of not knowing if he is alive or dead.'

'Best pray he's dead, if you ask me.'

'I can pay you.'

'Resistance, was he?'

I nodded, unsure if I should admit that or not, but it was too late now.

'In that case I don't want your money. But if we're caught you slipped in without me seeing. Is that understood?' He unlocked a door for me. 'You've two minutes. I shall be in the yard.'

The room was long and narrow. Along each wall were shelves on which were placed grey-sheeted mounds. The air was rank and full of the pungent smell of formaldehyde; the light was dim but just about adequate. There was a dreadful silence, the only sound the rasping of my nervous breathing.

Felicity, my sister, was the only dead person I had ever seen. She had died in my arms, but she had looked as if she had fallen asleep. The only sign of violent injury was the mark on her forehead where beneath her pale skin her poor skull had been cracked by the dashboard. There was no evidence of the haemorrhage that had killed her. But here I did not know what to expect and Felicity was no preparation for what I saw when I finally plucked up the courage to pull back one of the sheets.

Although there were people here who did look asleep, as if death had come quietly, there were others who did not. The first person I saw had no face only a violent, reddish-purple pulp, like a squashed plum, where it should have been. I had to fight the wave of nausea and forced myself to look at his feet – feet that in death looked so sadly vulnerable; Didier's big toe on his left foot was proud of the next one. That day I saw no one with a toe like his. There were others who bore no scars but on their faces a twisted look of terror from when they had met an unimaginable death.

These poor people added to the misery inside me. I did not know if I was relieved or disappointed that he was not there. I rushed out into the clear air and stood propped against the wall gasping for breath, knowing that tomorrow I would have to return.

That night as I lay awake the images of the day raced across my mind, and when sleep came my dreams were peopled by the victims I had seen that day.

'He's alive and he hasn't talked. He's a brave man,' Luc told me, at our rendezvous in a park, both of us bundled up against the cold.

'I know.'

'How?'

'I go to the morgue each day. I look at the bodies,' I said bleakly.

'That can't be fun.'

'No. But they're not all victims. Some days are worse than others.'

'How many times have you been?'

'Four times. It's a week today, you realise. In a way it seems like yesterday and yet also that he was taken from me years ago.'

'Poor Clare. He really loved you, you know.'

'Don't talk about him as if he were dead!' I stood up abruptly, not liking this, wanting to get away from him. For all his sympathy, there was something about this man I didn't like.

'Look, Madame, I'm sorry for your predicament, but you can't come here any more. It's too dangerous. Each time I think I'm going to have a heart-attack from the anxiety.' The mortuary attendant looked at me intently as if unsure whether I understood his words.

'What if I didn't come each day? Maybe just three, two times a week?' I pleaded.

'No, I've made up my mind. I'm sorry, if you come here again I'm calling the police and you will be arrested for trespassing.'

'I understand. You've been kind to me. Thank you. But can I look just this last time?' I wanted to be here yet I didn't, so although I was appalled at his decision I was also relieved that he had decided for me.

He looked doubtful. 'Just this once, then, but be quick.'

I had time to look at only one body before there was a great commotion outside. The door burst open. Dark-uniformed French police, followed by German soldiers in grey, poured into the room. Two squat men who wore no uniform brought up the rear.

'Clare Dupont?' The policeman in charge demanded. I nodded miserably and winced as my arms were grasped and pulled roughly behind my back.

5

The impressions I had after my arrest were strangely fragmentary. I sat in the back of the car wedged between two short, burly men who wore black leather coats and black hats and who on any other day would have looked theatrically ridiculous and would have made Didier and me laugh. On the pavement I noticed a child of about four, playing with a ball, and found myself worrying for his safety. I was aware that the sun was shining: it was one of those pale, silver days that hints of spring and the stronger sun to come. I saw women in a queue, and wondered what they waited for. I was anxious about my bicycle and I hoped that the mortuary attendant, in the car behind me, would not be in trouble. What a silly thing to think! Of course he would be. For myself I had no fear. I felt detached, as if I were watching this happening to someone else, and, in a very odd way, I felt relieved – that the gnawing fear in my stomach every time I acted as a courier had gone for good.

We arrived at the headquarters in rue des Saussaies and I was bundled out. I made no move to resist so could not understand why each time we moved they were so rough with me. Forms were to be filled in. I watched nervously as a young woman in the grey uniform of the Nachrichtenhelferinnen, the female clerks, wrote laboriously, frowning frequently. All of

Paris called them field mice because of the unflattering colour of their uniforms. I smiled; she did not seem nearly as frightening now.

'Why you laugh?' she said, in heavily accented French.

'I'm sorry.' I hoped I looked sufficiently apologetic.

I was stripped and searched, a humiliating experience. My possessions were listed and then I was shown into a room. For over an hour I estimated – they had taken my watch – I sat alone. That strange feeling of detachment, no doubt caused by shock, had deserted me. Now, as my mind ticked off the minutes, my fear returned and mounted until every muscle and nerve in me was filled with dread.

'I do apologise for keeping you waiting, but I've got behind with my forms. And with nothing for you to do. We should have magazines, don't you think, to while away the time?' A pleasant-faced middle-aged man stood over me, smiling in a friendly manner.

'I don't mind,' I said unsurely. I had prepared myself for punishment not pleasantries.

'Right. I've a few questions to ask you.' He sat at the table opposite me and placed on it a pile of folders. He picked one up and laid it between us. Emblazoned on the front in capital letters I read Didier Pointe. It had obviously been placed there on purpose so not by the flicker of an eyelash did I let on that I had registered it.

'Monsieur Pointe tells me that you work together, in this pathetic organisation your comrades have recently formed and called . . . Let me see . . .' He shuffled the papers again. 'Here it is. The Movement United of the Resistance – MUR.' There it was again, the pleasant smile.

'I'm sorry, I know no one of that name. Nor anything about such a movement.'

'Then you must be very forgetful, Madame, for to my knowledge you lived with him. He told me so. Also that you worked as a courier for your group, busily cycling about Paris on errands.' He made it sound such a casual thing, a game, and his French was so perfect that, despite the uniform, I began to wonder if he was French.

Back and forth this conversation went, he insisting, I denying. I was convinced that Didier would not have mentioned my name.

The blow to the back of my head caught me unawares, I had not even known anyone else was in the room – I had seen no signal from the smiling man. I reeled, shafts of light danced before me and I was assailed by a feeling of sickness.

'So unnecessary, and such a pretty young woman too.' The smiling one leant forward. 'Make it easy for yourself. We have all day. Just tell me who the others in your group are and then we can all go home.'

'I've nothing to say. I know no one and nothing about any movement.'

I tensed myself for another blow. He leant back in the chair with a satisfied smile. In a fleeting moment I realised he was relishing the anticipation of me being beaten.

I had mistakenly thought that nothing would hurt me as much as the first smash to my head. I was wrong. I don't know how long I was there, only that it seemed never-ending. When it was over I could not stand up.

'Have a pleasant evening,' the smiling one said, as he left me.

Alone, I slumped on the table. I would have liked to weep but it seemed I was past crying.

There was a routine. Those prisoners alive at the end of the working day were transferred to a prison. The black van was waiting for us as another four women and I shuffled towards it. So it didn't just carry corpses, after all.

At the prison there was yet more form-filling, more searches – though where I was supposed to have acquired anything to hide since the previous search was a mystery to me. Finally we were placed in a cell.

It was dark and it took time for my eyes to become acclimatised to the low light from one meagre bulb set in the ceiling and protected by a metal cage.

'Are you all right? Are you in pain?' a voice from the gloom asked me.

'Yes and yes,' I managed a weak laugh.

'Let me see.' My face was held between two gentle hands and through my rapidly closing eyes I saw an old woman with improbably blue and kind eyes. 'How could they? Françoise, in that parcel you received today you had some ointment. And don't say you didn't because I saw it.'

'I don't know her, I'm not letting her have it. Why can't she have some of Christiane's?' a voice snarled from the other side of the cell.

'Because I say so. Just look at her.' I didn't like the woman's concern: I knew I looked a mess but from her voice it was worse than I'd feared.

'It's not fair!' There was a rustling.

'She can have some of mine,' a faint voice said.

'Christiane, you are an angel.' I felt a soothing cream that smelt of disinfectant being spread over my face. Pads with what I thought was witch-hazel were placed on my eyes. 'Have you eaten?'

'I can't remember.'

'Probably not. Our hosts are not famous for their hospitality.' She laughed. 'Here, this is a dry biscuit and we have a little water.'

'Why should she have what's left of the water?'

'Françoise!' the older woman said, in a tone that brooked no argument. With difficulty I ate the biscuit and, with relief, drank the water. It tasted foul but I was so thirsty and my mouth was so sore. 'There are only two beds, tonight so you shall have mine.'

'Madame, I couldn't possibly.'

'There must be no argument.'

'Madame Chloë, why the hell do you always manage to make me feel so bloody guilty?' another voice – that made four – complained.

'Martine, that is the last thing I should want to do.'

'What's your name?'

'Clare.'

'Well, Clare, don't let this old harridan con you as she has me. You'll sleep in my bed.' In her voice it was easy to hear that there was a true and affectionate bond between Madame Chloë and Martine.

In the morning when I awoke I was stiff yet rested. I opened my eyes gingerly expecting not to see but finding, with profound relief, that I could, even though my sight was a bit blurred.

'We let you sleep. We answered for you when they called your name.' Madame Chloë was sitting on her bed and had been watching me. We were alone.

'Where are the others?' I winced as I sat up in the bed – a misnomer for the plank on which I lay and the rough, somewhat smelly blanket that covered me.

'Gone for the day. Hopefully they will be back this evening.' I was not yet aware of the significance of that 'hopefully'. 'Now, I suggest you eat something.' Madame Chloë had to be in her late seventies yet moved with surprising ease to retrieve a small cardboard box from under her bed. Despite the dishevelled state of her clothing, she managed to look elegant. I couldn't work out why until I realised it was her hair, white as snow, brushed smooth and knotted neatly, since no pins were allowed, into a loose chignon. It was as if all her years of dignity were now concentrated in it – and in her eyes, which shone with kindness and, I was sure, goodness. She behaved very much as if she were at home and I was her guest, fussing over me as she served me a tiny biscuit, laid on a scrap of linen in lieu of a napkin, which she also had in the box. 'Even if it is difficult I believe we should improvise to maintain standards,' she explained. 'The food here is virtually non-existent. They allow us to have the occasional parcel from outside. Of course, it cuts down on their expenditure. Do you have family who can supply you?'

'No one.'

'Then I shall share mine with you. Martine will too. Christiane receives little and, as I'm sure you are aware, one cannot rely on Françoise.'

'Was that the woman who objected to me having the water last night?'

'Yes, poor dear. She is not adjusting well. She only gave it to you because she is more afraid of me than of starvation.'

'I should have refused it.'

'Nonsense. You must drink and eat whenever anything is offered to you, even if you have to force it down. You have no idea when you will next be given food.'

'How long have you been here?'

'A year.'

'How have you borne it?'

'I have learnt that one can bear far more than one at first realises. But I shan't be here much longer. They tire of me.'

'You always say they, never "the Germans".'

'I do not wish to dignify them by calling them that. I have many dear friends who are of that race and if they knew what was being done in their name they would die of shame. These people, it would seem to me, are not of the same nationality. They are mutants.'

'Should you be saying things like that?'

'No. And I have already been beaten for it. But I shall continue. I am not afraid of them, I have made my peace with God and they know it, and will now leave me alone.'

'They beat you? But you are—'

'An old woman? Was that what you were too polite to say? My dear, age and position mean nothing here.'

'I'm half Austrian,' I blurted out.

'Then tell no one. You shouldn't even be telling me. They would shoot you. And say nothing of significance in this cell. I fear that one has been planted here to report on us.'

'Who?'

'Better that you work it out for yourself, my child. Then you will be careful in front of everyone. I hasten to reassure you that it is not I.'

'I didn't for one moment think you were.' I managed a somewhat painful smile. 'Might I ask why you are in here?'

'I hid a British airman. Unfortunately my brother-in-law, always a fool, saw it as his duty to report me.'

'How awful for you.'

'It was, rather, and for my poor sister. But war does this sort of thing to families.'

'I've seen some of that too, not as bad but . . .' And I was able to tell her all about Fabien and his mother. 'So, you see, she didn't approve of me.'

'It sounds as if she is too aristocratic for her own good – or she would like to be.' She smiled knowingly. 'Either way she is a fool. Fools are fairly common with our noble families. We intermarry and, as a result, weaken the strain – just look at the idiot who is married to my sister.'

How strange it was to be sitting here in this gloomy cell, shivering with cold and discussing such matters. But it was comforting.

'What have the others done?'

'Dear Martine, she's not sure. She was denounced by a neighbour who, she thinks, was having an affair with her husband. It is genuine, I am sure, and she will be freed, I am equally sure. The little one, Christiane, she was caught stealing food from them, and dealing in the black-market. She is a prostitute and because of that she is not popular, but I like her. She is honest and generous. She had a miscarriage in here. They would not take her to the infirmary. We did what we could for her but . . . She's barely spoken since.'

Then I told her about Tiphaine and asked whether she had come across her. She pursed her lips. 'Bad enough to have been hiding Jews but to be one herself . . . After so long I think you should accept that she has already been deported to their camps in the East.'

'And the other woman?' I changed the subject not wanting to think that was Tiphaine's fate.

'Françoise was involved in the Resistance.' She said it in such a tight-lipped way that I was certain she was the suspected informer.

'Where are they now?'

'Gone for questioning.'

'Why weren't we taken too?'

'They know I know nothing. And you? Probably they are giving you a day to think of the horror of yesterday so that tomorrow you will be more likely to tell them what they want to hear.'

'But I know nothing. I have nothing to say to them.'

'Take my advice, my dear. Say something, anything, so that they can scribble their little notes. All the time you are talking they will not be beating you, now, will they?'

As evening drew on, we heard the banging of doors along the dank stone corridor.

'They're back.' Madame Chloë straightened her blanket and tidied her hair, as if preparing herself for visitors. 'Before they come, that little matter you told me about being half Austrian. You speak the language? Then, my dear child, when you get out of here I think you should use it in some way. Such a gift – you owe it to the women who will not be so lucky.'

'*If* I leave you mean.'

'No, *when*. Never give up hope, Clare, for if you do you are finished. Ha! The weary travellers return,' she said brightly, as the door to the cell crashed open.

That night I could not sleep: there was so much to keep me awake. This was a noisy place – there were cries in the night, a background of sobbing, doors banging. Over all was a thick miasma of misery which I could almost touch. I could not erase from my mind the terror of the day ahead. There was fear for Didier, and for Tiphaine. But on top of this I longed for my home. I wanted my father. I wanted to see him, to smell him, to have him hold me. I cried as softly as I could, but in the night it was Madame Chloë who comforted me.

6

The days melted one into the next so that I could no longer say what day of the week it was or how long I had been here. But Madame Chloë kept count. I was astonished when she told me eight days had elapsed.

Each morning they would come with their lists and call out the names of those who were to go to rue des Saussaies. The relief of those who were not named was expressed in a great sigh that ran through the prison.

'This must have been how it was during the revolution when they came to the Conciergerie for our ancestors to take them to be guillotined.'

'Madame Chloë, what a gruesome thought! Stop it do!' Martine wailed.

'They wouldn't have taken any of mine.' Françoise laughed.

'No, Madame, I'm sure yours were knitting as the tumbrils rolled by,' Martine snapped.

'Did they chop off the heads of any of yours, Clare? Were they from Lyon or Paris?'

'They bore their fate, we must bear ours,' Madame Chloë said briskly, neatly deflecting Françoise's question.

Some days the beating was more intense. On others they tried half drowning me, or talked to me, which was the most alarming of all. Without doubt the worst time was when I was being marched along an underground corridor and saw, coming towards us, two guards dragging a man between them. As they drew close one yanked up the man's head by his hair. The face was badly beaten but it was my Didier. He saw me I was sure of that. Neither of us reacted and we were dragged in opposite directions. What made it worse somehow was not being able to tell anyone I had seen him. I could not risk confiding even in Madame Chloë, for what if they beat her to make her tell? The following day they were particularly brutal but I felt exulted. He had not talked and I was paying for it!

What still occupied me was who had betrayed us. If I ever found out, the memory of my love, battered and half dead in that passageway, would be sufficient for me to kill them. But I could not marshal my thoughts: I was always either recovering from a beating or preparing myself for the next. I would begin to think logically through our circumstances and all those to whom we had spoken, but I could never reach a conclusion. I knew a clue was hidden somewhere, just waiting to be unlocked – if only I could clear the confused fog that was now my mind.

I slumped in the chair to which I was tied. I had been unconscious. As I came to, I pretended still to be out cold – they wouldn't waste their energy hitting someone who couldn't feel.

'We're wasting our time. I really begin to think she knows nothing,' the smiling one said in German to his brutal companion.

'But your informant was adamant. She knew her movements.' I heard him light a cigarette. The first spoke in an educated voice; the other's accent was thick and guttural. 'Don't forget it was she who told us she could be found at the mortuary. I say we carry on. She was living with that scum Pointe and she'll know the others.'

I realised I was holding my breath. Of course! A woman! How could I have been so blind, so stupid? Suddenly all the fear in me was replaced with a hatred so fierce it was like a great fire. It was Luc of whom I had been suspicious but it had been his girlfriend Louise. I had told only him about visiting the mortuary and he must have confided in her – but why had she done such a thing? Suddenly I had an image of her folding children's clothes. Was she afraid for her children? If only I could escape and warn the others.

'Throw some water on her. She's been out long enough.'

That night I could not sleep and not because of the pain in my body: I lay planning my revenge on Louise. As I worked out the most outlandish plans, hatred continued to build in me. But it did not last: after a couple of days, when the initial shock had begun to fade, I realised that I had to control it if I was to survive.

Several days had gone by without me being called so I began to hope that the smiling one had won and that soon I would be released. Then early one day Madame Chloë was summoned. We feared for her but within the hour she was back. She entered the cell without saying anything but acknowledged our joy that she had not been beaten. But I noticed she had taken her parcel from beneath the bed. Carefully she wrapped a minute sliver of soap in her linen napkin with her comb and gave it to me. With mounting concern I saw her take her precious packet of biscuits next and divide them into three mounds. She gave one to

Martine, one to Christiane and the last to me, each time with a kiss. Françoise she ignored.

'Madame?'

'Peace, my child. No recriminations.' Then she sat on her bed, put her hands in her lap and closed her eyes. She was praying.

When they came to take her we were all weeping, except Françoise, and even she looked sad. At the door Madame Chloë turned and smiled at us. 'Ladies, it has been a privilege to know you.'

Later that day we heard that they had shot her.

The days lurched on. I went nowhere. The others told me the weather was getting warmer: spring was coming. Many other prisoners communicated by banging on the pipes in Morse code. I had tried but I could never remember the sequences and quickly gave up. As I knew no one here I could not see the point in persevering. All I had was my thoughts: no one could take those or my memories away from me.

I thought of my home and prayed I might be spared, if only so that I could tell my father how wrong I had been: I understood his grief now in a way that, when I was thoughtless and immature, I had not.

Felicity was often in my thoughts and when I dreamt of her I always felt better, more composed. It was as if she visited me to tell me that all was forgiven.

Best of all were the times when I relived my life with Didier. I went over our days together, our lovemaking, our jokes. I found I could almost sense him with me, smell him even. I was so grateful for that time and that love, for I knew now, in my heart, that my darling was no more. That I would never again hear him tell me he loved me, that our plans would remain unfulfilled.

There was no logical explanation for how I knew. One day, alone in the cell, I had felt him there with me, even though I could not see him. He had brushed my lips, I felt the touch of his hands and, despite my sadness I felt a great sense of calm. I knew he had come to tell me he was dead.

Martine was released. 'I'll get a parcel to you both,' she promised. 'Any messages you want me to deliver?'

Christiane gave her the address of a friend. I was tempted: I wanted to warn the members of the group, I wanted to tell Hortense I was alive. But I stopped myself. What if this was a trick and Martine was not going to be set free – that at the last moment she would be interrogated and give up their names?

Once it became obvious that we knew what she was, Françoise had been removed from our cell. Christiane banged out a warning on the pipes that no one should trust her. We learned later that this had been so successful that Françoise had been moved to another prison.

Other prisoners joined us. I talked to them, of course, but I didn't want to grow fond of them. Madame Chloë's death had affected me badly. I could not risk having to go through that grief again.

One day I was taken back to the Gestapo headquarters and beaten mercilessly but still I had nothing to tell them.

'I wish you had talked, Madame – I might have saved you. As it is . . .' the smiling one shrugged '. . . you are to be deported.'

I forced myself to control my initial terror. Rumours abounded as to what that meant. We had heard of camps where people were forced to work until they dropped, of others where they disappeared. Once alone, though, I began to reconsider: without Didier, I did not care that perhaps death awaited me.

With the normal efficiency, forms were filled in and documentation completed. I had been handed back the coat I had worn on the day I was arrested, and my handbag, which even contained the few francs I had had. We were assembled in a large hall; then divided into two groups: those who were being freed, and us the next shipment of women to be sent by train to God alone knew where.

'At least it'll be a change of scenery,' rasped a voice from the next bench. The effort made her cough, which amused her for then she laughed. It was odd to hear laughter in that place – but it had been a pretty tinkling sound that triggered a mass of memories in me.

'Tiphaine!' I swung round. I would never have recognised her, but for that laugh. Her body was gaunt, her hair, which had once been fair, was matted, of an indiscriminate colour and undoubtedly crawling with lice. Her hands, which she held politely to her mouth were dreadfully scarred and bloody rags were wrapped round the finger tips. She had no teeth and the light in her eyes had been replaced by dread.

'Little Clare, is it you? What are you doing here?' She coughed and spluttered between sentences, just as poor Pauline had.

'I've been here just over a month, I think.'

'Time flies when you're having a good time . . .' Again, she was overcome by coughing.

'Are you being deported?'

'Yes.'

'At least we'll be together.'

'That's nice.'

'You knew my Didier?'

Oh, the unmitigated joy of having someone who had known him to talk to about him. We whispered to each other, and I supported her for she was so weak that just the effort of sitting vertical seemed too much for her. But, even though it cost her dear, she maintained her upright pose.

'They tell me you must look fit, otherwise—' She made a chopping motion with her hand across her throat.

It was our turn to move. We were pushed and shoved towards the tables where a row of 'fieldmice' were processing paperwork. We had each been given a number and Tiphaine and I were both headed to table four. As I felt the gun in my back, pushing me forward, I imagined wrenching it from the soldier's hands and shooting half a dozen of them before they killed me.

'Name?' It was my turn. I didn't normally look at them, I found it easier to deal with them if I didn't see their faces.

'Clare Dupont,' I said, but this time I stared as arrogantly as I could at the woman in her unbecoming uniform. 'Heidi!' I had said her name before I could stop myself. Oh, my God, what would she do now? She would denounce me for sure. They would learn that I was English. And they would arrest Hortense . . . The room swam and I had to clutch the table to stop myself falling.

'Clare, is it you? But what on earth . . .?' Heidi had also spoken before thinking; she looked nervously about her but the women on either side of her were too engrossed in their bullying to have heard her.

'It's a long story.' I managed to smile: I wasn't going to let her know how scared I was.

She riffled through a pile of folders. 'Dupont, you said.'

'That's right,' I said, as firmly as I could.

She found one with my name on it. She glanced at it and, as she did so, I saw her hand go involuntarily to her mouth as if she didn't like what she read. She reached for a form. I watched her scribble my name. Saw her stamp it – So much for friendship, I thought bitterly.

She leant across the table. 'Do you remember, at Madame Hortense's, we vowed that this war would never mar our friendship?' I nodded miserably. 'Then take this and go as far away as you can,' she whispered, and thrust a release form into my hand.

'Oh, Heidi, dear God, bless you.' I clutched the paper that spelt freedom to me. 'But . . . I have a friend here.' Frantically I tried to remember her real name. 'Rébecca Weil. She's been good to me. Please give her one too.'

Heidi took out another folder, glanced at it then at me. 'Clare, she's Jewish. If I let her escape I might be shot too.'

I pushed the form she had given me back across the desk. 'Then I can't accept this. She needs me. Give me the other form.'

Heidi looked at me in disbelief. She sucked her pen, looked at the bedraggled scarecrow standing beside me. 'You don't know me, is that understood? Get out of Paris today. If you're caught I don't know you, I made an error – overwork . . .'

7

'You can't stay here! What do you mean by coming here? It's not fair, it's so dangerous!' Hortense, jumping up and down around the stranded chandelier in her hall, was screaming at us. Her face was red, she was perspiring, I feared she would have a stroke.

'It's only for a couple of days until I can work out a way of getting us south.' I tried to sound reasonable but I was shocked to the core. I had thought Hortense regarded Tiphaine as a daughter, and she had only to look at her to see that she was on her last legs.

'Much good that will do you. They're everywhere, the Boche. The whole country is riddled with them. Everywhere!' She sobbed and pressed her handkerchief to her mouth. 'You have no right to endanger me in this way. And just look at her! She's crawling with lice. She's filthy. She's—'

'So? So am I. You're going to turn us out for that? We can wash, we can cut our hair. Have you no pity?'

'Don't you lecture me.' She had calmed down a scrap, and I thought she looked a bit embarrassed. 'Can't you see? She's ill, she needs a hospital. I can't have you, I have no facilities!' She began to wail again. 'The Germans who live here could be back at any minute,' she howled.

'Hortense, I understand your reluctance, but we have to stay and there's an end to it. We've nowhere else to go.'

'You always were selfish, Clare, always! Your father warned me. I just knew I hadn't seen the last of you.'

'Hortense, leave my father out of this. We're staying. I suggest you get Tiphaine to bed in the attic she made for her refugees. I'll wash and then I have to go out.'

'You can't speak to me in this way.'

'I just have. I'm sorry, Hortense, I understand your fear but—'

Tiphaine fell at our feet in a dead faint. A scarecrow she might have been, but to carry her upstairs took all the strength the two of us could muster. But she had to be moved at once.

'The main problem is that she coughs all the time.'

'Has she got TB?'

'How on earth would I know? She's ill, she needs care and warmth.'

'What if she coughs in the night and they hear her? They're young, not deaf old men.'

'Then put some rouge around your nose, pretend you've a cold. Make out it's you coughing.'

With Tiphaine finally settled, I had a bath – if one could call the two inches of tepid water I sat in a bath. But I washed my hair and managed to scrub the stench of that dreadful place from me, though I was convinced I would never get rid of it altogether. The feel of the bath towel around me was pure luxury. I was glad now that I hadn't taken all of my clothes south for I was able to put on clean underwear as well as top clothes. I burnt the ones I'd worn in prison.

Seeing myself in the mirror was a shock. I must have lost a stone at least, but once I'd brushed my hair, put on some vanishing cream and practised a few smiles I looked better.

Fortunately Hortense had not sold my bicycle – because she had forgotten it was in the garden shed. It had rusted since I had last ridden it. I thought longingly of the one the group had acquired for me that I had left at the mortuary. I had never found out what had happened to the man and I wondered if I dared risk going there to check if he was all right. Better not, I decided, as I put on my hat and gloves.

'I don't think you should go out. What if you're caught?'

'Hortense, I explained to you, I have my release documents. No one is going to hurt me and I have things to do.'

'What? No!' Her hands flapped. 'Don't tell me. I don't want to know.'

'I wasn't going to.'

I set off, not sure quite where to go. When the meetings had taken place in Didier's apartment only four were ever present – and I guessed that they had been just a small splinter of the whole network. Of these four I thought I knew where two might live, but I was not sure.

At the first flat I went to I had no luck: an elderly widow lived there and, while helpful, knew of no Antoine. I cycled on to where I hoped Claude lived. To get there I had to pass the square where Didier had his apartment. I wanted to go there, longed to. Just to see it one more time, to smell it – Did it still smell of him, I wondered. At the end of the street I paused: it was deserted, it would have been so easy, the temptation was so great . . . I got back on my bicycle and pedalled on resolutely.

At the next house a young woman answered: she had the expression of one who lived with fear and dreaded a knock on the door.

'I'm looking for a Claude. I'm afraid I don't know his second name.'

'And who's asking?'

'My name is Clare.' I said this quite loudly for I sensed that someone was in the dark hallway listening.

'We don't know anyone of that name. I don't know you.'

'I realise that. Look, I've just been released from prison—' At that she began hurriedly to close the door. I put my foot in the way to stop her, and we tussled inelegantly. 'Stop. Please listen to me. I think Claude was one of a group involved with my fiancé, Didier. He's dead.' That was the first time I had said those words and they cost me dear, as if by saying them I was making his death an incontrovertible fact. There was a catch in my voice that I could not hide.

'Clare?' A voice came from behind the woman.

'Thank God, Claude! I wasn't sure . . .'

'Come in. It's OK, *chérie*, I know this young woman. I'd heard you'd been taken.'

'I expected you all to have dispersed.'

'We had. I had to come back.' He nodded at the woman and now, in the better light from the windows in their small sitting room, I could see that she was heavily pregnant. 'Everyone thinks I'm mad but some things are more important in life, aren't they?'

'Does anyone know you are here?' I must say I thought he was pretty mad myself, risking his life to hold his wife's hand.

'No.'

'Are you sure? Especially Luc.'

'Luc's in Lyon. It's becoming an important centre of activity.' He smiled, proud of what the Resistance was beginning to achieve.

'Only . . .' I filled him in about my suspicions of Louise.

'Jesus! She's there with him, she's involved. She's doing courier stuff, same as you did. You've no proof?'

'None. But it has to be her. Luc was the only person who knew I went to the mortuary every day searching for Didier. And the Germans referred to a woman informant, not a man.'

'We should just thank our lucky stars he didn't tell her you spoke German.' At that I blanched at what might have happened if he had. 'It has to be her. Luc wouldn't do anything like that. It's not in his nature – and especially not to Didier, they went back a long way. He was in love with Didier's sister, you know.'

How long would I continue to find out things I hadn't known about Didier? I was hungry to know more, for our time together had been so short that there was still much to learn, yet the finding out was painful.

'I overheard you saying that Didier was dead.' He took my hand, as if he thought that might ease this conversation.

'I think so.'

'Then you don't know for sure?'

'I saw him . . .' I had to take a deep breath to continue. 'They engineered it, hoping we would acknowledge each other. Except we didn't. He looked . . . He couldn't have gone on much longer.'

'But he might have, Clare. He's young and fit and brave . . . Don't give up hope. He might have been deported. He might escape.'

'Yes,' I said simply. There was no way I could explain to this man, who I hardly knew, that I was certain Didier was dead, that there had been a moment when I felt his spirit leave. It had been so strong that he must have been thinking of me at the point of death and the solace that gave me was too dear to share with anyone.

'But tell me about the mortuary attendant. They arrested him too.' I had to change the subject – I felt too close to tears.

'He was released. He'd had a good beating and he won't do that again. But then, poor sod, he had to face his wife. He told someone he thought the Germans were more merciful.'

'Wasn't she just relieved to have him back?'

'No, he got a right telling-off for letting a pretty young lady persuade him to put everything at risk. I don't think she'll ever forgive him,' Claude said. 'Still, to business. We must get you and your friend south as soon as possible. Leave that to me. She's ill, you say? Can she not rest and get better?'

'Not really. The woman we are with is rather . . . agitated by our presence.' At that understatement I allowed myself to grin.

'Are you safe there for a couple of days while I set things in motion? You had better give me your address.'

I was reluctant to do so but I could not see that I had a choice.

'Maybe we can meet up. I'm going to Lyon too.'

'Why's everyone going there?'

'Well, you knew that working for the Germans – or, rather, slave labour – is now obligatory for men?'

'I hadn't heard.'

'They're having to combat their losses in Russia. Every able-bodied man is being taken from their factories and mines so replacements have to be found. Us.' He stabbed his finger at his chest. 'To avoid it, men are fleeing into the hills, and the Auvergne is such a wilderness that it is ideal for hiding. Lyon is close enough to the region to be a centre of activity. There is a lot of training to be done, camps to be set up, documents to be made, food and supplies to be got to them. We have the beginnings of a veritable army now. And we need it against the Milice.'

'Milice?'

'They were formed just before you and Didier were arrested. We'd heard about them but perhaps Didier didn't want to worry you. They're a new police force, and brutal bastards they are too – French, which makes them even worse. We know what to expect from the Germans but one's own countrymen!' He shook his head as though in disbelief. But then he brightened. 'Did you know that the Germans were defeated at Stalingrad in January? And they've been in retreat in Africa too.'

'Oh, that's such wonderful news. If only—' I knew how sad I looked.

'We all have real hope now. Things are beginning to move our way,' he interrupted, aware I was thinking of Didier again. How sad that he could never have known the tide was turning. 'Clare, if the worst comes to the worst, you've had the privilege of knowing Didier, the knowledge that he was in there fighting for his country.' I nodded mutely. 'Did you know he was one of those who marched down the Champs-Elysées that first Armistice Day in nineteen forty, cocking a snook at the Krauts? Oh, yes, he was there.' Another precious scrap of information. It made me smile. 'That's better.'

While we talked Claude's wife served us tea, and in an odd way it was all very pleasant, a glimmer of what life had once been.

'If it is Louise, I'd love to know why, if you ever find out.'

'Don't you worry, we'll find out and take the necessary action.' He spoke so ominously that I almost felt sorry for her.

It was while I was cycling back to Hortense that I began to count dates in my head. The last time I'd had a period was in January. I wobbled as the significance of this hit me. I was at least seven weeks' overdue. 'Oh, please, God, let it be so,' I said aloud. For the first time in weeks I felt happy and at peace with my world.

8

'Tell me, where are you going? I need to know, just in case.' Hortense didn't explain what she meant by that and I didn't ask.

'I'm not sure myself,' I replied evasively, although I knew full well where I was heading. Claude had asked me if there was anywhere I could go and I had said Anliac, without a moment's hesitation.

'You don't trust me, do you?'

'It's not that, Hortense, I do, but it's not just me and Tiphaine who are involved. Others are putting their lives at risk.'

'But I wouldn't breathe a word to a soul.'

'You don't know that, Hortense. Remember, I've been there, I know what it's like and what they can do to you.'

'But you didn't talk, did you?'

'I didn't know anything to tell them. So, you see, it's safer this way.' I talked to her as if she were a child. Only three years ago it had been she who had been in charge and explaining things to me.

'You didn't tell them about your man. Tiphaine told me. She said you had been so strong and brave. Now, isn't that a surprise?' I laughed at this. I knew Hortense didn't mean to be rude. Why, I had even surprised myself at the way I had behaved – if I could bring myself to think about it, which wasn't often.

'She shouldn't have. But, in any case, I knew nothing about Didier's work. I just didn't let them know I knew him, that's all.' We were in Hortense's room and, she had sorted some clothes for Tiphaine to take – not an easy task since most of her clothes were suitable only for night-clubs and restaurants – not for the countryside, to which we were headed.

'What was that?' Hortense clutched the petticoat she had been folding to her chest and looked wild-eyed at me.

'Your Germans?'

'No. It's too early for them. They're never here in the daytime.' The words were barely out of her mouth when there was a tap on the bedroom door, which swung open to reveal a middle-aged and rather portly German officer.

'Madame, forgive me disturbing you, I heard you talking . . .'

'Yes, Herr Müller, and what can I do for you?' She was all smiles, simpering just as she had with her old philosophers before all this had started. He was looking at me, standing in the middle of the room, holding a pair of shoes. I was shaking with terror – his was the first uniform I had been this close to since my release. 'This is the daughter of a dear friend of mine, the Countess of Vichy. She has come to collect some clothes for the poor,' she lied smoothly.

The soldier clicked his heels and bowed, which I acknowledged graciously, then said he was enchanted to meet me and I said likewise.

'Madame, I fear I must have caught your cold. I feel really rather unwell.'

'You poor man. You go to bed and I'll make you a hot-water bottle. Tell me, do you have any of that whisky you showed me? Splendid, then give me the bottle and I shall make you a tisane to comfort you and send you to sleep *immediately*.'

'Madame, you are so kind.'

'My pleasure.' She trotted off behind him and I had to sit on the side of the bed – my legs wouldn't hold me up. This was a disaster. Because of the curfew we were to be picked up at one – it would be a good time since the forces of occupation would be sitting down to their lunch, we hoped. There was no question of our meeting at an anonymous rendezvous, since Tiphaine was too weak to walk, and I had no means of contacting the person coming to collect us.

I could hear Hortense fussing along the corridor. I finished packing Tiphaine's bag and crept out of the bedroom.

'Now, you try to rest. I'll pop back and check later if there is anything you need.' Hortense was standing in the doorway of what had once been Mab's room.

'You are so kind . . .' came his voice from the room, as Hortense quietly shut the door. She put her finger to her lips, and I crept along the corridor then down the stairs.

'The Countess of Vichy – what on earth possessed you to say that?'

'The Germans respect order and status. Is he going to query someone so far above him socially?'

'But I hardly look like a countess.'

'Rubbish. You looked positively regal with him. In any case, I have him eating out of my hand. His marriage, you know, has not been a success. He finds French women totally absorbing.' She fluttered her eyelashes. I didn't know whether to be shocked at the implication of her words or whether to congratulate her.

'What on earth do we do now?' I said instead.

'There's no problem, my dear Clare.' She picked up a small bottle from the table and tapped it. 'The joy of a hot toddy – even without lemon – is that the honey and whisky will mask the taste of the sleeping draught I put in. He'll sleep like a baby now until nightfall.'

'Hortense, you're wonderful.'

'I must say, I was rather pleased that he was so taken in by my pretending I had a cold. Maybe I should have gone on the stage as my mother wanted. Now, while we have this bottle in our custody, I think we have earned a nip or two, don't you?'

It was almost time to leave. Hortense had crept up to the officer's room and reported that he was snoring like a volcano.

'Hortense, you've been such a brick, especially when you didn't want us here.'

'Don't remind me, Clare.' She shook her hands, as if pushing away the memory. 'I'm so ashamed. It was the shock, you see, seeing you standing there and poor Tiphaine such a wreck. Now I am loath to see you go.'

'You can't pretend to have a cold for much longer. His Nibs would get suspicious.'

'Poor Tiphaine, she's not fit to travel. I fear I shall never see her again.'

'Don't talk like that. I'll look after her, I promise.'

'Take this.' She pressed a hip flask into my hands. 'It's some of that whisky, and here,' she thrust the remains of the sleeping pills at me, 'you might need help to keep her quiet on the journey.'

'You think of everything. But won't he be suspicious that half his whisky has gone?'

'Bah! I shall say I felt exhausted and helped myself. That, or I'll top it up with brown water – he won't have the sensitive tastebuds of a Frenchman!'

Claude's brother-in-law had a lorry in which he travelled to the countryside to pick up produce for the Germans. Built into the back was a small hiding-place into which we could squeeze with reasonable comfort – Tiphaine was on a mattress on the floor and I was propped up against the bulkhead. The only problem was, it was very cold and the lorry was old and wheezed its way, juddering and wobbling, out of the city. I watched Tiphaine with mounting anxiety – she needed sleep, which, in this vehicle, was out of the question.

Getting in and out of the city we had been told would be the most difficult and dangerous part. We had our papers, certainly, but by now perhaps it had been discovered that Heidi had let us go. It was safer to be hidden. In fact, Tiphaine was safer than I. Hortense had dug out her papers in the name of de Bourbonnais, which she had left with her when she ventured out as Rébecca Weil. In my bag were my incriminating English and German passports, which could cause me untold problems but which I could not leave behind, although sense told me I should – or destroy them. But I couldn't bring myself to do either.

Once in the countryside and on back roads we had been assured that our passage would be less interrupted and safer – I hoped they were right. I willed Tiphaine not to cough at the several roadblocks we had to pass through. At one she had to stuff her fist into her mouth and went the most alarming blue colour. After twenty miles we had to change to another vehicle. What could we say to the kind man who had transported us? 'Thank you' seemed woefully inadequate.

We moved slowly through the country, passed from one person to the next. At some houses we were hidden, in an attic or in a barn, at others we joined the family at the table – all these anonymous people, helping two women they did not know, who they would never see again, and knowing nothing about us. The retribution if they were found out was too awful to contemplate. They might not be blowing up bridges and railway lines but their courage was as great. And the punishment would be no less: death.

All went smoothly until we reached a small town north of Le Puy. The lorry we were in – delivering potatoes this time – ground to an abrupt halt. We were in the back but not hidden.

'There's a roadblock ahead – you've got to get out. They're looking for someone.' The driver's eyes rolled with terror. I wanted to tell him to pull himself together.

'We agreed. I gave you enough money to get us to Le Puy.'

'I didn't know we were going to meet a bloody roadblock of Germans, did I? Out!'

'But my friend, she's ill, it will soon be night and she can't walk far.'

'I'm not a bleeding ambulance.'

'Look, we have our papers. We agreed the story – I'm taking her to her parents to be looked after. They'll swallow that.' I said this with a conviction I was far from feeling.

'And what if they don't?'

'Can we skirt the roadblock by going through the fields and meet you on the other side?' I pleaded. From his expression I could see that his answer would be no. 'Oh, sod you, then. We'll manage. I just hope that one day you find yourself in the same position and that it's up to me whether you're helped or not. Come on, Tiphaine.' I helped her off the tailboard. 'Quite honestly, I don't want to ride in your lorry any more. I'm rather particular about the company I keep.'

Unfortunately I had no map – I hadn't thought we would need one. Of necessity we plunged into the countryside away from the main road and the roadblock the driver had seen. The more I thought about it, though, as we trudged along the more sure I became that there had been no roadblock, that he had just wanted rid of us, having pocketed the money only ten miles further back. Soldiers would have thought the stopped vehicle suspicious and would surely have come to investigate.

'Clare, I'm going to have to sit down.'

'Tiphaine, I'm so sorry – I wasn't thinking. Look, there's a little copse over there. We'll rest for an hour.' We had packed too much, that was certain. Tiphaine couldn't carry her bag so I had to, and my arms were aching already but we had only walked a few miles. 'You rest and I'll go and have a recce.'

I left her and climbed the steep slope to the top of a hill. I hurried for the light would be fading soon. There was something familiar about this landscape. I was close to Vorey, I knew, and if I could see a landmark . . . I breasted the hill, and there it was: a volcanic peak rose out of a lush valley with the Loire serenely flowing through it. What made this peak different from all the rest was the cross I could just make out on its rocky summit. I knew it: I had been to the tiny village that clung to its side with Fabien. We were approaching his home from the north-west.

I ran back to Tiphaine. 'We're safe, I know where we are. If you could manage just a little further, I know a place we can rest the night out of the cold.'

She had such courage, that woman. Each step with her poor aching lungs must have been torture, each breath she took must have torn her apart. 'I'm going to leave this bag here.' I shoved it into a bush of bracken. 'I'll come back for it later. Now you can lean on me more easily.'

What could only have been a couple of miles took us a good four hours to cover. Once among the trees, progress was slowed by the denseness of the undergrowth. Tiphaine was weakening at every step. 'Nearly there,' I said, knowing how hollow it must sound, since I had already said it so many times. 'There it is!'

'Wonderful,' was all she could say as we stood, in the moonlight now, in front of the little cottage in the wood that had been Fabien's and my secret place.

Chapter Six

April 1943 – February 1944

1

It was bitterly cold in the cottage. The mattress and blankets Fabien and I had put there felt damp, there was no light and I had to fumble about from memory. As I barked my shins for the umpteenth time, and cursed, I acknowledged that there was one advantage in there being no light: I could not see poor Tiphaine's face. By now, exhausted as we were, she must look awful, and I probably looked a wreck myself.

'Tiphaine, you sit down on the floor – there's a rug here.' It was easy enough to find her in the dark: I followed the sound of her laboured breathing. I helped her to the floor. 'I'm going to have to go back for the bag. We'll need the extra clothing. You'll be all right?'

'You don't want to go back there now. We can cuddle up together.'

'It'll only take me an hour at the most.'

'Take care,' she called, as I let myself out into the pitch-black night.

Trekking back the way we had come, alone, was not a pleasant experience. With Tiphaine, I had not been aware of how noisy the forest was at night. Creatures scurried in the undergrowth and I remembered Fabien's tales of the fearsome wild boar that roamed these parts, who could kill a man with ease. The wind made a strange moaning sound in the trees. It was as if the whole hillside was alive with alien, unseen forces. If I'd looked a mess before setting out I must have looked a positive fright within a few minutes. I fell over I don't know how many times, I tore my coat, I lost a shoe and wasted ages finding it again. And then I couldn't locate the bag and had to fish around with my hands in the brambles getting scratched for my pains.

The night must have been almost over by the time I returned. I pushed open the door gingerly and paused, listening, afraid there would be total silence. I sagged with relief at the sound of Tiphaine's noisy breathing. I rapidly extracted clothes from the bag and piled them on top of her then lay down beside her, holding her tight, trying to transfer some of my warmth to her.

Lying in the darkness listening to her I remembered the last time I had been here. Then it had been Fabien close to me and his breathing I had listened to. How in love I had thought I was. How mistaken I had been – or had I? It had been a real enough emotion that had consumed me but it hadn't been like . . . I shut my eyes tight as if that might stop me thinking of Didier. I wasn't ready yet. If I allowed myself to dwell on him and what might have been I would become so overwhelmed with grief that everything else would cease to exist. I had to control myself for Tiphaine. I could not yet afford the luxury of mourning my darling. I expected to have difficulty getting to sleep for my stomach was aching from lack of food and my teeth were chattering with the cold. But exhaustion took over and I drifted off.

A snuffling noise woke me. Hot fetid breath alerted me. In a second, terrified, I was awake and sitting up. A dark face stared at me. A corkscrew tail was wagging back and forth like a metronome. The dog's tongue was lolling – it was pleased to see me.

'Fifi, where are you?' The door burst open and Madame Chambrey cannoned into the cramped room, searching for her pug. 'What have you found, you naughty dog?'

'Me,' I answered, rubbing my face with my hands. Tiphaine was sleeping peacefully.

'Clare, is it you?'

'I'm sorry I look such a mess, Madame.'

'But I don't understand . . . My poor child, what is all this? What are you doing here of all places?' There was urgency in her voice.

'Fabien and I – Oh! No!' Against one wall was a pile of blankets, against another a stack of tins. On the third side stood a large wooden box. 'We were freezing. We got here in darkness. I didn't see any of those things.' In a trice I was on my feet and I grabbed one of the blankets, which I laid gently over Tiphaine. 'My friend is ill.'

'So I see.' Madame Chambrey bent down and laid a podgy hand on Tiphaine's brow. 'She has a fever. You can't stay here – she needs warmth.'

'This was the only place we could go. I didn't want to go to the village and compromise everyone there. And I could hardly call on Fabien's mother, could I?'

'Just as well. The castle has been requisitioned by the Germans. It's a good lookout point – it covers the river and the main road into the valley and even the railway line. We are packed into three rooms on the top floor. Hardly conducive to harmonious living.'

'How has it been?'

'Difficult. I work on the principle that if I ignore them then they will ignore me. It's worked so far. Fortunately.' She indicated the room with a sweep of her hand.

'What is all this?'

'Not now, Clare. I think it would be better if I went to get the doctor, don't you? You stay quiet. If a group of men arrive, tell them where I am and to take everything quickly.' She bustled out. I was left with the frustrating sight of food and no tin opener. I sat on the floor, one of the blankets around my shoulders, and waited. Tiphaine, thank goodness, was still sleeping. In sleep, the strain had left her face and she looked more as I remembered her.

It seemed an eternity before the door burst open again and Madame Chambrey, with Dr Forêt in tow, bustled back into the room. Seeing him was too much for me: I was on my feet, clinging to him, with his arms round me, and crying as if I would never stop. Eventually Madame Chambrey prised me away so that he could examine Tiphaine, and she held me as I sobbed. Now there was someone else to take responsibility and I felt the dam that had held back my fear and worry give way.

'I'm afraid she's in a coma.' The doctor stood up straight.

My hand shot to my mouth. 'How could I have been so stupid?'

'You look drained, Clare. Is it surprising?'

'She'll be all right, though?'

'Perhaps, if we can get her to some warmth.'

'Madame Verdier will take them in and she's nearest,' Madame Chambrey offered. 'But how do we get them there?'

'They didn't come?' Dr Forêt gestured at the blankets. 'Then it's best we move quickly. If we can get your poor friend strapped to my horse, do you think you could walk to the Verdiers'?'

I nodded, so overwhelmed with tiredness that I doubted it. For Tiphaine's sake, though I would have to try. In a desultory way I began to pack up our belongings.

At a sudden muffled noise from outside we all stopped what we were doing and looked up. 'It's them,' said Madame Chambrey and, swiftly for one of such bulk, she crossed to the window and peered out. 'Yes, it is.' The relief in her voice was almost palpable. She opened the door and three young men entered stealthily, looking back over their shoulders as they did so. They were swarthy and unshaven, their clothes were muddy and looked as if they had been slept in for weeks. 'Have you a cart?'

'Yes,' the oldest answered, eyeing Tiphaine and me. 'Who are these people?'

'They're all right. I know Clare and she's one of us,' the doctor reassured them.

The man and his companions looked doubtful. 'We have just escaped from being deported,' I said, thinking some sort of explanation was necessary. I was right: their attitude changed immediately and they smiled.

'I nearly had a heart-attack when I came this morning to check and found the stuff still here and these poor souls,' said Madame Chambrey.

'There was a patrol in the night. Unexpected. We hid in the forest.' With a start I realised I had been blundering about in the forest with a German patrol in the vicinity and these men of the Resistance. Either side might have shot me.

'Is it safe to be here in daylight?'

'Yes, Doc. We watched from daybreak. The whole caboodle, Oberst and all, have gone off to the east – must be a bit of a disturbance somewhere.' The man smiled knowingly.

'Clare, there's a camp close to here where the young men of the Resistance are being trained. These provisions are for them.'

'And you work with them?'

'I do my best. I couldn't go home.'

'When I was in Anliac I heard you had escaped. Thank you for my letter, by the way.'

'A bit late in the delivery but there is a war on.' He grinned. 'I hope it was good news?'

'Not particularly, but it led to something very good. I'd heard about the Maquis when I got out of prison.'

'Was it awful?' The doctor asked kindly, not in a nosy way.

'I can't even begin to describe it.'

With Tiphaine loaded on to the cart and me on the doctor's horse we left Madame Chambrey and her dog and made for the isolated farm of Madame Verdier.

As long as I live I don't think I'll ever forget the feeling of bliss when I was put to bed in crisp clean sheets, my head on a goose-feather pillow, a bowl of hot soup in my stomach, with the comforting feeling that someone else was in control, that I could let go.

When I awoke I felt ashamed: I had let Tiphaine down by sleeping instead of guarding her.

'What a silly notion, girl,' Madame Verdier said kindly. 'You couldn't have gone on as you were for much longer. Your friend would be the first to forgive you, I'm sure.'

'How is she?'

'She has pneumonia. Only time will tell.'

'I must be with her.'

'Not till you've eaten this omelette. Madame Violet is sitting with her.'

'But I thought she'd gone back to the château.'

'She did. Then she told the stuck-up bitch she's forced to live with that my lumbago was playing up and she was coming to help out. I welcome her but not that snuffling dog – she sleeps with it, you know. It isn't natural.'

'Does Fabien's mother know about . . . well . . . everything?'

'Heavens above, no.' She raised her hands as if in supplication. 'She'd have us all arrested and no doubt take pleasure in it.' It was most satisfying that someone else disliked her as much as I did.

'Is it hard with the Germans here?'

'Very. Both my boys have taken to the hills. And now they're being armed I can't sleep at nights. Last night they got the radio they've all been waiting for. They said there'll be drops now from aeroplanes – more guns, no doubt.' She shuddered. 'It used to be so peaceful here, but never again.'

We took it in turns to sit with Tiphaine. For three days, twenty-four hours a day, there was always someone with her. She lay, looking old beyond her years yet with a serenity that I almost envied. When it was my turn I would talk to her non-stop. I told her stories of the past, when we had all lived together at Hortense's. I reminisced about Mab, about Tiphaine's Henri. I talked to her about England and my home – anything to keep her brain working – for I was convinced she heard me. Eventually I allowed myself to talk to her about Didier and how we had loved and laughed, and how I knew I would never be happy ever again. I began to cry at that, for my lost dreams and hopes.

She died as I cried. And I knew I would never forgive myself that at that moment I had been talking to her of myself, instead of about her.

2

It seemed as if, with the death of Tiphaine, my soul felt free to give in to all the misery and anger inside me. It was made worse when a couple of days after we had buried Tiphaine in a wood, in a small and beautiful clearing, I felt the familiar ache of an oncoming period. That must have been the moment of my greatest despair: it was as if I was losing Didier all over again.

I remember little of the following days, weeks even: I was immersed in my own hell and there was no one to lead me out of it. I was aware of Madame Chambrey and the doctor visiting. They would talk kindly, sensibly to me. They meant well but they repeated the same refrain time and again, like the members of a chorus:

'Life must gone on . . .'

'It will get better . . .'

'You will be happy again . . .'

'You must try to pull yourself together . . .'

What no one could understand was that I felt I belonged in this cocoon of anguish, that there was no world outside it. I was safe there, I understood it, whereas in their real world I no longer understood anything. Most importantly for me, in letting go I felt closer to Didier. He came to me often in my dreams. Sometimes we made love and I would awaken in a haze of happiness, smiling to myself.

Even as I fought their admonishments I knew I could not stay in this hinterland of despair, much as I longed to. One glorious spring day, sitting in the sun, I was listening to Madame Verdier say that soon the swallows would be back and realised that I felt better. My prolonged, hysterical grieving – for now I could see it as such – had passed. Though I knew it would never entirely leave me, I felt cleansed of it. I wanted to live again, I wanted the world to know of my Didier. It was still a form of mourning but tinged with hope, something I had never thought to feel again.

'If anyone could find me a bicycle, I think I would like to go to Anliac to see my friend Arlette.'

Such dear kind people! Immediately they were galvanised into action for me. A bicycle was found, a train ticket purchased and, with many kisses, hugs and good wishes, they sent me on my way.

As I pedalled down the hill to the station, I felt a great load lift from me. I would survive. I had to. I had things to do.

'Clare, my dear, we've thought of you so many times. How have you been?' asked Arlette's mother.

'Fine,' I answered. I was in their flat, denuded now of possessions – no doubt sold for food. She looked as if in one year she had aged twenty. 'And Arlette?'

A frown flickered across her face as I asked and for one awful moment I thought something had happened to her. But 'She is well,' she said. 'You missed her wedding. We even managed to make a cake.'

'David?'

'Who else? And did you find your Fabien?'

'No, but someone much better – Didier.'

'I'm so happy for you.'

How strange, I thought, that only last week I could not talk of him.

'Have you a place to stay? You are most welcome to remain here.'

'It's most kind of you, Madame.' I didn't want to stay there but how best to get out of it without hurting her?

'But I expect you would prefer to stay with the young ones. I understand.'

It crossed my mind that maybe Arlette wouldn't want me there when they had only been married three months.

'It will be more convenient for you, I'm sure David will be happy to find you employment. He has never been busier than now with the Germans here, you understand.'

'Are there many? I saw the flags on the town hall, which was a shock. I hadn't really expected it – as if I could return and find everything the same!'

'If only that were possible. Yes, the town is full of Germans. There is a garrison here and in the town hall they have set up a regional headquarters. Poor David, he hates to serve them but what can he do?'

'I think he's wise to. You can learn far more by being friendly, can't you?'

'That's what I say, but I hear people muttering that he should close shop. And I say to them, "What good would that do? He would starve!" But people can be so cruel.'

'It's all right for them. They haven't got businesses to run, have they?' I wondered if she knew of David's activities. 'You have no one staying here?'

'No, the strain of hiding them was too much for me. It became a deluge of poor people fleeing. I felt so useless, so unhelpful . . . and I can tell you . . .' she paused '. . . scared. So terribly afraid all the time. Isn't that pathetic?' She imparted this as if it was a shameful secret.

'No, I don't see it that way. It must have been an appalling time for you. You have done your bit. No one can ask more.'

'Bless you for those words, Clare. You see, I feel so guilty not doing anything but in the end it made me ill for months. My nerves affected my heart, the doctor tells me, but with no drugs available there is nothing to be done. It was shocking news of the doctor's mother-in-law, Madame Chadrac, wasn't it?'

'What news?' Even before she spoke I knew what she was about to say.

'She was shot.'

'Oh, no!' Tears flooded into my eyes. 'How?'

'She was being loaded on to a train to be deported, saw an opportunity and ran. They shot her in the back. An old woman of seventy! As if she could have run far.'

'So the friends she trusted didn't help her as she hoped.'

'And who can blame them? When your own family is put at such risk, is it fair to help? That is what I have begun to ask myself. One's family must come first, don't you think?'

'I haven't really got one, not any more.' There it was, one of those moments when I saw everything clearly and knew things would change – even if I didn't want them to. I had to help David and Arlette. I was the ideal candidate – who would be sad if I never returned?

Walking through the town was unnerving with so many Germans about. That was odd: I was used to them in Paris so why not here too?

My welcome from Arlette and David was more than I could have hoped for. They were insistent I stayed with them – so much for my fears that I would not be welcome. 'You don't want me around, not newly-weds like you.'

'Nonsense. We have several lodgers – they come and go.' She smiled in a conspiratorial way. 'You can give us a hand in the bar if you like, can't she, David?'

'Actually, I was rather hoping I could get a job with the Germans.'

'But you said you never would!'

'Something happened to me, Arlette. Somebody, a person I respected enormously, said I should, that I owed it to the people who would not survive this war.'

'Now you're talking, Clare.' David leant forward with an eager expression. 'We've got people working there but none who speak the language as you do.'

'David, it might be dangerous for her.'

David looked at me keenly. 'I don't think she cares if it is.'

One problem I had not thought of was that after my experiences the very sight of a German in uniform made me nervous and distracted. And my loathing of them extended to their language: the words I had spoken all my life, which had once given me such pleasure, now sounded discordant. At least with David's plan I wasn't going to have to speak to them: I would be there to listen. No one must know that I understood a word.

David had organised an interview for me. I was applying for a cleaning job, one that we hoped would get me into many offices. There might be documents lying around that I could peek at. As I crossed the great square in front of what had once been the town hall the familiar knot tightened in my stomach. I looked about me at the plane trees that had stood for so many years over the parades, the markets, the old men and their games of boules. Now only German soldiers strutted about.

Arlette had lent me some makeup. 'They seem to choose the prettiest,' she explained, as she fussed over my hair and applied mascara to my eyelashes. It was her own special dye that she used on my legs to make it look as if I wore stockings. She chose my clothes – I was too nervous. It was in her wedge-heeled shoes that I clattered up the front steps, her blue scarf I rearranged in the neck of my grey suit, and her matching blue hat that I wore at an angle on my head. She had set my hair in convoluted waves, which I was not sure I liked.

Five other women were after the same job. Who would have thought that a cleaning job could be considered so desirable? I nearly walked out when I saw that one applicant was a sad, beaten-looking woman, who told us she'd four children and no husband. Another was elderly: she had lost both husband and son. They needed this job. But then, I thought, if I got it I would be helping them in a roundabout way.

When it was my turn I was shown into an office and told in excellent, if a little stilted, French to sit while the officer at his desk finished some paperwork. That was a ploy to make me more nervous, I was sure, but at least it gave me time to study him and decide how to behave with him – two could play games of stratagem. He was not old so demureness wasn't called-for. Nor was he middle-aged where a degree of flirtatious sycophancy would be in order. Major Karl Schramm was young for his rank and far too young for a desk job. He was the archetypal German, broad-shouldered, blond, but his eyes, instead of a cold icy blue, were a lovely gold-flecked hazel. He had a nice smile too.

'I must apologise for keeping you waiting, but I've got behind with my folders.' When he looked up he was evidently puzzled by my horrified expression, but he had used almost the same words as the smiling one when he had first met me in prison. I began to sweat. 'Are you all right, Mademoiselle Dupont?' he asked, with what sounded like genuine concern. 'Some coffee, perhaps?' He shouted an order towards a half-open door.

'I'm sorry, I felt faint – nerves, I suppose.'

'Just like my sister. She faints at the drop of a hat but, then, she's always forgetting to eat. I hope it wasn't nervousness at meeting me?' There it was again, the pleasant smile that I knew might cloak evil.

There was a tap on the door and one of the fieldmice was scurrying in with a tray of coffee. He poured mine, and asked if I took cream or sugar.

'Black, thank you.'

'Like me.' He handed me the cup. It smelt so wonderful I took a second just to sniff it.

'It's real coffee,' he assured me. He shuffled some papers. 'Now, let's get organised.'

Again I had a moment of indescribable panic and knew that I sat rigid, waiting for the blow to fall. 'I need this job, that's why I'm nervous,' I said in explanation.

'I have to tell you that the cleaning job has gone.'

'Oh.' I looked and felt downhearted.

'There was a poor woman with four children – I had to give it to her, you understand?'

'Of course.' Why was he so nice? Where was the trap? When would it snap shut?

'But we are in need of someone to help out in the mess – to help the stewards clearing the drinks, helping at table. Would that interest you?'

'Very much.'

'Please, I don't want to offend you but after a hard day all the men prefer to have a pretty lady serve them.'

I thought I was about to be sick.

3

On my first day at work at the German headquarters I was terrified. The town hall was an enormous structure, which fronted on the main square. To either side and behind it was a park, where in another time people had walked for pleasure, a band had played in the ornate iron bandstand, and children had visited the exotic birds in the aviary. Now only Germans were allowed in. At the front of the building were the fine reception rooms for entertaining and the mayor's suite, but behind its elegant, pillared façade, it stretched far back in a warren of offices, some large, most small. Here, French bureaucrats had spent their days pushing pieces of paper around desks. Now it was the turn of the Germans. The man in the street still maintained his scant respect for authority, but it was heavily disguised now, for fear swaggered along the hallways and offices in a way it hadn't before.

'This room you uniform change. Here store your clothes you will.' The fieldmouse banged the tin locker noisily. She spoke execrable French and I made no effort to help her. 'You will in officers' mess and dining room work. You not to speak them to. The canteen of lower ranks you not enter.' Each time she said 'you' she thrust her forefinger at me aggressively. 'If you steal one lump of sugar you will be prosecuted.' At least she had that sentence off pat, obviously learnt by rote. The knowledge that I spoke well both her own language and the one she was massacring gave me a comforting feeling of superiority.

'What about time off?'

She looked at me as if I was something unpleasant from the gutter. 'You no time have. Myself clear I make?'

'As mud,' I muttered.

'What did you say?'

'Nothing, miss,' I said, all meek and mild, but thinking that, with her pursed mean little mouth and beady eyes, she looked remarkably like a mouse I had once owned called Greta – after Garbo, because we hardly ever saw her.

Two French girls worked with me, both about my age, and one, Madeleine, was likeable. She was pretty, flighty and nothing seemed to get her down for she laughed constantly. She reminded me a little of Tiphaine. She said constantly how much she hated the Germans and boasted of how she spat in their food. She claimed she had once peed into a bowl of punch. 'To improve the flavour, you understand?' She had been working here since the Germans had arrived last November.

Sylviane, in contrast, was morose. She had been recruited a month before me. At my interview, Major Schramm had said they preferred pretty women to serve them but Sylviane missed being so. She might have been, had she smiled more, but her looks were flawed by the spiteful character imprinted on her face. She said little but when she did it was a discontented diatribe. Evidently her life had been a sorry disappointment to her: everyone and everything in it was against her.

I hadn't needed David's warning not to trust anyone: I had enough experience now. As soon as I set eyes on her I decided that if anyone was going to cause trouble and be a tell-tale it was Sylviane.

'Madeleine, honestly, I don't think you should talk about spitting and things like that in front of Sylviane. She might tell on you.' We were in the locker room, changing into the ridiculous uniform of black dress with lace collar, starched white apron – which we had to launder ourselves, despite the lack of soap – and black stockings. I liked the stockings: they were the first I had had in years.

'Sylviane? Nonsense! She wouldn't do that, she's French.'

'I've learnt that not everyone can be trusted, whatever their nationality.'

'And where did you learn something like that?' There was a sly look about her as she asked.

'Round and about,' I answered evasively. Sylviane was not to be trusted but perhaps Madeleine was the same.

*

'Are you settling well, Mademoiselle Dupont?' I was counting the knives and forks for lunch and giving them a final buff.

'Yes, thank you, Herr Major Schramm.'

'If anything or anyone ever bothers you, come and see me.'

'Thank you, I will.'

'Or if you ever feel like a chat.'

'You're very kind,' I replied, with mock humility. Yes, I thought, get me in your office, get my clothes off – no, thank you, Herr Major.

We were really fetchers and carriers, and had to wash the silver and glasses. Most of the serving was done smoothly and ably by soldiers. I was relieved since I had had nightmares at the prospect of trying my hand at silver service, knowing I was sure to drop food on some immaculate uniform. We weren't allowed near it – I supposed in case we tampered with it, or poisoned it. I wondered why Madeleine had lied.

The first few weeks went smoothly enough, despite the fieldmouse constantly snooping and yelling at us: I soon learnt that if I kept up a constant barrage of apology she quickly ran out of things to complain about. I was aware of the way the officers looked at us, in a bold, appraising manner. Sylviane and I kept our distance, pretending not to notice, but Madeleine was content to flirt with them – so much for hating them. I didn't know for sure but I had the distinct feeling that sometimes she did more than flirt. I tried not to be censorious but it was hard, after my experiences.

Every day, at some point, Major Schramm was guaranteed to appear. Some of his pretexts were transparent: surely it was not his job to check that the cupboards were tidy – but then perhaps it was since I didn't know how an army was run.

'I think he likes you – a lot,' Madeleine teased me one day, when he had turned up searching for a teaspoon.

'Of course he doesn't.'

'Haven't you noticed the way he looks at you? He's smitten.'

'Well, he can stay smitten. If the last man on earth was a German I'd die celibate.'

'I wouldn't! Especially if it was our Major Schramm. He's divine!'

'You are so silly, Madeleine,' Sylviane said.

'And you are sour enough to turn the milk in the churn.'

Unfortunately we were not the only ones who noticed his interest in me. The fieldmouse did too. And she was not pleased. 'You!' Finger waving in the air at me. 'To officers, no speak.'

'He spoke to me.'

'You heard me!'

'If I didn't answer him he would be angry with me, wouldn't he?' I wanted to laugh at her stupid, twisted expression. She was jealous! She wanted him herself. And it was unlikely that he would return her interest: she had too much facial hair.

At first I was clumsy, unused to working at the speed expected and, in any case, always nervous. There was also far more to learn than I had at first thought, for there was a ruthless routine to each meal served and woe betide whoever interrupted it. Learning where everything was stored, how to clean, in what order to wash, stack and put away was bewildering at first. All orders were shouted. The fieldmouse did not have one gracious word in her vocabulary, and took pleasure in showing us how much she despised us. And with Karl Schramm's constant visits, her spite towards me increased.

She had been wrong: I did have time off, even if the hours were appallingly long. I had to be at work at six and we could not leave until the last officer retired to bed. This might be at two or even three in the morning. There was a curfew and at first I feared I would not be allowed to live outside the premises, but fortunately accommodation was short and we were given a dispensation to be out at night, provided we never deviated from our route home.

With the help of the barman, a friendly middle-aged soldier from the Black Forest, we devised a shift system so that we worked late only one night in three.

I discovered that the officers were amazingly indiscreet. It seemed that it had never crossed their minds that any of us might understand a word of their language. I learnt who had been unfaithful to his wife, who was secretly homosexual, who had money problems, who they thought was responsible for a string of thefts, their opinion of their senior officers, and once, excitingly when three young men confessed that they loathed and despised Hitler.

'But they never talk of troop movements, or where they're going, or anything that might be in the least useful to you,' I complained to David one evening when, as usual, I reported to him what little scraps I had heard.

'Anything, Clare. Just tell me everything you overhear. We can never tell when a snippet might be useful, when information about an officer might come in handy.' He tapped the side of his nose, no doubt to make himself look villainous but he was too honest to look anything of the sort.

I was less convinced than David. How could a band of resistants blackmail any member of the army of occupation? I felt I was having to work too hard at a job I found tedious for nothing. I became despondent, especially when the better weather came and I was cooped up serving a group I hated and held responsible for the loss of two important people in my life. And then . . .

I was removing glasses from a table where three officers were sitting with a map spread in front of them. 'It's an impeccable source . . . He's trusted by the fools. Next month . . .' The officer glanced up at me, frowned and waved his hand dismissively. I dropped a glass. 'You stupid whore! Watch what you're doing.' I did not react to the insult, appearing not to understand his German, and apologised meekly, but glanced swiftly at the map, registering the name of the town that was ringed. I bent down and took time to mop up the drink on the carpet. 'I have organised . . .' He dropped his voice and I could not hear. But I was certain he said 'drop' and 'shambles'.

Unfortunately it was my night to work late and it was long after three by the time I returned. David was asleep in the bar. I would normally have left him and crept away to my bed but I had to shake him and tell him what I had overheard.

'Jesus! Clare, it's been worthwhile after all.'

'Is there a drop?'

'I don't know. But I know who to tip off in case there is.'

For the first time in the six weeks I had worked there I went to bed feeling reasonably contented.

4

'I wondered if you would care to take a walk with me?'

Engrossed as I was in sorting linen I was startled by the voice behind me. I swung round expecting that Major Schramm was talking to someone else, but he wasn't. The invitation was for me.

'I can hardly do that.' I was flustered. Part of me was angry at his presumption, another was afraid and a third quite flattered.

'Why not? Are you too busy? I can arrange that you have the time.'

'I'm not allowed to talk to you.'

'Who told you that?' He had stepped into the room, which was the linen closet. Given his size and its smallness I stepped back involuntarily feeling uncomfortably crowded.

'I was informed.' I clutched a pile of napkins to me rather like a shield, I thought, and lowered them feeling even more silly.

'No doubt by our own dear "Greta Fieldmouse".' He leant forward as he spoke and smiled in a conspiratorial way. I stepped back again. 'Mademoiselle Dupont, you need not be afraid of me.'

'I'm glad.' Like hell, I thought, stacking the napkins on the shelf and ticking the number in the ledger.

'Please leave that task, Mademoiselle. It makes talking to you very difficult. How about this walk?'

'I just said.'

'But what if I made it an order.'

'Then I couldn't refuse, but you wouldn't.'

'And why wouldn't I?'

'Because you're a gentleman.' It was my turn to smile.

At that he threw back his head and laughed. He had a lovely laugh, and, despite myself, I laughed, and felt myself relax. 'Of course, you are, I hope, correct. I could not bring myself to order you, but it would make me very happy if you accompanied me. I love to go and watch the birds, don't you?'

'I've never seen them. We're not allowed in the park.' Honestly, I'd have thought he would know that.

'Then please give me the pleasure of showing you.' His courtly, precise way of speaking was lovely.

I felt self-conscious as we walked down the wide avenue leading into the park. It was shaded by great poplars, and in the distance we could hear the distinctive cry of peacocks. 'It embarrasses you to walk with me?'

'No, not at all.'

'The only French here are the gardeners, and I see none at present, do you? You will not be compromised.'

'Honestly, it's of no . . .' Importance I was going to say, but instead found myself admitting that I found it difficult.

'You have lost someone, then? And you blame all Germans and that includes me. How sad, for you and for me, for then we are both losers.'

'Yes, something like that.' I knew I sounded rather crass after his sensitivity.

'He was a soldier?'

'Yes,' I lied – but, then, was it a lie? Didier has been fighting for his country, even though he had no uniform. I felt the familiar constriction in my throat, and put up my hand to relieve it.

'I understand. Just thinking of them hurts, does it not? But it will ease, I promise you. I know. I, too, have lost people I loved.'

'I'm sorry.'

'My brother in Russia. My parents in Berlin. My fiancée too.'

'I'm *so* sorry.' I genuinely was. How did someone survive such losses? I would have preferred to be untouched by this, but I could not be. I looked at him from the corner of my eye as we walked along. He was a good-looking man with a kind face. If only he had not been in that hated uniform we might have been friends.

'I knew when I first saw you at your interview that you had suffered – it was in your eyes. We are marked people, you and I.' I was moved by this, as if at last I had met someone who understood how I felt instead of trotting out the usual polite platitudes. We stopped in front of a large cage where some of the exquisite birds were housed. 'I particularly like these Chinese pheasants, don't you? Such lovely colours, and they're so touchingly dignified in such undignified surroundings.'

I averted my eyes: I didn't like to see them like this, imprisoned, their freedom taken from them.

'You are not interested in the birds?'

'They're lovely.'

'I hate to see them in these cages, don't you?'

'Yes.'

'Creatures should be free, don't you think?'

I was unsure what to say. I had an overwhelming feeling that his conversation about the birds had been planned. But why? He couldn't know anything about me surely . . . Unless . . . It took all my willpower not to react to the thoughts that were scudding around noisily in my head, screeching alarm at me, making fear pour like a torrent over me. Had my name been reported? Had Heidi been found out? I forced myself to take control of these fears. Change the subject, a voice in my head told me.

'What is your job here? I'm never sure what everyone does. You're a soldier and yet . . .' Should I have asked him that? Would it show too marked an interest?

'No, I'm not a member of the catering corps.' He found this funny and laughed again. 'I'm in overall charge of the smooth running of the place, though any fool could do that. I am seconded from my Panzer division, I was wounded, you see, and had to be put on lighter duties.'

'Not badly, I hope.'

He stopped in his tracks and looked down at me. 'Ah, Mademoiselle, I like that little word "hope". Might I dare dream that you begin to feel at ease with me?' I made no reply. 'It only bothers me when it rains – the wound, I mean.' He smiled his attractive, lazy smile. 'But I was sent out of harm's way because there were people who did not like the way I was thinking.'

'Really?' I tried to sound noncommittal.

'They were good friends to me. At first I was sent to Berlin – not the best place to be if you think as I do. They felt I risked too much.' He paused as if he expected me to comment, to ask him what these thoughts of his were, but I had no intention of doing so. What if it was a trap to lull me into saying things about the Germans that I might live to regret? We had moved on from the birds and were now in front of a cage with a small deer inside, which distressed me even more. 'So they sent me to France, to this backwater. Not that I mind, I love to speak French.'

'You speak it very well.'

'I should do. I studied it at university and I lived in France for three years before the war.'

'Where?'

'Here. It was where I met my fiancée. She was French, you see. When I arrived here it was – How shall I put it? It was as if I was coming home. I'd never experienced that before. There are times when I feel very much a part of this country.'

'I understand that.' He had no idea how easy it was for me to know how he could feel that way.

'I wonder if you do. It is very difficult for me since I have my fiancée's relatives here too. Do you understand?'

'A little. But if you were indiscreet in Berlin, why send you somewhere where you might have divided loyalties?'

'Did I say I was indiscreet? Did I say my loyalty was divided?'

'Well, no . . .'

This conversation was like a game of cat-and-mouse. I felt he was trying to say something to me but if I was wrong I might be in serious trouble.

'Cigarette?'

'No, thank you, I don't smoke.'

Whatever it had been it was over, for we turned to literature and art. I confessed to a lack of reading, which made him offer excitedly to compile a list of books for me. And we talked about food and wine, about which he knew an enormous amount.

'We have talked about art and me – too much about me. Tell me about yourself.'

Oh dear! This was the last thing I needed. 'I was born, I live, I work for you.' I tried to sound light-hearted.

'Where were you born?'

'In Lyon . . . My father was in the silk trade. We . . .' I told him the tale I had learnt – had it been only last year? It seemed like a lifetime ago. Why had he asked me when he must have known all that from my application? The wariness returned. However, he seemed genuinely interested and asked a few questions. He appeared to accept my answers as true. Perhaps he had just been curious.

'When this wretched war is over I hope to return here. Buy a house and become a wine grower.'

'Won't you miss Germany?'

'Not now my family is no more. I have one sister left and we have never got on. And, in any case, maybe when I return you would not be so scared of me if I wore no uniform.'

That evening, in the darkened bar I was recounting my walk. 'I felt he was trying to say something to me but he kept taking everything back. I'd think him friendly and then just as quickly think he was the enemy.'

'You should be careful, Clare. He might know something about you. Your name might be on a wanted list.'

'What makes you think that, Arlette?' David asked.

'What was the name of the woman who stamped your papers? Heidi? Well, what would you do if you were her? She might have given you a couple of days to get clear of Paris then reported that she had made an error. They would check where you had come from—'

'A bit far-fetched, isn't it? They're deporting so many at such a rate that they can't possibly keep a check on everyone.'

'She could be right, David. The Germans are so obsessed with order. Lists for everything. You should see the amount of paperwork involved with one pantry for the officers' mess – heavens, they note everything down.'

'It still seems unlikely to me. And if so, Arlette, then why hasn't he had Clare arrested?'

'Because he's infatuated with her, David. Don't you see?'

'Hardly!' I laughed.

'Clare, don't be so modest,' Arlette said. 'You told us he makes a point of searching you out every day. He invites you for a walk. Has he asked any of the others? And, on top of that, he's in love with France and, presumably, the French.'

'That's odd, isn't it? If you were his superiors would you send him to a country he undoubtedly loves. He's a risky proposition to them.'

'Maybe they don't know.'

'But, Clare, you've just said that they're so efficient they'd know even the nationality of their officers' grandparents – especially with this pure Aryan thing they're obsessed with.'

'To me the interesting thing is that perhaps he's sympathetic. Perhaps he wants to help us – perhaps talking to you is his way of putting out feelers.'

'Who's being far-fetched now?' Arlette chortled.

'Not so. Clare herself told us of that conversation she overheard, about the dissatisfaction with Hitler. They have had setbacks – Russia, Africa. The bombing is appalling in Germany, they say – hell, this man lost most of his family, his future. This is maybe the start of a general discontent with the whole regime.' The words were pouring out of him in his excitement.

'Well, I've never heard anything so silly. A German! Wake up, David. I think Clare should watch herself. It might be the other way round – have you thought of that? Perhaps he's a plant to ensnare us and knows full well who Clare is, who she lives with. Oh, David!' Arlette looked wild-eyed with sudden fear.

'Arlette, I'm sure he's not.' I wasn't anything of the sort but I couldn't bear to see her look so frightened. 'The trouble with this war is it makes us doubt everyone. Why, I even find myself doubting one of the girls I work with – and then today she shared some chocolate she'd got with us and I felt so disloyal.'

'Where did she get chocolate?' Arlette asked, with suspicion.

'I didn't like to ask!' I laughed. 'It was delicious all the same.'

'Do you like him, Clare?' David asked suddenly, with a penetrating stare.

'David! No!'

'I haven't said a word.'

'I know exactly how your mind is working, David. It's asking too much of anyone.'

'Do you like him?' he persisted.

'Well, despite myself, yes. He's a nice man, and in another place and time, I could like him enough to do what you're about to suggest.'

'Would you get to know him better – see what you could find out? It would be such a help, Clare.'

'I don't know. It's hard . . . I don't even want to speak German again – let alone . . . I'll have to think about it.'

5

For a week I had thought long and hard about what David wanted me to do. After a lot of shilly-shallying and pretending that he hadn't meant what I had thought, he had finally spelt it out: if we became lovers Karl, at some point, would be indiscreet.

'I think it is unfair of you to ask me to do such a thing,' I said, all hurt dignity and pride. 'Friendship, perhaps, but this!' He had the grace to apologise – he had to, with Arlette telling him what an immoral man she had married. A pimp, she called him.

My first reaction stayed with me for some time: I reasoned that if I went to bed with him I was no better than a prostitute – but less honest. That in doing so I would be betraying Didier and all I held dear.

The longer I thought, however, other ideas and theories occurred to me. What would Didier have counselled? He had been prepared to lay down his life for the Resistance. Would he think that in such times sacrifices had to be made?

And was it so important anyway I was hardly a blushing virgin. If I wanted to, if I enjoyed it, that would be different. Perhaps I could close my eyes and pretend it wasn't happening. And if I was careful . . . Back and forth the arguments went, round and round in my head.

Insidiously, and not at my invitation, another thought began to worm its way into my mind. I liked Karl – I had meant it when I had said that if times had been different . . . And then I was shocked at myself and hated myself. And I had to ask myself whether if he was old and ugly I would be having such a struggle with myself – and I was not happy with the answer that came back.

Surely if I did it for a reason it was not a betrayal of Didier. If I did it because of my personal feeling for Karl, it was. That decided it. I wouldn't.

Karl Schramm could not have been kinder to me, nor, as I had first perceived, did he behave in any way other than that of a gentleman. We went for walks, we talked, he had kissed me chastely on the cheek and on the hand, but never on the lips. He had made no attempt to seduce me, and I really began to think he wanted only companionship. Unfortunately for my peace of mind, I had to admit to myself that my relief was tempered with disappointment – did he not like me enough?

Anliac was fortunate in that the German commandant was a man of culture. It seemed, from what we could ascertain of what was going on in France generally, that if the local commandant was uninterested in the arts the populace suffered brutality. If he liked Mozart and paintings, atrocities were less likely to happen. Certainly I had heard of no one suffering in Anliac, though it had to be admitted that many were sent away.

With our commandant, there were concerts to attend, exhibitions to see. His passion was fine porcelain and Karl, because of his excellent French, was often sent as an emissary to view a particularly fine piece, photograph it and then, if his superior officer was interested, negotiate a price for him. 'At one posting I had, the commandant purloined whatever he wanted but old Johann is a man of honour – he offers a fair price.'

'That's good,' I said, though I longed to add that he was only able to do so because the people selling were desperate for money to enable them and their families to live. As we bumped down the road of a particularly dilapidated château with the exciting news that the dinner service we had just viewed was undoubtedly Sèvres, I thought of how my life, in the space of six months, had gone full circle. This was what Didier had done, helped negotiate a fair price for the French when selling *objets d'art*.

Our trips were clandestine. Work rotas had to be altered – which annoyed the fieldmouse and, given her suspicions about Karl and me, made her even more unpleasant to me. We would arrange a place to meet, on the outskirts of town, to which I cycled, on Arlette's awful bicycle, and he drove. I had no desire for any French people I knew to see me with him, and he did not want anyone at headquarters to find out he was with me.

While I enjoyed our trips to see the china, the pleasure I felt at getting away from the grind of work was spoiled by the way I was greeted by the owners of the objects. They looked at me with contempt and only spoke to me if it was unavoidable: they did not want to annoy the German officer. I knew what they were thinking: that I was a 'horizontal collaborator'. I longed to explain that we were not lovers, that I was with him under instructions from the Resistance. Instead I had to endure those cold, bitter looks. It was hurtful, and so unfair. But, then, I was fully aware of just how unfair life could be.

Karl was a generous host and the dinners we had together were memorable – I drank wines I had previously only heard of. He gave me perfume, soap, lovely things, but then, when I thought of how the others were living, I felt such guilt. At those times the *filet mignon* in my mouth turned to sawdust. When I confessed this to Arlette, she said, 'Don't be so silly, Clare. There isn't one citizen out there who doesn't envy you your good fortune. They would grab it themselves – and the *filet mignon* – with both hands if it was offered to them.'

'But when children are undernourished . . .'

'There is nothing you can do about that. But at least you are trying to do something for them and for France.'

There were times when I forgot who I was supposed to be and why I was there. On one particular occasion we had taken a picnic up into the hills. It was a perfect summer's day and we lay in the grass, watching the skylarks and the swallows, heard the buzzing bees, saw the flash of gaudy butterflies. For a time I could forget the war and all the horrors that I knew existed. I could enjoy the loveliness of the day, the pleasure of the simple food and wine we had with us. I was a young woman with a handsome young man . . .

'What are you thinking?' He had propped himself on one elbow and was looking down at me, tickling the end of my nose with a blade of grass.

'How I would like . . . I was pretending there was no war and we were not enemies.' It was the wine I had drunk in the heat that made me so incautious.

'Can we not forget it altogether?' he said softly.

'Fleetingly I think it's possible – but that's all.'

'Do you really see me as your enemy? I'm not, you know.'

'Officially you are.'

'I hate to think of you feeling that way about me.'

'But what if I asked you something? What if I wanted you to do something that would be harmful to your country?' I must be mad, I told myself, but once I had started it was difficult to stop.

'I could not betray my country.'

'Then, you see, you have to remain my enemy. And . . .' Inexplicably I was close to tears.

'And . . .' he prompted me.

'I hate it. I don't want to feel like this. I want us to be friends. I would like . . .' I stopped.

'To be lovers?'

'Yes.' I looked away from him, miserable at my admission, miserable at my disloyalty, appalled at my betrayal of Didier.

I felt his grip tighten on my waist. I knew he was going to kiss me and, God help me, I wanted him to, longed for him and his lips . . . As they searched for mine I sighed, I heard it, it was heartfelt. I had to put away a crowd of thoughts – Later, I told myself, I'll think about this later. And I surrendered to him and marvelled at our self-control that it had taken us so long to reach this point. And love, in a second, conquered noisy guilt.

'He's such a nice man, David. I feel guilty that I have this ulterior motive.'

'He's a German. He's the enemy.'

'Not to me he isn't – not any more.'

'Christ! You're not falling in love with him?'

'Don't be silly! Me fall in love with a German? Never!' In denying it I felt as if I was betraying him. But if I admitted it to David I risked severe censure from the group – I'd heard tales of women disappearing for such a crime. Whether they were true or not I did not know, but I feared they might be. The injustice of this was something I would have liked to argue about. I was permitted to sleep with him as a spy, but in no way was I to

love him, feel for him or, I supposed, enjoy his lovemaking. It began to
look remarkably hypocritical to me.

'He's told you nothing?'

'He's the wrong person, I'm sure. He's in charge of the organisation of
the garrison, that's all, just as he said.'

'A Panzer officer? Don't be stupid, Clare. They wouldn't waste him on
housewifery duties.'

'It's hardly my fault if I've ended up with an officer who appears to
know nothing. And I'd appreciate it, David, if you didn't call me stupid.'

'I'm sorry. I shouldn't have. But there's so much going wrong at the
moment. In Lyon last week, so many important people were arrested,
betrayed. Just when everything was going so well.'

'Well, none of that is mine or Karl's fault, is it?'

We needed each other constantly. Sometimes we made love in the
countryside but it was difficult for both of us to get away too often in the
daytime without rousing suspicion. He gave me a key to his room, and on
those evenings when I did not work I would steal up to it, high in the
eaves of the building, pretending I was on an errand, dusting, inching my
way there. Once on his floor we were safe; his was the only room. The very
secrecy imposed on us gave it an added sweetness, as if we were doomed
lovers, for we never talked of any future together. Neither did we speak of
love – the time was not right – but it was always there, this unspoken
longing. When peace returned, then . . .

Madeleine was aware of what was going on and quizzed me, but I ignored
her. As the weeks passed and our relationship strengthened it became
something I could not joke about. I found myself looking out for him, my
heart lifting when he walked into the mess. I waited for the secret looks he
gave me. Longed for our time alone.

My guilt over Didier had died. It had died in the strange way that
Felicity had forgiven me: in a dream. He came to me, he kissed me gently
and I knew that what I was doing was fine. It was a resolution for me.

It also helped that, in so many ways, Karl was like Didier: they had the
same passions, music, literature, they both had a quirky sense of humour,
not often found in either nationality. They were both gentle and kind. I
couldn't have stopped myself feeling as I did.

Then one night Karl let slip some information. But it was not what any
of us wanted to hear.

'Clare, my darling, you live at the Golden Bear, don't you?'

'I used to. I seem to spend most of my time here in your quarters now.' I
laughed but a sixth sense was warning me.

'Then I think you should move out.'

'Why?'

'I'd rather not say.'

'What's David done? Selling black-market wine? I bet every bar-owner in France is doing that.' Still I laughed even though my stomach was churning.

'Nothing like that. Far more serious. I wish I could have mentioned this sooner but I did not know.'

'Know what?'

'That you should move out.' I could get nothing else from him. We argued after that over something so trivial: I'd had a bad day with the fieldmouse and I didn't think it would be unreasonable for him to say something to her.

'I couldn't do that. It is I who am in the wrong in having a relationship with you. Fraternisation is frowned upon.'

'Thank you! So that's all I am to you! A little wartime pleasure.' I was off the bed in a flash and putting on my clothes.

'Please, Clare, don't interpret it like that.'

'How else should I?' I snapped, and made for the door. At least it gave me an excuse to storm off and warn David.

The streets were dark as I raced through them. His warning could mean only one thing: the arrests in Lyon a fortnight ago when the leaders had been betrayed had led, we knew, to a big mopping-up operation in all the surrounding areas, as those who had been arrested talked.

'That's all he said, David.' I watched as David methodically packed up his radio transmitter – a recent acquisition – and hid it in its secure place in the wall of the attic we were in. 'It's an obvious warning. They must have got wind of you, or the transmitter – I told you they were stepping up the searches for them. You have to get out of here. As quickly as possible. Tonight.'

'But I can't. We've a drop tomorrow, agents and weapons. It's too important.'

'Then take to the hills. David, please!'

'I'll go tomorrow night, I promise.'

It was a promise David was unable to keep. The next night, as the aeroplane from England circled the field, and lined up with the flaming markers placed by David and his group, the Germans were waiting. They waited until the plane had landed, the equipment and agents unloaded and then they swooped. All of them were arrested. Only the crew of the aeroplane escaped.

6

By early morning, everyone knew what had happened to David and his group: bad news *does* travel fast. The Germans were smugly triumphant, the French workers downcast. Somehow I worked, though I shall never know how, for every time a door opened, a phone rang, I was certain they had come to get me. But in the mess it was frantic: Madeleine had not shown up for work and Sylviane, according to the fieldmouse, was ill, so that just left me to help the stewards.

Eavesdropping on the officers' talk at breakfast I heard that David had been taken to Lyon. I nearly dropped the stack of dishes I was holding. That was bad news, for while we had heard no stories of brutality here in Anliac, in Lyon things were different. There the Gestapo held sway, and there was a man called Barbie whom everyone feared. There was no reference to Arlette, so I could only hope that David had spirited her away. Fortunately, having made up our argument, I had spent the night with Karl. Had I not, I would now be in custody with David but nothing was said about me, though I heard Madeleine's name mentioned several times.

It was mid-morning when the fieldmouse, broad grin on her sour face, came to tell me I was wanted. 'Fast!' she screamed, and I quite expected her to kick me as I went past. I was led into a large crowded room. I had not been alone living at David's: there had been a motley crew of lodgers who came and went with such frequency that I knew few of them, and all of the people who worked for him were there too. Without exception, everyone looked frightened.

As I sat and waited on the bench for my turn my fears were mounting. My papers were secreted at the inn: if they did a thorough search they would find them and then . . . I would be shot. At the thought my stomach lurched. With difficulty I tried to control my mounting fears, which bubbled up inside me like lava in a volcano.

Other people's dread fuelled mine; when Brigitte, the woman who did the cleaning at the inn, began to scream hysterically, then fainted dead away, I thought my heart would burst, it was pounding so hard. The pot man, Hubert, sat silent, rocking back and forth. I wondered how many of them hid secrets, like me, that they feared would be exposed.

Arlette's mother was brought in, looking bent and so old that I didn't know whether to acknowledge her or not. If I did, and I was found out, it might be bad for her, so I looked at her and tried to convey that it was best we did not speak. I don't think she even registered that I was there: she was alone in her own world of unimaginable horror.

'I thought I'd find you here. What a drama!' Madeleine slumped on the bench beside me.

'What are you doing here?' I asked.

'Would you believe I was found nicking some salt and one measly onion? You'd have thought I'd robbed the Reichsbank, or whatever they call it.' She laughed gaily enough.

'You seem very cheerful.' I was on my guard: as far as I knew, she had had nothing to do with David's activities so was it *just* coincidence that she had been arrested at the same time as me and put in the same room?

'Bit crowded, isn't it? I hope this isn't going to take too long. Last time after a night here they let me out with a caution. I expect they'll do the same today. I mean, with you lot already here they're going to be very short-staffed, aren't they? What have you done? They virtually tore your locker to shreds. And gorgeous old Karl was last seen stomping about looking very stern.'

'Nothing.'

'Oh, come on, Clare, it's me you're talking to.'

'I repeat, I've done nothing. I don't know why I'm here.'

She was asking too many questions. She was too happy. She seemed not to have a care in the world, while the rest of us . . . I looked at her with disdain. And I had been so convinced that it was Sylviane I had to watch.

'I heard they'd arrested David. Nice bloke. I must say, I rather fancied him but that Arlette got to him first. I've always found her a bit stuck-up, haven't you?'

'You never mentioned you knew either of them.'

'Didn't I? Subject never came up. Poor David. Mind you, it was only a matter of time before he was arrested.'

'I don't know what you mean.'

'Everyone knew what he was doing. He wasn't very discreet about it, was he?'

'I haven't a clue what you're going on about.'

'Did he have a radio, do you know? Was he in contact with the Maquis? Are they really up in the forest over Aubenas way?' The questions poured out of her.

'You're a fine one to talk about David's lack of discretion. You're not remarkably good at it either, are you?'

'Now it's my turn to be mystified. What are *you* going on about?'

'Madeleine, I'm disgusted with you and that's all I have to say.'

'Well! Thank you, and I like you too. What the hell has got into you?'

'I don't want to talk to you, is that clear?'

'Fine by me. Just because Schramm has you as his fancy woman, you needn't get shirty with me.'

As I got up and walked away from her to sit on the other side of the room, I felt frozen with anger but I was also sad. I'd liked her. What had turned her into a traitor?

This waiting was intolerable. I had David to worry about, Arlette, and now Karl. Why had he looked so stern? Was he at risk too? He'd said they were not supposed to fraternise. But other officers had dealings with French girls and everyone turned a blind eye to them. Why not Karl? Had he said something? Or was he worried that they knew he had warned us? If they thought that, he would be classed as a traitor and executed as such. I shuddered at the image this conjured up. That would be so unjust. Maybe I should speak out and tell them it was all my doing, that I had overheard somebody else talking. And then I realised that if they knew what Karl had told me it could mean only one thing: that David had talked and by now they would know why we had had an affair. Worse, maybe Karl thought that was the only reason too. What if I never saw him again? He would leave convinced that I had used him, that I felt nothing for him. This was the hardest part of all to bear.

The anticipation of what might come was dreadful. Last time I had not known what to expect; this time I did. I could not face another beating, I knew I couldn't. If only I could close my eyes and die, then everything would be over.

'Clare Dupont.'

Every organ in my body realigned itself. I held my arms tight to me so no one could see I was shaking. I was led into another room where three soldiers sat at a long table. No Gestapo yet.

There were no preliminaries, no good afternoon. Simply, 'And what do you know about David Pointe's activities, Mademoiselle Dupont?'

'Nothing,' I replied – but what else did they expect me to say? 'He's my landlord.'

'You need not look so scared. We don't want to hurt you,' another man said quietly. Despite his uniform he looked so like one of the men who had questioned me in Paris that just looking at him made me break out into a cold sweat.

'And I don't want to be hurt.' What could I tell them to keep them from hitting me? I sat silent, they looked expectant. I tensed, expecting a blow from behind at any minute.

'You must know something.'

'No. Monsieur Pointe was always going out and about. But he had been a councillor so that was to be expected. And he had the business to attend to, and a large family to care for . . .' I waffled. Was I being disloyal to David? Was I saying too much?

'He's a senior member of the Resistance – or don't they now prefer to be knows as the Maquis? I read it meant undergrowth. Is that so?'

'Why yes.' I was flummoxed by his conversational tone.

'Yes, that it means undergrowth? Or yes, that he's an important member?'

'David? Never! Really?' I said, making myself look wide-eyed with astonishment, hoping my voice mirrored my expression.

'You have a relationship with a German officer, I gather?'

'I don't know who told you that. It's a damned lie.' Why the sudden change in tack? Did it mean they believed me? A tiny glimmer of hope began to emerge.

'That is most commendable of you.'

'I don't understand.'

'That you should deny it. I presume because you don't wish the said officer to get into trouble.'

'How could he when he doesn't exist?'

'You see, Mademoiselle, when a young attractive woman like yourself begins a liaison with one of our men and she's living in the house of a member of the Resistance, we must begin to wonder if our officer has not been set up. If, in fact, you yourself work for them.'

The questioning went on and on – I lost track of time. They got nowhere, and I grew more and more afraid that they would soon lose patience with me. I watched, with mounting alarm, as they huddled together and talked about me but too softly for me to hear.

'Very well!' The senior officer neatly shuffled the papers in front of him. 'You may go.'

'I beg your pardon?' Fatigue must have made me deaf.

'Go. Report back to work. We are finished with you.'

I should have experienced a great rush of relief, but I felt nothing. I stumbled from that room, and once outside I collapsed on a bench. I fought great waves of nausea, and blackness closed in on me. An elderly woman came up to me and asked if I was all right. 'Fine,' I answered. 'Just fine.' At that point, I realised I had to get out of there – and fast. Ideally I should leave Anliac as quickly as I could. I stood up and made for the door. Outside I could hear a dreadful commotion of women wailing.

Madeleine was standing with a small group, some crying, some white-faced and silent. Two soldiers were pointing their guns at them.

'That's a friend of mine. May I speak to her?' Stupidly I asked one of the guards in German, but I was so shocked by the scene and by Madeleine's appearance that, for the first time, I made the mistake of using that language. She stood wan-faced, tears falling down her cheeks. She looked so forlorn that momentarily I forgave her. The guard gave his permission and didn't seem to have noticed that I had spoken to him in his own language.

'Madeleine, what's happened?'

'I'm being deported to the camps. For one bloody onion!' she said in despair.

'You mean it's true?'

'I'd hardly be here if it wasn't, would I? It's not a bloody holiday camp they're sending me to, is it? And I sodding well confessed I'd done it. I thought it would mean I'd get out sooner.' She wiped away her tears with the back of her hand as if irritated with herself for crying in the first place.

'Madeleine, I don't know how to apologise to you. I'm so sorry, I thought you were a traitor, a plant,' I whispered to her.

'You what? Me? Clare, how could you think such a thing?'

'Please, don't shout, Madeleine. Please. It was just . . . Well, David and everything, someone must have told them.'

'And you decided it was me. Thank you, Clare, I thought you were my friend. I thought—' She stopped in mid-sentence. 'Oh, my God, it probably was me! Oh, dear God in heaven, what have I done?' She gestured to me to come closer. Nervously I glanced at the guards, but they were too busy talking. 'It's Sylviane. Ages ago she asked me if I knew any way of joining the Resistance. She said she understood a little German and she might be useful. I was offhand at first, said I knew no one, knew nothing. But then she told me a sob story of losing her boyfriend at Dunkirk and how she wanted revenge. Well, don't blame me, it's not totally my fault, and David made no secret of his activities did he? And my uncle . . . Well, he'd been doing some deliveries for the Maquis up in the forest . . . Oh, God, my poor uncle – You don't think—'

'That's enough, Miss, you'll have to go now.' The guard advanced on me.

'But . . .' Madeleine's eyes grew bigger: he had spoken in German and I had understood.

'Say nothing,' I whispered urgently. We had time to kiss and I promised to see her mother. Then, finally, I fled.

7

Instinct might have told me to get out of the city but love, as always, held sway. I ran through the corridors and up the sweeping front staircase of the town hall – no time for discretion now. I ignored the stares of the curious and gave way to no one as I was supposed to do. I sped right up to the top of the building and to Karl's room. I banged on the door. No one answered, but a sixth sense told me he was in there. I knocked again.

'Karl, it's Clare. I want to talk to you.' Nothing happened. 'Please!' I begged.

The door opened a fraction.

'I'm not so sure I want to speak to you.' He began to close it again.

Behind him, on the bed, I could see a half-packed case. I pushed at the door. 'You're leaving?'

'I am being posted elsewhere, yes.'

'Where?'

'I hardly think that is any of your business and, in the circumstances, you don't think I'm going to tell you? Now, if you don't mind, I've things to do.'

'Karl, I need to talk to you, to explain things. Please don't be like this with me. Don't you understand? I love you.' At which, unable to stop myself, I burst into tears.

'Five minutes, then,' he said gruffly. He held open the door for me. Once in the room I didn't know whether to sit or stand. It was our familiar room yet the atmosphere now was uninviting and cold. Karl decided for me: he moved a pile of clothes from an easy chair and indicated I should sit.

'I want you to know that it isn't as it seems,' I began.

'And what is that?'

'I wasn't using you nor was I trying to trap you. I genuinely love you and want to be with you.'

'And why should I believe that?'

'Because it's the truth. Because I don't know how to explain to you – what to say.'

'Maybe you would find it easier in German?' He spoke in that language as he pulled his briefcase towards him. 'Or, perhaps, English? Such a clever little linguist, aren't you?' At which he took from the case my passports and threw them on the bed. My tears stopped in an instant, and the familiar fear swept through me. Even though I was sitting down I felt myself sway, the room move as if I was on a boat.

'Where did you get them?' Who had found them? Was I immersed in another cruel game? Was I about to be re-arrested?

'I found them. You were fortunate it was me. Not the most sensible place – a loose brick in the cellar, the most obvious place for us to check. Oh, Clare, aren't you taught better than that? What shoddy tuition – or weren't you listening at that particular lecture?'

'I don't know what you mean. I've been to no lectures, I've not been taught anything. It isn't like that. I'm not a spy, I swear to you.'

'Then what were you doing with these? And what were you doing with me? And what is your connection with David Pointe?'

I sat feeling bleak. He had my passports. It was inevitable that he would denounce me, I had nothing to lose by telling the truth. 'Very well, I'll tell you. David arranged the interview for me to work here – he hoped that with my German I would pick up information. It was he who asked me to have an affair with you and to find out anything I could. I didn't want to initially, I was afraid of everything German – I had been imprisoned in Paris and I suffered.' He closed his eyes at that point as if in pain. He said nothing. 'But for freedom one will do anything – or so I thought. But I didn't do as David wanted because it was what *I* wanted. Quite simply I had fallen in love with you. I would never have betrayed you and I didn't. Before I got to know you I told him what gossip I had heard in the mess, once an important piece about a planned raid on a group of resistants – I don't even know what the outcome of that was. From you the only information I ever gave him was what you told me, to get out of Golden Bear. And that's the absolute truth.' I was surprised at the way I spoke, no pleading, no histrionics: it was as if I was too tired even to try to persuade him.

He looked at me for what seemed an age. 'And the Resistance?'

'I know nothing of them here or their activities. I took some Jewish children south ages ago in forty-two. I didn't even want to do that but somehow got sucked into it, despite my better judgement. In Paris I was a courier. I delivered clandestine newspapers and occasionally forged papers, but I did not know the people I gave them to, nor did I take part in anything else. I was in love and I did it for him, but my fiancé was murdered. That's all there is to tell you. I can't make you believe me.' It would all come out eventually; there seemed no point in holding anything back.

'And these?' He pointed at the passports.

'I am English. I was trapped in France at the beginning of the war. It was my own fault, everyone told me to leave, but I thought I knew better. But also I am half Austrian and have dual nationality. I used my German passport once to get a permit to travel south. I nearly destroyed them I don't know how many times but—'

'These are too incriminating.' There was a metal wastepaper bin under his desk. I watched as if mesmerised as he systematically tore up the passports and placed them in the bin. From a bureau he took a bottle of lighter fuel, poured it over them and, with a whoosh of flame, set light to them. I put my face in my hands and sobbed with relief. I was aware that he was kneeling in front of me. 'Clare, my darling, don't cry. It's all right, I never intended to tell anyone anything. I was hurt for myself. I wanted you to love me as I love you.'

'Karl!' I flung myself into his arms. 'I've been so afraid that you would hate me and that I would lose your love. Don't go, please don't leave me.'

'Sweetheart, I have no choice. Although they are certain you know nothing – they very much approved of you refusing to compromise me, by the way – all this has left a question mark over you. So, they now think that by knowing you perhaps I am not reliable. How right they are!' He smiled ruefully, looking at the still smoking ashes in the wastepaper bin. 'It's only because the commandant was once in love with my sister that I, too, wasn't initially arrested under suspicion. Instead he sent me to search your premises, no doubt working on the theory that I would be so angry with you that I would want to hurt you and would tear the place apart to incriminate you. But, then, no one knew how we really felt about each other, did they? I could as much hurt you as stop breathing.' He was stroking my hair.

'When do you leave?'

'In an hour.'

'So soon? Where are they sending you? No, don't tell me, I understand, I really do.'

'I don't know myself yet. But no doubt it will be to where the fighting is worst. I'm sure they will be very content to hear that I have been killed.' He laughed bitterly.

'No!' The word emerged as a cry of pain.

'I'll write when I can.'

'You promise?'

'Promise. I love you, Clare, my darling.'

'As I love you.'

'Our tragedy was that we met each other in the wrong time and in the wrong place. But my darling, keep our memories safe in your heart.'

Karl had advised me to remain where I was for the time being. If I disappeared suddenly it would look suspicious and they would come searching for me. I would be on wanted lists and would be a fugitive not only from the Germans but from the Milice as well. But it was hard. To be where he had been and not see him made it doubly so. Stupidly there were moments when I thought I heard his footfall and looked up expecting to see him but, of course, he was never there. And not knowing where he was was agony.

As news filtered through, I discovered that things were not going well for the Germans: we knew within days of the Allied landings in Italy, how a month later the Italians had declared war on the Germans. Defeat for the Axis powers began to seem possible. In November when the Maquis descended from the hills and, on Armistice Day, occupied several towns, flying the tricolour for the first time in years, the joy of the French was wonderful to see. I was happy for them but I found myself torn – wanting the Germans beaten but for my Karl to be safe.

And there was Sylviane to contend with. I hated to be in the same building, let alone the same room, with her. I avoided her as much as I could. Nothing was said between us: I was worried that if she knew I was aware that it was she who had betrayed David she would make trouble for me. All I could do was to warn the other French workers to be careful with what they said in front of her and hope that none of them were collaborators too. How complicated our lives had become: we did not know who was friend and who was foe, who to trust and who not.

Once, I met Arlette's mother in the street. I wanted to cry when I saw her and what this cruel war was doing to her. She was desperately thin and she seemed to have aged even more. She was able to tell me that thanks to my warning, Arlette had taken off to the countryside, but where she was now, dead or alive, she had no idea. As I worried for Karl, so she was in torment for her daughter.

And I had Madeleine's family to visit too. Of her there was no news, not that they expected any. Her mother, however, was one of those women blessed with eternal optimism – I could see where her daughter had inherited that characteristic: she was convinced that Madeleine would come home. Whenever I could I took food to them and to Arlette's mother too. I did not make the mistake of stealing it: I asked for it to give to friends and, as often as not, the cooks allowed me to take some. As I had known all along, there were good as well as bad Germans, just like the French.

I was lonely, desperately so. I'd always had Arlette to talk to and then Karl. Now there was no one I considered my friend, to whom I could unburden myself and explain my desperate longing for him.

Every day I waited for a letter – something he had touched. The fieldmouse, of all people, was in charge of the post for our department. I fretted that she was keeping his letters from me. I didn't dare ask if any had come or she would destroy them. Eventually one arrived.

She eyed me enviously as I put it into my pocket. 'We all know who that's from.' She sniffed. 'Don't think you can take time to read it during working hours because you can't.'

It was torture working all through the rest of that day knowing it was in my pocket, longing to read it, wanting a private quiet place to be with it.

He loved me! He repeated it time and time again. He wrote of his dreams for the life we would lead one day in the future. The censor had blacked out one line, which drove me mad with frustration. I held it in vain to the light, desperate to see what he had said. I did not know where he was, on which front, but of course he could not tell me. I gathered news to me of German movements, where the Panzer regiments were fighting, frightened every day that something would happen to him.

The lengthiest relationship I had had with a man, I worked out, was with Fabien. We had known each other longest and I had spent more days and hours with him than with the two men who, I could see now so clearly, were the ones I had truly loved. With Didier I had had just over two glorious months. Karl and I had been lovers for three months before he was taken from me. But with him I still had the hope that one day we would be reunited. I prayed for that every night.

That Christmas I received a second letter – no present had ever meant as much to me. As the Germans saw the New Year in, for some the enjoyment was not the same, the celebrations were muted compared with other years. As for the French, as much as they would have liked to celebrate, they had nothing to commemorate with. But all of us had that one precious commodity, hope.

But all through January there was no further news. February came. I plucked up the courage to ask the fieldmouse if any mail for me had been mislaid.

'Mislaid! What meaning you? We no letters lose.'

'But it's such a long time.'

'Perhaps he's dead,' she said coldly.

'Don't say things like that.'

'You are rude! Be careful.'

Hope kept me going until, a week later, she called me into her office. She enjoyed telling me, that was the awful thing. She smiled as she told me Karl was dead, his tank blown to smithereens. The room darkened for me, I swayed with shock.

'You now work.'

Work? Now? I couldn't. I fled from her satisfaction. Not again. Not that awful despair. I could not survive this, I did not want to. I wanted to die . . .

'Dupont, where you think you going to?' she yelled at me. I ignored her as I ran to the changing room and collapsed there in grief. She followed me. It did not matter to me what she said, what she threatened, for I was past caring. 'Listen to me. Do as I say.'

'Shut up!' I screamed, as I raced past her and out into the cold snow of winter.

Where I went I have no idea, I just walked and sobbed. I ranted at the heavens, I cursed man, machines and God. And I railed at the unfairness of my life. I would like to have curled up in the snow and gone to sleep and let it all be over.

'Mademoiselle, you will die of cold if you stay out on a night like this. You haven't even a coat.'

I looked up to see the concerned face of one of the junior officers. 'Leave me alone.'

'I can't do that. Here, come . . .' And, with no more ado, he lifted me up and carried me back to the headquarters. Someone put me to bed, I don't know who. When I awoke in the morning I had no idea where I was. For a few blissful seconds I felt content, then reality intruded and I cursed the soldier for saving me. What was the point of living in a world without my Karl?

Chapter Seven

February – December 1944

1

Life could never be the same again, but I did recover as, deep down, I had known I would. I'd wanted to die, certainly, but I hadn't killed myself, and if I had really thought I could never rebuild my world then surely I would have. Each trauma had left its mark, beginning with my sister Felicity, for without her death I would never have been in France. Then Fabien had used me. And there had been Didier and Karl.

Now I longed for this senseless fighting and the cruelty to end. I wanted to return home, to show my family how different I was and perhaps become worthy of their respect and love. Meanwhile I worked, my sadness so much a part of me now that I could barely remember what it had been like to be happy.

When I went to bed I hoped I would dream of Karl. I rarely did. I longed for him to come to me as Didier had, to reassure me that I could move on without guilt, but he did not. Now, I was in limbo. There were times when I allowed myself to hope that Karl was alive: he hadn't visited me in my dreams so perhaps there had been a hideous mistake. But in the morning I knew that could not be. I did check. I asked the fieldmouse if she was sure he was dead. She'd called an officer over. 'Tell this slut her lover's dead, will you?'

'He's very dead.' He grinned.

'It's not funny,' I said angrily. He hit me hard and they docked my pay for insubordination. If we hadn't been so short-staffed I would probably have been deported – such was the fate of those who crossed these people.

In the headquarters, life, while backbreakingly hard, had been bearable, despite the fieldmouse and Sylviane. The officers were generally polite, if arrogant. However, that changed at the end of February when the old commandant was replaced by a new man. Then it seemed that, with defeat a possibility, the Germans became crueller in their determination to quell opposition. Now there were large areas of the building where no French person was allowed. Late at night I could hear the cries of those locked in the basement where the Gestapo must have been at their deadly work. The dawn was often heralded by a fusillade of shots from a high-walled yard at the back of the building as some of the prisoners were executed. The frustration we felt at being unable to save them was indescribable. One of the gardeners said he was sure we would get used to the noise and become immune to it, but I hoped we wouldn't: if we were impervious to others' sufferings what would that mean we had become?

'You're wanted in the commandant's office,' Sylviane informed me grumpily, one March morning, as I worked in the pantry.

'Why?' I asked, my heart sinking.

'How should I know?'

I washed my hands, took off the long rubber apron we wore when at the sinks, combed my hair – anything to delay going. Anything to put off finding out whatever awaited me.

I pushed open the door of the commandant's outer office and entered the large room where clerks toiled at reams of papers, telephones shrilled, orders were barked and people rushed in and out.

'Clare, my dear!' I was enveloped in an expensive-smelling and smothering hug. 'I am so relieved to see you looking so well.'

'Madame de Rocheloire?' I stared inanely at Fabien's mother.

'I have permission to take you to lunch.' She smiled warmly but there was something agitated about her. From the floor beside the chair on which she had been sitting she picked up a wicker basket covered with a cheerful checked cloth. She took hold of my arm firmly and guided me towards the door.

'I can't do this. I've work to do. I don't finish until—'

'Of course you can come. I spoke to the commandant, a perfectly charming man, and he has said he can spare you. I've packed us a picnic. One can never be sure what they are serving in the restaurants, these days, can one?' She chattered away as we walked out of the office, waving regally to a sergeant, who jumped smartly to attention. 'Such a helpful man – for a German.' She waited for me to get my coat, for it was a chilly day, and we sallied forth, she inclining her head graciously at the armed guards as if they were doormen at the Ritz. I trailed along, hoping I was in a dream and that none of this was happening. I expected to feel the prod of a gun in my back at any moment.

'I've chosen the park – such a pretty one. And so convenient. Has it a bandstand? I so adore them – I remember when I was child dancing round and round one. Delightful.'

'We're not allowed in there. It's for Germans only.' She was mad, I decided.

'Rubbish. It's a French park and I'm a Frenchwoman,' she said defiantly, and I could not help but admire her courage as we swept through the gates. I was astonished no one stopped us. 'If one looks as though one belongs, who is to gainsay one?' she explained, reading my surprise. 'Here's a suitable place.' She looked about us as if checking for something or someone then took a cloth from the basket and flapped it over the bench before sitting down beneath a huge oak that was just coming into bud. 'I thought it safer here in the open air. No one to overhear us. I do hope it's not too cold for you.' She began to unpack her basket, stopped, looked at me, sighed, then shook her head as if clearing her thoughts. 'I need your help, Clare.'

'Mine?'

'I was unfair to you in the past and I misjudged you. I apologise.'

I was so shocked I couldn't speak.

'Well, I've apologised, I trust you will accept it,' she said sharply.

This was more like her, I thought. I felt on firmer ground when she spoke like that. 'Of course.' I would like to have said how surprised I was but as much as I disliked the woman I couldn't bring myself to be rude.

'Some time ago, before he became ... well ... a fugitive ...' she coughed delicately as if this was unpleasant gossip '. . . the doctor told me what you had done for his children. That was brave of you ...'

'I did nothing. In those days such a journey wasn't as dangerous as now.' I paused. 'And Fabien? I suppose you have no news.'

'That is exactly why I need to talk to you. Fabien is a prisoner.'

'Oh, no. I'm so sorry.'

She took out a scrap of handkerchief and dabbed her eyes. 'Yes, my poor brave darling, he was working with the Resistance. He was airlifted in, you know, by the RAF – such danger! But sadly . . . a collaborator, they say . . . He was discovered.' She really began to cry then and I was at a loss as to what to do: she wasn't the sort of person I could put my arm round and in any case I didn't want to. 'We have to rescue him.' She clicked open her handbag, put away the handkerchief and snapped it shut, as if putting an end to her tears.

'Rescue him? We? But how?'

'Time is of the essence, so please don't behave stupidly with me. I haven't the patience for it,' she said brusquely. 'You will marry him.'

'Me?'

'Oh, really! Yes. What's so odd in that?' She frowned. 'You were desperate to do so once, as I remember. Pray, what has changed?'

'Many things.'

'You're married to someone else?' she asked anxiously.

'No.' I had no intention of explaining to her about Karl and my unhappiness – I doubted that she would understand. Evidently my answer calmed her for she began to unpack the basket she had been carrying. There was a quiche, a half-bottle of wine, napkins, silverware, two cut-glass goblets – here was someone else who had no intention of letting a war change her standards.

'Then you should be pleased to marry such a fine young man.'

'Madame, I'm sorry, but I no longer love your son.'

'Love? What's that got to do with it?' She waved the corkscrew in the air. 'I need you to marry him, he needs you. You must. I have a plan.'

'Madame, I'm distressed for you that your son is a prisoner, but I can't see how my marrying him is going to help anyone.'

'But I haven't explained,' she said, exasperated.

'Then perhaps you had better. And while we are about it, Madame, perhaps it might be more helpful if you asked me rather than ordered me as you appear to be doing.'

'Am I?' She looked quite surprised. 'If so, I'm sorry. But you must understand what I'm going through. I can't sleep or eat. All I can think of is Fabien in the hands of those barbarians.'

'Where is he?'

'Lyon – in the Montluc prison.'

'This plan?' There seemed little point in explaining how grim the outlook was if he was there.

'I have been to Lyon, I have seen various people – members of the Abwehr, the SS. I have spoken to them about you. It is agreed that he is to marry you.'

'*What?* You had no right to do that. It's not fair to me.'

'What is fair is getting my son's freedom.'

'You didn't know what I was doing. You could have compromised me, got me into trouble, had me arrested.' I was angry: her presumption was breathtaking.

'Has anything befallen you?'

'No, but—'

'So I see no problem. Clare!' She grabbed my hand tightly. 'They have sentenced him to death—' Out came the handkerchief, and I found myself biting my fist to suppress my own tears. This was awful. I did not know what to say to her. I waited for her to compose herself. 'I have told them that you are pregnant and it is imperative for the succession of our properties that he makes an honest woman of you.'

'But—'

'It is lawful for such a ceremony to take place *in extremis*. And this is such a case. I will say this about the Germans: they have a fine respect for class and position. Fortunately it was a charming Junker I spoke to, with estates of his own, so he quite understood the urgency.'

'But if I marry him in prison, how does that help him get out?'

'Because this particular Junker – such a sensitive and understanding man, but then I would have expected that from one of his background – well, he also has an uncle who is a bishop, Lutheran, of course, and he quite understood my sensibilities that Fabien's own uncle should perform the ceremony. I explained that sadly he is infirm and cannot make the journey to Lyon. It will be performed in his private chapel. The mayor of that commune happens to be a cousin so all is officially recognised.'

'And they have agreed to that?' I laughed – I had to: it was all so ridiculous.

'I don't see what there is to be amused by.'

'It doesn't seem possible. It's so far-fetched. I can't believe they would allow it. It has to be a trap.'

'I would like to say that it was agreed on matters of social sensibilities, culture and compassion. Of the understanding that should be between noble families. But unfortunately a large sum of money and my Fragonard changed hands before an agreement could be reached.'

'So they have agreed. Then what happens?'

'I have already alerted his friends in the Resistance – that is where the dear doctor helped me. They will ambush the car and he will be saved. Those men would die for my son. They worship him.'

'Would it not have been a good idea to have discussed this with me first?' This was outright cheek.

'Clare, my dear, I didn't have time. I had to forge ahead for Fabien's sake. And you were always such a sweet girl, I was sure that when you knew . . .' She looked archly at me.

'There's just one thing. Is he to be rescued before or after the ceremony?' I asked politely. I still couldn't believe this was going to happen.

'Afterwards. The light will be failing by then, and on the mountain roads it will be easier.'

I slumped back on the bench. The whole plan was so preposterous it could never work. 'But there will be guards?'

'Of course.'

'With guns?'

'I should think so.'

'But I—'

'You're not going to say you're afraid?'

'No – Well, that's not strictly true, of course I'm afraid. But I was wondering, if this happens to come about, what happens to me? The

Germans are not going to like me very much, are they? They're hardly likely to welcome me back with open arms.'

'A plane will be sent from England to pick you both up. You will not be put in any danger. I have asked your commandant to release you to marry my son and he has agreed.'

'You have told the commandant that I am pregnant by a member of the Resistance? Oh, really, how could you be so stupid?'

'I told him my son was terminally ill and that was why you had to marry – nothing about him being a prisoner.'

'And he would know that I haven't been anywhere to get pregnant.'

'I did not mention your supposed condition to him. You are to return with me and he expects you back here in two days. So? Will you help me?'

I sat there and gazed into a future that I did not like the look of one little bit. Marry Fabien? How times had changed. Once I would not have had to think twice – but now? Still, if it meant saving his life, why not? When the war was over, we could divorce, or have the marriage annulled. And there was England, the idea of finally getting home. I was aware that she was watching me anxiously and I wouldn't have been human not to enjoy the situation, but I had to put the poor woman out of her misery. 'Yes,' I said. 'I'll do it.'

'Dear Clare, I knew you would never let us down. Fabien was sure you would help him once you knew all the details.'

'You've seen him?'

'I have. He's a changed man, Clare. So thin and sad. You will never regret this day. My family will owe you a debt that we shall never be able to repay.'

2

Once in the car, and presumably content that she had me in her grasp, Fabien's mother ceased talking to me. I didn't mind: I had time to think, which was not so good for I found that I didn't like what I was thinking.

Provided everything went to plan then the outcome would be splendid. But the operative word was *provided*. The more I thought about it, the more ludicrous the whole scheme seemed. I wondered if I hadn't fallen into the fantasy of a deranged mother, for what woman wouldn't plan the most extreme stratagem in the faint hope of rescuing her child?

It did cross my mind as to why she had decided on me? Why not Céline? After all, she was the favoured one.

'Why isn't Céline marrying Fabien?'

'She left for America years ago. She'll be married herself by now, I'm sure, a beautiful creature like her.'

I nearly said, 'Not that many years'. I had seen her in 1942. And I couldn't agree on the beauty: I had always thought she looked like a ferret. 'How did she manage that?'

'Her father was a diplomat. He had contacts with the Italians.'

How convenient, I thought.

As we motored along in the aged car it struck me as odd that she had managed to get petrol, such a precious commodity. Then it occurred to me that maybe she had been given it to transport me to the Gestapo in Lyon. Suddenly I felt trapped and panic hit me square on. Until I examined the idea and rejected it: why would they go to such lengths to arrest me when I had done nothing except know the wrong people – or the right ones, depending on which side you were on? That made me smile.

'Something is amusing you?'

'No.'

'I dislike people who say that. Have you ever tried to think of nothing? It is an impossibility.'

'It wasn't important. I was wondering how you got the petrol to drive all this way.'

'My friends and relations are intensely loyal. They gave it to me when they knew my mission was to save Fabien.'

More likely she had blackmailed them into handing over their precious coupons, which made me smile again. But this time I looked out of the window so that she could not see.

We drove over the mountain roads where sometimes there was no surface. Had we crashed and I had been the only survivor I would have had no idea where I was. A long way back I had seen a signpost to St Paulien and La Chaise Dieu. Then I must have fallen asleep for the next sign was to St Étienne, which I knew was a big city. We skirted Lyon by a long way and drove into burgundy country and an area unknown to me. To give her her due, she was a competent and tireless driver. We passed vineyards, some sadly neglected and weed-choked, others newly prepared for the summer. We saw little traffic and fewer people. The villages we went through for the most part seemed deserted as if the end of the world had come.

I must have slept again, for the rattling of the car woke me as we turned sharply off a road, through a gateway and on to a rutted drive, then went through overgrown trees until we arrived at a great sweep in front of a large, mainly shuttered house. It was old, falling down and heartbreakingly beautiful. With a start, I saw that it was built of stone the colour of butterscotch and the front was covered in what looked like a wisteria. It looked like the house of Didier's dreams.

'This is my brother's residence.'

'It's lovely.'

'You are not here to admire the architecture.' The time for gratitude was over, then.

A man who might have been Fabien, tall and slim, though older, raced down the steps to greet us. Since Madame de Rocheloire made no attempt to introduce him he did so himself. 'Mademoiselle, I am Philippe Boyer. I am enchanted to make your acquaintance. I am in awe of your courage.'

'I can't imagine why.' I had to suppress a giggle: middle-aged men who spoke so elaborately always made me laugh. He was friendly, appeared much nicer than his sister and, I was pleased to note, calmer. But I was on my guard: he was too much like his nephew for me to feel relaxed with him.

As he ushered us into his house he made small-talk. Inside, to my astonishment, the hall was panelled in pale, almost white wood.

'Did you know a Didier Pointe?' I asked.

'Pointe? No, I don't think so. May I ask why?'

'He was a friend of mine, but he described this house to me once – even this hall. It's quite creepy.'

'I do hope that won't affect how you feel about my Manoir des Hirondelles. I love it as if it were a person.' He smiled kindly at me. 'Are you cold?'

'Only a little,' I lied, unable to explain what had made me shudder. Didier had lived in the Place des Hirondelles and he had described the Manoir des Hirondelles to me. Had he been describing somewhere he knew?

'Is this your family home?' I asked, finding it difficult to imagine bad-tempered Madame de Rocheloire living here, for it had a lovely atmosphere of calm and security.

'No, I bought it ten years ago. I intended to retire here, but the war accelerated that retirement.'

'You ask too many questions, child.'

'And why shouldn't she, Constance?'

This house reminded me of Hortense's: it had the same faded, battered charm. The curtains and wall hangings were so old that I was sure that if anyone disturbed them they would die of dust inhalation. The furniture was in sore need of a polish, and the objects on it, without exception, had a fine rim of dust around their bases, as if they had not been moved since they were first set in place. There was a lovely scent of apples, and to my joy two large dogs bounded up to introduce themselves.

'You haven't still got those monsters, Philippe? What are you thinking of? They must need so much food, and with the shortages!' Madame tutted and pushed them away, which only made them pester her more.

'They hunt for rabbits.'

'You look to me as if you feed them your rations too. Just look at the state of you!'

'Will you want me to serve supper in the dining room, Monsieur?' An oldish woman had appeared, dressed from head to toe in black and with no smile of welcome on her face.

'Wherever's most convenient, Nelly.'

'Of course we shall eat in there. Whatever next? How are your feet, Nelly?' asked Madame.

'I get by.' She did not look at Fabien's mother as she spoke, and I was sure I had heard a sniff – the sort of sniff our cook at home gave when she didn't approve of something or someone. She shuffled out, her slippers flip-flapping as she went.

'You should get rid of that unpleasant old crone.'

'She suits me.'

'Useless woman! Just look at the dust.'

'I suggest, Mademoiselle, that once we have dined, perhaps you should rest. It will be a long and tense day tomorrow,' Monsieur said, ignoring his sister. I liked him more and more.

'Tomorrow?' No one had told me it was to be so soon. 'Not here, surely? I mean, afterwards, wouldn't Monsieur Boyer be put at risk . . .?' I tailed off because I was not sure how much he knew of the cock-eyed plan.

'No, no. You are going to a village some fifteen miles from here. I shan't be involved.'

I thought I heard Madame say, 'Coward,' but I couldn't be sure.

We ate our meal in the dining room, at a table beautifully set with silver and glass. There was no electricity and the candles made the scene look so romantic that I almost failed to notice how tough the meat was. And, indeed, the dogs' bowls seemed to contain a lot more than our plates.

The next morning the tension was almost palpable. Madame de Roche-loire, criticised her brother and me incessantly.

'Why are you so pale?' she said accusingly to me.

'I don't get out much.'

'Then you should. It's unhealthy at your age to be cooped up all day!' I didn't bother to explain that my German masters did not encourage me to take the air.

'Maybe it's a good thing if she's meant to be . . .' Philippe coughed delicately '. . . in a delicate condition.'

'Why have you no makeup? All young women have makeup.'

'I've never really used it much.'

'Well, you should. It might smarten you up a little.'

'I think she looks perfectly lovely as she is.'

'It's of no interest to me, Philippe, what you are thinking.' She stood back and looked critically at me. She had dressed me in a cream suit, which almost fitted but not quite. The skirt was just a bit too loose and long, the jacket too baggy on the shoulders, and I didn't like the collar. 'You don't look . . . you know . . .' Further flapping of her hands ensued.

'Pregnant?' It wasn't a word I would normally have used in mixed company but I felt like shocking her.

'Precisely. Can't you put some padding under your skirt?'

'And have it fall out at an inopportune time?'

'This is no joke, Clare. You have to look the part.'

'I'll stick my tummy out. That'll help.'

'I think she looks charming.'

'You, Philippe, wouldn't know charm if it knocked you over.' That was hardly fair, he had more charm in his little finger than she had in her whole being.

'Sister, what a sweet person you are.' And so it went on, carp, snipe.

'Please, will you both stop this? I'm so nervous and you're making me feel worse,' I said eventually, and for good measure I stamped my foot.

'Well!' was Madame de Rocheloire's response.

'I do apologise, unforgivable of us,' said her brother.

Madame de Rocheloire had a piece of paper to which she constantly referred, glancing at her watch. 'They will have left Lyon one hour ago, they should be with us within the hour.'

'Don't you think Mademoiselle should have gone to the prison to meet Fabien there?'

'No. If we had done that they might have suggested performing the ceremony there.'

'How many guards will he have?'

'I asked the Junker to be discreet. I'm hoping just two.'

'I think this is all so foolhardy, Constance. I feel that the Germans are permitting this for their own ends.'

'Think what you will. I'm not interested in your opinion.'

They were off again. I had five minutes before we, too, left so I went and sat on the front steps and waited. The garden in front of the house was lovely. Uncared-for in these times it looked natural, not man-made. In the distance I could see the terracing on the southern-facing slopes where vines had once grown. But no more: now it was a tangled mass of weeds.

Only the landscaping indicated what had once been there. It was a perfect spot and I allowed myself to dream of how wonderful it would be to live here in peace, with the man I loved, to tend the vines, to drink the wine and . . .

'Are you all right, my dear?'

'I was admiring the view.' I made room for him to sit beside me.

Philippe jack-knifed his slim length and lowered himself on to the step. 'Once the vineyard was my pride and joy. No more.'

'Did you have to supply the Germans?'

'Wine was taken, yes, but that did not matter too much – I've plenty bricked away from prying eyes. No, I gave up when the Vichy authorities came to inspect the wine – to use it in fuel alcohol for the Germans! That I minded but there was nothing I could do about it. It was when they poured heating oil into the barrels to ruin the wine and to ensure we could not drink it that I gave up.'

'But why, if you didn't mind them taking it?'

'Because they ruined the barrels. The barrel is important in the wine-making process. The older the barrel the better the wine. Some of mine were older than the century. They could never be used again – the stench of the heating oil can't be got rid of. So!' A Gallic shrug.

'But some vineyards are still in production.'

'The growers are made of sterner stuff than me. Some, you see, can't bring themselves to let the vines die and others who would carry on have no workforce left to tend them. Wars can mean hard choices. As you are making. You do know what you are doing?'

'Not really. I think it is the most madcap scheme I ever heard of. But once I was happy with Fabien and if I can help . . .' I shrugged but not as expressively as he had. 'I just felt that in the circumstances I could not ignore his mother's request.' Still he did not respond. 'After all, I'm sure Fabien would help me if our roles were reversed.'

'You think so.' I looked at him, puzzled. Had that been a question or a statement? 'And after the great escape?'

'If all goes to plan then I shall return to England and my family. So they will be doing me a favour too.'

'Just in case anything goes wrong, take my address.'

'Thank you, I will.' I took the proffered card. With my fingers I could feel that it was engraved, a relic from that other time before all this madness started.

'Time to go.' It was Madame de Rocheloire's sharp voice. 'Don't sit there, Clare, you'll make your skirt dirty!' I stood up wearily, climbed into the car and allowed myself to be driven to my fate.

3

Madame de Rocheloire, her cousin the local mayor and I awaited Fabien's arrival. We were gathered in a small, simple, whitewashed church – more a chapel, really. There was a font, a rough slab of stone for an altar, on which was a cross made from two rough branches nailed together. Apart from that there was no decoration, no stained glass. It was a place of worship for countryfolk; no fripperies here. But there was a wonderful atmosphere of serenity, which I tried to grasp and keep with me. Karl would have loved this place, and how wonderful if I had been waiting for him to marry me – how happy I would have been.

Madame de Rocheloire was a blur of movement, pacing back and forth, checking her watch, fretting. It was interesting that she was as irritable with the mayor as with me, as if Fabien's lateness was his fault. But the man seemed not to mind being snapped at. In fact, he seemed resigned to it and, once or twice, amused by her. He was pleasant to me, welcoming me to his family, saying what a lucky man Fabien was.

'How can you say that, Jules? After what my Fabien has suffered. Lucky! What rot you speak!' The mayor winked at me. Then, 'At last!' Rapidly she made for the door as we heard a vehicle grind to a halt. I knew from the heavy rumble that her hopes of only two guards were to be dashed. I reached the church door. Outside a car had drawn to a halt and behind it was a troop carrier from which jumped half a dozen soldiers. In one languid flow of movement a German officer emerged from the car. My heart missed a beat: he wore the dramatic black uniform of the SS. 'Madame.' He bent low over her hand, the noble Junker, no doubt – but not so noble that he couldn't be bribed. 'And this is the pretty bride?' It was my turn for the clicking heels and the low bow and I tried to look suitably bridal while quaking inside. Then Fabien appeared.

It was strange to see him again after so long and when so much had happened to us both. Before, when I had seen him at the château, he had been desperately thin. He looked far fitter now. Then I had noted a wariness in his expression, but now that look was even more pronounced, and there was a tension about him that reminded me of a wild animal. He licked his lips constantly, as does one who has something to fear, and who could blame him? I preferred not to think what agonies he had gone through.

Mindful of the Germans present I raced to him and flung my arms around him crying out his name. For a moment he looked taken aback but recovered quickly and engulfed me in a hug, calling me darling loudly. I felt as though I was being held by a stranger. It was weird to be with him and to know we had once been lovers. I could no longer remember how he had made love, how he had felt and smelt. Odd, when I could easily conjure up Karl, his scent, his touch.

'Shall we proceed?' The officer held wide his arm, gesturing towards the church for all the world as if he were the host at a normal wedding. I was horribly aware of the soldiers, guns at the ready, who followed us in and lined up at the back of the small church.

'The Bishop? Where is he?' The officer swung round.

'Unfortunately my poor cousin has been taken ill, Herr Oberstleutnant.'

'Not seriously, I hope.'

Oh, really, I thought, these social niceties seemed ludicrously out of place. 'You look a little pale, Mademoiselle. Are you all right?'

'I'm not too happy in the mornings, if you understand. Herr Oberstleutnant.' I simpered, touching my stomach discreetly.

'Only too well, my wife was the same. Still, as we have the mayor here, I suggest we begin.'

The mayor, who had been placid with Fabien's nagging mother, seemed now to go to pieces with the Germans present. I didn't know the wording of the French marriage ceremony well but the way he was gabbling it out made it incomprehensible. In minutes we were married, even if it was no marriage. The forms were signed. Fabien took our copy. I'd have liked one myself as a bizarre souvenir.

'Please may my wife ride with me just to the crossroads? We have so little time. Then she can transfer to the mayor's car,' Fabien asked the officer, who looked doubtful, but my woebegone expression persuaded him and I was allowed to sit in the back of the staff car with Fabien. I was not happy with the arrangement: I had presumed that we would part there and then, that I would scuttle away to safety and meet up with him later. I had no idea where the ambush would take place and I didn't want to be part of it. But I thought it best not to disrupt any plan he might have.

The cars lined up. The troops went first, then us and then the mayor. Madame de Rocheloire had already excused herself: she was about to visit her ailing bishop cousin, she said. Off we set. Fabien seemed remarkably relaxed. He had his arm round my shoulder and he was nuzzling me just as one would have expected a new husband to do. It was not pleasurable – in fact, I was irritated by his heavy breathing in the nape of my neck. Then I felt him stiffen, and glanced out of the car window. We were passing a farmyard. Inside, their engines running, were two troop carriers. We had far more than six to guard us!

'Is this the crossroads you meant?' the officer asked and swung round in his seat as the top of his head exploded. My cream suit was suddenly scarlet with his blood. I opened my mouth to scream but at the taste of his blood, I shut it fast, gagging. The driver was dead too and the car skidded into the bank so that Fabien's door wouldn't open.

'Move, for Christ's sake!' he shouted, leaning across me, grabbing for the door. He wrenched it open and shoved me out into the road. 'Run!' he yelled. Scrabbling to my feet, bent double, I did as he ordered as soldiers cascaded from the troop carrier behind us, guns firing. With a howl of brakes they were joined by the other vehicles we had seen hidden in the farmyard. The world had erupted into a shouting, gun-firing maelstrom with men groaning, cursing, screaming and blood spurting. Fabien and I ran hell for leather into a copse of trees. It was then that I realised the soldiers were not firing at us but at the hedges along the roadside. The mayor was in the centre of the road, whirling around, holding out a sheaf of papers as if they could shield him. I saw his mouth open wide, then he fell to the ground, blood pouring from his chest, his papers scattered about him. He crawled agonisingly slowly towards them, grasping at them. And then he was still. I stood up as if to go to him but Fabien pushed me back. 'Don't be a bloody fool, he's dead. Come! Quickly!'

I stumbled behind him, branches whipping across my face. The air in my lungs was like scalding water, and my heart and head were pounding painfully. There was no way of telling how far or for how long we ran but just as I thought we could go no further we dashed into another farmyard and raced up the outside slope of a barn. Fabien had to drag me up the rough wooden ladder to the hay-loft where I collapsed on the floor.

'It was we who were bloody ambushed! What a fiasco,' I heard him say, and looked round to see three men at the window, guns pointing out the way we had come.

'We heard the shooting. What happened?'

'They had more troops there lying in wait at the farm just down the road from the church.'

'But that was checked.'

'I'd like to know by whom.'

'But your mother was so certain . . .'

'Of course, it was always a possibility. We knew that. But some trigger-happy fool killed the officer.'

'So? One Kraut less.'

'I sent specific instructions that he was not to die. He could have been useful to us. He was open to bargaining.'

The men looked unimpressed. 'How many have we lost?'

'God knows. I didn't stop to count but it looks bad. We were lucky not to have been shot ourselves.'

I listened as they debated back and forth. There was something about Fabien, something in the way he spoke, with which I did not feel comfortable: he was excited, elated even. He looked too pleased with himself as if everything had gone well. I wondered if he had known that this was going to happen. It was not luck that we hadn't been shot, since no one had been shooting at us. Was it too far-fetched to believe that the deal his mother had done was for him not to be hurt in an ambush they both knew would take place? It was a dreadful thing to think. But it would not go away.

'We should leave here, and fast,' one of the men said urgently. Fabien slid down the ladder and someone helped me. I could not have made it unaided: not only was I tired from running but I felt an unreal weakness in every part of me. I was shaking yet I was not cold.

'It's shock,' explained the man, who had introduced himself as Jean. 'We'll get you in the warm, then you'll feel better.'

They loaded the guns on to a hay wagon, which they covered with sacks of potatoes. One of the men helped me climb up. When I looked down and saw the state of my suit I began to retch.

'Take deep breaths – it'll help. My mother will find you something else to wear,' Jean said kindly.

'You don't have to come, Clare,' Fabien said, as he climbed up beside me.

'And where else do you suggest I go?' I asked, with heavy irony. I wriggled my way as far forward on the wagon as I could get before the men covered us with tarpaulins. In the darkness as the wagon lurched from side to side, the intolerable shaking took over my whole body.

'She needs rest,' I heard a woman say. I was wonderfully warm. There were sheets on me and a soft pillow under my head. Had I been asleep or unconscious? I struggled to sit up. 'There, there, my dear, you rest awhile yet,' she said, in a soft country accent. 'Drink this, it'll help you.' I sipped at a warm but bitter liquid she held to my lips. Strangely, its bitterness was pleasant and the warmth I felt as it sped through my body delicious.

'Thank you, you're so kind. What is this?'

'My own herb concoction. For the nerves.'

'Have I been asleep long?'

'Bless you, no. Only a couple of hours.'

Only! 'Where is everyone? What has happened?'

'Your husband's downstairs with the other men having some food.'

'My husband?' I must have sounded like an idiot. But then I remembered, and the awful scene came flashing into my mind. 'Dear God, the men, what . . .?'

'Six dead, two taken – God help them.' She crossed herself. 'What a catastrophe.'

'Did any escape?'

'By a miracle, yes. Six are safe, my son included. And your fine husband.'
I felt such anger at her words, for if I was right then she, her son and his
companions, like me, had been duped. And yet . . . had I imagined the
irony in her tone? 'I'll let you rest now. You try and sleep. You've a big day
tomorrow.'

'Have I?'

'It's a full moon. They heard on the wireless that the plane is coming
for you and your husband.'

I couldn't sleep. The images of the dead, the dying, the awful screams,
Fabien's uncle would not leave me. Finally I gave up trying. Perhaps
company would help blot them out. I dressed in the clean clothes the
woman had thoughtfully laid out for me and ventured downstairs. The
men sat around the long table in a kitchen that reminded me of Arlette's
grandmother's. There were several pitchers of wine and a large platter of
cheese and bread.

'Hello, everyone.' I felt shy suddenly.

'Are you hungry?' Jean leapt to his feet and pulled out a chair for me.

'Now that you mention it.' No bread or cheese had ever tasted better
and the wine was sublime. I sat quietly as the men talked amongst
themselves, evidently planning the next day's escape. Fabien's expression
was self-satisfied, petulant. Had he always been like this and had I chosen
not to notice?

'How are you, wife?' He grinned at me, as if suddenly aware that I was
staring at him.

'Better now that I've had something to eat.'

'I should thank you for making this possible.'

'It was nothing. You'd have done the same for me. I'm glad it succeeded
– to your satisfaction.'

'I hear you've been working in Anliac. You should have come with me
when I left – you'd have been useful to them instead of wasting your time
stuck behind a German bar.' I couldn't be bothered to explain myself to
him. 'I hope once I'm back in England that I can be recruited in some
capacity.'

'Undoubtedly. Mab is.'

'You've seen her?'

'You could say I have.'

'Is she an agent? Only that card I got, you remember, telling me you
were well?'

'That was Tubs.'

'I didn't like him at first but he turned out to be a good friend. How is
he?'

'In Africa, last I heard. He got over Mabs eventually but it took time.'

'She ditched him? How sad.'

'Fell for another. These things can't be helped.'

'It was you, wasn't it?'

'Clare, what an accusation.'

'It doesn't bother me if you were lovers.'

'No? Well, I *am* offended.'

'Then don't be. And you were parachuted in as an agent. That was brave of you.'

'It was quite good fun until I was captured.' He laughed as if it had all been nothing.

'Were you tortured?'

'Quite honestly, Clare, it's something I'd rather not talk about.'

'I'm sorry.' I couldn't think what else to say to him, so I decided to go back to bed. 'Well, if you'll excuse me, I think I will be able to sleep this time.' I was suddenly so tired that even climbing the stairs took effort.

At about midnight the door opened. 'Hello again, wife.' Fabien was grinning at me as he walked towards the bed, unbuttoning his shirt. He took it off and flung it on a chair. In that split second I noticed that there was not a mark on his body.

'You know and I know that I'm not your wife, so stop saying it.' I moved back in the bed.

'Oh, come on, Clare, don't be stuffy. You used to love me.'

'Not any more, Fabien.' I pulled the covers closer.

'And you used to enjoy it when we made love.'

'That was because I didn't know better. Now, would you please get off my bed?'

'Don't be a spoilsport.' He lunged towards me and, from his breath, I knew that he was drunk. I shrank further away from him, but he followed me and grabbed at the borrowed nightdress.

'Don't touch me!' I shuddered.

'Clare? What has got into you? You're so unfriendly,' he whined.

'I hate traitors.'

'What does that mean?'

'You know damn well. Your mother certainly did that deal with the Germans – your freedom in exchange for as many resistants as would be there to help you. You're a cruel, selfish bastard, Fabien.' I was not prepared for the force of the blow and my head jerked back painfully.

'Don't you ever say that again! You understand?'

'So it's true. God forgive you, I can't.'

Once more he lunged at me, ripped at the nightdress, tore it off me, then placed his hand firmly over my mouth so that the others would not hear my screams as he raped me.

4

During the night, while Fabien slept, I crept out of the room and out of the house. It was cold but that was nothing to the ice I felt inside me. There was a pump at one side of the yard, and there in the moonlight, I stripped and scrubbed myself. The water was freezing but I was glad for it seemed to purify me.

Back in the house, the fire, though low, still threw out some warmth. My teeth were chattering. An old coat was hanging by the door. It smelt of animals, comforting. I wrapped it around me and lay on the wooden settle built into the side of the fireplace. It stretched almost the length of one wall. On the opposite wall was a cupboard, made from cherrywood, which contained a clock that wheezed away the minutes. I huddled as close as I could to the embers of the fire. A mouse scurried by on some mission. Normally I was terrified of them; tonight I watched it with detached curiosity. After my ordeal it had lost the power to frighten me.

I felt such a muddle of emotions: anger, yet a weird passivity as if everything was beyond my control, as if what had happened had been inevitable. Perhaps it was a punishment on me for loving the others and not Fabien. Was it my fault I'd fallen out of love with him? And where had my feelings for him gone? I had not imagined them: they had been as much part of me as he had been. And if I had loved, how could I hate? It was such an ugly word. I felt tears of self-pity begin to fall. Then I sat up, pulling the overcoat closer to me, I mustn't cry, it wouldn't help. I had to overcome this, quench the fear that was bubbling close to the surface as if that one violent act had stripped me of all self-confidence. But I could not give in to shame. I needed to hate him. Hate! Such an ugly emotion. I paused, pulling my knees up close and holding them for comfort. But wasn't love akin to hate? If I gave in to it I would be honouring him with my extreme emotions. I would not do that.

I would go to England. I would inform the authorities, let them deal with him. But what would I tell them? If I told of the rape he would deny it. Should I tell them here? The woman might believe me – but they adored him, they would not want to hear. Still, there had been that tone in her voice last night. And who had told me he was adored? His mother. Should I tell? The thoughts played tag around my mind. His betrayal of his colleagues – that I would tell, that could never be forgotten. I would ignore him and expunge him from my life as if he had never been.

How disappointing people could be. I really didn't mind if he and Mab had been lovers, for what was he to me now? But as far as she was concerned she had gone to bed with her friend's lover – and I would never have done that to her. But why should I be surprised? She had lied to me about her father, so why shouldn't she betray me with Fabien? It would seem she lived by a different set of rules from others. Here was someone else I would remove from my mind and my life.

There were good things to think about – better to concentrate on them. Soon I would be home, and I made myself plan my return, what I would say, what my father would say, how happy they would be and me . . .?

It was fine to imagine my welcome home but what if I was the last person they wanted to turn up? What if they were dead? I shuddered at that. No, Clare, think of . . . Karl, unlock those precious memories . . . I fell into a deep sleep.

'Whatever are you doing here, my dear?' It was Jean's mother. The dawn light was filtering through the curtains and she was dressed, a large basket of logs in her arms. I peered up at her but the blackness flooded back and I shuddered. 'Clare? You don't look well.'

'I don't know your name. Last night I never asked you.'

'Antoinette.'

'I'm fine, really.' And then I burst into tears.

'There, there, what's happened?' She scooped me into her arms and rocked me. Her breasts were large and soft and, for a sweet moment, I could almost feel like a child again, held in my mother's soft embrace. When had I last thought of her in this way? Not since I was a child.

This was the moment I should tell it all. I should warn these good, honest people that they had a snake in their midst. Let them mete out what justice they thought he merited. Let others deal with him . . .

'Marriage isn't all it's made out to be,' I decided to say instead, and laughed weakly through my tears.

'Was he rough with you? It's the drink – it gets some of them like that. Why men have to drink the way they do has always been a mystery to me.' She clucked about me, smoothing my hair, wiping away the tears with a handkerchief that smelt of rosemary. 'What you need, my dear, is a good bowl of porridge.' She bustled away and the moment was gone.

The men appeared. Fabien was one of the last. 'Good morning, wife,' he said, with a grin, as if nothing had happened between us. I wondered if he remembered what he had done. I chose to ignore him.

We had a long day ahead of us. The aeroplane to take us to England was due to arrive just before midnight, and the hours from now until then had somehow to be filled. I helped Antoinette. We pottered about her large kitchen, she seemingly relaxed, I a bag of nerves waiting for the Germans to appear at any moment.

'Don't you worry, Clare. If one soldier appeared in a twenty-mile radius, we would know. The police here are with us, not them. Now don't fret and, if you like, you can help me with this bread. I've a whole load to make for our boys in the mountains. When the arms come tonight they'll be hungry.'

'You're very brave.'

'Me? What nonsense you talk. I only do what any woman would do.' She pushed at the dough as if pushing my words away but she looked pleased for all that.

'I don't think every woman would. I think there are special women and you're one of them.' I wondered how many more there were like Antoinette, prepared to risk all for their own people. There was Madame Verdier, who'd cared for Tiphaine, Arlette's mother and grandmother, Madame Violet. All of them had said much the same, that they weren't doing anything important.

Antoinette couldn't have found me a better task for as I kneaded the dough I was able to vent my inner tumult. The dough was Fabien. As I kneaded and pummelled it was his face, his body I attacked – Oh, I felt so much better.

Antoinette insisted that I rest in the afternoon. I could not bring myself to lie on the bed but sat in a chair, having taken care to lock the door. For good measure I pulled a chest in front of it too. Why hadn't I told them? The explanation was simple, I decided: they were quite capable of killing him and I didn't want his blood on my hands. It was best to leave it until we got to England. But then I wondered if perhaps this wasn't true: without him would the plane still come and would I have my passage home? I had been through enough now, and nothing would stop me going to England.

At last it was time to depart. We were all dressed from head to toe in black – I must have looked a fright for, with no clothes of my own, I had been kitted out by Antoinette. Since she was at least four times larger than me, everything hung off me in folds. I must have looked like an old elephant whose skin no longer fitted. In the dark it would be impossible to tell if I was man or woman – and in the circumstances there was some comfort in that.

The vehicles we used were old and rusty, the wood-burning stoves that powered them snorted and wheezed like an old man dying. Thick, pungent smoke billowed out. As if that wasn't enough the exhausts threw out clouds of acrid fumes. As we rattled noisily along I hoped that Antoinette had been right about the Germans, for the noise we made should have attracted a battalion.

We arrived at a lane where we all had to get out. The vehicles were hidden under branches and we had to walk through trees, not easy in the dark for no lights were allowed. Eventually we arrived at the landing site – a large field where, in the bright moonlight, I could make out figures standing. 'They'll light the beacons,' Fabien explained.

'Don't talk unless you have to,' Jean whispered urgently. 'No smoking. Hide in that ditch. Do nothing until I say so.'

'Cheeky sod!' Fabien was not used to taking orders from peasants.

'Silence!'

We huddled together in the ditch. I was not happy being so close to Fabien, but there was no alternative. Crouched alongside us were several other men – I was the only woman. Two were unmistakably English. They smiled politely but we were all so nervous that none of us was in any mood even to whisper. I would have liked to practise my English. I had not spoken it for so many years now that I feared I had forgotten it. But this was not the time.

My ears ached from listening for an aeroplane.

'Shit!' I heard Jean mutter.

'What is it?' Fabien asked.

'See the mist rising from the ground? It's common around here – it's the river. They might not see us.' At which point we heard the drone of an aeroplane, coming in low. Jean gave the order and a light flashed, a beacon was lit. Once it circled, twice, three times, and then we saw it bank and fly away.

'Bastard!' I heard Fabien mutter.

'He couldn't see us. Or maybe he saw something he didn't like the look of,' Jean said. 'We should get out of here fast.' My heart lurched. Surely Fabien was not about to betray them again? Was a platoon of Germans about to appear and arrest us all, or kill us?

The beacon was doused. As quickly and noisily as we had come we returned to the farmhouse. No Germans appeared, no ambush. I was jumpy. Could he bring himself to jeopardise his own escape?

The waiting began all over again.

For three nights nothing happened, three nights during which the tension and frustrations mounted. For three nights the BBC did not send the code: '*Argent sera libre*' – silver will be free. Our message. Each night I locked the door of my room and dragged the chest across it. I need not have bothered for Fabien and I were no longer speaking. He had tried once or twice, but each time I had whispered back, 'I don't speak to rapists and traitors.'

'Why don't you say it out loud? They'd never believe you,' he goaded me.

'Because I prefer to bide my time,' I replied.

It was a dreadful time, not just for we escapees but for the brave people who sheltered us. I was scared and yet, I learnt, they had done this many times. It was implied, but never said, that the attic of Antoinette's house was a veritable armoury. That was courage, for if the Germans ever came there would be no trial: they would all be shot in their own yard. When I heard them talking about the Germans and their hatred for them I often wondered what they would think of me if they knew about Karl. Certainly I would not be sitting here in this kitchen sharing their food. I would be an outcast. Would his being dead make a difference? I doubted it. But I had always known that, and it had never affected my feelings for him. How many of us were there who, despite themselves, had found love with the enemy? My longing for him never decreased. If anything it had grown stronger – I felt far more for him now than I had felt even for Didier. Yet at the time I would never have thought that possible. Had Karl lived I would not be here. Had he not died I would not have gone through this ludicrous marriage to a man I now hated. The Germans of whom they spoke were not like my Karl. I was convinced of that.

The message from the BBC came on the fourth night. Once more we said farewell, although, this time, Antoinette refused. 'If I don't say it, perhaps you will have more luck and go.' This time the plane circled over the flares the men had lit and then, surprisingly softly for something so large, it landed, engines running. The door in the side of the plane opened, supplies were dumped, followed by two men, who were immediately whisked away by some of our men. Fabien, the two English agents, three others I had not noticed before and I raced across the rough field. I could see the cheery face of an RAF sergeant at the door of the plane. He helped the men inside. I put up my hand for the man to pull me in.

'Sorry, Miss. We can take no more. We've instructions for six only.'

'But I'm one of them.'

'There's been a mistake.'

'Fabien, explain to this man,' I yelled over the noise of the engines, for the airman was already leaning out to shut the door.

'Explain what, Clare? This is an RAF plane. You've not been booked in by Thomas Cook.'

I grabbed the side of the doorway but the plane was beginning to move. Fabien leant out. 'I warned you. You should have kept your mouth shut.'

'You bastard!'

'Yes, that's me.' He gave a jaunty wave as the door closed and the engines revved. Jean pulled me clear as it taxied away and took off for England and freedom.

5

'That man was never to be trusted. He'd a snide look about him. Too much charm. I thought that the minute I set eyes on him,' Antoinette said bitterly as we sat around the kitchen table eating a huge breakfast. Because of my disappointment and anger, I was not enjoying it.

'You never said, Mother.'

'Would you have listened?'

'Probably not. But you should have said something.'

'It was a feeling only, I had no proof. There's several you've brought here I've had no time for, but what good would it do us if I told you what I thought? You'd put it down to female tittle-tattle. I know you. You're like all the men.' She cut more bread. 'And you're angry, Jean, but what about poor Clare? You must be so upset.' Antoinette patted my hand comfortingly, but it didn't help: I was too miserable. I had lived here in France for five years, resigned to the fact that I would not see home until the war ended. To be given a glimpse of freedom only to have it snatched away had been hard. It was interesting what Antoinette had said. I had been right about her.

'Have any of you thought how odd it was that at the ambush he wasn't hurt? Neither was I, for that matter. They weren't firing at us but at you.' I might just as well tell them.

'Weren't they? You never said.' Jean was looking very angry indeed.

'I . . . It was . . .' Maybe I shouldn't have told them. Would he think me part of the conspiracy?

'Give the poor girl a chance. She'd just got married. Was she likely to tell us? She was hoping her interpretation was wrong.'

'It wasn't that simple, Antoinette. I'm ashamed to say I kept quiet about my doubts because I didn't want to jeopardise my return to England.' There, it was out now and I was glad. But I sat tense, knowing there were likely to be repercussions.

'You did what? You selfish bitch!' Jean thumped the table. I winced, afraid he might hit me next. 'Do you realise fifty men have been shot in reprisal for getting that bastard on a plane?'

'No, I didn't know.' My voice emerged like a squeak.

'What did you think was going to happen? That the Germans would pat us on the back and say well done?'

'Jean! Shut up for a minute. Let's get to the bottom of this. You don't mean you were going to keep quiet about it? Let him get off?' Antoinette looked shocked.

'No. I intended telling the Military Police, or whoever should be told, in England. Let them deal with him.'

'Bastard traitor. I'd have killed him with my bare hands. Madame, do you realise six children have no fathers because of that shit?'

'Cursing won't help, Jean. You know I don't like language like that in my kitchen.'

'Jean, please listen to me. I'd no idea until it was all over and I began to think about it. Even then I wasn't certain. Had I known before I would have told you, you must believe me. He's no friend of mine either.'

'Our falling out isn't going to help. Stop hitting furniture and listen to the poor woman, will you? We must report all we know and all we think we know. Fabien knew the identity of too many resistants in this area for comfort. We must ensure we limit the damage he might have done. Claude is due here this morning – he's coming to collect much of the cache we were left last night. He'll know what we should do.'

All morning I waited, not allowing my hopes to rise too high since Claude was such a common name. At lunchtime, smiling broadly at the sight of me, the Claude I had helped in Paris, the man who had worked with Didier, strode into the kitchen.

'What was it?'

'A boy. We called him Didier – after a fine and courageous man.'

'How lovely.' Tears filled my eyes. 'And your wife?'

'Well in health but moaning that Lyon isn't a patch on Paris. But you know Parisians – nowhere in the world is.'

'And Luc?'

'Ah, well. We've had a problem with Luc. Since Louise died he's gone crazy. He's too wild for his own good and ours. He's been shipped out of harm's way. We've got a friendly doctor who took him to his clinic . . . you know.' He made a circular movement, tapping his temple.

'Poor Luc. How did Louise die?'

'Luc killed her.'

'Oh, my God.' I had to sit down with a bump. 'It was I who named her. It's my fault.'

Claude leant forward and took hold of my hand. 'It was only one person's fault. Louise's. If she hadn't betrayed us she would be alive today.'

'But why? She always seemed such a pleasant woman.'

'*They* had her mother and son – they threatened her that if she didn't tell . . .' He made a chopping motion with his hand across his throat. 'She made a choice.'

'But an inevitable one. What woman put in that position wouldn't have done the same? Poor Louise.'

'Poor Louise my arse! She killed your Didier as surely as if she'd put a gun to his head, and you, too, if you hadn't been out that morning. Never forget that.'

'It's just that I wonder, if I'd had children, what I would have done.'

'All she had to do was confide in us. We could have fed them false information. All those people dead, and Luc might just as well be. He's completely off his head, I doubt he'll ever come out. And she didn't save her kid. It's been deported. *Kaput!*'

Once I had seen everything in such simple terms: there was a right and a wrong and that was that. But I had learnt that life was rarely like that and in war even less so; the choices that had to be made in the world we lived in were every shade of grey. If I was right, then Fabien was a traitor to his comrades and his country. But that poor woman, what had she been? Undoubtedly a traitor to her friends and country but not to her family and her child. To them she had tried to be a saviour. It was all so complicated.

'What will you do now, Clare? You're welcome to join us in Lyon. We always need discreet couriers.'

I laughed. 'No, thank you, Claude, I've had enough excitement to last me a lifetime.' I noticed Jean was no longer looking at me with such a surly expression.

There was a problem, though. Where could I go? Anliac was out – they'd be surely looking for me there. If I went to Paris I would put poor Hortense at risk again. The doctor was still a fugitive. Fabien's? Hardly. At that my thoughts screeched to a halt. Of course, Madame de Rocheloire had known all along what was to happen: she had known that Fabien had betrayed his friends, for it was she who had set the whole thing up. She'd have known they were not taking me to England. She had lied to me so convincingly – and I'd felt sorry for her too. With no money what on earth was I to do?

'You can stay here, Clare.'

'It's very kind of you, Antoinette, but I think I should move on.' The truth was I would love to have stayed but I couldn't, not where Fabien had harmed me.

'I hoped you meant your invitation, Monsieur.'

'It has never been my way to extend one if I did not wish the person to accept. You are most welcome.' Philippe Boyer ushered me into his house. 'You look tired, Madame. I suggest we drink a glass of Madeira.'

We sat in the shabby drawing room. I remembered my own home where everything had been of the best Maples could offer and shone with its newness, and realised I preferred the old and faded look of this house – it had a reassuring quality that made me feel it would last for ever and I would be safe there.

'While I am delighted to see you, Madame, you must be bitterly disappointed not to be in England.'

'There just wasn't room on the aeroplane. They made a mistake on the numbers.' I had decided not to tell him that Fabien was a Judas. After all, Monsieur Boyer was his uncle. There was no way of knowing how he would react and I didn't want to risk being thrown out.

'But there was room for Fabien?'

'They wanted him back, no space for mere passengers.' I tried to smile but my feelings were still too raw, and it was a stiff little *moue* I made instead.

'I am amazed that the British sent a plane just for Fabien.'

'Oh, they didn't. They delivered . . . other things,' I said lamely. How did I know he was to be trusted? He might be like his sister. Yet, watching him, I couldn't believe he was.

'But he promised you, or rather my sister did – acting, I assume, on his authority.'

'Yes, well . . . This is such a lovely room Monsieur Boyer.'

'He never intended to, did he? It was a trap, wasn't it?'

'I'd really rather not say.' *I need a roof over my head, I don't want to upset you, please change the subject.*

'Madame, I feel I should apologise to you on behalf of my other decent relatives, who would be as appalled as I. Unfortunately there's bad blood in my family.' At this I sat forward in my chair, agog to hear more. 'My sister . . .' He paused as if he was fighting with himself. 'She is my step-sister. She had a bad start in life. Though why I make excuses, I don't know. I think you deserve an explanation after all you have done for them. The bald truth is, she will do anything and harm anyone to further her own ends. Quite honestly, I think she's mad. While Fabien is not as bad as her, he is appallingly arrogant and selfish.'

'Oh dear.' What a limp remark, but what else could I say?

'Your discretion earlier does you honour, Madame. But I am no fool. When Constance told me of her plan I feared it was a charade. I worried that you had been duped. It was something of a relief to discover that you were not in love with Fabien – my sister had assured me you were. Given those circumstances, I wondered if you were simply a saint or whether you in your turn were using him.' He smiled when he said this, so there was no criticism in his words: he was simply telling me what he had observed.

'You certainly are no fool! I didn't want to tell you the truth and have you send me packing.' I smiled properly this time. 'I wanted to get home. So, yes, it's a moot point as to who was using whom. It probably serves me right that I was left behind.' It was better to leave it at this and not tell him my real fears.

'Did you come because you had nowhere else to go?' His hand flew to his mouth. 'My dear, I have said that in such an unwelcoming manner. Please, I am happy for you to stay here as long as you wish. You do understand?'

'That is most kind of you. It would be wonderful if I could lie low for a couple of weeks. But I worry that they might look for me here.'

'The locals are loyal to a man. You must stay as long as you wish. I shall enjoy your company.'

He poured us more Madeira – he was more generous with the drinks than his step-sister, that was sure. 'I've been wondering if I should join the Maquis.' I didn't want to, but I thought I should: the men shot in reprisal haunted me.

'In the hills? I hardly think that's suitable.'

'They need anyone who can help. I can teach them how to be a courier – I was good at that.'

'Some of those young men are, of course, sterling people, but some . . . how shall I put it? . . . are not in the mould of heroes. I hear they are a motley band. Criminals and hooligans who have joined to avoid the enforced labour.'

'You can't blame them. And they will all have the same cause in mind.'

'I trust your faith is not tested,' he said, with a wry smile.

'You know, Monsieur, the real reason I came here is, I suppose, quite odd. Do you remember I told you about my friend who had dreamt of this house, to the very details of the architecture, even to the wisteria? I suppose it sounds silly but I wanted to be here because of him.'

'I remember well. If he dreamt of this place then maybe while you are here you might touch his spirit.'

I understood then why I liked this man so much.

My plan to join the Maquis wasn't mentioned again. I was glad. I hadn't really wanted to live rough in the hills and I was afraid now of fear: I remembered it too clearly, the clenching of my stomach, the bitter taste in my mouth of real dread. I loved it here and I was sorely in need of the peace of this place. I was tired – not just my body but my mind too. As the days passed I felt the atmosphere soothe me, taking away the anger and bitterness. At the back of my mind, though, was a tiny nagging voice that kept reminding me I should be doing something.

We got on so well. I had never before met someone so much older than myself with whom I felt so relaxed. He enjoyed talking to me of art, music, wine – his passions, as they had been with Karl and Didier. In turn I could talk to him about almost anything. I was able to tell him all about Didier and I knew he understood. Didier, yes, but Karl – never. And, a new experience for me: I found with him that I enjoyed silence. In the evenings we would sit, the windows wide open, the cooling breeze making the candlelight flicker, and there was no need for words.

As the war turned against the Germans, and as rumours of liberation flew about us like the summer swallows, Philippe began to think of replanting the vines in the autumn. His wine maker was called to the house and I was privy to their excited plans. And he began to make designs for the garden – me, interested in gardening!

Nelly looked after us, but while she was good at housekeeping her cooking was dire – she was the first Frenchwoman I had met who couldn't cook. I tried to work out how to offer to take over from her without offending her – difficult, since she made no secret of her dislike of me. She was suspicious of the friendship I had with her master whom I now addressed by his Christian name.

The tiredness persisted and I was becoming very lazy. Worrying that I might be ill I decided to have a check-up. At the beginning of this war I had been an innocent child: I had known nothing of the world, men and sex. I thought I had learnt. I hadn't. Why else had I not realised – for over three months – that I was pregnant?

'Are you sure?' I asked the doctor. He looked less than pleased that I should question his judgement.

Having cycled here, the bicycle a present from Philippe, I wondered if I should cycle back or whether that would harm the baby. At that thought I got off my bicycle and sat on a bank. I needed to think. I went over how I had felt when the doctor first told me. Had there been a glimmer of pleasure? Or had it just been a shock? Another lie from Fabien. Sterile! What a fool he had taken me for. Now I would be suspicious but then – God, I'd been so young. I shuddered at how lucky I'd been, the number of times we had slept together – I didn't want to think of it as making love – when I might have become pregnant. What would he have done? Deserted me, that was for sure. Did I really want this man's baby? Conceived in that brutal way? The answer was a resounding no so I got back on my bicycle and pedalled furiously, hoping to damage it in some way.

Philippe was at the door waiting for me, his face tense, his movements agitated. 'Clare, my dear, you can't go to the hills. Not now!'

'No? I know.' I smiled at him. 'You tell me your reason then I'll tell you mine.'

'There has been a dreadful ambush in the Auvergne. The Germans are attacking the massed forces of the Maquis. They will be slaughtered.' He was jigging up and down, he was so upset. 'My poor child, you look white as a sheet. Are you ill?'

'Dr Forêt, he's with them, perhaps others I know. And I'm pregnant.' I hadn't meant to blurt it out quite like that.

'My dear Clare, how exciting. I shall be a great-uncle, a fine and honourable position. You must sit down immediately. Nelly, a tisane for Madame, quick,' he called, into the back regions of the house where she held sway.

'Honestly, Philippe, don't fuss, I'm fine.' But I wasn't, and he saw the bleak expression on my face.

'But, Clare, I am so insensitive. You would have preferred this not to happen, at this time and in the circumstances. My poor child. But I will take care of both of you. When that wretch returns – if he ever dares to return – he must be made to accept his responsibilities.'

'I'm pleased, Philippe, really.' There was no point in trying to explain. I could not embarrass this dear man by telling him the truth – how already I loathed the child I carried in my belly.

6

News travelled in the most amazing way and, given the way we lived, with extraordinary speed. A snippet heard was repeated along the chain from town to village from hinterland to the sea. Some was gossip, some wild rumour, but the rest was fact. For too long any news had been depressingly bad, and now things changed for the better.

June had begun badly when the Germans began their severest offensive against the Maquis, massed on Mount Mouchet, which led to dreadful losses. But then came the exciting news that the Allies had entered Rome, which was overshadowed when we heard that the liberation had begun with the landings in Normandy; the longed day had arrived.

'I have been saving this bottle of Romanée-Conti for today,' Philippe told me, as he carefully decanted the precious wine. Nelly had killed a duck for our dinner. It seemed hard on the creature to have survived so long only to die when liberation was close.

'Years ago, at a friend's birthday lunch at Maxim's, I decided that this was my favourite wine.'

'Young as you are, you are a woman of discrimination to choose the greatest Burgundy.' He raised his glass to taste the wine, an expression of rapture on his face.

'I fear our liberation may take some time,' he said suddenly, the elation replaced by sadness.

'Philippe, don't spoil today. Let's worry about that tomorrow.'

He was right, our joy was shortlived when a few days later we heard of the massacre of a whole village: men shot, women and children burnt alive in retribution for the successes of the Resistance. I knew so many villages now, so many good honest people. I feared for them all.

'The enemy will not give up without the most appalling fight, I think.'

'Then I have to help.' Here I go again, I thought, just when everything was secure and comfortable. I seemed to be destined to help a cause I supported passionately but which I wished could get along without me.

'Clare, not in your condition.'

'Bah! Philippe, I am young, fit and capable.'

My moods were strange even to me; I hoped it was the pregnancy and that I wouldn't always be like this. In the morning I might wake content with my lot but by lunchtime I was irritable and angry, by supper depressed and by nightfall content again. My decision to join the Resistance again was a prime example of my instability. While knowing I would be afraid, and dreading that numbing fear, I also felt excited. While I wanted to live, I did not care what happened to me or the baby. The thought of peace filled me with joy yet when it eventually came who would be there for me to share it with?

Philippe might have pretended to be aloof from everything to do with the Maquis but this was far from so. Unbeknown to me much had been hidden in this rambling house, which now began to emerge. 'Old houses are so useful with their hidden rooms and bricked-up cellars,' he said, as a cornucopia of stored food appeared, with an arsenal of weapons he'd been hoarding for this time. His gardener was an active member and soon I was doing my errands, cycling hither and thither to deliver messages. Philippe's objections to my working for them had been overruled by the Maquisards. Who better than a pregnant woman as a messenger? Who would suspect her? Who would search her? Too indelicate for words!

There were times when, puffing along on my bicycle, I imagined what it would be like to use a gun, lay a fuse, blow up a bridge. It would be far more exciting than what I was doing but such activities were reserved for the men – 'Fighting is a man's job,' I was told, so often I could have screamed. I heard of women doing sabotage but they were mainly agents flown in, not the women who had endured so much and who, no doubt, would have thoroughly enjoyed blowing up a train full of German troops.

At least I was now a constant source of news for Philippe who always waited anxiously for my return. It seemed that, after weary months of fear and inactivity, everything was happening at once.

'Last night, Philippe, the Americans dropped the largest amount yet of weapons and food for our boys. They are a proper army now. They'll really be able to fight.'

'If they don't get carried away.'

Sadly he was right: news of fighting and ambushes of the Maquis, by both the Germans and the Milice, filtered through. Philippe was certain that, at last, with sufficient weapons, their courage had soared and they had felt themselves invincible so the toll of young men's lives mounted.

'Clare, Clare!' Philippe was running as I struggled up the driveway. 'Have you heard? There's been an attempt on Hitler's life.'

'It can't be true.'

'If the BBC says it, it must be.'

At the end of July when the Allies broke out of Normandy, and we heard that the Free French were with them, that the liberation was real, that they were not going to be pushed back into the sea this time, Philippe opened a bottle of Château Latour 1929. It was divine. 'Of course, in a great year Latour is almost immortal,' he said.

'At this rate you'll have nothing left for victory.'

'Don't you worry about that, Clare!'

When Marshal Pétain denounced the Milice we laughed – 'Too late,' said Philippe, with glee. 'That won't save your bacon.'

'There'll be those who'll be saddened at the old man facing defeat and admitting he was wrong – like your sister.'

'Winners and losers, Clare, that's what war is about,' he said.

And then it wasn't just the north celebrating, it was the south too as our troops landed in Provence, and we drank Château Mouton-Rothschild. Three days later it was Château Haut Brion after the gardener rushed to tell us that Pétain had been taken to Belfort, in the east, by the Germans. 'He'll be in Germany before he knows where he is.'

'Where he belongs!' said the gardener.

I thought often of Hortense and wondered how she was faring. 'Wouldn't it be wonderful to be in Paris? Imagine the excitement as they get closer.'

'Imagine the losses too. The Germans won't leave without a fight.'

And Philippe was right again: throughout the country the Germans and the Milice massacred people, showing no mercy.

'At least they have arms to fight back now. There's only one good

German and that's a dead one.'

'You're getting overexcited, Philippe,' I said, when what I wanted to shout was, *'You're wrong, there were good men too.'* But I couldn't, I dared not.

De Gaulle, we heard, had marched down the Champs-Elysées and we had champagne, Dom Pérignon. How I envied all those who had seen it: they would know it had really happened. For always, at the back of my mind, was the feeling that this was all a dream, a mistake, and we would wake up to brutal reality.

'Philippe, I shall be away for a week. Maybe longer.'

'Where are you going?' He looked bereft. I sometimes found myself pretending that he was my father – he certainly cared enough about me for that to be so.

'There's to be a meeting. I have to travel to Anliac with some documents.'

'But that is too dangerous for you. You might be seen. They have no right to ask you to go. And now it's September and the chill . . .'

'Pooh! Philippe, you are so French with your fear of chills! I have to go. The woman who was going has chickenpox, would you believe! Her replacement's mother has died. There's only me left.'

'It's essential?'

'I think so. This meeting, I'm sure, is to plan for when the liberation reaches us.'

'Take care, please. What would I do without you?'

I stood on tiptoe to kiss him goodbye. I didn't like it when he spoke like that, as if he knew something that I didn't. 'I'll be back as soon as I can.'

Journeys had been irksome for so long but now they were even more fraught with tension. But this one, for me, was the worst of all.

Anliac had not changed – I can't imagine why I thought it should have. At the station there was the usual knot of police and Milice to check documents. I stuck out my stomach to look even more pregnant than I was and passed through with no trouble. To get to my rendezvous I had to cross the square in front of the town hall. I did not look: I did not want to see where Karl and I had made love, or the park where we had first walked.

At the café which was my rendezvous I did as instructed, walked past once, glancing in. There seemed nothing untoward and no Germans, which was always a relief. Then I had to walk round the block, checking that I was not being followed before entering. The man I was to meet would have a folded newspaper in front of him and would be doodling with a blue crayon. There was no man. I wasn't to wait, that was rule number two. I moved towards the door.

'He couldn't make it,' a woman's voice said behind me. I ignored it. It might be a trap. 'Madame, did you hear me?' A hand tugged at my arm.

'I beg your pardon?' Anyone, even a deaf man, must have been able to hear my heart thudding. Slowly I turned – and threw caution to the winds at the sight of Arlette. I flung my arms around her but had the sense not to call out her name.

She grinned at me. 'Well, this is a surprise. You're supposed to be forty.'

'She's sick.'

'We have to get out of here fast. The Milice are everywhere – they've got wind something's up. Remember the milliner's? Meet me there in an hour. You'll need transport.'

It was a long time to wait, so I walked about the town with a purposeful air. It was odd to be back in this street with the houses steep and tall making a canyon of bricks and mortar. Arlette had two bicycles. She looked at my stomach doubtfully, 'Can you, do you think?'

'How far?'

'Twenty miles. Remember my grandmother's?'

'How could I forget?'

We set off with ten minutes between us, me going first since Arlette thought I would need a head start. Arlette's bicycles had not improved – in fact, the worn seat made cycling agony. I had to stop and pad it with my hat. We had divided the documents between us, so that if anything happened half would still get through. I was stopped at a checkpoint, and my bag was searched but presumably they didn't like to search a pregnant woman's knickers for that was where the coded messages were.

The farmhouse looked exactly the same, as did Arlette's grandmother when she opened the door to me.

'Little Clare! Well I never – but not so little any more.' She patted my stomach. 'Not one of those Parisian babies?'

'No, Madame, an honest Auvergnat bump.'

'Well, I'm glad to hear that. You'd better come in and have something to eat.'

I had to smile: here was something else that hadn't changed one iota.

7

'Any news of David?' It was the question I had put off asking but since Arlette had said nothing I had to ask.

'Nothing. He was in Lyon and then . . .' She shrugged in that expressive

French way, which I feared I had never mastered. 'He might be a prisoner, but I don't allow myself to hope too much. And I try not to think of him.' She lied of course: no doubt she thought of him every minute of the day. 'Any news of Fabien?'

'I try not to think of *him*.' I explained what had happened. 'When I first met him I thought he was the love of my life, was the love of the century even. I must have known he wasn't for why else was it so easy for me to stay with the doctor's family? I was too pig-headed to admit it, even to myself.'

'I did that. I was going out with someone else when I met David. You know, he waited over a year for me, while I was trying to make a dead relationship work. Everyone warned me, I just didn't listen. I could have had another year with David if I hadn't been so stupid. I might even have had his child – you know, just in case . . .' She pressed her hand to her mouth, not wanting to say what she thought.

'Poor you.'

'You're a fine one to talk.' Arlette gave a sympathetic smile. 'Look at you, pregnant and abandoned.'

'Pregnant, yes, but not abandoned. Fabien's uncle is wonderful to me.'

'Pity you didn't marry him.'

'Don't be silly. He's old enough to be my father – he's forty-nine!'

'So? They often make the best husbands.'

'He's invited me and the child to stay there – for ever, if we want. He'll educate it, pay for it. He's very kind.'

'And will you? Perhaps he hopes you'll begin to see him in a different light. Sounds like it to me, from what he's offering you.'

'I'm tempted but I think not. I'll go home to England. There are too many memories here.'

'Karl?'

I nodded mutely. Now it was my turn to keep a tight rein on my emotions. 'He was killed.'

'This bloody war!' We were in her grandmother's kitchen. After serving us one of her wonderful meals the old lady had long gone to bed – fortunately upstairs, not in her cupboard bed: she used that in winter, she had told me. I wanted to talk about Karl but I wasn't sure if I could without breaking down.

'Do you despise me for loving him?' I dreaded her answer but I had to know.

'No, why should I? If you chose to love him he must have been a good man, not one of the bastards. I'm not so naïve as to think that a whole nation is bad. Look at us – look at the maggots in the Milice. War is never simple. Neither are our emotions. I'm sad for you that it can never be resolved, that he died. You deserved better than you have ended up with.'

As she spoke I knew I was going to cry, that I wanted to and needed to. I had kept Karl a secret locked inside me for too long. It was such a release to be able to talk to someone about him, to someone who understood and did not sit in judgement. She listened patiently to me as I talked of my love, my longing.

'There was a long time when I hoped he was still alive. I didn't *feel* he was dead. Do you know what I mean?'

'Yes. I'm sure that David is still with us. I'm convinced that you can't love someone and not know it here if they are no more.' She put her hand on her heart. 'But you speak as if you are now certain that Karl was killed.'

'It's never been as it was with Didier. He came, and he told me. It was as though he was in the room with me. That's not happened with Karl. But, then, maybe he didn't love me as much as Didier did. Who knows?'

'Then you still hope?'

'No. I checked with one of his fellow officers. He confirmed he was dead. In any case, it's all unimportant now. I no longer care what happens to me.'

'But you've the baby to consider, you must try and care. Oh, God, listen to me, I'm sounding like all the old women who must have been saying that to you.' She looked at me, her head on one side, as if wondering whether to continue. 'You always refer to the *child* or *it*. You don't love it, do you?' she said, the truth dawning. 'I shouldn't have said that. I'm sorry.'

'Yes, you should. It's true. How can I possibly love a child conceived as this one was and by a man I now hate?'

That evening, I realised yet again how fortunate I was to have such a friend as Arlette. I could talk to her honestly without fear of recriminations or criticism. Here was someone I could trust with my soul. Years ago, talking to Mab about my sister, I had felt the unburdening that confiding had given me, and tonight it was even more so.

'Perhaps you should think about adoption,' she said finally, and gave me a funny look, which I wasn't quite sure how to interpret.

'I hadn't thought about that. Maybe I should. But all we've done is talk of me. How about you?'

'Of all the Germans to die I have to regret that one was Karl. It was he who saved me. That night when you warned David he sent me packing. I came here to my grandmother. But even then I wasn't safe. My uncle – you remember the pompous fool with the shopping list, Paul Brives? – he advised the Milice to look for me here.'

'Your own uncle?'

'Oh, yes. For good measure he told them my grandmother was hoarding food.'

'How could he? Was she arrested?'

'Yes. But apparently the local mayor and the gendarmes kicked up. They weren't going to let the best cook in the area, who always shared what she had with them, rot in jail and released her.'

'With you French it's your stomachs before all else.'

'Isn't it sad, though? She'll never speak to that side of the family ever again. I liked my aunt. We're all having to make sacrifices of a greater or lesser degree, aren't we? And guess who's volunteered to join the Resistance. None other than my dear uncle Paul.'

'Because he sees he might have chosen the wrong side? Philippe said there'd be an upsurge in recruits, that when this is over there'll be masses who claimed they fought when they didn't.'

'But we'll know. And that bastard gets in over my dead body.'

'They didn't find you, though?'

'No, I'd already gone into the hills. I normally only come back here for the odd day – to wash, get clean clothes. You've no idea what it's like with the Maquis. Half the time we're starving and lousy. But I've met such wonderful people – I've made friends for life.'

'What do you do there?'

'They all have to have new identities. The movement is growing all the time. As boys reach the age for compulsory labour in Germany they join us – so we have a never-ending supply of new recruits. We arrange the paperwork for them and my job is to teach them their new backgrounds, how to remember their false persona, how to avoid being caught out. That sort of thing.'

'Maybe I could help. After all, I've had enough practice. I get so bored cycling back and forth.'

'No, thank you, Clare. It's a kind offer, but it would be impossible for a pregnant woman. We have to move camp too often. And, in any case, hopefully our days are numbered. Once the French army can fight its way south, liberty at long last!' She grinned and raised her glass.

'Have you come across Robert Forêt?'

'The doctor? Yes, he's fine. He works with us, tending any wounded, and he helps those who help us. It's amazed me how many people have put their own safety at risk by giving us food, allowing the sick to rest in their homes. Do you remember my cousin Fleur who ran the bar? She's our quartermaster, keeps us supplied with masses of things.'

As I lay in bed that night, still too excited to sleep, I envied her. She was doing something useful, and there were days when I was sure I wasn't. This trip had been important, bringing what I now knew were false papers for these boys and a set of codes for the big push that everyone was expecting. But sometimes when the gardener sent me pedalling off I often wondered what the messages were for; and once or twice I had wondered if I wasn't delivering a love note to his mistress.

Arlette had some odd ideas, though. Marry Philippe? What a notion! He'd never shown by a single word or look that he thought of me in any way other than a relative by marriage who needed help. What a ridiculous idea! He was so old. But then . . . he was kind, and I'd be safe and he was quite good-looking in a patrician way. Rubbish! Being pregnant was making me soft in the head. I turned my pillow over searching for a cooler side.

'Have it adopted.' That was an even odder thing for Arlette to have said. But maybe it was the best solution for me and the child. After all, it hadn't asked to be born, and life was hard enough without a mother who hated it. With such a weight off my mind I was soon asleep in the tiny room in the eaves, which Arlette had told me had been hers when a child.

When it came the noise was like the end of the world. I sat up in the bed and listened to the coarse shouting. Germans! There was no banging on the farmhouse door, they had simply broken it down.

'Clare, climb in the cupboard – there's a door. I'll get out the back. Keep quiet!' Arlette said before she raced down the stairs.

Her grandmother was adding to the racket. 'Keep your hair on! Can a body not be left to sleep?'

I heard no more for I was in the cupboard that was placed at an angle across the tiny room. It was full of clothes. I fumbled in the darkness and felt a knot in the wood. A panel slid back and a small opening appeared. I crawled through it with difficulty, and found myself in an alcove in the roof big enough only for me. I sat hugging my knees, so afraid that I thought my heart would stop there and then. How could I face imprisonment again?

The house was being searched. I could hear them banging and crashing about. Then they were in the small room I had slept in. I heard the clothes being ripped from the cupboard, the rasp of a hand over the panelling. I stopped breathing.

'Here! We've found them! A bloody arsenal!' a voice shouted and the heavy tread of men rushing to it made the house shake. Then there was an eerie silence. The sound of boots now came from the yard. I heard a guttural order and a fusillade of shots ricocheted off the walls of the old house and echoed in the hills.

8

When you are that afraid you don't count minutes. It was as if time had frozen, and me with it. There had been a tragedy out there that I did not even dare think about. All night I listened so hard that now it was virtually impossible to hear. I was aware of the blood rushing in my ears and little else.

When daylight came I decided to risk moving. Gingerly I slid back the panel. The room was wrecked. But I had been lucky: in their haste and with their pleasure at finding the weapons my bag had been pushed under the bed. My papers were intact. I dressed quickly, grabbed a few things and threw them in my case. As silently as I could I crept down the stairs. The chaos of my room was repeated here. The fine kitchen where we had spent such a pleasant evening was no more. Everything was broken, the furniture upturned and hacked to pieces. The door was wide open, swinging on its hinges. I took a deep breath and stepped out into the yard.

Lying in a lake of blood, looking at me with unseeing eyes, was Arlette's grandmother. Her body was riddled with bullets, her face, untouched, wore a strange smile, or so I thought. From the kitchen I took a curtain and covered her, I didn't want to leave her like that. I searched through the house and farmyard when instinct was telling me to get away as quick as possible. But I could not go until I was sure that Arlette was not lying there too. I did not find her.

When I cycled away from the farmhouse the sickness of fear went with me. But added to it was anger that such an old lady had been treated so. And where was Arlette?

'What a relief you're back, Clare. I've been so worried. You were much longer – Clare, what is it?'

'My friends . . .' And the words tumbled out to make everything I had seen real instead of the nightmare I longed for it to have been.

'You must stop this work you do, Clare. The risks are too great.' He made me lie down, insisting I drank some brandy, which I didn't want.

'I can't, Philippe. Don't you see? Now it is imperative that I do all I can. What if they took Arlette? What if they tortured her? And her grandmother . . .' And I was off again. It seemed to me that I would never stop crying. I had bottled up the tears all the way home.

Philippe was kind to me but there were days when I wanted to scream at his concern. I threw myself into my courier work with a vengeance. I felt that if only I could do more, push myself, volunteer more than anyone else, I would not have to feel so guilty. For I did, dreadfully so. It was no use telling myself that it was not my fault Arlette's grandmother had died and that Arlette had perhaps been taken prisoner: I blamed myself. In this war, whenever I had become close to someone they had died.

The tiredness was the hardest thing to deal with. I was not used to feeling like this – all the fault of the baby! And how could I keep taking from Philippe, giving nothing in return? One evening, sitting with my feet up, as ordered by Philippe, I watched him as he pottered about his study pouring us a drink, thinking, as I often did, what a kind and gentle man he was. I wondered if I could live with him as his wife. Was it such a ludicrous idea? I had blithely said to Arlette that I would go home to England, but would I? Did I have a home to go to? What would my welcome be? And there was another problem. I had no papers, nothing to say that I was Clare Springer. Would they even let me into the country? Perhaps I would wait and see what happened. If he mentioned it, maybe I would say yes, but I'd have to divorce Fabien first. And how did one do that? It was all so complicated. 'Thanks.' I accepted the glass of port he held out to me.

'You look deep in thought, Clare, and so serious.'

'Do I? I wasn't thinking of anything in particular.' I lied. Probably better to leave things as they were.

At seven and a half months pregnant I fell off my bicycle. It had been raining and when Philippe saw my bedraggled figure I thought he would have a fit.

'That's the last time, Clare. It isn't safe for you or the baby. There are plenty of others who can help out. It is to cease.'

'Very well, Philippe.'

'I beg your pardon?'

I laughed. 'Don't look so surprised. I agree with you. I can't do it any more.' Philippe had not yet heard that General de Gaulle had ordered the French Resistance to lay down their arms. Not that I thought there was much chance of that: they'd waited too long to get them! But I was able to wallow for a few days in the glow of being regarded as a sensible woman – for once – until Philippe found out.

The Germans were in disarray in their scramble to return to their homeland. In France courts were set up to try collaborators. I thought of Fabien and wondered if he would ever dare to come back to France. I wondered whether to make an accusation against his mother – but what was the point? In doing so I'd be tainted, in a way, and become like them. I did nothing. But I hoped that someone had reported Sylviane – I blamed her for so much. Had it not been for that woman, David would perhaps still be with Arlette. I wouldn't have married Fabien and been carrying his child. Without her Karl would soon have been on his way home. Would I have followed? Of course.

There were other courts too – kangaroo courts.

I had walked to the local village on an errand. I liked to walk each day, even though I tired easily. As I reached the main square a young woman ran screaming from a side road, a baying mob right behind her. She stumbled on the cobbles and fell but was quickly up, unaware that her leg was bleeding.

'Stop her!' they screamed. 'Grab the bitch!'

Just by the butcher's another group cornered her. I saw the wife of our next-door neighbour grab at her dress, then the chemist's wife snatched at it. Within a moment other hands were reaching out for her, tearing at her clothes, their faces distorted with anger and all the while the girl was screaming for help and everyone ignored her.

'What's the matter?' I asked our gardener, who had ridden up on his bicycle and was watching the proceedings with a wide grin on his face.

'Bloody whore. Been sleeping with a Kraut, hasn't she? Serves her bloody right!'

The crowd parted. Standing in the middle the girl was naked now and trying to protect her modesty. But not for long as the baker's wife appeared, a large pair of dressmaking scissors in her hand, and bore down on her. Another woman held up a hank of her hair. The crowd was silent, but the girl still screamed. 'Help me, someone, please!' And the villagers, those kind souls I knew, cheered and jeered. I was shocked that these gentle people could become, so quickly, a violent, malevolent, dangerous mob.

'Madame, please, help!' she cried, looking straight at me, her hands held out in supplication. I looked away, and to my shame I ran out of the square needing to distance myself from that caterwauling crowd. I turned the corner as a great cheer rang out. I paused, out of breath, sick inside. And I shuddered at what they would have done to me if they had known.

When the truth of what had been happening in the concentration camps was discovered, I feared for Madeleine and Arlette. If only I had known what was going on I would have done so much more. I had felt proud that I had helped the doctor's daughters to escape and the other children too, but the memory was tarnished now. I was miserable that I had done so little and hated myself – but I was not alone in thinking that way.

My condition was not good: my skin was dry, my hair dull and lank, my gums bled, and I was too thin for a woman entering her final month. We had been too long without a balanced diet. I was luckier than most in living here: there always was food of a sort – even if invariably ruined by dear Nelly. She had accepted me now, especially with the baby due. But the plight of women in the cities was dire, I was told. Liberty might have come but essentials hadn't come with it.

I resented the pressures the child exerted on my body – as though it was a parasite growing inside me, taking all the energy and goodness out of me. When it was born, I didn't even want to see it.

We had so hoped, back in August, that peace had come but the fighting continued as if the Germans were incapable of acknowledging defeat.

I finally went into labour on 19 December, just as the German troops had begun their surprise counter-attack in the Ardennes forest, the Battle of the Bulge.

I shouted, screamed and cursed. There were no drugs to help me, only Nelly with her countrywoman's remedies. The poor soul, how I cursed her for every wave of pain I suffered. Until finally, with one great push on my part, it was over and from me slid a baby girl.

And I promptly fell in love.

Chapter Eight

January – December 1945

1

Karla Felicity I called her. Most people commented on her first name and said how nice, how different, things like that. But I didn't let on why I had chosen it. It was my secret, my personal tribute to him, and one that I could never share even with my daughter. Arlette would have known, but Arlette had died.

All those months of worry over her and she had been safe in the hills with her comrades – she had got away that dreadful night when her grandmother had been executed – until she was killed by a drunk driver in Anliac, who did not even stop. It was a cruel thing to have happened when everyone had thought the danger was over. And to die in such a way after she had survived all manner of perils. I grieved for her and what made it worse was that I had not known. She had been dead for three months before I found out. I felt I should have known instinctively, rather as I had when Didier died.

Too many friends had died and I hadn't: it didn't help my feelings of guilt that I had survived. I hadn't been brave like them, or taken the risks that they had. We would never know how many lives Arlette, David and Didier had saved in their quiet way. And, to add to my shame, there were those times in the past when I had wished myself dead – so wicked of me.

It came as a big shock to me, loving Karla as I did. Other mothers, wanting the little creature growing inside them, build that love for their baby before it is born, but, my hatred had turned to love in the instant I saw her tiny face. For days I reeled with the intensity of it.

Second to me in adoring her was Philippe who fretted over her as if he were her father. Nelly brought up the rear of this triumvirate of love – never had a child been so cherished.

'But, then, never has such a beautiful child been born,' Philippe pronounced, looking down into the bassinet that, lace-trimmed and delicate, had been his when he was a baby.

She was lovely. No doubt other mothers think the same, but I was sure there was not a baby alive who could compete with my Karla. She was dark when born but at four months promised to become blonde – I liked that, I didn't want her dark like her father. When the dark eyes of the newborn began to look as if they were to be a light hazel, my prayers were answered: I would forget Fabien's existence and pretend to myself that she had had a different father. If I worked on it hard enough I was certain that, given time, I would convince myself she was half German. These, of course, were my personal fantasies shared with no one – they might have thought me mad.

There had never been a time in my life when I had been so content. Philippe fussed over us both and I felt protected against the world and everything bad in it. Once I had thought he cared for me simply as a young friend; now I was not so sure. I sensed he felt more, though he never said so.

My days were filled with tending my daughter – what joy I took from calling her that, which I did frequently. I never ceased to be amazed at the time it took to look after one so small. She ruled that house with her demanding ways, but none of us complained.

The war carried on but for me it had finished. I didn't want to know of the last desperate fighting, the bombings, the death camps. I wanted to be calm and happy for my baby so that no bad thoughts would pass from me to her in my milk. Philippe continued to follow the news avidly but soon learnt not to tell me about it. But of course he told me when, in May, peace in Europe finally came.

'My last bottle of Latour, twenty-nine.' Philippe was decanting the wine. His expression of concentration as he poured it was endearing.

'It's a good job it's over. We might have become alcoholics.'

'Do you think you should have a glass? The baby?'

'One glass will do us no harm, I'm sure. Heavens, you fuss! Look at all the Frenchwomen who drink wine and successfully feed their babies.' I giggled at him standing there, looking worried. 'Or perhaps that's your justification for drinking it all yourself.'

'I want no harm to come to either of you, ever. And as long as I live it won't.'

'Dear Philippe. You are so good to us.'

'Clare, forgive me for saying this, but I think I love you.' He looked shamefaced as he spoke and was taking a great interest in the pattern of the carpet at his feet.

'Philippe?'

'Have I spoilt everything by talking like a fool? I didn't mean to. I had promised I would never say anything, but you looked so pretty . . . And I . . . I'm sorry.'

'Then don't be. I love you too.'

'I mean I love you as a woman, Clare. Not as a daughter. I have to be honest with you.'

'I know.'

'How long have you known?'

'For some time I have felt it. In a way I wanted you to speak out, and in another way I didn't want you to think like that. I'm talking in riddles, aren't I?'

'A little, yes.'

'I suppose I was scared. And then I thought I might have imagined it. I didn't want anything to spoil how we are. How pleasantly our lives have worked out. Perhaps if you said it it would change everything, distance us from each other.'

'That was what I feared. And has it?'

'Would we know immediately?'

'It's done now, so I might just as well say everything that is in my head.' He coughed nervously. 'I would like to marry you, Clare, to take care of you always, you and Karla. I know I'm older than you and maybe too old for you to see me in that way, but if anything should happen to me I'd make sure you were both all right.'

'Philippe, you're so sweet. I wouldn't even contemplate marrying you for money. And you're only fifty, I know, Nelly told me – hardly in your dotage.'

'You mean you're not rejecting the idea completely?'

'I can never love you totally, but I do love you in my way. I'm so happy here, and the way you feel about Karla means everything to me. If I can disentangle myself from Fabien, I would be honoured to marry you.'

How strange it was that after all my agonising it was such an easy decision to make. I had been honest with him: I could never love him in the way that I had loved Didier and Karl, but I loved him more than anyone else. And had I never known them, perhaps my love for him would have been complete. I could honestly say that my feelings for him were strong enough for me to know that I was not using him. I could make him happy, I knew. And my Karla would be secure – which was what we both wanted.

When I saw how happy my decision made him I was glad I had agreed. He seemed to have shed years. After so much unhappiness it looked as if I was about to embark on a happy phase of my life.

'Let me come with you, Clare.'

'No, I want to do this myself. I don't want them to know I'm living here. I don't want them even to get a hint of what we're planning.'

'Why not? What business is it of theirs?'

'They will spoil it. I don't know how but they will. They'll make remarks, they'll malign us. Honestly, Philippe, I'll be fine. I've written to the doctor and he says I can stay with him. He'll look after me.'

'Promise me you won't go to see them unless the doctor is with you.'

'If it makes you happier, yes. But they're not going to hit me, are they? All I'm asking for is an annulment. Fabien, no doubt, will want one as much as me. Stop worrying. I'll be back as quickly as I can.'

There was another reason I wanted to go alone but I didn't explain it to Philippe because I was worried that he might misinterpret my motives. I hoped Fabien would be there for I wanted him to see our daughter. To show him how lovely she was, how content I was with her. It would prove to him that what he had done to me had not destroyed me, that good had come out of it. And also I wanted him to see what he was missing.

It was strange to be entering Fabien's village again. I had told myself on the journey that nothing would have changed – I had laughed at my obsession that because I had changed everywhere else would be different too. But this time I would have been right. The village *was* different. To begin with, wherever I looked there were window-boxes and baskets from which bright red pelargoniums cascaded, making it look more like the villages in Austria I had seen as a child. There was a bustle in the main square where the shops once more were stocked and in the middle was a market of local produce; several of the women recognised me and shouted greetings though there were several men I did not recognise.

The doctor was out but I left my case in the hallway. Although he had known I was coming I had been unable to say when. Nothing in this vast country was back to how it had once been: the rebuilding would take a long time. I had been warned that train journeys were even more delayed than before: so many railway lines and bridges had been destroyed. But that day there were remarkably few hold-ups and I was astonished when I arrived at Vorey station to find a taxi I could hire.

The woman who worked for Dr Forêt said he would not be home until late afternoon. I couldn't wait that long: I would have to break my promise to Philippe and go to see them by myself. He was being a bit fussy, I thought, insisting I had an escort – I'd tease him when I got back.

I climbed the hill to the château. Despite the steepness, and the weight of Karla in my arms, my step was light. Once more the château seemed to be protecting the village instead of threatening it, which was how it had seemed to me the last time I was here. The noise of the large boss-eyed lion knocker reverberated through the house.

When she opened the door the windy one was still bent double but no longer mute for, looking up at me, she let out a small whimpering noise. 'Hello, Belle. Is your master or mistress at home?'

She looked unsure as to whether or not to shut the door in my face. I made up her mind for her: I pushed it wide and walked into the gloomy hall. I shivered: despite the July heat it was chilly inside. 'Could you fetch either of them?' I said, with studied patience, and watched her scuttle off into the back of the house, like a giant beetle. I was not sure whose footstep I was expecting to hear – the click-clatter of hers or Fabien's heavier tread. As I sat there I realised that both were approaching and at speed, which was gratifying. I also realised that I felt nothing. Certainly no nerves, no fear – not like last time when I was all a-tingle with nervous anticipation.

'Clare? Is it really you?'

'What do you want?' Fabien's mother said sharply.

2

'What do you want?' Madame de Rocheloire repeated, once I had been ushered, at unseemly speed, it seemed to me, into the drawing room and presumably away from Belle's ears. There was a gap on the wall where the Fragonard had hung – so that bit had been true, at least.

'And how do you do to you too, Madame?'

'You always were insolent.'

'Mother!' Fabien smiled apologetically at me.

'I resent the assumption that I have come here for something. I don't want any arguments.' I was standing; no one had suggested I sit.

'You'll get nothing from us.'

'There you go again. Fabien, would you please explain to your mother, since she seems intent on not listening to me, that I am here to discuss matters calmly and sensibly?'

'Did you hear that, Mother?' He grinned. I don't think he was nearly as put out by my visit as she was.

'I want an annulment but before we do that, I want to make sure that—'

'Of what?' Madame de Rocheloire snapped, not letting me finish, all the time pacing the floor with that restless energy.

'Have you forgotten already, Madame, that your son and I were married

285

in March nineteen forty-four? Surely you remember the dramatic circumstances? And that you told me this family would be grateful to me for ever.' I laughed bitterly.

'I said no such thing. You see, Fabien, she's after some recompense.'

'No, just an agreement to have the marriage annulled. I'm sure Fabien wants to get on with his life as much as I do.' Since Karla was getting heavy I sat down without being invited. Fabien took a seat opposite me. His mother continued to pace. Neither said anything about the baby in my arms.

'How can you have a marriage annulled that didn't take place? There was no marriage because you were using a false identity.' She stopped, came to where I was sitting and loomed over me, threateningly. 'You are not Clare Dupont as you claimed.' She stabbed the air in front of me. 'That woman never existed. The documents are null and void.'

Not by an inch did I back into the cushions. She stared angrily at me. I stared back.

'In fact, Clare, I tore it up.'

'Tore what up?'

'The certificate of marriage my uncle gave me.'

'Then what about *our* child? Where does that leave her?' I looked down at Karla, who was sleeping on my lap, blissfully unaware of the scene swirling around her.

'You're not fobbing off some bastard on my son.'

'I'm not trying to fob her off. This is his daughter. She is not illegitimate and don't you dare say that she is. She has a moral as well as a legal right to have her father acknowledge her.'

'Clare, you expect me to believe you?' Fabien asked.

'Yes, Fabien, I do,' I said quietly. He had the grace to look away.

'Did you sleep with her? Did she force herself on you?'

'*Me* force *myself*? Tell her, Fabien! Tell her what you did.'

Fabien looked out of the window.

'Then I'll tell her. Your son raped me, Madame, and this is the result.' I shifted Karla a little.

'How convenient a tale. And how do you propose to prove it? You are a fantasist. My son would never do such a thing. If he took you it was because you wanted him to. I know women like you who say no while egging the man on.'

For a second I was speechless and, had I not been holding Karla, God help me, I would have jumped up and struck her. I took a deep breath to calm myself. 'Perhaps it would be better if we had this conversation in private, Fabien. We shall get nowhere with your mother here.'

'I think it's better she remains.'

'You don't believe me either?'

'Come on, Clare. I'm supposed to believe that we make love just that one time and that baby is the result? I wasn't born yesterday. Whose is it?'

'Don't debase the word "love" for what you did to me. You are even more despicable than I thought. In the circumstances, I regret you are her father but nothing can be done about that. Most days I manage to forget the truth myself. At first I was afraid I wouldn't love her but I do, despite everything you did. But don't think for one moment that I am trying to pass off another man's child as yours. How dare you?'

'Bah!' Madame de Rocheloire snorted.

'I don't need anything from you, don't you understand? I just wanted that charade out of the way so that I could remarry. And at some point in her life Karla will have to know who her father is.'

'Not me.'

'Look, Fabien, I don't wish to be nasty but at this rate you are going to force me. If you won't acknowledge what happened, if you just pretend it never happened, then I shall go to the authorities and tell them about you and that ambush. I shall tell them who set it up, and who is morally responsible for the deaths of those poor men.'

'Really, Clare, you talk such rubbish. I think motherhood must have addled your brain.'

'Fabien, you should take me seriously for your own good. I've said nothing so far but I will, I promise you.'

'And what will you tell them? Don't waste your breath. Clare, my dear, it has already been investigated, both in England and – because those damn peasants denounced me – here too.'

'And you got off?' I said, with disbelief.

'But of course I did. What was there to accuse me of? That I was lucky enough not to be shot? Is it my fault the soldiers' aim was so bad?'

'Why wasn't I called to give evidence?'

'No one knew where you were. If you will rush off and not leave an address what do you expect?'

'But Antoinette had my address.'

'Did she? She never said. She must have lost it.' He smiled so smugly that I knew he was lying. I was sure Antoinette was above being bribed so Fabien knew something about her and had blackmailed her – I knew, better than most, that he was capable of anything.

'I should have been there.'

'What could you have said? What would your accusations have amounted to? How would you have proved anything? Be realistic, Clare.' The awful thing was that he was right. Like the rape, it was his word against mine.

'I shall have to get a copy of our marriage certificate, then. Go through the process of sorting out this mess myself.'

'How? I told you I destroyed the certificate. And the only record would have been with my uncle who, as you know, was shot.'

'You are unbelievable, Fabien. I am just amazed that I ever loved you. I must have been so blind and stupid. Even more so than when I agreed to go through that charade with you. As for you, Madame, I shall prove that this is your grandchild. You need not think you can cheat her out of her inheritance. I know the law of France – I am aware that a child cannot be disinherited. She is entitled to her father's estate when he dies. And she shall have it.' With that I stood, rearranged Karla's shawl, and swept from the room. I had to get out, I was shaking with rage. I had to distance myself from these people. I raced from the house and down the steps, I was virtually running by the time I reached the market.

'Mother! Stop!'

I swung round to see Fabien in hot pursuit of his mother, who was running down the hill, shouting at the top of her voice. As she got to the market, she stopped and drew breath.

'Stop that whore! She's a collaborator.' She stood like a mad thing, waving her arms wildly. I wanted to run, but sense told me to stand my ground. If I fled it would make what she said look true. There was a muttering around me and I realised that the people who earlier had been all smiles and welcome were looking at me differently, which made me feel uncomfortable. 'She denounced members of the Maquis,' she shouted. At first the people looked shocked but then menacing. 'She had a German lover,' she screamed, spittle flying. They were angry now. 'That spawn in her arms is the result.' She was purple-faced with rage. The stallholders and shoppers were still. Then, *en masse*, they moved towards me.

'It's not true!' I heard Fabien shout.

'Bitch!' shouted one woman. They were in no mood to listen to him.

'Fifty-six died because of her!' Madame was shrieking. 'Do you hear? She came here blackmailing us – she would say it was my son's fault they died. Lies, damn evil lies.'

Like an army the crowd moved as one. One step nearer me, and I could see the incensed expressions. Another step, and I saw the pure hatred. I could see their mouths screaming abuse at me but I heard nothing. I stood rooted to the spot with terror and clutched Karla to me so tightly that she awoke and began to cry.

My child's cries drew me to my senses, made me speak, defend myself. 'It's she who's lying, not me.' I knew the woman who struck me first – I'd helped her with her children. I looked at her in disbelief. She saw my expression for her raised arm wavered, but to no avail for a second woman's blow landed. Karla was torn from my arms and I heard her wail. Black terror descended on me and I too screamed – for my child. I started fighting the mob, searching for her. But the blows rained down.

'Don't do this. Stop it!' I heard Fabien cry.

'She's a stinking whore!' his mother shouted. I sank to the ground, my arms above my head in a futile attempt to protect it.

'Stop this!' a new voice bellowed, and a dog yapped. '*What* do you think you're doing? Stop it, this instant. Stop it, I say.' The blows lessened, I heard a snuffling sound and was aware of being licked. I opened my eyes to see a pug fussing about me. The crowd was moving back a pace. And there was Violet Chambrey, holding aloft her furled parasol like a sword and taking swipes at them as she berated them. 'You fools, you blind, stupid sheep. She worked for the Resistance. For you! God knows why, she shouldn't have bothered!'

'Karla! Where's my baby?' It was as if my legs had no strength in them, for as I tried to stand I toppled over again.

'She's here,' a woman called, and brought her towards me.

'Are you hurt?' It was Fabien helping me up.

'Of course I'm bloody well hurt!' I snapped at him, grabbing Karla from the woman, frantically inspecting her to make sure she was not hurt.

'You note the child's name, Karla. Her German lover was called Karl. Odd coincidence, wouldn't you say?' Fabien's mother had not finished.

But Violet pushed her to one side. 'I know nothing about the name of this child. But I'll tell you a thing or two about the mother. This woman has been tortured by the Gestapo. Did this bitch tell you that?' The crowd shuffled and had the grace to look embarrassed.

'Bitch, am I? Well, Violet, I suggest you find alternative accommodation.'

'I shall be doing so with pleasure. But, my friends, know this: Clare was ordered by the Resistance in Anliac to have a relationship with a German officer. How many of you would have done that? Answer me that! She acquired invaluable knowledge for us. And if you don't believe me, ask the doctor.'

'It doesn't alter the fact that it's his child.' Madame was pointing dramatically at the baby.

'How can that be? She's not seven months old until the nineteenth of this month. I have not seen him since September 'forty-three. But why should I tell you? What do I care? I can't be bothered any more. Think what you will.' I wrapped the shawl tighter around Karla and began to

Clare's War

make my way to the doctor's house, aware that I was limping. But I turned
round before I got there. The group, shamefaced now, were still watching
me. 'But I'll tell you this. I would far prefer that Karl Schramm, an
honourable man, was the father of this child, rather than that poor excuse
for a Frenchman standing there!'

'Excuse me, don't I know you?'

I hadn't noticed the woman who barred my way. I was still too wound
up to notice much. 'I'm sorry?'

'It's Clare Dupont, isn't it? Do you remember me? Céline? I'm Fabien's
wife.'

<h1 style="text-align:center">3</h1>

Such a fuss was made of us both. I would have preferred to be left alone for
a few minutes to collect myself, but it was not to be. Violet was ordering
the woman who worked for the doctor to get a basin and bandages. Two
young women hurled themselves at me with squeals of delight, squashing
me and the baby: Dominique and Yvette back from Spain and so grown
up. And finally the doctor bustled into the room, concern on his dear face.
Once more Karla and I were at risk of suffocation as he, too, hugged me as
if he was never going to let me go. At which point Fleur from the bar
rushed in with a bottle of Cognac she had been saving.

'You were magnificent!' She planted a kiss on my cheek. At which, to
my annoyance, I burst into tears. If anyone had asked me why I was crying
I could not have answered: it was a mixture of pain, frustration, fear, relief
and joy.

'I think we should let Clare have some peace to compose herself. She
looks exhausted,' the doctor said.

'But we haven't seen her in years!' Dominique complained.

'I'm all right, really, Doctor. Perhaps some coffee . . .'

'My brandy.' Fleur thrust the bottle forward.

'Well, it's against my better judgement. Are you in pain anywhere?'

'My ankle. I must have twisted it as I fell.'

'I've asked the maid to get us a basin to soak it in. See.' Madame
Chambrey pointed at my swelling foot.

'The whole village is so ashamed, Clare.' Fleur held out a brandy glass to
me. 'In the bar they asked me to come and apologise.'

'It's all right, I understand, I really do. Those accusations would have made any group of people mad with anger. They weren't to know they were lies.'

'Clare, don't be so reasonable. They behaved outrageously.'

'Dear Madame, I'd have felt the same way if I'd heard those things. After all we've been through, revenge is understandable.' I spoke so reasonably because, lurking just below the surface, was the knowledge that what the crowd had been told was a half-truth. Would I have got off so lightly had they known I loved Karl?

'It's that lot up at the château who should be beaten up.' Fleur was pink with indignation. 'That's the last time that creep comes into my bar.'

The door banged open again – the room was becoming crowded.

'I've just heard, my poor Mademoiselle. What a to-do!'

'Madame now, Monsieur,' I said to the *curé*, who had bustled in dispensing dry skin to left and right.

'And a baby! What glorious news.'

'Bernard, you're a fool. She was almost lynched.' Violet was different, I decided. There was confidence about her now as she took control. With Karla awake and restless she ordered Fleur and the girls out of the room and told them to look after the baby. 'We need to talk. Now, Clare, tell us everything.'

I was almost too weary to do so but I needed help and perhaps these were the people to give it to me. It took some time to describe everything that had happened. 'But I swear to you we were married. I admit I only did it to help him escape to England, but we were.'

'Was there a priest?'

'No, just the local mayor. A cousin, if memory serves me right.'

'Jules Boyer.' Madame Violet nodded sagely. 'Unfortunately dead as she says, Bernard.'

'We must try to get confirmation in writing. Were there other witnesses?'

'A German officer, and Fabien's mother signed the papers. And there were about half a dozen soldiers present. The officer was later killed.' The more I looked at it the bleaker it became.

'Certainly the Germans with their efficiency will have noted the names of all the troops there – they'll be somewhere in their archives. If they haven't all been killed.'

'It's going to be a hopeless task.' Despondency crept over me.

'The one piece of good news is that the authorities are going to allow marriages to be legal between members of the Resistance who used their aliases. Also those that were conducted with no earlier formalities, such as the normal notification to marry, as yours evidently was.'

'Honestly?' I looked at the *curé* with relief. 'It's not for me, you understand, it's for the baby. She has a right to her inheritance. But I met Céline and she said she was his wife.'

'And a pretty muddle they've got themselves into. Her father will not be pleased to learn that his son-in-law is a bigamist.' Madame Violet was grinning in a most impish way.

'And certainly the courts won't like it either.' Dr Forêt looked equally pleased.

'The poor woman.'

'Clare, what did I say? Stop being so reasonable, do!'

'I'm sorry, Madame, but that's how I feel. I don't know her, I've nothing against her. I feel sorry for her. And you, Madame, because of me you've no home to go to.'

'But I have.' She smiled but not at me. The doctor's grin spoke volumes.

'That is the most wonderful news!' I exclaimed.

'But we haven't said anything.'

'You don't have to, Doctor. Congratulations. When did all this happen?'

'Last year, Robert, wasn't it? Robert helped the Maquis as you know, and I did a little.'

'A little? Violet, you were wonderful. In dead of night she used to bring my supplies and help me tend the wounded.'

'I'm glad I could be of use. I had always wanted to be a nurse but, of course, my family would never hear of such a thing.'

'You know, I keep meeting women who did so much and they all said it was not important, that they were just helping. But the Resistance would not have worked as well without them, that's for sure.'

It took me ages to reach Philippe. The war might be over but we were resigned to it being years before the telephone system would work properly. I had been obliged initially to send him a telegram explaining briefly what had happened and how I lacked the necessary proof of my marriage. But it was an inadequate way to explain the complications. When we were finally able to speak on the telephone, the line was dismal, crackling, fading, then booming. I managed to assure him I was safe, that I would be home as soon as possible, that my twisted ankle was healing fast and that I loved him.

'He's a good man. He will look after you and the baby well.'

'I've been very lucky, Madame.'

'Do you really love him? Impertinent of me to ask, I realise, but I have known Philippe all my life and . . .?'

'I love him, not as he loves me, but we are honest with each other.'

'As Robert and I are. He will never love me as he loved Pauline and as I loved my husband, but love can come in many shapes and forms. Was there someone you loved especially? Not Fabien, I trust?'

'No. There was a man in Paris. It was like a madness, our love for each other. I wanted to die when he was murdered.' The familiar ache came in my throat. We were in the small sitting room, the windows open wide for it was hot. The doctor was out on a call and the girls and Karla were asleep. I felt so relaxed with this kind woman. 'I . . . There was someone else.' I looked down at my hands, not certain whether to continue, but knowing that I could not deceive her or the doctor. 'He was the German soldier in Anliac. I didn't mean to but I fell in love with him, I couldn't help myself. He was killed.' There, it was out. What would her reaction be?

'You poor child. And you feel guilty about him, because of his nationality?'

'No, that's the point. I can't. He said to me that our tragedy was that we met and fell in love at the wrong time and in the wrong place. I can't deny my love for him, that would be such a betrayal. Keeping silent about him is torture enough.'

'Is that why you have told me?'

'Yes. It's like a great bubble inside me that I am always afraid will burst. I long to talk about him, explain him. But it's nearly a year since I had that luxury. The memories are alive inside me, and I want to tell people, but I know I can't. And everyone this afternoon, I was deceiving them too and I'm so confused about it all.'

'Have you told Philippe?'

'No, I'm afraid to.'

'Does anyone else know?'

'A friend, but she was killed in a motor accident. David, her lover, never returned from the camps – they were the only ones who knew.'

'Although I think, of all people, Philippe would understand, I advise you to say nothing. I have always thought that if something needed to be a secret in the first place then perhaps it should remain so. Secrets when told have a habit of taking on an added significance that you never intended in the first place. "Why didn't she tell me in the beginning? Doesn't she trust me?" I can just imagine the way his mind might work. Meanwhile it is safe with me, and if you ever need to talk about him you can phone me.'

It wasn't really what I wanted to hear, not that I was clear what that was. My face must have shown my disappointment for she got up, crossed the room and kissed me gently. 'And how were you supposed to stop yourself falling in love? Don't be sad, Clare. Treasure your precious memories.'

4

On the train travelling home Karla had gone to sleep after a fretful start. I had made a bed for her on the seat beside me. It was hot in the carriage but I did not dare open the window for I risked soot or worse falling on her. The engine was billowing out dark clouds of cinders. 'Lousy coal,' the guard had informed me.

Victory should have made everything right again, but instead there was a pall of depression everywhere: too many people were still searching for lost ones; others were still coming to terms with the death of those who had not returned from the camps; there was not enough to eat; new clothes were rare still, jobs hard to find – and we had been victorious!

The journey gave me time to think over what Violet had said. I decided she was wrong: I could not begin this marriage on a lie. If Philippe was disgusted then it was better to find out now, before we married, than afterwards, with all the accumulated hurt and complications that would mean. She was right, he was a good man, and as such he should be told the truth. And maybe he would understand the situation I had found myself in.

Being away from him had shown me one thing: I had missed him – and our talks, our jokes, the calm security he gave me. On hearing the news the doctor had asked me if I was perhaps looking at him as a father. I had thought about that too on the journey, and I could honestly say I didn't think so. Our relationship might have started off in that way but it had changed. And I had never missed my own father like that.

It was just as well, I supposed. Since the war had ended I had sent three letters but had had no reply. So much for forgiveness. I leant my face against the window and gazed out at the glorious scenery of the gorge made by the Loire. I missed this magical landscape, but nothing else from that period of my life. I looked at my watch. If I was lucky and there was a connection at Lyon I would surprise Philippe and be home in time for an *apéritif* before dinner.

At the local station I found my bicycle where I had left it. It was dusk but there was still light enough to see. I had had a huge basket made for Karla, which was strapped over the back wheel.

She loved the bicycle and as I cycled along through the gathering gloom I heard her chuckling away in the back. I nearly fell off when a car shot past me, horn blaring. 'Idiot!' I yelled. At the driveway I got off: it was too rutted for me to cycle safely, especially with the baby in the back. 'Nearly home, Karla. I can almost smell the wine your new papa is decanting.' I frowned at seeing the car that had nearly killed me parked outside the front door. The door was open and as I approached I saw with a lurch of my heart that it belonged to the local doctor. I ran the rest of the way, the basket bumping and Karla laughing.

I tore into the house, calling his name, the baby in my arms. She must have sensed my distress for she began to cry. I met Nelly on the stairs. 'Madame . . . It's Monsieur. His heart . . .' I thrust Karla at her and taking the stairs two at a time, ran up to his room. I didn't knock, but burst in.

'Clare is that you?'

'Oh, my darling, what is it? What has happened?' I was at his bedside. He looked so small and frail – yet he wasn't. He was a tall strong man. Why should he look like this? The sheet across his chest fluttered as his poor heart pounded painfully. The doctor stood on the other side of the bed. Almost imperceptibly he shook his head.

This angered me. 'I'm home now. Whatever it is I'll make you better. Philippe, my darling, is there anything you want? Anything I can get you? What do you need? Tell me?' Words, garbled and muddled, tumbled out of me.

'Just you, my darling. I waited for you.'

'What do you mean you waited for me? What are you telling me?' I knew my voice was rising hysterically.

'Papers . . .' He waved his hand at an envelope on the bedside table.

'Not now, my sweet. Later, when you're better.'

'I wanted you with me, holding my hand.' It was difficult for him to talk. His face was ashen grey, and his mouth was blue. 'My darling, I'm so sorry . . .' he said, as his body arched in a terrible spasm. A fearful groan of pain escaped him, and he gasped for breath, hands flailing. Then he died.

It was my fault. I could not get that idea out of my head. Round and round it went. I had truly loved three men and they had died. There was a curse on me. If I dared love someone it was a death sentence for them. I was responsible. I had never been repentant enough about Felicity, I had made excuses for her death when it was I who was to blame. I had rejected penitence and this was to be my punishment for ever more. No one could do anything with me, no one could help me. I was ravaged with guilt and remorse and loss.

I went to the church and I tried to pray, to confess my guilt, but it did not help me. The doctor gave me pills and I flushed them down the lavatory. If I took them I would be denying my culpability, I had to be punished. This time I could not even wish to die: I had Karla to care for, and I had taken her secure future from her.

'You can't stay, you do realise that?'

I looked up at Fabien. He had used the same words as he had before – how long ago? A lifetime, it seemed.

'I know.'

'I inherit all this, lock, stock and barrel – but, of course, you would know that as an expert on the inheritance laws. In the circumstances, well, it would be impossible to have you here.'

'I understand.'

'I can't believe you were really thinking of marrying the old fossil. You've had a lucky escape, I'm telling you. He'd never have satisfied you, ever.' And he laughed.

Was it his words or the laugh? I leapt up and, with all my strength, I hit him right across his cheek. He reeled from the force of the blow. 'I wish I had the guts to kill you!' I shouted, as I raced from the room and up the stairs.

I pushed open the door of Philippe's room. Until now I hadn't been able to enter it – I'm not sure why, I wasn't afraid of his ghost. I had loved it in here, large, airy, with the smell of him. Now it seemed to be a shell, like his body. I flung myself on the bed. His covers had gone and a new counterpane had been placed on it. I wondered who had done that. If only I could cry. Would that make things better? On the bedside table was an envelope. Idly, I picked it up. My name was written on it in his distinctive hand. Of course. The papers he had wanted me to see. I opened it, and slid them out. I recoiled – they were covered in something dark that looked like dried blood. It was the names that jumped out at me: mine and Fabien's. They were the documents I had last seen on the road when we were ambushed, the mayor's papers. Proof that I had been married.

Philippe must have had them all along. Perhaps, as he was the mayor's relative, someone had scooped them up from the road and sent them to him. But why hadn't he told me? The pages answered that for me: they were so stained that Philippe, so protective, wouldn't have wanted me to see them. He'd been so afraid that I would not realise what they were that he had stayed alive long enough to point them out to me. I folded them back into the envelope and put them in my pocket.

In my own room I packed my bag, washed, changed, collected the baby's clothes and toys and boxed them up. Then I went down the stairs. I felt incredibly calm. There was the comfort of knowing I had my certificate but, apart from that, I had no intention of debasing myself in front of him again – I had lost control when I hit him. I wouldn't let go again. I didn't want him to know the depth of my grief. He had no right to know.

'Fabien, might I ask you a favour?'

'Ah, Clare, there you are. Had a wash and brush-up? You look quite pretty once more. Are you going to hit me again?' He rubbed his cheek ruefully.

'I'm sorry I did that,' I lied.

'It was the shock.'

'Probably.'

'So, what is it you want?'

'There's an old Citroën in the garage. Philippe gave it to me when he taught me to drive. May I take it?'

'Going on a trip?'

'To Paris.'

'Very wise. Take it, it looks like a heap of junk to me.'

'And there are several jerry-cans of petrol. I'll need them.'

'I could get a pretty penny for them, with petrol so scarce.'

'I have no money. I have nothing.'

He looked away. 'Take them,' he said gruffly. He dug out his wallet and handed me a bundle of notes. I'd no idea how much was there – I didn't even look at it.

'Thank you.' I turned to go out of the door.

'Clare . . .'

'Yes?' I faced him.

'I'm sorry.'

I said nothing just looked at him.

'The little girl.'

'Yes?'

'Is she mine?'

Again I said nothing, I looked long and hard at him, turned on my heel and left the butterscotch-coloured stone house, the wisteria about to bloom for the second time that year, and I was sure that my heart would never be light again.

5

'You should have warned me that you were coming,' Hortense fretted at the sight of me on her doorstep. But then, 'My dear Clare, what has happened? Tell me, do.' She showed me into her drawing room, the large room with the doors that led out into her garden. 'And a baby! Sit down and I'll get us a restorative.' I laid Karla on a sofa, barricading her in with cushions. I felt restless being here, in this room, where we had once had such fun. I looked about me, trying to remember what I had been like. Had any of the spirit I had had then been left behind here? I could do with some of that now. 'And how old would the baby be?'

'Seven and a half months.'

'And her name?'

'Karla Felicity de Rocheloire.'

'Ah, most satisfactory.' She looked relieved and began to pour small glasses of a sticky-looking liqueur, which she served with tiny macaroons that I had not seen since before the war.

'Hortense, why are there great mounds of earth in your garden as if you've been invaded by giant moles?' I turned away from the window.

She looked put out. 'So silly. I . . .' She tilted her head to one side, the bright little bird I had once known. 'I can admit it to you, but don't breathe a word to another soul. I buried some things in the garden to hide them from the Germans and I can't remember where.'

'I know where they are.'

'You do?' She looked astonished.

'I was with you when you buried them.'

'Were you? What a relief. I can't tell you how worried I've been. I have so little now. You see, Clare, I'm getting old and my memory . . .' She motioned vaguely with her hand as if waving goodbye to it.

'I'm not surprised you forgot. It was a very tense time for us all. And you had so many things to think about and organise.'

'Did I?' She smiled at that. 'How kind you are. And Tiphaine? Have you news?'

'I'm afraid . . .' I didn't have to say any more. Hortense clutched at her throat, closed her eyes and breathed deeply.

'I thought as much. I sensed her magic had left the world.' She spoke with difficulty. 'Later you can tell me the details.' I was glad to respect her wishes: I found it hard to talk about any of them. She left the room on a lame excuse and returned five minutes later, looking pink-eyed, but she smiled. 'You must have second sight. Mab is here. Isn't that wonderful news?'

I felt part of me close up. It was far from good news. Of all the people who had been in Paris she was one of the last I wanted to see. 'Staying here?'

'Gracious me, no. She's married – perhaps you didn't know – to an American diplomat. She lives at the embassy. She's promised to get me an invitation to one of their parties. She's changed but, then, haven't we all? Why, look at you, a little mother! Whoever would have thought it!'

'How has she changed?' I might not want to see her but I needed to know.

'Still bossy, of course – so unfeminine I always think. But perhaps a little more dignified.'

'She probably had to quieten down a bit, with a position like that.' I hoped she was very different: it would be hard to find her the same after all I now knew. 'Did she say what had happened to Tubs?'

'He was a prisoner-of-war, and he hasn't fully recovered, she says. They're still friends, which I find strange. Only the English or the Americans could have such a barren relationship. Men and women should love or loathe each other, not be friends. Where's the passion in that?'

I had to laugh. 'And you?'

'Lonely, Clare. So many dead or disappeared. And no money.' She shrugged. 'But I've an interest.' She brightened up. 'I've invested in a little bar near the Parc Monceau – the best part of Paris, you will agree, a select clientele. No rough workmen.' Hortense hadn't changed. 'Do you want your old room back? I shall have to charge you, I fear. But you know how it is . . .' More expressive hand movements accompanied this.

'For a few days. I have to get a passport then try to make arrangements to get to England.'

'A few days! My dear, you were always such an optimist. That will take you weeks. The embassies are besieged by hordes trying to get out of Paris, though I can't imagine why anyone would want to live anywhere else, can you?'

'No,' I said, out of politeness. Once I had wanted only to live in Paris. Now all I could think of was where I had come from and how I longed to be back there. 'Are times still hard here?'

'If you have money and connections life is virtually back to normal, but for the rest of us it's difficult. The shortages! And, dear Clare, you would not believe the prices. And the denouncing – all the time! People telling on each other, who consorted with the enemy, helped them, why even if you had dinner with them. Perhaps it's as well that Tiphaine . . .' She paused. I wondered how she herself stood, what with her soldier who had been billeted on her whose wife didn't understand him. 'But, of course, there have been glorious times. When I saw our *dear* General de Gaulle striding down the Champs-Elysées like a colossus, I wept.' There was a change in her. How did she regard her *dear* Marshal now? 'I think the trials are pointless but people will have their say.'

'What trials?' I asked, all innocent.

'Why, the Vichy traitors! We who have done our bit, Clare, we can hold our heads with pride. But the little one is stirring. May I hold her? Do you think such a Germanic-sounding name is a good idea? But then I shouldn't interfere. And you must tell me all about what has happened to you.'

'Have you got a month?'

Hortense had been right about the difficulties of getting a passport. Not having one to renew made it doubly difficult.

'You see, Madame de Rocheloire, you have no proof that you are who you say you are.'

'But my marriage certificate?'

'Yes, but that doesn't tell us you're English – quite the contrary, it says you are Clare Dupont and that doesn't sound very English to me. You're going to have to get your family to send out documentation and that is likely to take a long time. So many records were lost in the bombing. There's confusion in Britain too.'

'Could I not go and prove who I am when I get there? You see, my family have not answered my letters – I fear something may have happened to them.'

'Madame, I'm sorry but no. Half of Europe, with the mess it is in, wants to cross the Channel. I accept that you sound English but I'm afraid there is nothing I can do.'

'Thank you. I understand.' I stood up despondently.

'And to have burnt your British passport was a serious offence, Madame.'

'It didn't seem like it at the time,' I said, with a heavy irony that apparently was lost on him.

'You could get a French one. You might have more luck there.'

It raised my hopes, but only momentarily: I had no papers proving that I had been Clare Springer, and with no identification in this country one was lost.

'Of course, had you applied as Dupont, I might have been able to help you.'

'Couldn't you now?' I cheered up.

'But you've told me these are false papers.'

'I thought I should be honest with you.'

'An unfortunate error, Madame.'

Bad news always made Karla heavier, I decided, as we walked along despondently. Now what? If I stayed here, how long would I be able to exist? I could continue to be Clare Dupont but what would happen if the real Clare returned to Lyon? Images of being imprisoned as an impostor jumped into my mind. I had thought that having helped the Resistance everything would be so simple, but it wasn't. Thousands were now claiming that they had fought with them – if they had, the war might have been over earlier. I could just imagine how Arlette and David would despise those making such claims – pretending to be heroes when they had spent the war safely with their heads below the parapet. It was an insult to the others, I decided, as I sat down at a pavement café and ordered an iced tea and some water for the baby. At least one still had this amusement. I watched the parade of people passing by.

Mab could never have hidden: she was too blonde, too tall and had too much personality. I spotted her, striding along, when she was still a good twenty yards away from my table. There was a row of potted shrubs in front of me; I hoped they were high enough to hide me.

'It isn't! It is! Hon!' Mab yelled, so loudly that all the passers-by looked at me. She danced round the shrubs, almost knocked a waiter flying, jigged excitedly towards my table, swooped on me and I disappeared in an all-embracing hug.

'Hello, Mab.'

She put her head on one side. 'So what's with the coolness?'

'You should know.'

She sank down at my table, clicked her fingers, ordered champagne, opened her handbag, took out and lit a cigarette, all in one seamless movement. 'What's the problem?'

'Fabien.'

Mab hooted. 'Six years of war with God knows what trials and tribulations, and the first topic of conversation you choose is that asshole Fabien. Well, you haven't changed one iota, Clare, have you? Except – good Lord, is that a child I spy? Whose?'

'Fabien's.'

'Oh, Clare, no! You didn't marry him! I thought you'd eventually see sense.'

'I did. I only married him to save his life. No romance.'

'How intriguing. Tell me all. Do you live in domestic bliss?'

'No. I have never lived with him. I'm getting an annulment.'

'Thank God.' She rolled her eyes.

'It's not a subject I want to talk about. I had stopped loving him years before so it didn't matter when I found out you had been lovers. What upset me was that you didn't know I had fallen out of love with him, and you did it all the same. You weren't to know it wouldn't break my heart. But I was hurt that you thought so little of our friendship. It's not how I work – and I didn't expect you to, either.'

'Do you smoke?'

'You know I don't.'

'Then I think you should start. Perhaps then you wouldn't be so ratty with me.'

'What did you expect?'

'I don't think "Hi, Mab, great to see you" is too much to ask when, for

301

one thing, we haven't seen each other in all these years, *and* we've
survived. And I never slept with that bastard Fabien.'

'He says you did.'

'So his word is more to be believed than mine? Some friend you are too
Clare.'

'You lied about your father so why not about this? And don't tell me
you didn't because Tubs told me.'

'That I hadn't shot him?'

'Yes.'

'That was stupid of me.'

'That could be one description, yes. I could think of others.'

'I shouldn't have lied but I wanted you to feel better.'

'And I'm supposed to feel better because of your lies?'

'I felt so sorry for you and I so wanted you as a friend and I thought it
might help you – and, shit, I was an idiot. And I'm sorry for it. But I was so
scared that day we met – and I so wanted us to get on. And, well, I was silly
and young, and all I can do is to ask you to understand and forgive me.'

'You were scared?' I was astonished at this information.

'Quaking.'

'How extraordinary. You positively oozed confidence.'

'I'm a good actress.' She grinned.

'And you didn't sleep with him?'

'Hell, no! I slapped his face – in public, in the Café de Paris actually, in
the middle of an air raid – when he tried it on with me. He was mortified
as only a Frenchman would be. He warned me I would live to regret it.
And I do, if it means you and I can't be friends.'

'Oh, Mab. I've missed you so much.'

'And I you.'

'There's so much to tell you.'

'Looks like it.' She nodded towards Karla. 'I think this calls for some
more champagne, don't you?'

6

Once before, way back in '39, I had thought that God had decided he had
punished me enough and had sent me Mab. Now I thought the same way
again. Mab took control of everything.

'It's what I'm good at – organising people. It's my bossy nature. It's what
I did so well in the war.'

'But you were a spy?'

'I *wanted* to be, but they said my appearance was too distinctive. Bloody cheek.'

'You might have had a problem being incognito.' I smiled at the very idea of such a striking woman lying low. 'So what did you do?'

'I helped train the agents. It was interesting but frustrating – I so wanted to be in the thick of it, like dear old Tubs. Isn't it extraordinary that you got my letter? Still, we digress. To business! I know the very lawyer you need to get a divorce and I'll get my husband Hank to talk to the weasels at the British embassy.'

And she did. I could not understand what Hortense had meant when she had said that Mab had changed. She was exactly the same, it seemed to me. She made an appointment for me to see a Mark Dupuy to discuss my affairs. To secure Karla's future inheritance, he recommended that I seek a divorce rather than an annulment, for then there could be no question of her legitimacy. Since Fabien was now a bigamist, he doubted if he would make any difficulties to my charge of abandonment and violence. If he did I could always threaten to expose him. But he warned me that it would take a considerable amount of time to achieve: divorce in France was not a simple matter.

The officials at the British Embassy were told, not to put too fine a point on it, 'to get their asses off the ground'. Fine diplomatic talk. It did not endear me to my fellow citizens but at least wheels cranked into motion.

'What you need is a nanny. You can't trawl around Paris with that baby slung on your hip – you look like a displaced person.'

'I can't afford a nanny. And, before you say it, you're not paying for one.'

'Then let me lend you the money. You can add it to your divorce settlement and Fabien can pay for her.'

'I don't want a settlement. I don't want anything from him but my freedom, and for him to acknowledge that Karla is his.'

'Sometimes, Clare you talk such rubbish. Of course you must have some alimony. Why, the economy of the United States would founder if all women thought like you. You saved his life, he raped you, you've got his child. He must pay for it.'

'Put like that . . .' I said, but I was not sure. I couldn't explain to Mab, because she wouldn't understand, that by taking money from him I was dependent on him and I didn't want that.

She found a nanny. But, I insisted, part-time only, a woman I could call on whenever I wanted to go out and who, by eking out my money, I could just afford. She was a young widow, Marie, who could not go out to work because she had two children of her own. It was a good arrangement for both of us.

Hank was lovely. He was just as I imagined an American should be: big and bear-like, blond, friendly and courteous.

'You always had such good taste in men,' I said one day, as Hank climbed back into his car having settled us in La Coupole to his satisfaction – even to the extent of ordering the wine for us.

'We can just about totter to a table, Hank hon,' Mab had protested.

'I don't trust these Frenchmen,' he had replied.

'I'm glad you like Hank the Hunk. He is adorable. Makes every day sheer bliss.'

'What happened with Tubs?'

'Dear Tubs. He really is a sweetie. But I just could not deal with his mother. She would have preferred that he was still in nappies! Made me want to puke. And she didn't like me, thought I was too vulgar for her precious.'

'But you and Tubs could have weathered that.'

'Probably, but silly Tubs got it into his head that he wouldn't use a penny of my money – honour and all that malarkey. Well, I wasn't going to live in genteel poverty because of his sensibilities. I'd have been as miserable as sin and our marriage would have collapsed before it even began.'

'So Hank doesn't have such reservations?'

'Hank, darling, is richer than I am! It's an ideal arrangement. He understands money. It's a mistake to marry someone poor.'

'But no one rich will ever marry me.'

'I shall find you someone.'

'I don't want anyone.'

'Nonsense, of course you do! You can't go on mooning for poor Karl all your life.'

'I know.'

'It's not having seen him buried, you know. It's quite a syndrome.'

'That's American speak if ever I heard it!'

'I'm serious. If you could see where he was killed you would feel better. It would be a finality for you. I'll get the Hunk to look into it for you.'

'Do you really think it would help?'

'I don't think, I know.'

True to her word she set Hank on the trail of finding out what he could about Karl. I thought it would be a hopeless task since I'd no idea where he had been fighting. And Mab, true to her word, introduced me constantly to eligible men. I should have been grateful, but I wasn't. I knew what she would not accept: that I would never fall in love again, that there was no spark left in me to be ignited.

'You talk like an old spinster. Good God, woman, you're only twenty-four.'

'Nearly twenty-five.'

'Hardly on the shelf.'

'Oh, no?'

Not being a mother she could not understand my contentment with Karla. That the love I felt for her left no room for loving anyone else.

I went out to dine and to dance with these suitors and I enjoyed myself, but that was all. I would say goodnight, kiss them on the cheek, ignore their blandishments and go to bed with my daughter.

The lawyer, Mark Dupuy, was very encouraging about my position since I had my bloodstained marriage certificate.

'Fabien's not to be bothered about matters to do with money. I can manage and I will. I want a divorce as quickly as possible, and I want Karla acknowledged as his legal heir. Nothing else,' I'd explained to him. He foresaw no complications. And, I reasoned, now that he was married, even if bigamously, to Céline, Fabien would want to sort the problem out.

Mab, who had been with me at the meeting, was all of a flutter later, as we talked over a glass of champagne. 'Some lawyer I introduced you to.'

'I liked him.'

'He should have insisted you went for Fabien, got what you can from him.'

'He understood how I feel about taking anything from Fabien.'

'That's misplaced pride, and it's a luxury you can ill afford.'

'I'll decide what I can and cannot afford, if you don't mind, Mab.'

'Think of Karla. You owe it to her.' But she was on dangerous ground and she appeared to realise it, for she changed tack. 'After all you've done for Fabien, it doesn't seem fair.'

'So many things aren't fair. He survived and good men died – that's grossly unfair in my eyes. But this is Europe, Mab, not the States. I'm not going to get any great alimony sum. Things aren't like that here.'

'Well, they jolly well ought to be.'

'Good gracious me, Mab, you sounded almost English then.'

She laughed and we agreed to close the subject.

'Isn't Mark lovely? And have you noticed his divine *derrière*? He's not married, you know.'

'Mab!'

Paris was a shadow of what it had once been but meeting up with Mab made it better. There was a greyness everywhere, as if the buildings were still licking their wounds, and a weariness in the population, who had believed that with peace all would be well, only to find that the daily grind to survive was the same – although the numbing fear had gone.

Hortense and her business were doing well, mainly thanks to Mab, who ordered the embassy staff, the army, the politicians – anyone who visited Paris – to patronise her bar. Never happier than when taking money, Hortense seemed to glow. 'I'm getting married, Clare. Imagine, after all these years!'

'Hortense, that's wonderful news. To whom?'

'A customer, such a dear man. Impeccable background, of course. Such sensitivity!'

'Will you be moving?'

'I fear so, my dear. But you must not worry, I shall find you alternative accommodation.'

This was a blow. I knew she would try but, being so busy with her bar when would she find time to join me in my search? Finding a flat that could afford would not be easy: with so many people returning to the capital accommodation was at a premium. I still needed somewhere to live for, even with Mab's intervention, my passport was taking an incredibly long time to come. Karla was the problem now: she was a French citizen and they did not take too kindly to her father not knowing she was about to go to England – as if I were a kidnapper, as if Fabien cared a toss. But he had to be contacted and his permission sought and, being Fabien, he was happy to make me wait. So the summer had gone and the autumn chill was there each morning as a glorious September became October.

Money, as always, was a problem. I still had some of what Fabien had given me, but not much. I was determined not to borrow from Mab, so had the added problem of pretending I was fine and having to keep up with her. I was running out of excuses not to go shopping with her. Soon I realised, I would have to get a job. I hated the idea for it would mean would spend so much less time with Karla.

It was no surprise when Hank reported back that there was no record of a Karl Schramm having been killed. 'Of course, that doesn't mean he's alive, Clare. Most of their army records in Berlin were destroyed, while others are in the hands of the Russians and mighty unhelpful they are too.'

'I know. I didn't really expect you to come up with anything. It was for Mab, really.'

'I can go on searching for you.'

'I don't see the point, Hank, do you?'

'Quite honestly, no. I'm sorry.'

Hortense was to marry the next week. Her cousin was taking over the house immediately – he had said I could stay on for a while but I didn't like him. I never felt safe alone in a room with him. He didn't just have lecherous eyes, he had lecherous fingers too. Not that he had ever done anything: it was just that I expected him to at any minute.

The two-room flat I had just viewed had sounded perfect – but it was full of fleas, no doubt vermin too, on the fifth floor and had no hot water. As I came out of the building I realised that around the corner was the square where Didier and I had lived. Could I see it without bursting into tears?

My heart lurched as I approached it. I could remember the scene so clearly of that bitter morning when I had seen the ominous black car parked outside our flat. Today the square was almost deserted, an elderly woman walking her dog, a young mother scurrying along dragging a recalcitrant child. A weak autumn sun shone down on the building, twinkled on what had been our windows. I leant against the wall and allowed my pulse to slow. There were no ghosts here – only memories.

I made myself walk to the entrance and peer into the hallway. There were the stairs I had once raced up two at a time in my haste to get to him. My own personal stairway to Paradise! I smiled as I saw the dirty steps, in desperate need of sweeping, butt ends on the floor. Had it been like that when I lived here and I had never noticed? I inhaled the odd mixed scent, of so many Parisian hallways, of cigarettes, oil, piddle and cabbage – the smell at which tourists wrinkled their noses but which I loved. What if the apartment was to rent? What would I do? I was excited to see one was available but I was not sure if I was relieved or disappointed that it wasn't his. Dare I go up?

Slowly I ascended the stairs. At each landing I pushed the button for the timed light, which was so dim that I had always joked it made little difference whether it was on or off. Always there had been a race to get to the next landing before, with a whirring click, we were plunged into darkness again. What if I got to the top and the door swung open and he was standing there and it had all been a mistake and he hadn't been killed? What would we do? I smiled at that. Silly question. There was only one thing we would do.

The top landing was the same. It smelt the same, looked the same, except it never could be. I put out my hand to touch our door, to stroke it, I can't imagine why. But even as my hand hovered, the door opened. A middle-aged woman smiled at me. 'Can I help you?'

'No, thank you.' She looked curious. I had to give her some sort of explanation. 'I used to live here. I came for old times' sake.'

'Would you like to come in?'

'No, thanks. This is far enough.' I swung round and fled down the stairs far faster than I had gone up them. No, this would not do. Never go back to where you've once been happy, someone had once told me. It was right. Seeing that door and someone else in our flat had not helped me, it had made me feel bleak. And I couldn't afford that.

'Bury the dead, Clare,' I told myself. 'Let him rest.'

7

Everything conspired to stop me getting back to England. After my passport problems had been resolved I had thought it would be the simplest thing to buy a ticket and go. Not so. The whole of Europe, it seemed, was on the move and the majority of it wanted to go the same route as me. Places were restricted; there was a waiting list. I had to wait.

We had found a small bed-sitter in a house in Passy, owned by an elderly woman, who was afraid of what she thought were hordes of marauding troops of different nationalities swarming about Paris. She would feel safer, she said, with someone else in the house. How Karla and I were to protect her from these drunken masses was never discussed.

The area was lovely and there was a large garden, not that it was warm enough to sit in, with November fogs whirling around. But, if the worst came to the worst and I was still here in six months' time then it was somewhere pleasant for us to be. I need not, however, have planned so far ahead. Our tickets arrived.

It was 1 December when I arrived at the Gare du Nord to catch the boat train. I felt sick with excitement and apprehension: I had still had no news from home and had no idea what awaited me.

Mab and Hank came to see me off, and Hortense rushed up at the last minute with toys for Karla, chocolate and magazines for me. She was crying.

'Hortense, you're behaving as if you're never going to see me again.'

'I have this dreadful feeling here that I won't.' She struck the centre of her chest dramatically.

'You won't get rid of me that easily.' I made myself laugh when the truth was that I, too, wanted to cry.

We were bundled on to the train.

'Why aren't you travelling Pullman?'

'Mab, darling, third class will do us fine.'

'It looks like a cattle truck,' she said, which offended everyone in the carriage in one fell swoop.

'Go, get off, all of you. I hate long goodbyes.'

'Take this.' She thrust a small packet into my hands before, with tears in her blue eyes, she pushed her way back along the corridor. I waved from the window until I could not see them any more. Once back in my seat, the bleakness I was so determined to eradicate assailed me. Fortunately Karla was sick, which distracted me.

It was my turn to be sick next. The crossing was mercifully short but not short enough for many of us as the ferry pitched and rolled. The deck was crowded with people and there was little comfort below decks, but we were outside because mines still bobbed about in the Channel waters. If we hit anything at least we would stand more of a chance.

Customs took what seemed for ever as bags were searched and passports scrutinised. It was strange for me to hear nothing but English being spoken and, for one fleeting moment, I heard the language as if it was foreign to me. Then, seconds later, I was an Englishwoman in her native land with her mother tongue being uttered all around her. But as we settled on the train to take us to London I wondered just how English I was now.

If I had thought Paris battered and grey, nothing had prepared me for what we now saw. This poor country was so damaged. We passed streets with great gaps in the terraces where houses had been bombed. It looked as if a mighty dentist had been pulling teeth at random. Children, resilient as ever, played on the bomb-sites, where grass and weeds grew. I wished Hortense could have seen this. She had always had the fond idea that the British were safe on their little island. We'd known fear ourselves, but here there must have been another, different type of fear.

Once at Victoria station I took Karla to the ladies' waiting room and only when we were safely inside, and in a corner where no one could see, did I open the packet from Mab. It had been wise not to open it in front of everyone: it was full of American dollars. And there was a note: 'To see you through.' Dear Mab, I was going to miss her here.

The package decided my next mode of transport for me. I took a taxi. The driver couldn't believe it as I negotiated a price with him. 'Only foreigners haggle, yet you sound English.'

'Just call me half and half.'

It did strike me, as we bowled along, that this was almost a modern version of a Victorian drama. Here I was, the prodigal daughter, returning home, a baby in her arms, fearful of her reception. It made me smile despite my nervousness.

My heart was pounding deafeningly in my ears. What would I find? Why had they not written? As we turned the corner of my avenue, it was as if I already knew what I would see. Nothing. The house had gone!

*

The taxi driver deposited me at the local hotel. When I had lived here this hotel had been comfortable, with good food, a fine cellar and well thought-of. My father's Rotary meetings had been held here, and Christmas parties. On Saturday nights there had always been a dinner dance. I had longed to go to one but had never been allowed to since the 'fast' set might have been there.

I barely recognised it. The heavy brocade curtains needed cleaning, the paintwork was chipped, the ornate chandelier in the entrance hall had gone. Instead of jumping up to enquire what I needed the receptionist concentrated on filing her nails. It had always been a man before. Overall there was the smell of stale tobacco and food.

Had I just remembered it as grand, or had it always been like this? Perhaps it was one of those places I should not have returned to.

'How many nights?' she finally deigned to ask me.

'I'm not sure.'

'I have to know.'

'Well, three, then. Would it be possible to have a cot?'

'I'll try.' She did not hurry to the registration form I had filled in. 'Ration book?'

'I don't have one.'

'You've got to have a ration book.'

'Where do I get one?'

'At the town hall.'

'It's Saturday. You mean I can't eat until Monday?' She had a fine line in shrugs. 'Could you tell me if you know anything about the bomb that fell in Furnbank Avenue?'

'It was big. Room twenty-two.' She dangled a key at me.

'Isn't there a porter?'

'No.'

'Would you help me?'

'Not my job.' She scurried back into the cubby-hole behind the desk, which was apparently her lair.

Three cases, two bags and a baby – it took me some time to lug everything up to the room. But down I went one more time where my request for a sandwich and something for the baby was met with a puzzled expression.

'This is a hotel, isn't it?'

'Lunch finished an hour ago. Chef's off. And you haven't got a ration book.' And that was that. I had felt sorry for the English as the train had chuffed through battered and tired towns and suburbs. Now I wasn't so sure. Back in my room I rootled through a bag: there was a little food left from the journey, stale but still edible, and some of Hortense's chocolate.

'You needn't think this is what you're going to eat from now on, my darling.' I laughed at Karla, who grabbed at the chocolate and within seconds was a sticky mess.

The room was grim: everything needed mending or replacing; the windows were filthy, as was the skirting board, and the smell of stale food had followed us. And the English fret about the French being dirty, I thought, as I whipped back the bedcovers to check the sheets, just in case. I took the bedspread and put it on the floor for Karla to sit on – I didn't like the look of that rug at all.

I sat on the one chair and allowed myself to think of the implications of my family home being a pile of rubble. The odd thing was that I had delayed doing so until now. I didn't feel in the least depressed or worried. I was sad that the house was no more, I had loved it and had had a happy childhood there, but I was certain somehow that my family were all right. I just had to find them.

After I had tidied Karla, then washed and changed, I sallied forth to do battle with the charm-school graduate in reception. She wasn't there. Instead, a middle-aged man was in charge.

'Can I help you?'

That was more like it. 'I'm trying to find a family called Springer who lived in Furnbank Avenue. The house that's bombed.'

'Old Mr Springer?'

'Yes. Well, I presume so.' How odd to hear my father referred to in that way. Middle-aged, yes, but old?

'He's living with his daughter out on Balmoral Way. Nice houses up there.'

'Do you happen to know the number?'

'No, but it'll be in the telephone directory, no doubt.'

'Could you call me a taxi?'

Now I felt nervous. What if they were still not speaking to me? 'Pity you didn't think about that earlier,' my inner voice replied. As we sped through the town I began to wonder what I was doing here. Everything looked run down, the people on the pavements so depressed. Could I get work here? Could I support Karla? I should have thought of all this before I set out.

The house was detached with bay windows. The front door opened into a porch in which there was another door with stained glass. 'See the pretty peacock, Karla.' I pointed to it as I rang the bell. It seemed an eternity before anyone answered. Then I saw a bulky shadow.

'Yes?' asked my sister Hope, much larger than before and far older-looking than she should have been.

'It's me. Clare.'

'Good God! We thought you were dead!'

'No, I'm very much alive.'

'So I see.'

'Could I possibly come in? It's damp out here.'

'What do you want?' She peered anxiously at me, her eyes small in her plump face.

At that I laughed. She sounded so like Madame de Rocheloire. 'I thought it was time I came home. I couldn't get here before now. There's been a war on, you know.'

'Still sarcastic, I see. Well, you'd better come in.' I accepted my sister's gracious invitation. 'Father!' she called. 'Look who's turned up like the proverbial penny.'

I felt sick: if this was her welcome, what would his be like?

An old man in carpet slippers appeared from a side door. He put his hand up over his eyes like a seaman scanning the seas – just as he always had.

'Hello, Father.'

'Clare? Is it you? Really? At last!' And he stumbled along the hall towards me and Karla and I disappeared into his arms as he hugged us tight. It would have been impossible to say who was crying the most.

Chapter Nine

December 1945 – March 1950

1

'If you're just going to sit there and stare malevolently at me I'll go back to the hotel,' I said to Hope, who was perched on the arm of a chair in the corner of the room looking as if, at any moment, she was going to take flight. Our father had pottered off to get a bottle of champagne to celebrate my return.

'What did you expect? You refused to come home six years ago. God knows the worry you've caused, and I'm supposed to hang the flags out?'

'Communication has not been easy.'

'You could have written.'

'I did. It's hardly my fault if the postman didn't deliver my letters, is it?' How extraordinary. Here we were, after such a long separation, wrangling with each other just as we always had, as if none of those years had ever happened. In an odd way it was comforting.

'The glasses, Hope. Have you got them ready?'

With a disgruntled sigh Hope hauled herself from the chair and went through connecting doors into what was evidently a dining room. She came back with three champagne glasses. I looked about me. It was a nice, substantial house, though the rooms were a bit small for my taste. The decoration was unadventurous, and the furnishings were old and battered but presumably new furniture was impossible to buy. Father uncorked the bottle.

'How big is this house?'

'You can't stay here permanently,' Hope said.

'I wasn't asking to. I was just making conversation.' I turned my back on her, bad-tempered creature. 'I'm sorry about our house, Dad.'

'It was a sad day but then no one was hurt, so we must be grateful for that. We managed to rescue a few bits and bobs – they're in storage. Getting anything built to replace it is nigh on impossible. We're renting this place. You have no idea of the rules and regulations, permits needed for everything, building materials in short supply. Here, this will cheer you up, Hope, my dear.' He handed us the glasses but I doubted if anything in the world would cheer Hope, least of all me. 'The annoying thing was it was one of the last bomber raids. They used to drop any bombs they hadn't unloaded. Usually Kent got them and it was our bad luck that one fell on us. Still, it was only possessions.' I would never have expected him to say anything like that: he'd always set such store by what he owned.

We sat politely sipping our drinks, Karla on my lap. No one said anything, as if they were too embarrassed to ask – I certainly was. I wanted to know who Hope was married to for a start. Nothing had been said but she'd a ring on her finger. However, the telephone was listed in my father's name. And I was nervous too: my father's welcome had been warm, but would it last? It had been unlike him – he had always been so withdrawn. I did not really know him, as he no longer knew me. Certainly he didn't look nearly as fearsome as he used to.

'Well . . .' my father and I said in unison.

'You first.' We spoke like a choir. We laughed. My father deferred to me.

'I had better explain. This is Karla. She's a year old this month.'

'Does she have a father?'

'Hope!'

'She could hardly have been a virgin birth,' I said shortly.

'Not with you as a mother.'

'Hope! If you can't be polite to your sister, kindly leave the room.' Karla, sensing the animosity, began to cry.

'Have you a biscuit I can give her? She's hungry. And some milk?' I called, after Hope's retreating back.

'Try and be patient with your sister, Clare. Things haven't worked out for her as she would have liked.'

'It happens to most of us.' I smiled at him. 'Is she married?'

'Why yes, back in forty-three. To Cyril, of course.'

'Of course.' I had to suppress a tiny smile. 'Was he in the army?'

'Cyril?' My father gave a little snort of amusement. 'Not him. Got out of it, something to do with his feet. But I was in the ARP. I quite enjoyed it – that is, if you can call war enjoyable.'

I didn't answer that. I didn't want to spoil this time with him by explaining how my war had been. There was time enough for that.

'But you've changed, Clare. You were always a pretty little thing but now you're lovely – so like your dear mother.'

'Thank you, that's a nice thing to say. I think I've changed as a person too – not so wild, you'll be pleased to know.'

'You were only a child. We've all changed. I doubt you expected to come home to this old codger.'

'You're not an old codger!' But you have changed, Father, I thought. You're not the strong upright man I left.

'I'm sorry there was so much bitterness before, that we were both so pigheaded. You cannot imagine how I missed you and feared for you. I wished so many times that you'd come back with the others.'

'Not as often as me, I'm sure. If I'd had wings I'd have come here a dozen times. I was stupid and foolhardy and selfish. All the things you said I was. I hope you can forgive me. There's little else I can do or say to make amends.' Would I have given up those years? No, not even with all the pain. But I couldn't say that to him.

'I forgave you years ago.'

'And I should never have written that letter to Lettie. It was unforgivable and I don't blame you for banning me.'

'But you were right. I didn't want to know the truth. Poor Lettie, I should never have married her. I was the selfish one.'

'But . . .?'

'She left me a year into the war. She'd always been in love with another man. Her mother persuaded her to marry me.'

'I hope my letter . . .'

'No, nothing like that. She would have gone eventually. The war made many people face up to things and act before it was too late. I don't hold any grudges. She has a little boy now and lives in Watford. She's happy.'

Such changes! Was this my father talking? He hardly sounded the same man. Or had he always been like this and I had been too young to see it?

'She's a fine little girl. Don't you think she has the look of Felicity about her?' He was looking at my child so lovingly it brought a lump to my throat.

'That's her second name. I wanted . . . Oh, Dad, I'm so sorry.' I burst into tears and Karla joined in. Now he had two of us to comfort. But at last the barriers were torn down and we were able to say the things we should have said all those years ago and hadn't. This war, which had caused such agony, might have been beneficial too.

'I allowed grief to cloud my judgement. It was a dreadful accident. When we didn't hear from you I feared that my stupidity might have been the cause of your death too.'

We were open and honest with each other. It was going to be all right. I could have wept tears of joy too.

Hope must have walked in, and seen us then left again for it was a good half-hour before she returned with biscuits and a glass of milk. 'Thanks for giving us that time,' I said.

'I don't know what you mean.' But I knew she did.

Now Hope served us tea, and I sensed her becoming more relaxed with me, as if, with the shock of my arrival over, she was dusting down her pleasant side. We even began to discuss the possibility that I should stay here until I finalised my plans. And then, at about seven, a key grated in the front door. Cyril walked in and the atmosphere changed again. Hope bristled and was on her guard, wanting me out, and quickly. I longed to tell her I would not touch her stout, moustached husband with a barge-pole – never very attractive, he had changed for the worse.

'Good God. This is a surprise! The wanderer returns!'

He *would* say that. I did not much welcome his kiss on my cheek, especially with my sister watching every move like a suspicious toad.

'Cyril, how nice to see you and looking so well!' Oh, the hypocrisy.

'Where have you been?'

'In France.'

'All through the occupation?'

'It wasn't that easy to get out.'

'You must be fluent in the old lingo.'

'Quite good, yes.'

'How could you bear to live with all those Frogs?'

'I like them. And don't forget my daughter is French too.' I hoped the xenophobia wouldn't continue – I owed the French too much to suffer it in silence.

'I stand corrected, Madame.' He smiled, pleased with himself. Had I really enjoyed his kisses once? How disgusting, I thought, as I smiled in response.

'Cyril, Clare is booked into the George, but Hope and I want her to stay here. Could you perhaps run her down to collect her baggage?'

'My pleasure.'

'We've hardly any petrol coupons left, Father, and there's the Christmas shopping to be done,' Hope fretted. What had one to do with the other? I wondered.

'I can get a taxi – if you'd let me leave Karla here.' I couldn't bear the anguish on Hope's face, and Cyril was the last person I wanted to drive me anywhere.

At the hotel I packed my bags and manhandled them down to Reception to pay my bill. 'Everything all right?'

'Yes, thank you, I found the Springers.'

'Good, but I meant the hotel.'

'Yes, everything was fine,' I heard myself say. How long had I been here? Already I was being so English. I should have told him about the dirt, the rude receptionist. I would have done so in France. But here, I knew only too well, was different.

Back at the house, the so-solid and respectable house on Balmoral Way, dinner was ready. Hope served a soup of indeterminate origin, we had a piece of incinerated lamb, pale, watery cabbage and jelly. The others ate with relish. It was puzzling: Hope had always been a good cook: what had happened? Was this how the food had been before? Surely not. But then maybe it had and, knowing no better, I'd liked it. No longer, though. I politely refused seconds. There was no wine, only water, which for me was strange.

'I quite forgot, I've presents for you,' I said. In the hall I undid the bag and returned with a bottle of cognac for my father, perfume for Hope, and a small packet of cigars, which I gave to Cyril.

'How kind, thank you very much. You mean you can buy things like this still in Paris?'

'Well, yes, things are getting easier.'

'They get worse here.'

'Brandy! What a treat.' My father promptly began to pour us one each. I grabbed mine like a dehydrated soul in the desert. I wished I'd brought more now. It was a good job Mab wasn't here: she'd fade away in England at this rate.

'When's Karla's birthday? We must have a tea party?'

'But who could we invite, Father?' Cyril asked.

'Oh, I don't know, we must know someone with children.'

'Too many,' Hope said, with a resentful twist to her mouth. She's so bitter about something, I thought. Was it that she had no children herself? I'd watched her throughout the evening and caught her looking at Karla, as if she didn't want to like her but couldn't bring herself not to.

'How's the business, Dad?'

I would have had to be blind to miss the look that passed between Hope and Cyril.

'Impossible. With all the rationing it's been hard going. No fancies or tortes during the war. But I live in hopes we'll soon get it back on an even keel. The problem then will be if people can afford what we make.'

'No expansion into Europe?'

'Why? Were you thinking of running a shop in Paris?'

'No, Hope, I wasn't. It would be a bit like taking coals to Newcastle. The French pâtisseries were wonderful.'

Something was going on here but I wasn't sure what. Hope and I had always argued, but we had loved each other, I knew that. Now she no longer loved me, I was certain. How bizarre. I had imagined that all the

problems would be with my father yet he was genuinely pleased to see me.
It was my sister who wanted me out of here.

'What do you intend to do, Clare?'

'In what way, Cyril?

'What work, or have you unlimited means?'

'No, I haven't. I thought I would get settled and then worry about it.'

'Just the same, aren't you?'

'I don't know what you mean, Hope.'

'You're one of those people who always presume that something will
turn up, that others will look after them.'

'I suppose I was like that once, but I can assure you, Hope, not any
more. Too much has happened to me out there in the real world for me to
presume anything any more.'

'Like what?'

'I don't think you're ready to hear it yet, Hope.'

2

'What's wrong with it?' Hope said accusingly.

'Nothing. It's fine.' I looked up from my plate of Spam fritters and boiled
potatoes – potatoes that had been in the clamp so long that the smell
warned you not to eat them.

'Ever since you got here you've been sneering at the food and the way
we live.'

'I've done no such thing.'

'You have, don't deny it. You and your Frenchy ways. I see the food's no
longer good enough for you.'

'It must be very difficult for you with the rationing. I understand
completely. There were times in France when we had nothing.'

'But you had your black-market, didn't you? I bet you weren't averse to
using that when it suited you.'

'Yes, I admit it, along with millions of others. What were we supposed
to do? Starve? And don't tell me it doesn't exist here too. I saw several
spivs on the high street only yesterday.'

'They're about but we don't patronise them. We're law-abiding citizens.'

'More's the pity,' Dad muttered, from his end of the table.

Stoically I began to eat. This was not working. I had been here less than
a week and the constant sniping from Hope was getting me down faster

than I cared to admit. I had tried talking to her several times but she always made excuses and left the room.

'So, Clare, have you thought any more about how to use that legacy your great-aunt in Devon left you?' I could have kissed father for getting me out of the firing line.

'I'm not really trained to do anything, am I? And it's only small, so I won't be able to live off the income.'

'I didn't get anything.'

'She was Clare's godmother, Hope.'

'Well, it's all right for some.' She stood up, noisily collected some dishes. 'If you'll excuse me, I've washing to do.' Hope never *left* a room, she crashed out of it, so ensuring that everyone understood how busy and pressed for time she was.

'Try not to let her get you down.'

'That's easily said. She's so angry all the time, Dad. Why?'

'I told you that life has proved a disappointment to her.'

'Is Cyril the let-down?'

'Maybe. Obviously we don't talk on that level. He is rather a stick-in-the-mud, don't you think?'

'He was that when they got engaged.'

'That's true. Both Lettie and I tried to warn her, but she wouldn't listen. She feels a failure that she can't have children, of course.'

'Can't she? How sad. She's so good with children too. She plays with Karla all the time and Karla adores her aunt. Does she know it's her? Maybe it's his fault.'

'Really?' My father looked at me with a surprised expression as if this was a totally new concept. He sighed. 'I don't understand people. I've listened to your story and the horrors you've seen and the grief you've had, and now a divorce! I can't imagine what your mother would have to say.' I couldn't look at him. I don't know why, but I'd told them I was already divorced. 'All that,' he continued, 'and yet you're not bitter and twisted like Hope. It's as if she blames the whole world for her problems, that none of them can possibly be of her making. Why are you different?'

'I don't know. But with both Didier and Karl I found great happiness. I've those memories and I'm grateful for them. Perhaps that's why.'

'You talk as if you'll never find anyone else.'

'Quite honestly, Dad, I don't think I will – and in any case I don't think I even want to.'

'I felt like that when your mother died, but I found Lettie – even if I lost her.'

'So it's the same?'

'No, it jolly well isn't. I'm always on the lookout for someone suitable. I don't want to end my days with those two miseries. My secret!' He put his finger to his lips.

Ideally, I would have liked to return to France. But it seemed I had burnt my boats. There was the expense of getting back, which I could ill afford – and how could I earn a living there? I knew only too well how difficult that might be. I'd given up our room and I was fully aware of how hard it was to find accommodation in Paris. I could not face working in a shop or bar again and, in any case, the hours would be too long so I would see little of Karla. I thought about teaching languages, but the money I could charge would be little since I had no qualifications: the French, war or no, set great store by them. And even if I could, the last thing on their minds would be English lessons: they were too busy picking themselves up and restoring order. If I could run a business of my own so that I could fix my own hours . . . but how would I start it up? I had my legacy, but there were such tight restrictions on the movement of sterling that I would never be allowed to take it out of England.

The atmosphere generated by my sister was making life intolerable so, I was looking for somewhere else to live, but any accommodation was snapped up before it was advertised. At least here Karla had the security of her grandfather, even though his money was sadly depleted. But I felt I no longer belonged here. In nearly seven years I had become more French than English. When Karla had a sudden temperature it was brought home to me when we called the doctor. I had left England with the vocabulary of an eighteen-year-old, I had returned a woman and a mother, knowing only the French words for illnesses and their treatment. Why, even my own inner bodily functions I knew only in French. I had to relearn parts of my own language.

'Hope, I'm truly sorry I can't find anywhere to live. I have tried. It's unfair on you having us here. You've been so kind.' I was making one of my periodic attempts to get Hope to talk to me. It was just after Christmas – and a dismal affair that had been.

'I love having Karla here.'

'I realise that. You're wonderfully patient with her.' I decided to ignore the implied rebuke.

'There's something I want to discuss with you.'

'I'm all ears.' This was a surprise.

'Cyril and I have been talking. And we think . . .' She began to fold a pile of laundry. I waited patiently, dreading one of those conversations littered with pauses when the words won't come. 'We've given it a lot of thought and we think it's the best thing for everyone . . . We were wondering if you would let us have Karla.' She said this in a rush, all in one breath, then bent down to pick up a napkin that had fallen on the floor. Or had she dropped it so that she didn't have to look at me?

'You mean for a little holiday?' I said, though I feared that was not what she meant.

'No. Permanently. We'd be happy to adopt her, make it all legal.'

'Hope, darling, I couldn't do that.'

'Why not? What sort of mother can you be? You haven't even got anywhere to live.'

'That's true, but I will have. I'll buy, if necessary.'

'With the famous legacy, I suppose.' This was tinged with her own brand of bitterness. Oh dear, I thought. 'And you've no man and you'll have to work. What will happen to her then?'

'I shall make adequate arrangements, as many women do. I know she has no father but I shall make up for that. I love her enough for two.'

'Cyril says she's illegitimate.'

For a second a red mist flashed before my eyes. I took a deep breath to control myself. Losing my temper wouldn't help. 'Does he? Then he'd be wrong. I am married and I am getting a divorce. Why should I lie to you?'

'Where's the proof?'

'I wouldn't have thought I needed any. But even if she were a bastard – the word Cyril used, I'm sure – what would it matter? She would still be sweet Karla, wouldn't she? Or does Cyril see himself as rescuing her from a life of shame?' It was my turn to sound bitter.

'You needn't take that tone with me. I'm only trying to help.'

'And I appreciate that. But don't you see, Hope? I adore that little girl. She's my whole reason for being. You might just as well offer to adopt my arm.' I waved it at her.

'I see – rubbing it in that I can't possibly understand because I'm barren.'

'I didn't mean that at all. I'm sad that you're so unhappy and I wish there was something I could do to help you but you're so touchy, Hope, it's difficult.'

'You've never wanted to be friends with me. Why, you even tried to seduce my husband.'

'Not that again, Hope, please. That was years ago, and I didn't. You know deep down it wasn't like that.'

'You turn up, and what happens? You're all lovey-dovey with Father, sucking up to him, trying to get out of him what is rightfully mine.'

I stood up then had to sit down again. I was so angry that my legs didn't want to support me. 'That's a disgusting thing to say.'

'Near the truth, though, isn't it? I'm the one who's lumbered with him, not you. I'm the one who has to look after him, the one who'll care for him when he can no longer look after himself. And who does he prefer?

Light-of-his-life Clare.'

'Lumbered! What an awful thing to say. He's been a good father to all of us, he's loved us – yes, you too despite your self-pitying stance. And to repay him by saying you're *lumbered*! Hope, you're disgusting. I presumed he was here because you loved him, not because of his bank account.'

'It's the truth, though, isn't it?'

'No, it isn't. I've enjoyed these weeks with Father, getting to know him and him getting to know me. I'd lost a lot of time with him and we've been trying to make it up. I've said till I'm sick to death of saying it, I was a stupid child. I should have obeyed him but I didn't. But, take it from me, Hope, I've paid in spades for my disobedience. If Father can forgive me I don't see why you can't. But perhaps, I can. It takes heart to forgive and I don't think you have any. And you want to adopt my daughter? Someone as mean-spirited as you? No, Hope. How long before you'd be saying you were *lumbered* – such an elegant word – with her?'

At that I stood up and stormed out, slamming the door with such force that a decorative plate in the hall fell to the floor with a resounding crash and broke into a hundred pieces. '*Merde!*' I yelled to the rafters.

3

How long was I to be judged because of the silly, thoughtless, selfish child I had once been? Was it just me or did other people suffer for the rest of their lives for what had happened so long ago? My father and I had spent hours going over the past. We had been able to talk about Felicity and what had happened that awful, tragic night. But in spite of that I could reach only one conclusion.

'It's no good, Father. I have to go. It's impossible for me here.' He had found me packing our cases.

'Where to?'

'London. A friend has lent me her flat.'

'Just as we get to know and appreciate each other again. It seems such a shame.'

'We'll keep in touch and when I get a place of my own you must come and stay with me for as long as you like.'

'She hasn't been going on about me to you, has she? That she feels lumbered?'

'Her very words.' I was able to smile because he was amused by it.

'I wouldn't give them the satisfaction of being right. She tells everyone that – it's most insulting. Do I look that old to you?'

'Greyer but no, not particularly.'

'I feel at any moment they're about to inspect my teeth.'

'Poor Father.'

'Not at all. Don't you worry about me. You've got Karla to concern you. In any case, keep it under your hat but I met a particularly pleasant lady last week. Widowed, nice house. I'll keep you informed.' He winked at me. 'Look after my little angel, won't you?'

As for angels, Mab had stepped in once more. I had written to her, not to moan about the situation here, but clever Mab had read between the lines. She had sent a telegram last week to tell me to use her London flat whenever I wanted.

When it was time to leave Hope had the grace to apologise and I, with equal grace, accepted it. But I had the satisfaction of seeing her blush to the roots when I told her quietly that once I was settled I would be happy to take Father off her hands. The pull of his money however, was, too great. 'That won't be necessary,' she said.

Mab's flat was typical of her: it was small but immaculate – and the white carpets and upholstered furniture were sufficient to strike dread into the heart of any mother. I carefully packed away all objects and covered everything with sheets to be on the safe side. The fridge – unusual in England at this time – was full of champagne and nothing else. The neighbours were most unfriendly, no doubt a legacy of the many parties Mab had undoubtedly thrown here during the war years.

Although I had no rent I budgeted carefully – Hope would have been proud of me. Work was of paramount importance and hard to get, but I secured a part-time job in a public house, just around the corner. I worked in the evenings when Karla was in bed. I was terrified every minute she was alone, convinced that the building would burn down, we would be burgled, she would choke, fall out of her cot or smother herself. Every ambulance or fire-engine siren I heard made my heart leap. I had arranged with the caretaker's wife that she would go and listen at regular intervals, but judging by her complexion she had an enthusiastic acquaintance with the whisky bottle so she was of little comfort to me, even though I paid her handsomely in cash.

The night had been long – the landlord had a group of regulars he allowed to drink after hours. My feet were killing me and, when I finally let myself in, I could have wept at seeing the lift not working – some fool had left the door open on an upper floor. It was the last straw in a trying evening, which had not been helped by the overtures of a drunk.

I let myself in to the flat and felt faint at the sight of a light burning in the sitting room. I'd turned everything off, I knew I had – my fear of fire made sure of that. Who was here? Quietly I opened the door. There, sprawled on her sofa, fast asleep, was Mab. She might have let me know, was my first thought. I tiptoed to the second bedroom to check Karla, who was fast asleep, her favourite toy penguin clutched in her podgy hands. In the kitchen, I made myself a pot of tea.

'That stuff will poison you.'

'Mab! You gave me such a fright.'

'Sorry, hon, but there was no time to let you know. I rang but there was no reply – well, there wouldn't have been, would there? You weren't here.' She stood up and, with her sinuous walk, crossed to the fridge. She took out a bottle of bourbon that hadn't been there before. 'I must say, Clare, you're keeping this flat like a palace, but why all the sheets? That décor cost me king's ransom and you drape everything so that no one can see it. Drink?'

'I was frightened Karla would make a mess.'

'Silly sweet. As if I'd mind.'

'No, but I would.' We walked with my tray of tea things back into the sitting room. With a deep sigh of relief I slid off my shoes and sank into one of the huge squishy armchairs.

'So how's tricks?'

'Fine.'

'It's Auntie Mab here, you can tell me all.'

'Hard.'

'I thought as much.' She nodded sagely. 'You've a job?'

'Barmaid at The Admiral round the corner.' Mab pulled a face. 'It's not that bad, the boss is OK – as bosses go. But . . .'

'Karla?'

'It's a worry. Gladys Fuller pops up to check her for me. I don't want you to think I just leave her.'

'As if I would.'

'And at least I have the whole day with her. We've been lucky. I've been working there for six months now and she hasn't had one day ill when I couldn't go in – I don't think the boss would like that. He said when he took me on that he'd accept no excuses. That's a miracle with a child of her age. There's usually something wrong. What happens when she's older I don't know – already she's beginning to climb out of her cot.' I knew I was burbling but I had been wanting to voice all these fears to someone for such a long time, and now the words were tumbling out so fast I couldn't seem to stop them – not that I wanted to.

'You can't go on like this. You look done in.'

'What else can I do?'

'Come back to France.'

'It would be the same problem there. I'd still have to work, and who would look after Karla?'

'They'd be more understanding about a child, that's for sure. Better than you English. Is money a problem or is that a stupid question?'

'I get by. The tips are good – in an area like this they would be. And I've a small legacy. I've only raided it a couple times. If only I could think what to do to make it work for me.'

'A language school.'

'I thought about that but the English just aren't interested in learning languages. You know how it is, they're proud of not knowing any and just shout louder at the natives. When I advertised to do private lessons I got four replies, and three thought I was on the game!'

'France. Open one there. They're hungry to learn.'

'I've no qualifications.'

'Employ those who have. You supervise – with your languages you'd be able to check, maybe do the odd private lesson on the QT. What would it cost?'

'Heavens, I don't know.'

'I'd go in with you like a shot. And I'll tell you another thing. We've got the premises – Hortense's house is for sale. I've been to see it and I've been dickering over buying it for old times' sake, you know. I need a permanent base in Paris – I'll never get it out of my system.' She lit a cigarette – she was so excited. 'We could do what she was doing – but properly, no cut corners. A super finishing school. It would be bliss, the closing of the circle. You could offer languages, cooking, art appreciation, deportment. Why, you could be the second Hortense.'

'What a great idea.' I smiled indulgently: her enthusiasm was endearing. 'But, Mab, hang on a minute. You're letting your ideas run away with you. Slow down. Why buy a house you're interested in then do this so you can't live in it? Hank won't like that idea.'

'Rubbish. He'd invest in you too.'

'You don't know that.'

'I do. I'd tell him to.'

'That's hardly fair. And you're very kind, but how can I? I don't want to do this since I can't show my faith and put my money in.'

'But you said you had a legacy.'

'Yes, but it's here, the exchange restrictions won't let me move it out of England. We're only allowed to take fifteen pounds out. That wouldn't keep you in champagne for a week!'

'That's no problem. We'll do what everyone else is doing. You give me the money here and I'll give you the equivalent there. No problem at all.'

'But that's illegal.'

'So?'

'I can't break the law.'

'It's a stupid law. They're meant to be broken.'

'I couldn't.'

'Of course you can – who's to know? You'll be helping all manner of economies. Get the one in Paris going and you can open one here. What shall we call it?'

'Les Hirondelles.'

'Pretty, but why?'

'Because that bird has been lucky for me. Didier lived on the Place des Hirondelles and Philippe's house was Le Manoir des Hirondelles. It's an omen. But I can't do it!'

The argument as to whether or not I should become a criminal swung back and forth as we drank the tea, finished off the bourbon then opened a bottle of champagne. My head was going to be appalling in the morning.

'That's decided then. You will.'

'We'll see.'

'You can't spend your life being indecisive, Clare. It just won't do.'

'You make me laugh, you're so bossy.'

'That's me.'

'You didn't say why you'd suddenly turned up out of the blue.'

'Didn't I? I had a bloodbath with Hank. He's impossible. He's so bossy too. I left him.'

'Oh, Mab, no. But hang on, you've been talking about him as if he's to be involved in this plan of ours. How can he if you've split up?'

'Did I say it was permanent? I'm just teaching him a lesson – show him who's boss.'

4

It would have been nice if the school had been a success from its inception. Sadly, that was not the case. For four years it had been hard work and constant disappointment. Starting such a business in a city still reeling from the effects of war had been foolhardy of us. Both Mab and I had thought blithely that all that would be necessary was for us to decorate, buy some furniture, china and cutlery, interview a couple of teachers, get hold of some books and open. Not so. There were rules and regulations, planning problems, neighbours to placate, officials to satisfy. I watched my small inheritance slip through my fingers as if swept away in a torrent. Mab had bought the house, so I insisted on paying for the setting up. But I couldn't: my funds were quickly gone. Hank and his cheque book were summoned and then, about a month later we were joined by Don, an American friend of his who was interested in investing in us too. If they hadn't all been as rich as they were, I would have gone under in the first three months.

The first year we had three pupils. Not nearly enough. The second we had four, still not enough. If Hortense had been unable to manage with her six, I'd decided long ago that we needed at least twelve. And then miraculously, in January 1950, the enquiries doubled and the bookings with it. Perhaps, we were going to succeed. It was a close-run thing for I had given it until my thirtieth birthday, the following year, to succeed. If it failed, I would insist we sold up. Then what I would do, I'd no idea.

'It's still only eight, Mab, for the Easter term. We really need a dozen.'

'You're such a pessimist, Clare. They'll come, don't fret. If I have to go out and drag them in, we shall have pupils.'

'People prefer to send their daughters to Switzerland – there are still too many shortages here and the constant changes of government don't help. I'm sure the fathers think we'll be Communist soon. And the English are taxed out of existence and can't afford to come.'

'Doom merchant. Any chance of you coming out to dinner tonight? Mark's in love.'

'Really? How lovely. Who with?'

'You, you fool.'

'That *is* a joke?'

'No. I promised him I wouldn't say anything but the poor fellow is so down – you don't seem to notice he's alive.'

'Don't be silly. Of course I do. If it wasn't for him, I wouldn't be a free woman.'

'It took him long enough to arrange your divorce. I reckon he did it on purpose so that he could keep seeing you.'

'No, Mab, he didn't. This isn't the New World. Ending a marriage can take for ever here. I'm very grateful for all he's done.'

'I don't think he's interested in your gratitude.' Mab smirked.

'That expression doesn't suit you one little bit. I like Mark, you know I do, but not like that.'

'Couldn't you try?'

'No, not even for you. The spark is either there or it isn't. And in this case it's most decidedly the latter.'

'You're mad. Half of Paris would give their eye-teeth for him.'

'He probably wouldn't fancy them if they did.'

She was right, of course. Mark was a lovely man. He was in his mid-thirties, good looking, kind, considerate and rich – very. He had everything I should have wanted, only I didn't.

'Clare, Mab told me she had spoken to you about me. I'm really angry with her, she'd no right to do that. It's put us both in a difficult position.'

'Don't worry, Mark, I know Mab. She's always blundering in – she means well, she's always matchmaking, so don't be too cross with her. I shall forget she even said it.'

'I wish you wouldn't – forget, I mean.'

'Mark, I—'

'Clare, don't say it. I know what you were about to say. But you don't really know me, you might change your mind.'

After this conversation I did give him some thought . . . well, quite a lot, actually. It was just as it had been with Philippe: sense told me that this was a good man and my life would be easier. But my heart wasn't listening. I would lie awake at night unable to sleep with worry over the school and I would almost persuade myself that I should marry him, that I'd nothing to lose, that it would be wonderful for Karla who would be able to have whatever she wanted. But it never worked.

The problem was that I had been too lucky in love: two great loves and the third, dear Philippe, whom I had learned to love in a quieter, calmer way. Everything had to be compared with that. Was I hoping that another Karl would walk into my life? I told myself no, but in the dead of night when I was honest with myself I decided that that was probably true.

My lack of encouragement did not stop Mark: I was inundated with presents, flowers, invitations to dine. Sometimes I accepted, more often I refused. I hated hurting him when I liked him so much.

'What's that?' Mab asked, nosy as ever.

'I told you about the little girls I looked after down in the Auvergne, didn't I? Unbelievable as it seems, this is an invitation to Yvette's wedding. She was fourteen when I last saw her and now she's twenty – makes me feel ancient.'

'When is it? Can you go?'

'Two weeks before Easter. I'm just writing to say I can't.'

'Don't be so ridiculous. Of course you must go! You need a break. Go for a week.'

'I couldn't possibly. There'll be so much to do here. The students will be arriving a week after Easter.'

'So? What makes you think you're the only person who can manage?

You're not indispensable, you know. I'll hold the fort. You take a holiday, recharge your batteries. In any case—'

'What?'

'It'll do you good to get right away and then you'll see what an opportunity you're letting slip with Mark. If you don't see him for a week, ten days, you'll fall on him when you get back.'

'You never give up, do you?'

'Never. So you're going?'

'Yes. And I'd like Karla to see where she comes from. I think she thinks that Paris is the whole universe.'

'Just like dear old Hortense.'

This time, two weeks before Easter, the train journey was different altogether – no paper checking, just our tickets, food and drinks served. It was the first train ride that Karla would remember, and she was excited. I was glad we had come: with the school there wasn't much time for treats for her.

'Why, if you love it so much, did you move away, Maman?'

'The man I was going to marry died and I was too sad to stay.'

'But what about my papa, why didn't he look after you?'

'Because he was busy.'

'Shall we meet him?'

'Do you want to?'

'I don't know. He hasn't been very nice to us, has he?'

'Well, I expect he thinks about you.'

'I'd quite like to, if you want to.'

'Maybe he'll be there.' But, oh, how I prayed he wouldn't. From the moment of her birth I had realised that this time would come, a day when she would want to meet Fabien, and I had vowed it was her right to do so and that I would never stop her. But now, when it loomed so close, I wished to God I could. I didn't want him to see her, didn't want her to see him and maybe like him. I feared him saying he would like to see more of her. Then what would I do? Perhaps it was stupid of me to have come with so much at stake.

'Can we have lunch now, Maman? I'm starving.' I followed her along to the dining car. She bobbed along, long blonde hair flying, hazel eyes sparkling. When she was not aware of it, I often watched her, trying to identify anything of Fabien in her. But I could never see it. My father was right: she was so like my mother that it was as if his genes counted for nothing. Except that she was bright, far brighter than me, and she loved doing sums – so maybe something of him was there. But there wasn't his bad side, of that I was certain. My daughter shone with gentle goodness.

My dear Mab had arranged for the car of a friend to be waiting for me at the station in Lyon, which was wonderful since I would have far more flexibility. There was so much I wanted to show Karla. The owner was waiting with it. Another good-looking man of the right age and, from the way he was dressed, the right amount of money too – Mab was incorrigible. Serge offered to drive me if I wanted, he was entirely at my disposal, he said, nothing would be too much trouble.

'You're very kind but it would be so irksome for you. I have so many friends to see. We shall talk of old times, which would be tedious for anyone who hadn't lived them,' I said, praying he would agree, and feeling rotten at the same time: he was so keen it seemed churlish to turn him down. But I wanted to do this trip alone with Karla. 'I promise to guard your lovely car with my life.' I stroked the sleek lines of the Talbot Lago.

On the way I told Karla of my first adventures here and was gratified to see how impressed she was that I had walked all this way.

'Weren't you scared?'

'No.'

'I would be.'

'That's because you've more sense than your mother.'

She loved the scenery, she oohed and aahed much as I had as we bowled along in far more comfort.

'Maman, look, that signpost, it had my name. Rocheloire.'

'That's your village, where your ancestors have lived for centuries.'

'Isn't that a funny idea?'

The welcome we received at the doctor's was worth every mile we had travelled. I had insisted we would find a hotel and he had insisted that we stay with him. He was stronger than I.

'We thought you would like your old room.' Yvette showed us the way. 'Your daughter is beautiful, Madame.'

'Yvette, call me Clare. You'll soon be a married woman. Is he nice?'

'I wouldn't want to live in a world that he wasn't in.'

'That's lovely.' I remembered when I had thought that too.

'You never remarried?'

'No, the right person never came along.'

'She's got an admirer,' Karla piped up.

'Daughter, don't embarrass me. There's just one thing. I wondered if . . .' My voice trailed off, I didn't know quite how to put it.

'No. My father won't have either of them in the house.' She lowered her voice, glancing nervously at Karla.

'And his wife.'

'Céline, she's lovely. We all feel sorry for her. She doesn't deserve that woman as a mother-in-law, Papa says.' She looked around the room, checking that all was as it should be: she'd always been an efficient housekeeper, even as a child. 'I'll leave you in peace to unpack.' She turned to go but at the door she paused. 'There's just one thing, Clare. I never thanked you for what you did in the war. If it hadn't been for you perhaps Dominique and I wouldn't be here.'

'What did she do?' Karla asked.

'Don't you know? Your mother was a real heroine.'

'Nonsense. I did next to nothing. Now, Yvette's father . . .'

Violet rushed into the sitting room, her face aglow with anticipation. 'My dear Clare – and this is Karla! You can't imagine how bursting with excitement I've been. Do you like my hair? I went all the way to Le Puy to get it done.'

'It's lovely,' I lied. In fact, it was marcel-waved into a torturous shape.

'I think it's awful. I should have stuck with the girl in Vorey. Comes of trying too hard.' She tugged the beautifully worked bell-pull – I remembered Pauline embroidering that.

'How sad that Pauline won't be at the wedding.'

'But she will be, I'm sure. I often feel her presence. I tell Robert it's what keeps me from shouting at him too much.' She laughed and ordered coffee and cakes for us all from the timid little maid who appeared. 'I wish I'd seen you when Philippe died, my dear. That must have been such a shock for you. You know the house has been sold?'

'No. I have no contact with anyone but you two.'

'I should have told you, remiss of me. It took three years but eventually a Dutchman bought it. Very nice, by all accounts. Ah, coffee – fancy a smidgen of Cognac in it?' We settled with our cups. 'Now, tell me, any smart young man in your life?'

'Why does everybody want to marry me off?'

'She's got an admirer.'

'Karla, I do wish you'd stop saying that!' I pretended to be cross but spoilt it by laughing.

5

Apart from the weather, which was cold and blustery as only a spring in the Haute-Loire can be, the wedding was wonderful. There were drinks beforehand at which close friends admired Yvette and Dominique, who looked adorable in a pale blue shantung dress as the bridesmaid. Then there was the wedding, conducted by Father Bernard who grinned from ear to ear upon seeing me. Afterwards there was a cocktail reception, dinner and the dance. A mighty undertaking but, as it was pointed out to me, this was a quiet wedding. The celebrations for some went on for days.

In the church I had noticed one or two sly looks in my direction and several sheepish ones from those who had tried to attack me that last day I had been here. But I smiled broadly at everyone to show there were no hard feelings. Of Fabien and his mother, to my great relief, there was no sign.

The following morning I went to the bar for coffee, invited by Fleur, who wanted a natter for old times' sake. Without needing to turn round I knew he had walked in: the atmosphere had tensed when everyone saw him.

'Hello, Clare, this is a nice surprise. I wondered if you would be here.'

I glared at Fleur before turning round, but she looked surprised: evidently she had not told him I was here. 'Hello, Fabien,' I said.

'I thought I told you I did not welcome you in my bar?' Fleur stood, hands on hips, with a belligerent expression.

'He's here now, Fleur, it's OK.' I noticed he didn't have the grace to look embarrassed.

'And this is Karla?'

'It is. Karla, this is your father.'

'I hoped we would bump into you.' She grinned, bobbed, stuck out her hand, put it behind her back, then stood on tiptoe and plonked a kiss on his cheek. This time at least he looked surprised.

'That's nice. Well, thank you . . . daughter. Something to drink, some *sirop*?' Was I the only one to notice that pause?

'I've got some, thank you.'

'Perhaps you and your mother would like to come up to the château. Your grandmother would like to see you.'

'Please, Maman, can we? I'd love to see a real château.' She was jumping from foot to foot.

'You go. I'll wait here,' I said, with superhuman effort.

'You sure, Clare?'

'Positive.' Being so close to him I felt the hairs on the back of my neck stand on end. 'Just for half an hour. We have to be going.' I watched them leave the bar, hand in hand, and felt such a cutting wave of jealousy that I had to close my eyes to blot out the sight.

'That went well.'

'Did you tell him I'd be here this morning?'

'On my honour, no. I nearly died when he walked in. He never comes here. Violet said he'd refused to admit she was his daughter.'

'I expect he still does. I'm sure that was done for show. He'll fight tooth and nail against acknowledging her, according to my lawyer.'

'Then why?'

'So that you would say exactly what you have just said – *"That went well."* I don't trust him, Fleur.'

'Then why did you let her go?'

'She has the right.'

'He gave that up five years ago, if you ask me. Still, you're the popular one. There was someone else looking for you a while back.'

'Really?' I wasn't concentrating: all I was conscious of was my stomach churning. 'Is that them?' I rushed to the door, but it wasn't.

Waiting for them to return was the longest hour of my life – so much for thirty minutes. I felt sick with apprehension. I imagined them telling her bad things about me, kidnapping her, refusing to let me see her again. When I saw them strolling down the hill, still hand in hand, I wanted to rush and grab her from him. It wasn't my imagination: he had a proprietorial look about him as if he had accepted that she really was his daughter. As if, despite all he had said, he wanted her to be, that he was content she was.

'Robert, I know I was supposed to be here for another week, but I have to go.' I wish I could have said it so that it didn't sound as ungrateful.

'Do you have to? We're so enjoying your stay. We don't see enough of you. Too quiet for you after the excitement of Paris?'

'No, nothing like that.'

'She doesn't like the close proximity of you-know-who, do you my dear?' Violet arched her eyebrows and nodded towards Karla, who was drawing in the corner of the room.

'It sounds silly but, yes, I want to get her and me right away.'

'Where will you go? Back to Paris?'

'I thought of going to Lyon, to show Karla the city.'

As always it was hard to say goodbye to these people, who I had grown to love over the years, but they promised to visit us in Paris, so there were no tears this time.

'Do we have to go to a city, Maman? We live in a city and I'd like to stay in the country.'

'As you wish.' Where could we go, I wondered, as we crested the hill and the village disappeared from view? 'Would you like to see where you were born?'

'Oh, yes, *please*. The actual place? The actual room?'

'No, not the room but we can see the outside of the house.' As soon as I suggested it I began to regret it. What had I told myself in Paris? 'Bury the dead, Clare.' But I'd never buried any of them. I did not know where Didier's bones lay, or Karl's. Philippe was different: I could visit him.

We stopped for lunch in a restaurant high above the Loire, I had forgotten just how wonderful the air was, how well I felt here. Then we headed into the mountains and towards Philippe's house. It didn't matter to me who had bought it: to me it would always be his house.

'My father is nice, Maman. Why don't we see him more often?'

'We live in Paris and he lives here. It's a long way.'

'We could move here.'

'And leave Aunt Mab and the school?'

'He could come to Paris to live.'

'I think he prefers the country.'

'He said he'd visit us soon.'

'Did he? That's nice.' How I managed to say that I don't know: it was the last thing I wanted. But, then, I had told myself when she was born that it wasn't my right to deprive her of contact with her father. A fine sentiment, but hard to maintain.

'I didn't like Grandmother much.'

'No?' Well, that was noncommittal enough.

'She looks like the nasty Queen in *Snow White*.'

'She does a bit.' I laughed.

'Do you like her?'

'No, I never have.' I didn't see why I had to pretend about her.

'Good!' said Karla, and five minutes later she had fallen asleep. In a way I was glad: there was much on my mind. I found I needed time to compose myself before we arrived: it had been an emotional few days.

Several people in the little town paused at the sight of me, as if trying to remember from where and how they knew me. We inclined heads in greeting but I didn't want to talk to anyone, not until my task was over. We stopped at the florist's and I bought flowers – lovely spring flowers. Outside the town we stopped at the cemetery within its high walls, its tall monuments making it look like another sort of town.

'What are we doing here?'

'I want to say goodbye to someone.'

'Uncle Philippe?'

'That's right.' Sometimes I thought the child could read my mind.

'Didn't you go to his funeral?'

'No.'

'Why not?'

'I wouldn't have been welcome.' And because your bastard of a father had thrown me out, I longed to add. I wondered if one day she would ask him the same questions and what his answers would be.

For me there was always a sense of continuity in French graveyards, perhaps because they were so well tended, not like English ones, where the graves were sadly neglected.

The little photographs sealed on the tombstones made them so much more personal when you know what the person in the ground looked like. I knew where Philippe lay: he had once shown me the large ornate mausoleum that was the resting place of his family. It was grand, and there were no photos of him. Without thinking I sank to my knees.

'What are you doing?'

'Saying a little prayer.'

'Can I too?'

'If you want.'

The hard gravel dug into my knees. I placed my bright flowers on the slab of black marble on which his name was carved. I outlined it with my finger. 'Goodbye, my darlings, Philippe, Didier and Karl.' I felt desolate.

'Who are Didier and Karl?'

'I'm sorry?' Had I said what I was thinking? I hadn't meant to.

'Your *darlings*, you said.'

'Did I?' I managed a laugh.

'Who are they? I know about Philippe but the others.'

'Friends of mine I loved once.'

'In the war?'

'That's right.'

'Can we see the house where I was born now?'

'If you don't stop jumping up and down, you'll fall over. And this is no way to behave in a cemetery. What will the dead think?' I grabbed her hand. 'Come on, minx.'

6

It was only three miles from the cemetery to Philippe's house but it was a hard journey for me. Even after all this time I remembered every turn in the road, every bump. How foolish I must have been to cycle all those kilometres while pregnant. Had I known then how I would feel about

Karla I would never have risked her safety. I shuddered at the thought of what might have been.

'See there? That's where I fell off my bicycle one day and Philippe was angry with me for riding it in the first place. And you see that copse? That's where some of the men hid right at the end of the war.' I prattled on but she wasn't really interested in tales of that time. Why should she be? One day, perhaps.

We shouldn't have come, there were too many memories here, I should have left them in peace. But there was no going back now – Karla wouldn't have let me.

We reached the gates. The sign 'Le Manoir des Hirondelles' was freshly painted.

'Are there many swallows here?'

'Hundreds. They nest in the barns and in the attics. They come back year after year, to the place where they were born.'

'Like me!'

'Yes, but we can't keep coming back.'

The drive, once so rutted, was newly surfaced with gravel. The bushes were neatly trimmed. The new owner was caring for the house in a way that would have delighted Philippe.

'Do you think the people who live here will mind us coming?'

'I hope not.' I patted her hand. I felt ridiculously nervous and could not understand why.

On the slope of the hills that held the house safe, the vineyard for which Philippe had had such plans, had been replanted. Row upon row of vines marched up the slopes. How long before they would produce any wine? Whoever planted them must be a patient man. The ground around them was neatly weeded. At each row's end I saw a rosebush. How nice. If only Philippe could see this, how proud he would be.

We drove on to the wide sweep in front of the butterscotch-coloured stone house. The fountain that in my day had been weed-encrusted and empty now sparkled with water. 'Well, here it is.' I stopped the car.

'It's lovely, Maman. You never said it was such a pretty house and it's enormous. Which room was mine?' She scrambled out of the car and I followed her.

'That one there, on the first floor, to the right of the door. That was where you were born. And the window two along from it, that was your nursery.' I pointed to them.

Just then Karla tugged at my skirt. 'Maman, there's a man,' she whispered urgently.

I turned, ready with my explanation for why we were there, and froze. I felt dizzy with shock. I shook my head to disperse a cruel trick of light.

Walking towards me was . . . 'Karl?' I did not so much say his name as whisper it.

He stopped, a look of puzzlement on his face. 'Clare?'

'Maman said you were dead!' Karla piped, in her practical childlike way. I just heard her before I collapsed in a heap.

When I came to we were in the drawing room. I was lying on the blue velvet sofa. I felt its familiar softness. I had so often fallen asleep here, with Philippe sitting reading . . . I struggled to sit up. Had I imagined . . . Had I been dreaming?

He was kneeling on the floor beside me, holding my hand, looking anxious. Karla, her face white and tear-stained, crouched beside him.

'I don't understand. What has happened? Is this some cruel joke? Who are you?'

'It's no joke, Clare. But no questions, not yet. Recover first. Drink this, it will make you feel better.'

He held a glass towards me. I swiped at it, sending it flying across the carpet. 'I don't want a drink, I want an explanation!' I shouted.

'Maman, I'm frightened.' I scooped Karla into my arms and rocked her, comforting her – and myself.

'I'm all right really, darling. I just felt dizzy.'

'Clare, you are angry? Please don't be. Why?'

'What do you expect? I was told you were dead. Can you imagine what that was like? I grieved for you – God, how I grieved. And all the time you were alive and well and I didn't know . . .' I held Karla tightly to me. 'How could you do this to me? How could you be so cruel?' I was having to fight bursting into tears: Karla was frightened enough as it was. But it was difficult.

'Clare, I did nothing deliberately. You have to listen to me.'

'I don't have to listen to anything.' I tried to stand. All I could think was that I wanted to get out of here, away from this confusion, away from him. But the floor moved beneath my feet and I slumped back on the sofa, still clinging to Karla.

'Maman, you're hurting me.'

'Darling, I'm sorry . . .' I let go of her and buried my head in my hands. I felt cold. I had dreamt so often of this, and now that it was happening I was filled with anger and confusion. I didn't know what to think, let alone what to do.

'Karla – is that your name? Look, I have some toys here.' From a cupboard he pulled a cardboard box of toys and settled her with them on the other side of the large room. At the sight of the playthings my heart,

which was all over the place with shock, anger, elation and r
disappointment, plummeted into my shoes.

'Karla. That's a nice name.' He looked at me intently.

'No, she isn't.' How many times I had wanted her to be his and no
almost felt satisfaction in telling him she wasn't.

'If you don't want a drink, I bloody well do.' He stood up, and as
turned to go to where the bottles stood on a silver tray on the ta
Philippe had owned, I saw that he was limping.

'You were hurt?'

'I was.'

'I'll have that drink, then.'

I watched him pour them. It was so strange. The room was the same,
furniture, even the dusty curtains. The pictures on the walls,
ornaments. Everything was the same, but so different. It should have b
Philippe there but he was dead. Instead it was Karl and he was suppose
be dead too. Again I felt as if I was in a dream, that it would be all rig
would wake up. But if I did, that would mean that Karl was dead and .
no longer knew what I was thinking or what I wanted.

'Your drink. Scotch and soda. See? I remember.'

I took the glass from him and he pulled up a chair and sat close to
'Does the child speak German?'

'Yes. French and English too.'

'Clever, like her mother.' He picked up my hand and brushed it ac
his lips. I pulled it away. 'Such anger.'

'I don't know what I am.'

'I didn't deceive you. I looked everywhere for you. You must believe
When you didn't write, I went through hell. I wrote so often and nev
reply.'

'I had two letters. I wrote – I lost count of the number.'

'Two? But I wrote to you nearly every day. I expected some not to
through, but all of them?'

'They told me you were dead.'

'Who told you?'

'That fieldmouse, and when I didn't believe her, Bruno Meister.
confirmed it.'

'The bastards!'

'She said your tank had been hit and you were dead. They enjo
saying it. They watched my face and they were pleased with my pai

'Clare, my darling, I'm so sorry – for both of us, the lost time, the g
the loneliness.'

'And after it was all over why didn't you find me? I tried to find you it should have been easy to find me.' I still could not believe this was happening, it was all a game, and I was being tortured again.

'At the end of the war, my darling, you must have known of the chaos. The whole of Europe was on the move. There were days when everyone I met seemed to be looking for someone.'

'But no one ever came, no one ever told me anyone was searching for me. There are organisations – there is the Red Cross.' Disbelief was winning.

'When you are the victors, yes. Who cares about the vanquished? And, Clare, you have no conception of what Germany was like at the end. The country was in ruins, there was no organisation. Some days I thought it was a miracle any of us survived. There were too many people looking for loved ones and not enough to help us.' He paused. I don't know if he expected me to show sympathy for his wrecked country, but I didn't.

'Another drink?'

'This isn't a cocktail party. This is our life you're talking about.' I was irritated that he should think of drinks at a time like this.

'I was sure that it would take me years before I could afford to search for you. But then I had an amazing stroke of luck. Unbeknown to my sister and myself, my father, even before the war, had sent funds to Switzerland, as an insurance, I suppose. Suddenly I had the wherewithal to track you down.'

'I can't have been that difficult to find.'

'You were. I found Clare Dupont – living in Lyon, the right age, the wrong woman. She explained she had allowed you to use her name as an alias.'

'She wouldn't have told a German that, I'm sure. Not even now.'

'I told everyone I was Dutch. I still do. I realised it was early days for Germans to be welcomed with open arms. In Anliac I found a man who said he thought you had contacts in Rocheloire, so I went there. No one was forthcoming. I sensed that several people knew you but were not prepared to say so.'

'I've just been to a wedding there but no one said anyone had been looking for me.' And then I stopped. 'You asked in the bar? Of course, Fleur said – I just didn't pick up on it.'

'Then do you remember I once told you my dream had always been to settle in France and produce wine? I heard this house was for sale and the price was right. It had the vineyard too, so I came here. Then strange things happened. I felt your presence so strongly. I asked the man selling it if he knew a Clare Dupont but he said no.'

'Dear Fabien, he would.'

'I didn't know your real name, that was the stupidity of it all. If only I had looked at your passports properly I might have remembered. Dear God, Clare, what do I have to say to make you believe me?'

'It's strange, Karl, but there were times when I thought you were alive. Feelings I couldn't explain.'

'Then you hoped?'

'Endlessly.'

'So?'

'I don't know, Karl, I want to believe you, I really do.' I looked at Karla playing with the toys on the other side of the room, oblivious to the drama unfolding. He spoke as if he was free and yet – the toy box. I didn't want to be hurt again. I didn't want to see a glimmer of happiness only to have it snatched away. 'Who do the toys belong to?' I asked, when what I wanted to ask was if he was married, if . . .

'Those are for my nephews and nieces when they come to stay.' He sounded irritated, as if they were the last thing he wished to discuss. I welcomed the information. 'Is it too late for us? Clare, I'm almost afraid to ask you. Are you . . . married?'

'Divorced.' Never had the word sounded so wonderful to my ears.